T0381959

COME IN
AND SHUT
THE DOOR

COME IN AND SHUT THE DOOR

CHRIS PETIT

SCRIBNER

London · New York · Amsterdam/Antwerp · Sydney/Melbourne · Toronto · New Delhi

First published in Great Britain by Scribner,
an imprint of Simon & Schuster UK Ltd, 2025

1 3 5 7 9 10 8 6 4 2

Simon & Schuster UK Ltd, 1st Floor,
222 Gray's Inn Road, London WC1X 8HB

Simon & Schuster Australia, Sydney
Simon & Schuster India, New Delhi

www.simonandschuster.co.uk
www.simonandschuster.com.au
www.simonandschuster.co.in

The authorised representative in the EEA is Simon & Schuster Netherlands BV,
Herculesplein 96, 3584 AA Utrecht, Netherlands. info@simonandschuster.nl

A CIP catalogue record for this book
is available from the British Library

Hardback ISBN: 978-1-4711-8880-0
Trade Paperback ISBN: 978-1-4711-8881-7
eBook ISBN: 978-1-4711-8882-4
eAudio ISBN: 978-1-3985-2301-2

Typeset in Palatino by M Rules
Printed and Bound in the UK using 100% Renewable
Electricity at CPI Group (UK) Ltd

COME IN
AND SHUT
THE DOOR

Unbelief

One start began in that flat Puritan landscape to the east with the discovery of a woman's body, missing over sixty years. Or it began, 'He was aware of people staring.' Or it began with Parker's realisation that there was no God, which led him to quit studying for the priesthood. Or it began years earlier, upon being told, 'Come in and shut the door.' Or it began with another young man, about Parker's age, twenty-one or so, flying a heavy bomber through night skies over wartime Germany. Or it began after the war with the chance meeting of two men on a train, one of whom turned out to be Parker's grandfather.

His own start perhaps began after leaving the seminary, in the long tunnel between St John's Wood and Swiss Cottage on the London Underground, trying to decide whether the complicated dream of belief was over and this was the beginning of unbelief; either way, he was unprepared for anything that would happen, being a novice when it came to life.

Everything had been done for him in the seminary. The strictest order was applied to the day: 5am starts, 10pm lights out, calisthenics every morning, weather permitting, and endless service and contemplation. He had surrendered wallet and watch. There was nothing to buy, and time was regulated by bells, not unlike school or prison, for lives of prayer and profound silence. No revelation had occurred, only the growing stalactite of unbelief. Not that this was the end of it: perhaps Nietzsche's death of God meant God really had died as an external force and instead settled in us as a parasite and so was more alive than ever.

In the confines of the religious order, people hadn't stared as they did on the train. Emerging into daylight at Swiss Cottage, Parker was conscious of harsh brightness and a small child looking in horror, unable to tear itself away from the state of his skin.

His disfigurement was all people saw but they never commented, except to whisper or, like the child, bawl. Unfamiliar even with his own shadow after the gloom of the cloister, he felt as though everything was being conducted under a searchlight. In the daily exchange, he was tongue-tied. Everything appeared as though he was waking from a coma. The garish billboards, the yellow lines in the street – so much direction and signage. He avoided telling his parents he was out and decided to go to London to look for a job, without any idea of what that might be. He stayed at the Barbican Youth Hostel, where he was befriended by no one. When he tried to register for the dole he found he couldn't without a fixed address. He scoured Situations Vacant columns, applied all over and answered an ad in the *Evening Standard*'s classifieds for a Man Friday. He explained that he was new to the world, so to speak, mentioned the seminary and wrote in the expectation of being unanswered.

He was surprised to receive a postcard some days later,

inviting him to Kilburn. He took the Underground and found a large stucco house near the station on one of the better roads, down from Shoot-Up Hill. He rang the bell and a man's voice shouted out that the door was open. It didn't open easily because of junk piled in the hall, stacked from floor to ceiling in old boxes. The voice called for him to come up. The stairs required picking his way over more boxes. Parker found the man in the front room off the first-floor landing. He didn't see him at first because everywhere was crammed with old electronic equipment, stacks of TV sets, several on with the sound down, paintings leaning against boxes and more boxes, turning the place into a maze. The man was sitting in the corner in shadow. The first thing Parker noticed was that both hands were in plaster, resting on his lap as though in supplication. He held them up and said, 'Bust wrists.'

The baggy, double-breasted pinstripe suit had seen better days. Parker noted the large melon head and stubble; he supposed him about sixty. Sun shone through the window at an angle. Dust motes hung in the air.

'Can you read?' the man asked. 'Out loud, I mean. You can add reading to me to your tasks as I have trouble turning the pages. Because of my hands I need spoon-feeding. Until now I have made use of packet soups and a straw. Minestrone gets a bit tricky. I prefer Batchelors on the whole, not Heinz. I'm Robinson, by the way.'

He showed no surprise at Parker's appearance and said, 'You can start by making a cup of tea. There's no milk; two sugars and a splash of whisky for me. Kettle and cups next door.'

That room was just as packed with junk. Piles of old newspapers and magazines lay around tied up with string, with

3

names like *Knave* and *Penthouse*. Parker addressed himself to the kettle, which stood on a table covered with crumbs interspersed with mouse droppings. There was a Belfast sink and a cold tap to rinse the mugs. He thought about leaving quietly. Such chaos was the opposite of what he was used to. He wondered what the man did besides being a hoarder with no interest in housekeeping.

They sat among the squalor, Robinson holding his mug between his plastered hands like a chalice. Parker was surprised to find himself there as though called. He wondered how Robinson had managed to write the postcard, and again about what he did, to be told in due course that he collected stuff people didn't want in the expectation that one day they would.

'You'll be too young to remember, but after the fall of the Berlin Wall there was a good trade in Russian icons until everyone else crashed the act. I used to get about more in those days. Excuse me if I don't get up. There's quite a good example on the fireplace ledge.'

Parker found it behind more rubbish, two small panels. The icons, representing several of the great religious feasts, left him contemplating his lapsed state.

'Painted on wood with tempera,' Robinson said, 'and finished with gold leaf. Rather fine, don't you think?'

Parker agreed only because he didn't know otherwise.

Robinson snorted. 'Polish fake. What do you think of representations of the crucifixion? In general.'

Parker was familiar with them, of course, but hadn't given them any aesthetic consideration.

'Grünewald, for instance.'

Parker mumbled that he was more acquainted with the Stations of the Cross.

4

'You probably remember Huysmans on Grünewald.' Parker pretended he did. 'Christ's thighs greasy with sweat, ribs like staves, flesh swollen, blue, mottled with flea bites. One eye half-opened as a shudder traverses the expiring figure, while the mouth laughs atrociously.'

Parker bowed his head, thinking of what he had lost.

'Huysmans puts Grünewald's Calvary at the opposite pole from those debonair Golgothas adopted by the Church ever since the Renaissance. Are you familiar with Huysmans?'

Parker said he was not.

'You should be. Thanks to him, we learn that Grünewald was the most uncompromising of realists, but his sewer deity let the observer know that realism could be truly transcendent. Did you consort with fallen women and tax collectors in the seminary? I suppose not, as you would have been a registered charity. Now, to business. I am not a charity. I will pay you three hundred quid a week, which is all I can afford, cash, so there's no fucking around with the Revenue. You, on the other hand, get board and lodging here, gratis, and expenses for any travel on my behalf. In exchange, you shop, provide and do as I ask. You can use my bicycle, as I have no use for it after falling off.'

The thought of Robinson on a bicycle stretched Parker's imagination.

'There's a room at the top you can clear,' Robinson went on. 'It has a camp bed, probably too short for you, being a tall boy, but let's not ask ourselves about the state of your closet. For the moment, that's the best I can offer. I don't wish to be disturbed after six o'clock, as I drink. Agreeable?'

It wasn't as if Parker had any choice. In one employment agency he had been told that the sort of casual work he was seeking was getting harder to find – stacking shelves or van driving, which he couldn't do anyway. He had even tried a few parish churches in the hope of picking up something.

'I am agoraphobic since my accident,' Robinson announced, 'apart from seeing my "dear old mum" – said in quotation marks, you will note – in her care home up the road; quite doolally. I would expect you to walk me there, in case I have a panic attack, and collect me one hour later, unless I call in the meantime. I will give you a mobile phone. You will have to work out how to use it, as I don't bother with things technical. You may as well get started. There'll be a pen and paper somewhere. I will dictate a shopping list. Can you cook?'

'A bit,' Parker said when the answer was 'not really'.

'There's a microwave I can show you how to use. That I can work, after making the mistake of baking a potato for forty-five minutes.'

They sat in silence until Robinson said, 'I am interested in those who lose their faith.'

Robinson on the whole favoured dressing gowns, slippers and clothes that didn't require buttoning, which meant he could dress himself.

'As for shitting, that's my affair.'

Hot dogs, sausage rolls and Mars Bars he could just about manage, along with glasses and mugs, but the breakfast cereal he insisted on had to be spoon-fed. After Parker fed him another mouthful, Robinson said, 'My Rosebud was a submarine out of a Cornflakes packet that used baking soda to submerge.'

His days passed watching a lot of television.

'Daytime TV is the final frontier,' he said. 'Consider it part of your education.'

Parker struggled to follow the morning talk shows because he had no idea who the guests were or what they were all laughing at. They watched shopping channels. They watched repeats of old property shows and documentaries about the Second World War. Robinson wondered aloud about the connection in his mind between pointless renovation and wartime devastation.

'My old man flew bombers,' he said, 'and flattened large parts of urban Germany.'

Parker's duties included scouring local charity shops for anything Robinson might find of interest. His paltry offerings were usually greeted with no comment beyond the occasional grunt.

The only times they went out together were to visit Robinson's mother up the hill when Parker took and fetched him, often having to stop while the man caught his breath.

'Did or do you care for your parents?' Robinson asked.

Parker, thrown by the question, explained how they hadn't really got on, but Robinson wasn't listening and interrupted to say, 'My life is still conditioned by six-gun cowboys hiding behind rocks and whispering how it's too quiet. Any Westerns or Second World War films you find, I'll watch.'

They started with *The Dam Busters*, then *The Cockleshell Heroes*, with the actor Trevor Howard, whom Parker decided was how Robinson's father would have looked.

He next brought back a book found for 25p, W. G. Sebald's *On the Natural History of Destruction*.

Robinson said, 'Give it a go and let's see if it's worth the price.'

Parker began, and Robinson exclaimed, 'Not from the beginning! Pick a page, any page, and start there. Nothing more boring than reading from start to finish.'

Robinson grew impatient with the account of the wartime destruction of Darmstadt by the RAF.

'Probably pulverised by my old man. Your writer's quite right that a firestorm was the desired effect, and he reports the inability of the survivors to cope with the trauma as so vividly envisaged by him. He quotes Max Hastings' book *Bomber Command* without having appeared to have read it, as it records how huge efforts were made by the local authorities to counsel victims and the bereaved, a detail ignored by our writer friend that rather spoils his theory of unspoken trauma.'

Most afternoons, Robinson preferred reruns of stale old quiz shows with funny people, denounced by him as the tyranny of comedy. 'Watch enough of those and you soon realise a sense of humour is a liability. I resolved to seek out the humourless for companionship, hence hiring you.'

Parker couldn't tell if he was supposed to laugh.

'I should introduce you to Vod.'

'Vod?'

'What he calls himself now. Vod was a face on telly, once. The biggest show-off in a cage of monkeys on an ancient, coked-up improvisation show. I have developed a laboured thesis around the meaning of "crack" in relation to Vod — the drug of which the man took far too much; cracking up with laughter; crack as in cunt, chased with a vengeance; cracking a joke and crack-up as in full psychotic breakdown, which he had in spades. Cocked and coked up. Treated women like fuck machines to be ignored in restaurants. Been on the scrapheap for years. Terrified people will still recognise him and laugh. A man of several disguises. Pay no attention. He's convinced there's a gangland contract out on him. Drives for me occasionally but won't on his own, says he needs someone

8

riding shotgun in case he's attacked. The truth is he needs a companion or he goes into fugue states and ends up in Hastings when you've sent him to Colchester.'

'What is it that you have, if you don't mind my asking?' was Vod's first comment on seeing Parker's skin. Parker thought to himself that he did mind, as Vod had asked. He said it was called psoriasis.

Vod wasn't what Parker was expecting. Baby skin for a start; a short, polite man, maybe still in his thirties, with neatly parted hair, wearing a suit with a sheen and narrow lapels, winklepicker shoes, a pressed white shirt and a string tie like those worn by riverboat gamblers in Westerns. Vod used eye contact even less than Parker, and the deferential air reminded him of haberdashery shop assistants from his childhood.

Robinson was sitting in his usual afternoon chair watching a children's quiz show and barely looked up when Vod stood before him and gravely stated, 'The pack is afraid. Perhaps I am the only one to see that. Terror is an externalisation of the fear in themselves. Not enough terror or having to dish out too much terror.'

Robinson considered, then said, 'I watched a woman on a cookery programme earlier, preparing German white aspar-agus, unmistakably phallic, signalled by the rictus grin of the watching master chef. For a moment, I swear the close-up of the stiff asparagus coddled in the woman's hand morphed into an image of the priapic Mayor of London, to whom is attributed the remark: "I've got so much spunk in me." Now let's watch one of your old shows so Parker can see what you were about. I can't make up my mind about Parker.'

Vod addressed Parker. 'Don't mind him. Known him for

yonks, frequented the same Soho drinking clubs. He came and went. It's said he spent time in Ireland working in global fixing that involved power breakfasts with Bono and flying Bob Geldof in a helicopter to Hull. Enterprise. Rejuvenation. Regeneration. Became friends with that dodgy French writer Houellebecq.'

'Piloted the helicopter myself,' Robinson said, and he and Vod sniggered at this unlikely image.

Vod carried on as though talking to a larger audience than just Parker. 'Either he went legit, the Quango years, or he went illegit, or did both. There's never any real trail, just the floated story and anecdote. He'll admit and deny everything at the same time.'

Robinson shrugged as Vod addressed him directly.

'Convalescing for the moment, but we'll soon have you back in the saddle.' He turned to Parker. 'He had a telly company off Charlotte Street. Even then it was hard to say exactly what he did. Admits to doing porn in the 1990s.'

Robinson shrugged again.

'Some say you're in the business of laundering finance for the London Olympics. Others that you broker for rich Russians and government stooges. There's a film company registered in Jersey which seems to produce nothing, so it's probably a way of moving money.' Vod addressed Parker. 'I can never tell whether he's bankrupt or loaded.'

'Not much diff these days,' interjected Robinson.

'He has the soft hands of a spoiled priest, have you noticed?'

Parker hadn't, as they were in plaster. He was reeling from it all. A feeling that none of it was serious beyond the performative enjoyment of two men whacking the conversation back and forth. Parker was quite unused to repartee, let alone questions, which had barely existed in the seminary, which was all obedience and devotion, recital and silence.

Robinson said to Parker, 'Bring us tea and – talking of Vod – a plate of Jammie Dodgers, and we'll sit down and watch one of Vod's old shows. Did you bring a VHS?'

Vod patted his pocket with a satisfied smirk while looking terrified.

He watched his former self with fondness and horror. Parker supposed the programme about ten years old, from around the turn of the century, but didn't remember having seen it. Vod appeared not to have aged a day, other than to appear more embalmed, and was wearing the same suit.

Robinson said, 'It's pretty obvious the host is on Mogadon, given the lethargic timing of his droll asides compared to the jabber of the rest of you.'

Vod was on screen, improvising wildly. Robinson said, 'Look at the chemically enhanced performance. Lines of coke on the dashboard on the way there and home, I'll be bound, which brings us to domophobia.'

'Domophobia?' asked Parker in a state of confusion at the speed of everything.

'The terror of going home, that end-of-night funk at the thought, too pissed by then to drive. Faced with the prospect of the solitary wank, idle thoughts of sexual congress coalesce. The swift pick-up, shared taxi, same general direction; coffee? Neither party really wants this. Half-hearted or passed out before it can get half-hearted. Last-minute toilet nerves. The revved-up performer who kept breaking wind on air, requiring careful sound editing. Am I right?'

Vod nodded. 'Remember stories of your old man flying bombers. A group of men with little in common, sitting in different parts of the plane. That was us, too, caught in the glare of the spotlight, desperate not to get shot down.'

Robinson interrupted. 'They called it an aircraft.'

His father, Evelyn, had flown a stripped-down killing machine in which no part was designed for comfort. He dropped bombs for a living (28 quid a month) while others tried to kill him. Five pints for Dutch courage didn't interfere with his concentration, but sub-freezing temperatures at altitude could be murder on a full bladder. In the front of all their minds, the dread of annihilation; slow targets, of which the Germans said: They crawl like flies across a table top.

Robinson said, 'Vod was one of those nearly good-looking men on telly, the ones who hadn't quite got the full handsome kit, that fell into the category of persistent little fuckers.'

Vod hung his head. 'Insatiable.'

'Disguising a crushing neediness via projection and the hostile joke, with the ego transformed from quivering mollusc to impenetrable redoubt. Vod is a perfect impersonator. The one thing he is less successful at doing is himself: all over the shop. The moment of sloth before the insult.'

Vod became a nodding dog. 'The turning and the snarling.'

'As it was, it came down to altercations with Page Three girls or paying for sex while off your head,' Robinson went on. 'And options now in terms of lifestyle choices?'

Vod hung his head again. 'Presenter at the Adult Video News Awards show in Las Vegas this year. What about you?'

'Forget about me. What's your fancy? Suspicions are that you may not be much good at sex, like maths or grammar. Did you renounce the greed and pointlessness of riches, or was it all taken away?'

'I failed to understand that depression just short of full breakdown was a smart career move. Are you on medication?'

He was asking Parker, who said, 'Only ointments.'

'For your skin?'

Parker thought Vod had said 'sin'.

He didn't mention how he avoided his reflection in the mirror, or the bad days spent scratching until he bled, or the sticky tar bandages he had to wrap himself in at night, including his hands and head, until he resembled an Egyptian mummy.

His room at the top was more of a den, with space cleared among the clutter. He slept imagining himself safe in a burrow, though it offered no protection from the night's dreams. He often could not say what a dream was about, other than palpable terror, like he was in something crashing or about to be crushed, with guns being waved around. Most dreams appeared so alien that they felt like an external penetration, as though someone else or the house itself was dreaming for him.

The seven-man crew led by Pilot Officer Evelyn Robinson took off into the night skies on 29 May 1943 in what amounted to a flying coffin: 2,000 gallons of gasoline, which might not be enough to see them home; miles of pipelines with 150 gallons of flammable hydraulic oil; tons of high explosive packed into the bomb bay; 14,000 rounds of ammunition; and a portable Elsan toilet. It was not flushable. Its chemical disinfectant stank the length of the fuselage. It was exposed, uncomfortable and dangerous in rough weather or evasive action. Over 10,000 feet, anyone using it had to take a portable oxygen bottle. On long trips, it invariably overflowed. The Elsan typified the hell of war as much as any enemy.

Other crewmen could use the Elsan; Evelyn couldn't leave his seat. With pissing a problem, and access through thick clothing difficult, he'd had an approachable nurse come up with a contraption involving a Durex attached to a urine bag. Shitting either had to wait or involved a hasty change of clothes on landing. Some preferred to dump in an old shoebox rather than risk the Elsan. One gunner had the skin taken off his arse by its frozen seat on an icy night over Germany.

During the flight they all farted constantly because trapped wind could cause severe distress coming down from altitude. The endless Brussel sprouts fed to them in the canteen generated huge quantities of gas. They were also advised not to land on a full bladder because it could burst if they crashed.

The seven men flying that night were little more than boys, padded out with so much clothing that they struggled to walk to the aircraft. For six or seven hours they would fly in an unpressurised, unlit fuselage, often in sub-zero temperatures, facing the prospect of enemy flak, night fighters, frequently lethal weather and any number of accidents, from running out of fuel to crash landing after making it back.

Evelyn knew the aircraft like the back of his hand, yet each time he stepped on board was like entering an alien space, waiting for the turn of the dice, rather in the way that the men he flew with were familiar but complete strangers. Even their names hardly counted; in flight they addressed each other by their job titles: skipper, wireless operator, navigator, flight engineer, bomb-aimer, mid gunner and rear gunner.

Physical discomfort, paralysing boredom and gut-churning fear resulted in a desperate fatigue that could be seen in the prematurely aged faces of young men who had seen too much, or rather had had too much seared into their brains, because flying at night they saw nothing until the skies were lit up by searchlights and flak. The sight of cities in flames resembled a spectacle staged for their terrible entertainment.

Evelyn suspected they all kept mental lists of the different ways of dying, perhaps the cleanest being a mid-air collision or ambush by a German fighter, provided their aircraft exploded. Being hit by flak was a greater fear: a desperate dive in an effort to extinguish an engine on fire, with a chance of not pulling out. There were stories of men who had baled out being lynched by hostile Germans. The worst, Evelyn thought, would be a shrapnel wound. One bled more at high altitudes. He often saw himself lying freezing on the fuselage cot, with insufficient morphine and too much time to think about life ebbing away, knowing he would be dead on arrival while the flight engineer tried to get them home; not that Evelyn had much faith in him.

He was among the few captains that let their crews smoke, puffing out of the edge of their oxygen masks. The navigator got through forty cigarettes on every outward trip and twenty coming home.

'Home' was a Nissen hut in a mud field. Theirs had a bad reputation because previous incumbents hadn't come back, most after less than a handful of missions. It was of little comfort that their tenure had lasted longer because the chances were their number would come up. Sometimes odds of twenty-to-one looked quite favourable; then, in the cold light of a hangover, more like a process of inevitable self-selection.

He wasn't a particularly good pilot, having been made operational after insufficient flying hours. His crew wasn't up to scratch. All of them were undertrained. The mid and rear gunners were sitting ducks who would probably get themselves killed by a night fighter without getting a second to practise their craft. The rear gunner flew looking backwards, scanning the skies for any sign of attack. One moment's lapse of concentration and it would be curtains for the lot of them.

Sometimes Parker heard screams coming from the basement.

The door opposite his room was heavily padlocked and so scratched it looked as though it had been attacked by something with sharp claws. Parker supposed it could have been a screwdriver, but such was the atmosphere that he wouldn't have been surprised if some strange beast slumbered there.

The door from the hall to the basement where Parker heard screams was locked. He thought someone was perhaps being tortured, except the sound often stopped, started and repeated. He asked Robinson what was going on.

'I hear things,' Parker said.

Robinson said, 'I don't.'

Parker asked what was in the locked room opposite his, to be told, 'No one's been up there in years, except you.'

'The door looks like it has been attacked.'

'That would have been a rather pushy lot of Bulgarians. Long gone.'

'What's in it that needs locking?'

Robinson shrugged. 'Can't remember. Keys got lost. What are we saying here in the end?'

Parker had no idea.

'Other than the doing of it, the courage is in carrying on long after anyone has stopped listening.'

Among Parker's tasks was to buy a full selection of the morning papers, which Robinson went through while watching television. Scissors had to be placed nearby so Parker could cut out stories that took the man's fancy. An Albanian sex-trafficker found dead in a London cemetery, drained of blood, organs missing. A top scientist said to have been killed by a pagan sect, with a suggestion that the secret state employed satanic methods to disguise its intervention. The trial of a wizened, harmless-looking concentration camp guard. The story of a mysterious inhabitant living rough in a wood, who turned out to be a girl abducted ten years before, who now stalked her parents. Another about a kid snatched in an Asda store by two Dutch women, who were found in the customer toilet dyeing the girl's hair.

'It makes you think,' Robinson said, 'when millions of cameras track our movements, that someone goes missing every two minutes.'

He told Parker that his father hadn't been in touch for years and his aunt had vanished into thin air.

Parker asked what had happened, as he thought he should. Perhaps he was getting better at asking questions.

'She disappeared near the end of the war, before I was born. The old man only ever mentioned her a couple of times, almost as though it were quite normal for people to walk out of their lives. Not a trace since. Same place as where those children have disappeared.'

The news was taken up with two missing girls who had been gone for over a week from their village in the Fens, with an army of reporters and rolling news crews invading the area.

'The linens are having a field day,' Robinson said. 'Feeding the beast.'

Over 700 aircraft assembled for that night's raid on Wuppertal, flying in a convoy over six miles wide and two miles deep: safety in numbers, in theory, calculated odds and a built-in sense of acceptable loss by those that sent them up. Evelyn Robinson's operational career having been thus far so strangely uneventful only added to the foreboding. Never hit by flak, never caught in a searchlight, no sight of any German fighter, apart from once on a return leg when the rear gunner shouted, 'Corkscrew port!' Evelyn desperately chucked the crate around, waiting for bullets to rake the exposed underbelly. When nothing hit them, he decided the gunner must have been seeing things. He reckoned he had used up most of his luck anyway. He'd had to bale out of a crashing Wellington while training. Given their knackered and poorly maintained aircraft, annual training deaths ran to the thousands, though they kept quiet about that. Death was always sniffing around. There was the cruel fate of a mid-air collision – he'd narrowly missed one in a daytime training exercise on basic formation flying when an aircraft strayed off course, taking down the next plane in a huge explosion that rocked them from nose to tail. Later, on a mission, there was the night a 400-pound bomb fell out of the bay while they were taxiing for take-off and lay unexploded on the runway. The crew refused to fly, expecting to face court martial, but nothing happened, even after Evelyn told the CO, 'Fuck this for a game of soldiers,' and took the men down the pub to carry on drinking.

After his first tour, Evelyn had been transferred back to operational training as an instructor. It didn't take long to decide that teaching third-raters to fly was even dicier than missions, so he signed on for a second tour. He reckoned he would rather die in the dark, thinking, illogically, that death would be quicker by night.

If they were all going to snuff it before their lives had barely begun, there didn't seem much point in getting to know his crew any better. By his reckoning, at least three were virgins. The rear gunner would fuck anything and boasted the largest tool in the squadron, hence was known as 'Donkey'. As for himself, Evelyn Robinson worked on the principle of 'pick 'em plain, they're ever so grateful'.

Most officers were public school and didn't know how to screw around, being conditioned by male camaraderie. Singsongs around the old Joanna, practical jokes and needling repartee amounted to a superior form of defensive bullying. Evelyn was held to be an 'oik', having gone to a grammar, not one of the rugger buggers. He found it all a bit like school with death written into the contract.

The only unusual aspect of the flight that night was they had a woman smuggled on board. Taking a woman up was believed to bring luck as the kites that had were all still flying. Deidre Stocker, a young WAAF, was having a thing with Robinson and wanted to 'see the fireworks'. He agreed because Wuppertal was a soft target, with nothing like the flak and searchlights over the Ruhr's Happy Valley.

The crate was a heavy brute and that night seemed reluctant to be airborne; Evelyn sometimes wondered if it had a mind of its own. Get into formation. Don't crash into anything. Pray they would get through. Do the job (they had been criticised for 'creep back', a common fault of releasing bomb loads too early). Fly home, get the bloody thing down and fuck the living daylights out of Deidre Stocker.

One of the things he didn't know was that his sister Valerie was directly connected to the task in hand because she belonged to an obscure branch of Operational Research, the Incendiary Bomb Tests Panel. Based in Orford, she worked with the boffins on the shingle bank opposite, which was reached by a short ferry ride, where their task was to study the composition of German towns for natural landmarks, building construction and destruction potential. Baedekers were closely consulted. Fire insurance maps were pored over to determine the frequency of firewalls. The contents of the average German household, from attic to cellar, were examined for flammability. This extended to replicas of different types of accommodation being set alight to see what burned best.

Detective Sergeant Copper

Miss Robinson, aged twenty-one, was reported missing on 10/06/1944 by her brother, Pilot Officer Robinson, a young man to whom I did not take, after she failed to turn up at a pub (The Three Tuns) where they regularly met, as far as their duties allowed. Several weeks had passed without word. I pointed out that Miss Robinson's unit would conduct its own search and not necessarily involve the local constabulary. PO Robinson said her work was bound by the Official Secrets Act and therefore he had no idea where she was based, other than it being within travelling distance of The Three Tuns.

Being conscientious and a mite curious, I made telephone calls as and when, but could find no administration that knew of her. My application for a Missing Persons Enquiry seemed to have been passed around the houses because no answer came back. One desk Johnny told me, 'We don't nanny or nurse.'

The Military Police had its hands full and frequently turned to us local coppers about soldiers gone AWOL or cases involving the black market. It was during one such investigation that I found myself telephoning the landlord of The Three Tuns, which was said to be frequented by a gang trading in stolen gasoline (as the Americans call it). The landlord was unable to confirm as much, given the crowd he had in most nights, which more than once had drunk the place dry. He suggested I come and see for myself.

As a teetotaller, I rarely visit pubs and the few I had I'd found in reasonable order, with any excessive drunkenness sorted out by the landlord with a firm hand. My first visit to The Three Tuns had more people in attendance than at the Portman Road football ground before the war, so packed that there was little room to move, with drinks slopped as a sweating crowd jumped up and down to a band of Negro musicians. A bossy American woman from a London fashion magazine was in that night, photographing the band and a *Daily Express* cartoonist who played jazz piano with them. The sole purpose of their infernal racket seemed to be to loosen all social inhibition. Lascivious, gyrating Negro soldiers were paired off with white women.

As I left, I encountered PO Robinson. He was with a couple of what he termed 'mates' and several young women. They all had that glittering look that spoke of high excitement. I was addressed insolently as 'old boy' and offered a drink, which I declined. PO Robinson was celebrating his return from a particularly dicey mission, which he was lucky to have survived, after his aircraft flipped on crash landing. We had to shout to be heard. Either because he was drunk or from disrespect, PO Robinson kept his arm draped around one of the young women. When I asked to speak to him outside, she gave me a look that said I was spoiling her fun.

PO Robinson remained distracted and found it hard to concentrate. I informed him that his sister was proving difficult to locate, with so much red tape and for lack of any lead. I asked whether there was any young man who could perhaps throw light on her whereabouts. He seemed to find the question amusing and unwarrantedly observed that I appeared to have taken 'quite a shine' to his sister. Drunk or not, there was no excuse for the remark. Seeing me take offence, he was quick to add that he was joking.

It wasn't for him to tell his sister how to conduct herself, he said, but she had 'played the field', as well as having a disgruntled English boyfriend, who couldn't compete with the perks the Yanks offered: nylons, chewing gum, fizzy drinks and so forth.

While I told myself that the chance of a well brought-up young woman coming to harm seemed unlikely, I was bound to consider whether she had been a victim of loose Americans and their hot-blooded ways, often resulting in hasty marriages because a young 'un was on the way, illegitimate children or backstreet abortions. We arrested a district nurse for performing such tasks.

I visited The Three Tuns on subsequent occasions, asking after Miss Robinson. Some remembered her as a lively, friendly girl. Further enquiries led me to an embittered young English army subaltern, who complained that he had been 'chucked' for no reason and had not heard from her since. I found no cause to disbelieve him, as he came over as a decent chap.

I became acquainted with a young American serviceman named Turk, a Methodist, so we had that in common. He seemed an unlikely visitor to The Three Tuns until it emerged that he saw his role there as missionary. While he understood the pressure of war and the need to 'let go', he believed the evils of alcohol should be pointed out and the higher calling invoked. He admitted to not having much success and being indulged as what was called 'part of the show'. I suspect his sobriety amused them. But this young man had in fact known Miss Robinson. They met there by chance, and to his surprise she appeared to take his exhortations seriously, at least not laughing at him, going so far as to say, 'I think you are probably right.' This surprised Turk because he knew the man she was seeing at the time, a pilot named Merriweather who was known as 'a bad lot' and a dealer in contraband cigarettes. Turk provided the case's first possible lead. Merriweather had gone AWOL and was believed to be in London, where the Military Police were looking for him.

Turk was part of Airbase Security, which was how he knew about Merriweather; his job was probably why he wasn't laughed at more by his carousing colleagues. There was no note of Merriweather having absconded with a woman, but given the association it seemed as good an explanation as any. The man must have gone to Miss Robinson's head sufficiently for her to abandon her post. I did not tell PO Robinson this, as my conclusion was no more than surmise.

Some weeks later, Merriweather was detained, not in London, but York, and returned to base. Through Turk's intercession, I was able to talk to the officer in charge of the base police, a large Texan named Rawls, who allowed me to question Merriweather about Miss Robinson. I expected a shifty fellow of evident criminal persuasion and found instead a friendly and unrepentant young man, who spoke with a twang.

Miss Robinson he described as outgoing and generous, but their relationship was little more than what he called 'a one-night stand' and, although she was clearly a girl up for 'a good time', it hadn't crossed his mind to invite her to play truant.

A craftiness to his look left me questioning the man's apparent openness. He was anti-authority, and there was no reason he should treat me any differently. Perhaps he guessed I had developed a paternal responsibility towards

Miss Robinson, because what he said as I was about to leave seemed intended to spite me as much as to besmirch her. Miss Robinson was known as a 'bike'. He had to explain that meant she would let anyone ride her, including Negroes. Merriweather added that had he known this at the time, he would not have gone near her with 'what you Limeys call a ten-foot barge pole'.

I asked if he could identify any of these coloured gentlemen. There were too many to name, from what he had heard; then he added in his soft-spoken way that where he came from they held strong views about interbreeding. I tended to agree, but was nevertheless depressed that a young woman of good upbringing had allowed herself to become so defiled.

When Robinson was going through the papers and announced, 'A body has been found,' Parker supposed it was one of the children Robinson had taken to calling 'the wee missing'.

'No, a Jane Doe.'

A psychic had come up with a site where she believed the children might be buried. It lay inside an American Air Force base. There had been trouble gaining access on such speculative grounds, but with permission granted they found the remains of a woman thought to have lain there for years. She remained unnamed, but Robinson was sure it was his missing aunt.

'How many other women have disappeared there? I fear it must be her.'

Over eighty had she lived. The thought left Robinson panicky and his palms were sweating.

Vod was hanging around, eating a sandwich.

'Tuna and mayo. Want some? Terrible business, those missing kids,' he offered, chewing with his mouth open. 'Snatched by outsiders the press says – migrant workers, pikeys, foreigners passing through. A yellow car is being sought.'

Robinson snorted. 'It'll be the Yanks.'

'Yanks?' asked Vod.

'Turned up for the last war and never left.'

'How do you know it's them?' asked Vod.

'It's either a paedophile ring of airmen selling children into slavery or someone in transit back to the US from Afghanistan.'

Sensing their uncertainty, Robinson said, 'It's well-known that a ring has been operating since the Balkan conflict in the 1990s. Or it's soldiers back from Afghanistan returning in a state of advanced shock, resulting in firecracker incidents, hair-trigger stuff. A local man beaten half to death outside a pub, with the assailant shipped home before any investigation.'

Vod asked, 'Then why are none of the papers running with it?'

'They refuse to make the connections – in this case, Fort Bragg, North Carolina. The very same week those children disappeared, four wives in Fort Bragg were murdered – four! – by their husbands, all just back from Afghanistan.'

Vod said he couldn't see what that had to do with anything, then rather wished he hadn't.

'War fucks with a man's head!' exclaimed Robinson. 'He's trained to kill, then they give him pills that mess him up even more. US servicemen are given an anti-malaria drug whose side effects include psychosis.'

Parker asked if British troops took it, too, wondering if Robinson had it in for Americans.

'They take something else, which gives them the runs.'

DS Copper noted: Miss Robinson appears to have vanished into thin air. However much an untimely end seems likely, no remains have been found. A hushed-up traffic accident is most probable, involving narrow lanes, drunken driving and unlit bicycles. There are enough of those.

Time passed. Squadrons and army units were transferred. More white faces turned up at The Three Tuns. The Negroes took themselves off when it became clear they were no longer welcome.

An incident occurred at another pub, The King's Head in Ipswich, because of the hostility of the US Military Police towards Negroes fraternising with local white women. A riot ensued, resulting in some being shot and wounded. We were called in because it had happened on civilian premises. The American CO blamed the poor leadership of white officers and racial incitement on the part of the MPs. The result was further segregation, which was not altogether popular with the locals, who regarded Negro soldiers as friendlier and more generous than many of their white counterparts. Among those opposed to such mixing, it was said that the climate was unsuitable for Negroes.

I ran into Turk when he attended a Sunday service at our church. Only later did I have the impression that this encounter was by design. We fell to talking and walked around Holywells Park, which looked sadly neglected. Turk admitted he was suffering a crisis of faith. I told him he should consider such a test as a way of strengthening his belief, but I sensed he had more on his mind. I remember we had a conversation about the ducks going about their innocent business. Eventually Turk said he was being transferred and how he

26

valued our friendship. There was another matter, which he wasn't sure whether to pass on, as it was no more than a story going around about how a Negro had raped and strangled a young white woman. I asked if the man had been questioned, to be told he had since died – I presumed in action, until Turk reminded me that Negro airmen were restricted to ground crew, in itself a cause of resentment, as they were not being asked to put their lives on the line.

By this account, Miss Robinson's end seemed both tragic and inevitable.

The death of the Negro serviceman, whose name was Wilson, was listed as a fall from a high building. Turk thought that remorse may have played a part and Wilson had jumped. I began to think this was starting to sound like a penny dreadful and was inconceivable without the Americans. Had they not been there, Miss Robinson would, God willing, have gone her way unharmed, met the right man and settled down to a respectable life.

Again, I passed none of this on to her brother, telling him only that I had been unable to make progress.

Indeed, that was that, or so I thought until a colleague, Frank Benfield, told me of a bizarre incident witnessed by a local spinster, a Miss Elizabeth Mouser, who had been so traumatised that she had only just come forward, and then only because she knew Benfield as a neighbour.

Benfield wanted my advice on how seriously he should take her account because the situation was complicated by the woman having a history of mental illness. According to Miss Mouser, she had been walking home some weeks before at around ten o'clock. Her route took her along the fence of the airbase. In the fading light, she made out half a dozen men in white hoods carrying flaming torches and chasing a man, who was intercepted by more men in hoods, overcome and strung up from a tree.

Miss Mouser returned home in shock – she lived alone, so told no one – and when she returned the next morning nothing appeared untoward. Even though it was beyond her wildest imagination, she told herself that such an event could not have taken place and spoke to Benfield only because she kept having nightmares. Benfield returned with Miss Mouser to the spot, which she had trouble locating, and found her account so garbled that he was inclined to disbelieve her. What the woman described had all the hallmarks of a racial killing by the Ku Klux Klan, although she said she had been too far away to identify the colour of the victim. What Benfield wanted to know from me was whether the matter should be reported to the Americans.

I was bound to connect this incident to the dead Negro, Wilson, but told Benfield that whatever Americans got up to at home, they would not be reckless enough to apply their vigilante justice here. I don't know whether Benfield was convinced. I am not sure I believed it myself. Compared to us the Americans are primitive apes with too much money.

Benfield and I spoke with Miss Mouser, who claimed she was often followed by American airmen, which seemed unlikely given her age and demeanour. Her squalid domestic conditions indicated a woman who could barely cope, while her scatterbrained air suggested that she was away with the fairies.

But I was more perturbed by Miss Mouser's account than I cared to admit, as it seemed such an extraordinary incident to have imagined. I mentioned the matter to Rawls, after he agreed to see me. At bottom, I went seeking reassurance about the unlikeliness of such an event and any connection to the vanishing of Miss Robinson.

Rawls gave me what he called the possible 'low down': that Merriweather had got a gang together to hunt down Wilson as a result of sexual rivalry and a lust for revenge, then bribed someone to state that the Negro had died as a result of an accident, following which Merriweather went AWOL.

Was that what I was suggesting?

It hadn't occurred to me to put it as clearly as that. The obvious answer would be to exhume Wilson and perform an autopsy. (It turned out he had been cremated.)

Rawls, as it happened, was leading me on, putting forward his interpretation of my version to mock me for wasting his time with such 'horse shit'.

I said it seemed not out of the question that Merriweather had exacted revenge after Wilson had raped and strangled Miss Robinson.

Rawls dismissed that, declaring that Merriweather had been concerned only with saving his own skin by going AWOL and had given himself up because he knew he would be discharged and not have to fly again. He blamed Miss Mouser's overactive imagination. There was no reason to believe Wilson's death was anything other than as reported. Accidental deaths were only too common. A gasoline dump had exploded recently, killing six men and two women.

Rawls declared Merriweather a brave pilot who had flown many missions until he got the 'heebie-jeebies' and suffered from what we British call 'lack of moral fibre'. Rawls admitted 'off the record' that mental crack-up among aircrews was much higher than anyone cared to admit and that the men probably needed more rather than less 'mollycoddling'.

Wuppertal was noted for its narrow river valley, hillside housing, crowded old buildings with a lot of timber and an absence of any significant defence, having no obvious military target, other than a parachute factory. The point of that night's exercise, according to the briefing officer, was to target thousands of refugees who had gone there after the recent Dam Busters raid, which had flooded areas of the Ruhr and been a huge sensation in the British press.

Evelyn Robinson wasn't particularly bothered about bombing civilians. 'Hun hate' was widely preached, but usually briefing officers attempted to justify the targets – factories, rail depots and so on – since it was obvious to all that bombing cities would kill civilians.

Was it Evelyn's bomb that incinerated thirty newborn children and their mothers in the hospital with its red cross on the roof, or shrank one of the burnt corpses to the size of a doll, or left a woman naked in the street, her skin completely blackened?

Forty-five minutes out, there was a problem with the hydraulics that controlled the propeller pitch. Evelyn asked if the crew wanted an early return, which would abort the mission. They agreed to press on because it wasn't Berlin or Hanover, where you'd look for any excuse. The flight engineer said they could always pour fluid into the hydraulics to keep them going.

'Piss, in other words.'

With the exception of Evelyn, that was what they did, using several old mess tins, which they kept in the warmest spot in the aircraft to stop them freezing, next to the wireless operator. Deidre Stocker, being a good sport, cheerfully made her contribution, joking that she was relieved to have something to do.

That night was a rare example of no combat casualties, with the loss of just one aircraft which crashed on landing. It was probably as well that Evelyn completed the mission because he had been pulled up for lack of moral fibre, which was considered contagious. His former wireless operator had run amok mid-flight and had had to be coshed with a torch and put in an improvised straitjacket, and that was the last anyone heard of him.

The easiest way to abort a mission before take-off was running the engines with the magnetos switched off, causing the plugs to oil up. The first time, Evelyn did it accidentally. Over the coming weeks he had done it again, once when the collective feeling of foreboding on board became overwhelming, and the third time because he didn't feel like dying that night. At that point, he had found himself dispatched to Bournemouth to what was called an Aircrew Refresher Centre – in fact an open-arrest detention barracks. Evelyn knew from old lags who had done the course that it amounted to a holiday. They were aware the RAF couldn't afford to lose them, so they treated the centres like hotels, checking in for a break from the tedium and terror of flying.

Another thing he didn't know about that night's raid was the pathfinders whose task was to flag the bombing area with flares were using new radar technology. Nor did he know that other aircraft were carrying 30,000 phosphorus canisters.

Phosphorus was not a usual load. The bombs had been developed (by the Incendiary Bomb Tests Panel, for which his sister Valerie worked) to set fire to crops and fields. A large order was put in, but the weather was never dry for long enough and the bombs turned out to be damp squibs. It was decided to make a gift of them to Wuppertal after some backroom boy (for whom Valerie Robinson worked directly) realised that the town's construction and contents put it in the category of somewhere that would burn. The panel did its own testing, which showed that such a bomb igniting upon

31

hitting a roof shot out flames that could set a whole house alight in seconds.

That night, the valley and town were shrouded in mist, with no flak or searchlights to speak of, a sitting duck for a change, although some lights came on as a defence started to be mounted. Evelyn supposed that anti-aircraft units were being rushed in from nearby. Deidre Stocker came up to the cockpit to applaud the drama of it all; silly cow, thought Evelyn, who nevertheless had to admit it was like flying over Armageddon or watching the creation of a distant galaxy, and few were privileged to see such sights. In that moment he almost believed in a higher force as he doubted that humanity was capable of such destruction without the aid of a divine and vengeful agent.

At the altitude at which they flew, the size of the target area allowed a ten-second window for the drop; what they called the 'shit run'. The bomb-aimer was droning in Evelyn's headphones, 'Steady, steady, starboard a bit.' The temptation as always remained to drop short and get the hell out.

'Bombs away,' he heard at last, as though he needed to be told – it was obvious from the way the aircraft lifted after dropping its load. They were already a couple of miles away by the time their bombs hit the ground.

Coned on the way home, Evelyn had to throw the crate around, banking and diving in an effort to shake the searchlights. It was like being caught in a deadly celestial glow. He saw the first bursts of flak as the guns got them in their sights and was aware of Deidre Stocker hanging on for dear life, eyes wide, whether from excitement or fear he couldn't tell. He decided to remember that look for when he fucked her later, in the desperate hope that there would be a later. His adrenalin was through the roof. The aircraft shook in protest at being wrenched around in excess of 300 mph. They passed

360 mph. At that speed, the wings were likely to fall off; still no escape from the blinding lights, flak and cannon, all working together in a lethal choreography. The lights seemed almost casual now in their tracking. He must have blacked out, because his next conscious thought was that the altimeter was showing only 3,000 feet and they were still in the dive. He pulled back hard on the stick, thinking it might refuse to obey or come away in his hands, and suddenly they flattened out and were in the dark. What had felt like hours had been, what, maybe a minute? He didn't know what he'd done to get them out of it. His flying suit was soaked with sweat. He checked everyone was okay. Deidre Stocker had to ask for the oxygen bottle, as she needed the toilet. Evelyn was relieved that he had been too scared to have shat himself. It was like being caught naked in Oxford Street in broad daylight. The wireless operator thought he was bleeding. It turned out he was covered in the urine they had been using to top up the hydraulics, which reduced them to relieved hysterical laughter.

Everyone forgot about Deidre Stocker until the navigator announced that he had found her slumped on the Elsan in a state of undress, very cold, apparently not breathing, and he was unable to locate her pulse. It seemed the mobile oxygen bottle wasn't working and she must have passed out from lack of air. Fucking typical, Evelyn thought, you survive an op to find yourself with a dead woman on your hands. It was so bad it was almost funny. They continued to fail to revive her, and Evelyn was contemplating chucking her overboard when the elusive pulse was finally found and she was slapped about the face until she came round.

DS Copper wrote: Nothing further came to light regarding Miss Robinson until I found a young civilian with a diffident air standing on my doorstep and wondered what I had done to merit a visit at the weekend from a Mr Dyer of the Home Office. He asked if we could talk in the garden as he was there on a matter of some sensitivity.

My visit to Rawls had set off alarm bells loud enough to have been heard in London. Mr Dyer asked me to repeat the content of my meeting with Rawls, which I did, to which he said, 'I see,' although it was not at all clear what he did see. He asked what exactly the point of my enquiry was. I explained what Miss Mouser had seen, or thought she had.

Mr Dyer declared that Miss Mouser had since undergone a mental breakdown. As she was now in the care of Melton Asylum, she could not be considered a reliable witness.

Mr Dyer then asked what I knew about Miss Robinson. Only that she had a reputation where men were concerned, and beyond that next to nothing, her being bound by the Official Secrets Act.

Mr Dyer, like many Englishmen, was not direct. Nevertheless, I understood. I was being warned off. The case of Miss Robinson he dismissed as a 'wild goose chase', and I should stop behaving like 'an American private eye'. Mr Dyer announced that he was visiting on a matter of what he called 'public relations'. The job of the police was not only to keep order, but to ensure harmony existed between the several communities here as a result of the war. He was adamant that no such incident had occurred as described by Miss Mouser. This was said with the air of a man who didn't quite believe what he was telling me. For all his circumspect manner, Mr Dyer implied that he didn't have much time for Americans and was annoyed at having to come up from London on his day off.

I asked what he was there to tell me, as it wasn't clear. Was I being asked to desist in all enquiries about Miss Robinson?

More or less, he answered, still equivocating. The gist of it was, he said, in an effort to be straightforward, that the American authorities were alarmed by the growing incidents of violence involving black and white troops, including the riot at The King's Head. They were keen that such cases be 'swept under the carpet' for fear of further exacerbating racial tension, and it affecting the local population, hence the introduction of greater segregation. In this context, it was important that Miss Mouser's wild story be kept under wraps because it would give the wrong impression and damage community relations. Mr Dyer asked if I understood. I told him I did.

'There's a good chap,' he said and emphasised that there was no need for me to mention any of this to PO Robinson, as there was no proven connection to his sister, whose memory shouldn't be sullied by gossip. On top of that, there was no evidence that she was dead.

Upon reflection, Mr Dyer's visit made sense enough. A local copper was threatening to 'upset the applecart' by asking the wrong kind of questions and needed warning, which was better coming from the home authorities than the Yanks. I came to suspect that what I had been told had been 'planted' to disguise the true fate of Miss Robinson, but given the prevailing circumstances no investigation was going to get very far.

I started to drink occasionally, a beer or two. I continued to frequent The Three Tuns, for no reason other than the hope that Miss Robinson might walk in as though nothing had happened, not that I had any idea what she looked like, although I knew I would recognise her the moment I set eyes on her: a tall, slim young woman framed in silhouette as she entered. These parts are full of ghost stories, and although I am not a fanciful man, I came to see myself as haunting

35

that spot frequented by Miss Robinson in the expectation of seeing her, or her ghost, walk in.

Later on, in 1945, as we got used to our shabby peacetime, Benfield told me of a cousin of his who had been employed in some sort of secret local wartime business, perhaps similar to that of Miss Robinson. She was reported dead after 'a sudden illness', which had taken everyone by surprise as she was 'as fit as a horse'. No one knew exactly what went on in those secret coastal areas, although stories were starting to emerge about various mishaps, including one involving a system of pipes extending out to sea, which could unleash a petroleum inferno, causing the sea to boil, and this was the cause of some terrible, hushed-up tragedy. Benfield said he was bound to wonder about the official account of his cousin's death – and I, too, about Miss Robinson's fate, although no one had reported her demise 'after a short illness' as they had with Benfield's cousin.

Another thing Evelyn Robinson didn't know about that night's raid on Wuppertal was that an Englishwoman was on the receiving end. Recently divorced from a German doctor, Sybil Bannister was visiting her father-in-law with her son, nearly four, and intended to go on holiday the next day with her two sisters-in-law and their young children. It was her birthday and a mild enough evening to sit out. When the sirens went off, no one was especially alarmed; they often did, and the town had never been bombed. Nevertheless, they dutifully sheltered in the cellar, which became overcrowded once the bombardment began. The house next door was one of the first to be hit, with a deafening impact that caused their cellar windows to cave in. One of the sisters went upstairs to fetch a jacket and came back saying that the stairwell was in flames and the whole house on fire. They couldn't fathom how it could have spread so quickly through a four-storey building, even if a hundred firebombs had penetrated the attic.

They had torches and used them when the local warden ordered them to evacuate, through the small opening into the next cellar, and so on until they were told to take their chances outside. Sybil had hurriedly managed to find a heavy coat and leather shoes in the cellar storeroom to replace her straw sandals (one black shoe, one green, she found out later). She grabbed a blanket to wrap her son in.

The three women became separated. One sister ended up in the next-door public swimming baths, in which twenty others were trapped. To escape the intense heat, they had to keep jumping in the pool and wrapping wet clothing around themselves.

The young Englishwoman and her son were instructed to make their way down Adolf Hitler Strasse, the main street, practically the only straight one in town. The whole of it had been bombed with explosives, incendiaries and phosphorus. By then, she was on her own. Her son was shivering and getting too heavy to carry. She struggled as best she could through the flames, smoke and choking fumes, clambering over debris and sticking to the middle of the road because of burning trees and falling branches, but melting tar made walking difficult. Forced to turn round when a house collapsed in front of her, she found herself trapped when another went down behind her. She searched in desperation for a way through the flames where they reached only to her knees. She ignored the burns on her legs and struggled on until she was overcome by the smoke; her strength gave out and her son rolled out of her arms and lay on the ground, still wrapped in the blanket with only his legs poking out. When the flames touched them, he screamed in pain.

Just as she was thinking they must surely die, a spectral vision appeared, wearing a gas mask and riding a motorbike with a sidecar. How he had managed to get through, she had no idea. He told her to get in. On the way out, they saw one of her sisters-in-law with her child and bundled them in too. Then, at the end of the street, the most extraordinary sight: a still intact section of town. Sybil could see the remains of the lines of flares marking the target area. One side was smashed to hell and on the other everything stood as normal. She remembered thinking that it truly was precision work.

Only when they took shelter in a temporary dressing station did she feel any pain, being until then concerned only with her son's safety.

By daylight, they saw the whole city was ablaze. Everyone's eyelashes were singed, faces black with soot and burns blotching faces and hands. Sybil would encounter frizzled corpses, horribly shrunken, pass wailing creatures searching for lost babies or relatives. She heard of burning people throwing themselves in the river only to drown.

Again, she was struck by how the bombing area was marked by lines as accurate as though they had been drawn on a map by the raid's planners in England. Until then, she had been convinced she would never be killed by her own countrymen, yet there she was, a victim of their destruction.

Some weeks later, the RAF returned and carried on where they had left off, flattening the other side. The flares they dropped to light the target were known as 'Christmas trees'.

A reference to Christmas trees is shared in passing with Katharina Fischer, Parker's grandmother, who after the war worked for the BBC Overseas Service and at some point came to the attention of the organisation's security office, during internal vetting, because she had acquired a secret dossier – known as a 'Christmas tree' file, so called because they were stamped with a green upward arrow. She was suspected of political subversion and of being a communist agent for the East Germans, but we are getting ahead of ourselves.

Parker spent some of Robinson's cash on a sweatbox of a gym above a shoe shop on the High Road. Push-ups, leg presses, treadmills, dumb bells, bike machines and skipping, which he turned out to be good at – thwap! thwap! thwap! – his feet hardly touching the ground, almost as though he were floating. He took up running to give a spine to his days. His belly lost its prayer softness. One thing he didn't do these days was kneel.

Robinson fell into a meloncholy state after the bodies of the wee missing were found, in shallow graves in woods near a parking lot.

He took to his bed, where he existed on a diet of Mars bars and red wine brought to him by Parker. It was the first time he had been in Robinson's room, which was tidy and expensively done out in a style of high decadence, with a four-poster bed, black and gold wallpaper, expensive drapes and *fin de siècle* furniture. The overall effect was one of fussiness in dainty contrast to the man's bulk and the general mess. A glass-fronted bookshelf contained French and English first editions of Huysmans and Oscar Wilde and signed copies of Houellebecq dedicated to 'Le Grand Robbo'.

Robinson spent his days and nights drinking and drifting in and out of sleep, contemplating the press hysteria surrounding the wee missing.

The besieged parents no longer seemed to recognise themselves, seen through the distorting lens of the media.

Robinson told Parker, 'The hacks coming up with this hysterical drivel will labour on until they are unable to strip-mine
any more of the infertile ground they're tilling. Thereafter
they will turn on themselves, body and mind moving in advance of the flailing career – cancer, alcoholism, rare blood
diseases, cirrhosis of the liver, depression and dementia.
Opening whole new fields to write about, the collapsing
interior.'

He thought a lot about his father, not about death in the
air but drowning. Water could be cruel. He had been in
thrall to the old man. 'I want to be like you-hoo-hoo!' Boring
childhood, moody little bugger, he had rather fancied a crash
course in bentness. He admired his father because he wasn't
hypocritical; secretive, yes, but quite open about his dealings,
as in: this is the way the world is and this is how it works. His
father had once had a woman called Beatrice, who worked in
films, who said to him, 'There are only two basic emotions:
love and fear. Everything follows from that, which makes the
world both endlessly simple and endlessly complex.'

True enough, thought Evelyn, who was bent even by Met
standards, initiating his rookie son into the standard practices: brown envelopes, conspiracy of silence, free drinks,
tarts on the side, graduating to torture of suspects, in Evelyn's
case employing methods brought back from Northern
Ireland – white noise, headphones for the blokes doing it
and a Sainsbury's plastic bag (or maybe it was Tesco, or even
Asda, definitely not Waitrose).

The real reason Robinson had left the force was because he
had spooked himself, never admitted to others and rarely to
himself. Fall in the Thames around Hungerford Bridge and
you have maybe two minutes to live. The shock of the cold
water paralyses the limbs and you sink, carried downriver

by the tide, to resurface as far as four miles downriver at Limehouse. Any retrieved body ends up in Wapping in a stainless steel bath concealed by a tarpaulin.

He was there one freezing morning because it was thought that a body might be that of a missing young man. Bodies decompose very quickly out of the water. Skin and hair fall off. Even so, Robinson expected to be confronted by a bloated yet recognisable face rather than something that looked like it had been flayed; all part of the process of immersion. Bodies got hit by boats and barges and attacked by gulls. Robinson saw straight away that it wasn't the man they were looking for, but he was assailed by the uncanniest feeling that the features, battered beyond recognition, were his own, and in them he saw his death foretold.

Outside, in the High Road, another puking Saturday night, and Robinson missed that helium way girls talked, with an interrogative rise at the end of flat sentences and reflexive giggles. He nodded off, half-dreaming of a man who found himself thinking of the wee missing at the wrong moment and suffered erectile disfunction, and the woman with him, short of climax, who was months away from a brain tumour, and in eighty-one days the wife of her employer would die in a plane crash after being misrouted and finding herself transferred to a flight she had never asked to be put on, and this flight would open up a strange case of several dead microbiologists, all mysteriously killed, one of whom was a passenger on the plane and turned out to have had some kind of contact with the family of the wee missing. And it looped and roiled and swirled as a mother leapt off a bridge with her kiddie holding her hand, thinking of the wee missing as they plummeted; and the Mayor of London, barnet akimbo, thought of the wee missing – not deliberately, they

41

just popped into his head – as he pursued a bout of rigorous self-maintenance in his executive toilet, spaffing a load prior to a tricky meeting. And the *Toy Story* Prime Minister, what did he think of the wee missing?

Vod's cousin was a newsreader: a blank imposter, famous as a transmitter of others' stories.

Of great recent interest to Robinson were accounts of drift, of cars driving across Europe for little apparent purpose. He was fascinated by old terrorist operations reported by German police surveillance. Someone would drive hundreds of miles to meet someone in a Berlin pizzeria, or go to Sweden to pick up or deliver a suitcase that turned out to contain only clothes. Someone else drove a Mercedes-Benz down to Cyprus to swap it for another with a right-hand drive. None of it added up, as though any point or motivation had been removed from the equation. There were reports on the eavesdropped activities of a suspected bomb-maker staying in a flat outside Frankfurt while ostensibly on holiday. Hours of nothing. The man did nothing. His wife did housework while their young son endlessly played an electric organ. Or the junkie jazz trumpeter Chet Baker scouring Europe for drugs. Booked to play in Italy, he spent his free days driving to Germany to buy stuff over the counter which needed a prescription in Italy. The drugs were dissolved and injected. Accounts of the Baader-Meinhof Gang had the same urgent, desultory quality: endless, endless journeys, a succession of safe houses, committing themselves to a life underground, an unstructured existence, in which it must have been hard to remind themselves what their narrative really was. They had the spoiled petulance of rock stars, those revolutionaries. Robinson suspected that some kind of link existed

between this motivated, restless existence and Nazi regi-
mentation, but he wasn't sure what.

Parker found himself being ordered by Robinson to accom-
pany Vod on errands that required driving. Go there and pick
that up, they were told. Southend. 'A fucking foldaway bed,
for God's sake,' said Vod and, as they got back in the car, 'You
know he used to be a copper.'

'Who?'

'Robinson. Like his dad – and bent, too, which was why
he didn't last long.'

Parker presumed it was another of Vod's stories. Vod knew
he was naive.

'I'm telling you, both bent coppers. Years ago.'

'How do you know?'

'He told me.'

'You're having me on.'

'Scout's honour. Jumped before they were pushed,
Robinson because he no longer had the old man's protection.'

Parker wasn't sure what to believe.

Robinson told them to drop off several bulky padded envelopes to a young woman in Thurrock service station's car
park, whose registration number they were given.

'Should we take a dekko?' Vod asked, then changed his
mind. 'Better not. It could be dodgy money, to do with that
Russian film.'

'What Russian film?'

'Hasn't Robinson mentioned the lost Val Kilmer pic?'

'Not to me. Anyway, Kilmer's American.'

One thing Parker quite liked about Vod was the trouble he
had distinguishing fact from fiction.

'He has a bloke cutting it in the basement,' Vod went on.

43

Well, Parker thought to himself, that explains that.

'Does Robinson go down there?' he asked.

'At night sometimes, when he can't sleep or there's a full moon.'

Vod bayed to show he was joking. Parker wasn't so sure.

'Who's the man in the basement?' he asked.

'No idea, except Robinson calls him Christo.'

'How long have they been working on it?'

'Ages. Years. Before he became soldered to his armchair, Robinson materialised in Siberia to produce a Russian Western. Huge budget, oligarchs' dosh, a monster vanity project, with a psychotic twelve-year-old director making the modern equivalent of an Italian Western, a total revision of the official sanitised history, genocide, head-boiling, hardcore sex, witch hunts, Indians played by Tartars and Cossacks, mountains, deserts, a huge stew, vast studio sets. Rumoured to have starred Val Kilmer, or maybe it was his stand-in or a lookalike, no one's sure, maybe not even Val himself, unless it was him looking for roubles to finance his Mark Twain project. Included the Donner Pass story or a near equivalent, communities of cannibals. Rumours of footage so secret that no one has seen it. It was said human flesh was eaten on set. Wild improv, anachronisms, huge violence, graphic hangings, lynch mobs – as if Jackson Pollack and Roy Lichtenstein had got hold of history and chucked it in the blender with George A. Romero. Zombie communities. It was said Rudy Wurlitzer was flown in. We are in the realm of *El Topo* and *The Last Movie* with a big shuck of *Heaven's Gate* thrown in. Stories of Cimino lurking in drag as a consultant. The uncuttable film and endless post-production, hours and hours of two-shots with no cover, a motley crew of English-speaking actors brought in to do dubbing guide tracks before there was even a cut. The money men say that

Robinson diddled them, ditched the director, confiscated the film, claiming it was a masterpiece that needed time, then did a runner, promised to return and never has. These boys don't fool around. It costs them nothing to have business taken care of. Now there's a hit team after Robinson, which is why he doesn't go out and we're doing the leg work.'

'How do you know all this?'

'I was part of the motley crew brought in for dubbing.'

Later, when Parker asked Robinson what the editing equipment in the basement was for, he asked back, 'Who wants to know?'

'Vod says a film is being cut down there.'

'For God's sake, don't start or we'll never hear the end of it.' Robinson grunted, was silent for a long time, then said, 'Debauchery isn't going into the whore house. It's not coming out.'

Parker read more, picking up books from charity shops for 20p. One he bought because it was written by the author of the book on bombing. He told Robinson, who was still confined to his bed and listlessly suggested he read bits aloud.

Parker said, 'It's a novel, so maybe start at the beginning.'

Robinson grunted. 'Go on. Didn't make much of the last one.'

It opened in Antwerp station, not somewhere Parker was expecting, in a strange mood of restlessness and hypochondria, which reminded him of the house. It was more literary than he was used to, and he rather struggled until he decided what interested him was an aspect of intellectual thriller, the weight of its historical themes, and what seemed to him a cheesy, almost bogus quality.

Robinson quarrelled with the premise that a

45

boarding-school boy in the 1950s could have grown up igno-
rant of the basic facts of the Second World War, exclaiming,
'It was a major currency among all boys at the time!' He told
Parker to look for something more sensational.

In a charity shop – those ubiquitous sorting centres of coincidence – he found two novels with dog-eared pages and
cracked spines, offered for 10p because of their condition.
Parker was in an odd mood, perhaps infected by Robinson's
melancholy, which he had so far resisted.

He felt particularly squeezed that day by a sense of ver-
tigo, looking down when he had once looked up, because
the diabolical was on the march and he was a candidate for
its ranks. Temptation appealed to his vanity; none of which
could be discussed.

Why should he choose those books other than that they
were there, waiting? The two accounts of historical child
murderers Gilles de Rais and Elizabeth Báthory seemed to
tap into a mood he was trying to resist.

Parker thought of the wee missing as he read extracts to
Robinson. He ploughed on in dread and awe, knowing nothing of Rais' twisted love for France's greatest saint. He was
Joan of Arc's second-in-command, and in turn was burned
at the stake for the slaughter of untold young boys. In a perverse invocation of the martyrdom of the Holy Innocents,
they were lured, feasted and tortured with erotic refinements,
then burned in rites of necromancy, in the hope of converting
them to spiritual gold.

The other book was a narcissistic, pathological alchemy
of witchcraft, torture, blood-drinking, cannibalism and
slaughter. The Bloody Countess' many castles became death
factories where hundreds of girls were killed and processed
for the ultimate elixir of eternal youth: the bath of blood.

Although presented as belonging to a mythic, long-ago past, it all felt very contemporary to Parker.

Unknown to him, the Báthory book was written by the French wife of an Englishman who later married a famous American photographer, whose wartime consignments for *Vogue* magazine included a photo spread of the jazz scene in The Three Tuns pub frequented by Evelyn Robinson and his sister.

Robinson finally declared his return to the world, saying, 'I have developed a hankering for Angel Delight. Chocolate, not strawberry.'

Vod and Parker were dispatched to Suffolk with instructions to make a pick-up. Robinson told Parker, 'Fifty quid, try to get away with thirty.'

Out in the countryside, Parker found it hard to tell where the land ended and sky began.

Vod announced they were driving into M. R. James country.

Parker said he didn't know James.

'Ghost stories, characters quite like Señor Robinson. Men who are collectors of historical objects, which turn out to have malevolent qualities. The story I identify with is the one about the orphan boy who sees visions of other children whose hearts are missing.'

Parker stared, at a loss for words.

Their destination was a stultifying road of semi-detacheds on the outskirts of Ipswich. Parker walked up the short path and rang the bell. A woman around thirty-five answered. She had bright red hair, parted in the middle with a sharp line of pale scalp like a scar. She held a large envelope in her hand. Parker offered thirty quid as instructed, and they settled on forty after the woman said, 'I can't see what it's worth anyway,' giving him the envelope and shutting the door.

Parker was looking forward to getting back, but it turned out they had another errand.

He decided in the end that he quite enjoyed being driven around like they were in a road movie, listening to Vod jabber on about his low opinion of the area. 'Feral thugeroos. Rural rudeness. Bad-diet violence. Congested arteries. All the inner conflicts written large on a man's broken-veined face.'

A maze of high-hedged country lanes finally delivered them into open countryside, and it was dark by the time they arrived. Parker found himself looking at a big shed under a bright moon. The huge windowless box stood alone in a featureless field, looking like it had been dropped from the sky. It was surrounded by a high perimeter fence, and a security guard let them in after Vod wound down the window and had a word. It seemed they were expected.

A crowd of cars stood on the parking apron, mainly Land Rovers and aggressive pick-ups. On getting out, Parker could hear heavy bass music coming from inside. Vod stood sniffing the air.

Inside the huge hangar everything looked dwarfed. What appeared to resemble a demented medieval fair was taking place – tents, flagpoles, fast-food stands, the smell of burgers and onions, booze stalls, thump of bass, wire-mesh cages containing violent entertainment, each with its own bookie calling odds. Fighting dogs. Fighting cocks. Even a cage with fighting cats. Bare-knuckle men, stripped to the waist, knocked nine bells out of each other. The sharp tang of sweat and tense excitement. Significant amounts of cash changing hands. The crowd was all sorts, from gentry to tattooed thugs, with as many women in and children who chased each other or used the bouncy castles provided. No one paid attention to any such nonsense as an indoor smoking ban.

Parker spotted Robinson chatting to others, looking for all the world as though he was at a parish fête, and wondered how he had got there. He watched him talking to a squat, hugely muscled man wearing shorts and a waistcoat that showed off his biceps. They were joined by a tall man wearing a tweed cap and a whipcord jacket, who looked like a local squire. Parker had the sense that the men were deferring to Robinson, who appeared as confident as a farmer at market with fat goods to sell.

Vod sidled up and said, 'Maybe we will get to see the fabled room.'

'What room?'

'In the back of the shed.'

Robinson joined them and asked Parker if he had the envelope. It was in the car, and he was told to fetch it.

The contents were an old soft-covered file with a clip.

Robinson said, 'A copper named Copper.'

Vod parroted, 'A copper named Copper!'

'Suffolk name,' said Robinson as though that were obvious.

He had telephoned a woman at the local newspaper archive, who turned out to know Copper's granddaughter.

Vod said, 'Excuse me, but how do you manage to dial?'

'Push-button handset and a chopstick.'

Vod asked, 'Well, are you going to show us?'

Robinson looked as though he didn't know what Vod was talking about. Parker presumed he meant the document.

There was a crack of bone on bone, and a cheer went up as one of the cage fighters went down.

Vod gestured with his head in an exaggerated way towards the back. 'Go on, since we're here,' he nagged.

Parker wondered if these gatherings were a common part of Robinson's life. When Robinson wandered off, Vod nudged Parker to follow.

The shed was divided by a wall. Parker looked back, and the crowd now appeared tiny and far away. After a lot of fumbling, and asking for help, Robinson produced a ring of keys from his jacket pocket and showed Parker which one to use to unlock a steel door that was as thick as a safe.

He went in, turned on lights and beckoned. Parker hadn't known what to expect, but it certainly wasn't a gigantic version of the house. He was confronted by a warehouse temple of military salvage and surplus – army vehicles, motorbikes and sidecars, weapons, ammunition and rifles, even artillery, all of it from the Second World War and a lot with German markings. There were racks and racks of uniforms, and shelves and shelves of boxes.

Robinson appeared unimpressed, bored even, as he scuffed the ground with the toe of his shoe. He looked at Parker and laughed. 'My old man had a bit of a collecting habit.'

'What's it for?'

'Film companies. Prop houses. Anyone who's interested. That American movie brat whom it is beneath my dignity to name was beside himself when he came scouting for some flick he was making. All kinds. Sold an SS leader's greatcoat for fifty grand to a buyer in Qatar and a carved eagle and swastika to a Chinaman for twenty-five. Had one fellow wanting Hitler's ashes. He got palmed off with a fancy urn, any old ashes and a fake letter. He was going to pay a fortune, then got cold feet and reneged on the deal. Pity. Half a mill then. Double or triple that now.'

'But hard to authenticate,' said Vod.

50

Robinson shrugged. 'There's always some mug punter.'

'And David Bowie,' chipped in Vod.

'Didn't think I'd mentioned that.'

Vod laughed. 'You dined out on it for years.'

Robinson shrugged at Parker. 'Well before you were born, our David was going through his Thin White Duke phase, drugged up and too much money to know what to do with it. He was interested in, ah, memorabilia. He'd heard I had the pistol Hitler used to shoot himself; I wouldn't have sold it to him anyway. He had to make do with a spare pair of Himmler's glasses. Charming man, David. We went to Poland because I had contacts there. He was interested in a signed copy of *Mein Kampf*, which I didn't have. He'd also heard Hitler had a golden gun, which he wanted me to find. Anyway, we drive to Poland, he spends like a sailor and we get arrested at the border with a car full of Nazi booty, which David, off his head, thought was a hoot, and he couldn't stop giggling – which he might not have done if they'd searched him for drugs, which they didn't – costing me a hefty bribe and autographs all round from him. Anyway, he moved on to other interests and we lost touch, though I did sell him the Mercedes 600 convertible that featured in the photograph of him at Victoria Station snapping off what looked very much like a Nazi salute.'

On the way home, Robinson sat in the back and read Copper's report, with Parker turning the pages for him while Robinson wondered to himself how the humourless, upright Copper had coped with being so named.

Afterwards, he concluded sadly, 'Broad canvas, but it comes down to the same old tight spaces: cockpit, cell, room, grave.'

Parker didn't know what to make of Copper's account of

rampaging gangs and saloon-bar fights like in Westerns, other than to think they appeared more strangely remote than the occult worlds of Báthory and Rais.

He telephoned the local coroner's office on Robinson's behalf to ask if Valerie Robinson's body could be released to the family, only to be informed that the forensic report offered no conclusive evidence of identity, therefore it could not be proved she was in fact Valerie Robinson.

Parker was told that, as a member of the public, he could request a copy of the report. It didn't tell him much, other than unexplained high levels of radium had been found in the bones, with the coroner hazarding a guess that the woman may have had contact with radioactive luminous paint, which was still extensively used at the time.

Robinson, frustrated by the lack of any conclusion, volunteered little, other than to state that at any time as many as a thousand unidentified bodies lay unclaimed in mortuaries, many remaining in their final lodgings for years; he had wished to spare Valerie Robinson that fate.

He said the names in her story were like shiny pebbles: Merriweather, Copper, Turk, Mouser. Parker wondered if the letters combined to form anagrams with occluded meanings.

Sometimes he found himself thinking about the high levels of radiation noted and Copper's mention of secret experiments gone wrong. In the sort of thrillers Parker read, such information was shared, discussed and followed up. It would lead somewhere. He couldn't see where, so he forgot about it.

What they didn't know was that the unidentified woman was not in fact Valerie Robinson. DS Copper's hunch that the dead woman was the victim of a traffic accident was correct. Two drunken US servicemen had clipped her unlit bike, panicked, bundled bike and body into the car, dumped the bike in a slurry pit and got rid of the body where it was found years later.

As for Valerie Robinson: she was a tall young woman, and by the time the propellor of a Lancaster bomber's Rolls-Royce Merlin engine, with its three-bladed airscrew, thirteen feet in diameter and rotating twenty-four times per second, had done its job, there was nothing left of the unfortunate woman to speak of. Why she had wandered at night onto the rain-soaked runway where aircraft were waiting to take off and walked into one, no one was able to say, and what little was left of her was disposed of without fuss, ceremony or informing anyone. So the mystery of Valerie Robinson and the identity of the run-over woman remained. Sometimes you don't get answers.

Light Entertainment

What was once important, vital even to the very being of existence, fades to a shadow, and so it was with the war. Katharina Fischer supposed she'd had a good one, but all subsequent major decisions – including having a child (Parker's mother, Joyce) – were made perhaps for the wrong reasons.

Born in Berlin in August 1922, Katharina was raised in Charlottenburg, the only child of a well-connected family that survived social and economic turbulence through her father's shrewd investments in foreign currency. Herr Fischer, with an eye to essential services, had founded a waste collection company on the grounds that, however dire the situation, someone would always get paid to clear up other people's mess.

Katharina's mother played the piano to concert level, but nerves prevented her from performing. She couldn't act but was photogenic, and for a few years, encouraged by a friendship with a film producer, appeared in small supporting roles, playing the heroine's older friend and so on, with lines such as, 'You look so marvellous in that!' Her career ('pocket money') amounted to a handful of titles, either comedies (*And Who is Kissing Me?*) or musicals (*The Voice of Love*).

Katharina grew up with memories of social fustiness in heavily curtained, over-furnished and highly polished surroundings, with domestic servants when affordable. Whatever else was going on (hyper-inflation, starvation and riots), she regarded her blinkered existence as no different from any other: we are all born, live and die, experiencing a variety of common emotions from sadness to elation. Not altogether true, she knew, as we remain individual and the time in which she grew up was divisive and traumatic; even so, her childhood was regulated by the common segmentary lines of family, school and the usual anniversaries.

She was a sporty girl and played at the Tennisplätze am Kurfürstendamm. On Saturday afternoons, she was coached by a Russian émigré, an aspiring writer, who told her at her level it wasn't hitting winners that won games but getting the ball back and waiting for your opponent to make more mistakes than you. In that, she was complicit: much of her life was spent returning the ball, without any obvious sign of winning.

She grew up an average student with no professional expectations. She could see she was supposed to get married and produce a family. She taught herself to touch type, as it seemed more practical than her mother's piano keyboard, which was occasionally played for the after-dinner entertainment of assembled guests. Katharina when older attended to the music sheets (right arm folded behind her back, holding her left elbow while waiting to turn the page). She harboured a secret desire to write, about what she had no idea. (The family name on her mother's side was Schreiber, suggesting someone had once written for a living.) Katharina was a sharp recorder of banal observations, but her limited experience offered nothing compared to the dramatic events going on outside, taking place as though behind a thick pane of glass.

Her interest in a boy a little older than her, on whom she had a crush, appeared to be reciprocated, until her mother told her he was not of an appropriate background. Katharina couldn't see why not, as he had been there all of her childhood, a sensitive lad and bookworm whom she had ignored during her tomboy years but was drawn to when she started reading for herself. She knew there were Jews and *Jews*, some of them assimilated into her parents' circle. Their fathers had fought in the war, had been decorated and were as accepted as any other well-to-do family. If these people were good enough for her parents, why was their son not for her? The argument got her nowhere.

Her future was decided by a friend of her mother with a shared interest in haute couture. The woman was a haughty English aristocrat who retained her honourable address and her original married name of Schlegel after her second marriage to a banker who bred racehorses. Katharina was familiar with her only son, August, a slacker with a penchant for jazz and shoplifting, so he told her, who had been the first boy to kiss her, at a party (slippery tongues). Though nothing had come of it, they remained friendly, as it was a time of frequent social gatherings, normally stultifying affairs. August's mother suggested a trip to England might be the solution to Katharina's problem. She would be leaving school that summer. She could be fixed up with a post with English friends. Because of the obvious affiliation between the two countries, despite current political tensions, English speakers would always find useful employment as interpreters.

She was packed off to Zehlendorf for a three-month Pitman course, then went to England in the new year of 1939.

It was the first time she had travelled alone, waved off from the Lehrter Bahnhof by her parents on a train to Hamburg, where she caught the Cuxhaven packet steamer to Harwich (fighting off the attentions of an old English lecher), and from there a train to Liverpool Street, where she was met by the driver of her new family and taken to a village near Box Hill in Surrey, now best known as a gay trysting spot. What little she saw of London looked older and more cramped than Berlin, dirtier and less garish, with roads incapable of handling the heavy traffic. What was she doing there? she asked herself, wondering if she hadn't inadvertently severed all connections with her past, regardless of talk of her return for a summer holiday. Her parents had appeared curiously indifferent about her plans, perhaps because they had their own difficulties and would soon separate (infidelity; his; a secretary).

Katharina was desperate for the lavatory long before they got there, but was too embarrassed to ask, even at a garage where they stopped to refuel. When at last she arrived, instead of being offered the opportunity to freshen up, she had to submit to a long tour of the house and grounds, including the stables, until fearing she would lose control of her bladder she at last got command of her tongue. She asked for the 'toilet' when she should have said 'lavatory' and was corrected, the first of many such small social humiliations.

She grew homesick for a life she didn't miss much, but which was at least familiar compared to her new dank and draughty surroundings, lacking central heating, with its smelly dogs, two ungrateful children and parents who barely bothered with anything beneath their level. They lived in a large rented house, an early twentieth-century example of the stockbroker style. The gravel drive was deemed 'common', as was the 'ghastly rhododendron'. Katharina could not understand why her new employer was addressed as Lady Monica when her husband was Mr Richard Tate, until the older brat explained testily that it was because his mother was the daughter of a duke.

Rupert, aged seven, was hostile, telling Katharina he didn't need looking after. It was only then that she realised she had been hired as a nanny. Diana, aged five, was marginally more accommodating, but even at that age expert at what would become known as passive aggression.

Richard Tate (locally disliked and known as 'Dick Tater') was a stockbroker with a horse breeder's licence. The house came with significant grounds, including a large walled kitchen garden and stables managed by three Irish lads who smoked roll-ups and delighted in showing the children, and Katharina, the mares being 'covered' in the breeding shed. Katharina, both shocked and thrilled, wondered whether such entertainment was appropriate for the children, let alone herself, and whether to report it; she didn't.

As she had ridden as a child, she took to hanging around the stables when she had time, of which there was quite a lot, picking up the grooms' slang (Lady Monica was 'the old boiler'). Katharina ate in the nursery with the children, with instructions that they clear their plates. The worst punishment was leading by example and forcing herself to eat the inedible (ghastly cabbage and Brussel sprouts, cooked to death). A detente was eventually struck with Rupert, who turned out to be an admirer of the dynamic Führer (as was his father). Rupert snapped off Hitler salutes and moaned about how dull the Wolf Cubs were compared to the Hitler Youth. Rupert, she came to realise, was jealous of her being German, and life became easier. He sided with her when she asked if she might be allowed to exercise the horses in the paddock. Rupert fixed it with the grooms, bypassing his mother on the grounds that she wouldn't care. Later, when Lady Monica saw her in the paddock, her only comment was that she seemed to be settling in, meaning that she was expected to entertain herself.

The reason for the house rental, Rupert explained, was its proximity to the local hunt, with which his father rode. Katharina lived in fear of being invited to join in. Ambling around a paddock was one thing. She could manage an elegant trot, according to the grooms, and a passable canter, but she drew the line at gallops or jumps. Her reward was being allowed to curry comb and feed the horses. Her main memory of that summer was a pleasant combination of the smells of saddle soap and straw.

War with Germany slipped in almost without her noticing, despite some concern over the summer about whether she should stay or return. Lady Monica took the line that any war would be over by Christmas because anyone sensible knew they had too much in common to fight. She now regarded Katharina with the sort of affection shown to her dogs, coming under the general heading of properties and responsibility.

Katharina realised too that the Tates were quite without culture, which she rather relished after her mother's artistic pretensions.

The postman delivered twice a day, and any brown envelope or semblance of a bill was thrown unopened in a wicker basket in the hall. When irate creditors pressed, a couple were grudgingly paid by cheque, with no guarantee that it wouldn't bounce. That way, several letters from the Aliens Department of the Home Office were overlooked. It wasn't until a local constable was dispatched to follow up that Katharina's overdue attendance at an internment tribunal came to light. Lady Monica, regarding herself as inconvenienced, decided the Home Office shouldn't get its way.

Whether or not Katharina wanted to stay was not addressed. Lady Monica was a woman of assumptions. Katharina persuaded herself that she had an anthropological interest in this strange breed – casual, arrogant and sentimental, all to the point of indifference, though sticklers when it came to the done thing: the right way to hold a knife and fork, butter applied from the side of the plate to part of the toast, not spread on all at once. Katharina had even come to enjoy the English sense of lazy superiority, with its suggestion that Germans tried too hard and the French were beneath discussion.

The family driver took her to Woking for a fifteen-minute meeting with two officials who looked barely older than her. She was what was known as a rubber-stamp affair. Her character was vouched for by a local MP, a magistrate, a vicar and a doctor, none of whom she had met, apart from the doctor and then only briefly. Lady Monica further stated that Miss Fischer's family, while not Jewish, had suffered religious persecution and the young woman bore an excellent character and there was no doubt about her loyalty to the country.

Everything came up for revision when Richard Tate dropped dead from a heart attack in the orchard while picking apples. Katharina supposed him no more than forty-five and presumed that fatty breakfasts, constant pipe smoking and liberal amounts of whisky had all contributed. Lady Monica seemed unsurprised by the demise and put on a good show as the grieving widow. The children proved stoical as they had hardly known their father. Part of Katharina's duties had been to take them downstairs for their evening audience in his study, a ritual viewed with impatience on all sides. A well-attended funeral took place in the local church. Talk of burial at the family home in Northumberland was stamped on by Lady Monica, who declared that the last thing her late husband would want was any fuss. Petrol shortages were cited.

Lady Monica summoned Katharina to say she would be moving, and with the family finances in disarray – implied rather than stated, as money was too vulgar to discuss – she would not be able to keep her on.

'Rupert was to start boarding in September,' she said, 'but under the circs we think he should go for the Lent term.'

Katharina sewed Cash's name tapes onto Rupert's new school clothes. Rupert put on a brave face, but she could see he was terrified. Couldn't she take him back to Germany, he pleaded, so he could join the Hitler Youth?

As for her own future, Katharina was starting to resent others deciding her life for her. In the same offhand way as everything else, Lady Monica said she had arranged for Katharina to meet a 'racy cousin' at the BBC, who was 'practically a Pinko', but she should be able to fix her up. In the meantime, she could stay at the family flat in Bryanston Square, as no one was there, 'until she found her feet'. London would be fun, Lady Monica promised.

The name of the cousin at the BBC was Herbert; 'Miss,' Katharina was pointedly told. She was a bluff, middle-aged woman who kept a more or less open line to her bookie. Katharina by then knew enough about the English to see that Miss Herbert operated on the far side of eccentric.

Katharina was shown a Berlin newspaper and asked to translate a ballet review out loud, which she did well enough to be told, 'You start on Monday.'

It was difficult to gather what anyone at the BBC actually did. Miss Herbert ran her own department in Broadcasting House, to do with the European Service. Katharina's job, answering directly to Miss Herbert, not that there was much physical contact, consisted of going through German newspapers and offering English summaries of any articles, news stories, editorials and general morale boosting that might be of interest in trying to understand the enemy better.

She ate in the staff canteen, hoping to meet people. She supposed it was similar to Rupert at his boarding school, where anyone new was routinely ignored. He had written a short, desperate letter to her at Bryanston Square saying that apart from being questioned in class no one had talked to him in three weeks. She sympathised. BBC staff seemed so good at avoiding eye contact that she may as well not have existed. Perhaps her neediness showed. One conversation in a lift with a young man ended abruptly when he realised she was German.

Quite unexpectedly, Miss Herbert invited Katharina to lunch. The reason only became apparent when they were shown to a private room in Rules in Covent Garden, where a large, overweight man was waiting. He wore a dishevelled, tent-like suit, flecked with dandruff, and didn't give his name. Katharina had never dined privately in a restaurant. She supposed the man must be important but couldn't see why she was there unless Miss Herbert was matchmaking with someone old enough to be her father.

He insisted on a bottle of 1919 Moët Chandon, most of which he drank. He was aware that Katharina had grown up in Charlottenburg. As he had spent part of his childhood there, he knew it well. His perfect English retained a trace of an accent. They discussed the Berlin they had in common

and, while the conversation was unforced, Katharina suspected she was being assessed. She was aware of talking too
much. The man remained convivial and went out of his way
to put her at ease. She followed his advice to have the steak
and kidney pudding.

It was a lunch well beyond her means, so she remained
nervous in case they were supposed to go Dutch, which she
could barely afford. As it was, the man settled the bill, saying,
'Allow me.' He had volunteered nothing about himself or
what he did, and Miss Herbert contributed little, although
Katharina suspected she knew the man well. Only at the
end, as they were leaving, did he ask how she thought the
war was going.

She answered carefully, saying she wished she could do
more to contribute.

'Perhaps you should come and do some tests, see how you
get on.'

Katharina spent several days in a large house in Carshalton,
not unlike the one the Tates had lived in. With her were
a dozen young women, mostly upper class, an unlikely
German that Lady Monica would have deemed a guttersnipe
and two English boys who didn't look old enough to have
left school. Several staff, older men and women, discouraged
them from fraternising or speculating about why they might
be there.

The days were regulated by bells every forty minutes for
different classes. Meals were taken in silence, accompanied
by the BBC Third Programme. Katharina and the other
girls were given typing tests, without correction fluid, using
English and German keyboards. They were handed English
and German texts for translation, which reminded her of

school exams. She was questioned by an elderly, donnish man, who knew Berlin better than she did.

He asked how she came to be in England and when told said, 'Ah, the Schlegels. She's English, of course. What do you think of her?' Katharina said she didn't really know the woman, other than her reputation for throwing lavish parties and that she had once shared an opera box with the Führer, which she never tired of telling everyone.

'Thoughts on Dr Goebbels?'

She cautiously offered, 'He's obviously a brilliant propagandist.'

'Better than us, would you say?'

Katharina had a sense of traps being set.

A bowl of cherries stood on the table. The man picked it up and offered. Too polite to say no, Katharina took a handful and only after she started eating them did she realise she had nowhere to put the pits. Did she swallow them, keep them in her hand, put them in her pocket or surreptitiously stuff them down the side of the chair? The man looked at her in amusement. Katharina took the pit out of her mouth and chucked it in the direction of a nearby wastepaper basket. She could have got up and dropped it in, but she sensed a certain recklessness was called for and the cherries had been offered as part of the test. She was relieved to see it drop into the bin with a ping. She smiled at the man, who gave her an ashtray for the rest.

'You were saying,' he went on.

Emboldened, Katharina said the German service talks were very dull.

'Have you heard of The Workers' Challenge? he asked.

She hadn't.

'A supposedly left-wing programme, pretending to be

64

British, but in fact a fake station broadcast on shortwave from Germany to the South coast. Listened to avidly by old ladies in Eastbourne and Torquay because it uses the foulest language ever. They enjoy counting all the Fs and Bs.'

Which was, more or less, what she would learn to do.

Katharina was approved, along with three of the women, the German (who turned out to be a U-boat prisoner) and one of the English boys. They were driven in an enormous Daimler car to somewhere outside London; they had no idea where, because all road signs had been removed in case of an invasion. Their destination was a secluded country house with several additional compounds consisting of wooden huts. In a guard room manned by a police sergeant, they were given copies of the Official Secrets Act to read and sign.

Local pubs were out of bounds, and they were not allowed to leave the grounds without permission. Thus did Katharina enter the twilight world that would occupy her next four years.

She had her own sleeping cubicle in the main house, converted from a larger room, that allowed for a narrow bed, a chair and a small chest. She shared with three friendly enough girls, all of them so junior that they were referred to as the 'donkeys'. A sense of segregation prevailed. The dozen or so staff in her department consisted mainly of public school boys, casual in appearance and offhand in manner, so at first she had little idea what the work entailed, other than what they called psychological warfare, which they seemed to treat as an extension of amateur dramatics. However hush-hush the work, hers was disappointingly the same as at the BBC, trawling through newspapers, with the addition of listening to German radio stations. Only after a couple of months, when she was given scripts to type up in German, did she realise it involved a shortwave radio show pretending to be a secret broadcast between two disgruntled German officers, involving coded messages to non-existent agents, suggesting that they were part of a resistance group, with a lot of filthy language thrown in about corrupt Party officials. The hope was that any German listener stumbling across it would think it was an underground station rather than something concocted in a converted billiards room in the Home Counties, with a cast of two, led by a Pioneer Corps corporal who had been raised in Berlin and written detective stories for a living.

It all struck Katharina as rather hammy and juvenile, though the defamatory content was a lot more entertaining than anything served up by the BBC.

Other than top brass occasionally coming down from London for meetings behind closed doors, they were left to their own devices. Sometimes she saw the fat man who had bought her lunch, standing in hushed conversation in the hall or one of the corridors. He showed no sign of recognising her. For reasons never explained, he was universally known as 'Squirrels'. He had grown a beard, which gave him a piratical air.

Only when a vivacious Irish redhead named Molly Fitzgerald turned up did Katharina sense a potential ally. Molly appeared more worldly than the men. It was rumoured she had worked for the Special Operations Executive, which involved being parachuted into occupied France, and was married to a Hungarian diplomat.

'What do you think?' she would ask Katharina when no one else did.

Under Molly's supervision, they expanded from shortwave

to medium wave with a much wider broadcasting range. She told them in no uncertain terms that they were fighting a radio war and any trick in the book was permissible, as long as it was plausible. By then they were capable of monitoring the German wireless teleprinter service, through which they learned about military decorations and promotions, official communiqués and speeches. Even the sports news was relayed.

The fake Forces stations they went on to set up reached a large German audience. One supposedly based in Calais was on air throughout the night and was a big success, with its requests and disc jockeys. A new station for Atlantic crews involved Katharina spending weeks trawling through letters written and received by U-boat prisoners, noting every bit of gossip and family news. This enabled 'siren-voiced Vicky', the Sailors' Sweetheart, to display an intimate acquaintance with the private affairs of 'her dear boys in blue', down to congratulations for birthdays, births and medals awarded. Another station went out on a frequency so close to a German one that they were easily confused, so much so that most Germans believed it was authentic, including Dr Goebbels – to Molly's hilarity.

Molly's mantra was cover, dirt, cover, more dirt. Accuracy first. Never lie by accident or through slovenliness. No dishing on German top brass, but plenty of smearing lower officials, with an emphasis on inequality of sacrifice and pigs at the trough getting fat.

Katharina noted that German military hospitals informing the relevant local authority of a death did so uncoded and gave the deceased's name and family address. Without knowing why, she found herself drafting a letter to one of these relatives, saying she was a nurse and it had been her privilege to console their dear Gustav during his last hours; she hoped it was of comfort to know that he had spoken of his unshakeable faith in the ultimate victory and had asked her to pass on his final greetings.

She showed the letter to Molly, who took it seriously until Katharina pointed out that it was a prank. Quite a lot of that went on, because it was accepted that those in the business of deceit should be tested themselves.

Molly read the letter again and said, 'You're missing something.'

'A named local official, perhaps.'

'Always good.'

'Let's say Gustav had some memento, quite valuable, which he hoped to bring home as a present. The letter states that the gift has been forwarded to the named official, to be handed by him to them. Official does no such thing, because he knows nothing about it, leaving the parents believing the brute thinks nothing of stealing from a hero who died for his country.'

Molly said, 'A perfect example of how the little man suffers, and the story can always be aired: "Today, the sad news of a young soldier who made the ultimate sacrifice, whose final wish that his family receive his parting gift, et cetera."'

Katharina introduced a twist to the letters of condolence she wrote, saying that she could no longer keep quiet about the real circumstances of the death of young Hans or Ralf.

However unpalatable the truth, and whatever the parents had been told, she wrote that their boys had been assisted out of this world by lethal injection. Deemed expendable, with no chance of becoming fighting fit again, they had given their beds to soldiers with a chance of recovery.

The stunt of which she was proudest, though it later

sickened her, as did her whole correspondence, stemmed from a perfectly innocent German article praising blood transfusion units and singling out doctors and nurses for special mention.

The result was a 'doctor' compelled to post that most donors were Slavic prisoners of inferior stock and no antibody tests were done to check for syphilis, leading to unpleasant symptoms after transfusion because infected blood was being pumped into the men who had given their own clean blood for the Fatherland.

Both stories seemed to capture the German imagination. Katharina found them repeated more or less verbatim as fact in transcripts of secretly recorded conversations between prisoners.

Katharina and Molly developed an easy relationship, united in their antipathy towards the English public school boys.

'Don't forget I am Irish,' Molly reminded her and asked what she thought of the Calais station.

'It would be a lot better for playing decent music.'

The officially approved German jazz to which they conformed was anodyne beyond belief.

Katharina said, 'A friend in Berlin used to complain about jazz with strings! Before the war, underground clubs existed where musicians met to jam in the old style.'

It was the first time she had thought of August Schlegel in a long time, and she was surprised to be reminded. She wondered what he was doing now. Slacking somewhere, probably, which he had always been good at.

Molly agreed that broadcasting halfway-decent jazz, which official German stations would never do, would only make the Calais set-up more popular.

'Let's vamp it up,' she said.

Like many ideas put forward by the women, it wasn't taken seriously until it was appropriated, usually by Squirrels, who made out that he'd just thought of it. However charming the man was, he held that women should know their place, including Molly.

Katharina wasn't particularly surprised to hear about special recording sessions doing exactly what they had recommended. Later, she met the band leader, who had been a name when she was growing up. Taken prisoner by the English Eighth Army while touring North Africa, he now found himself in the unusual position of being allowed to play decent music. At least he had the courtesy to tell Molly and Katharina, 'I am told it's you I should really thank.' Whether out of mischief or not, Katharina couldn't say, she put in a request for her favourite tune, with a dedication to August Schlegel.

Once, when Robinson was out visiting his mother, Parker came across a ring of keys. Wondering whether they were the ones Robinson had lost, he tried them on the padlocked door opposite his room. They worked, but whatever was in the room there was a lot of it, because Parker had to shove the door. The first thing he saw was a large portrait of a man in uniform, whom he recognised as Adolf Hitler. The rest of the contents were a mini-version of the big shed, all Third Reich: pistols, uniforms, swastika artefacts, even some furniture. He presumed the same went for the dozens of boxes. Several photos lay around, including Polaroids of a younger Robinson with a giggling David Bowie and another of a gold-plated pistol.

Parker told Robinson what he had found.

'Snooping?' asked Robinson.

'I am just saying I found the keys.'

'And snooping. A lot of rich Russians buy that stuff, you know. See it as trophies. Long memories. Pay silly prices.'

Parker said, 'I thought you fell out with the Russians.'

Robinson looked at Parker inquisitively. 'Says who?'

'Vod.'

'Vod will say anything for a punchline. Not true. I didn't fall out with *all* of them.'

Parker continued to clip sensational newspaper stories for Robinson, who now delegated the job to him – including one about a murder in which a young woman's body had been found in a flat for sale in North Kensington. For some reason, Parker didn't know why, he thought of Vod.

He found a couple of old laptop computers among the junk. Robinson used the internet for what he called dabbling in the currency market. 'How else do you think I turn a shilling? Not from the crap in this house.'

The internet was largely unfamiliar to Parker, so he was surprised to find it quite easy. He started to fantasise about an electronic world in which his physical appearance was not an issue.

With one click leading to the next, he came to see how, in a celebrity-obsessed society, enticements of wellbeing and happiness would be accompanied by increased psychosis. The ubiquity of technology would lead to greater surface conformity, while internet pornography (in which, Parker told himself, as with the girlie magazines in the kitchen, he took a rather disturbed academic interest) would become increasingly calibrated in terms of controlling response, leading to a greater isolation. The pornography he didn't understand, any more than he would want to spend his time looking at dead moths. He thought it not impossible that a technological advance into any virtual world would be accompanied by a reversion to a biblical state, in which Satan made his presence known.

He learned how the internet operated as grazing grounds for conspiracy theories. He noted a report of a woman who had taken her husband into the woods for 'sex play', then cut his throat (not part of the play) and went off to see a man she'd met over the internet. (The husband survived.) Then there was the kindergarten help who abused children and was in touch with similar people she'd never met, other than through social networking.

Parker knew that the psychology of paedophilia was more complex than was generally allowed: the child could feel empowered for being singled out, and for many adults abused in childhood the greatest private fear was that they would in turn offend; at which point, he switched off.

Parker's parents had not exactly become estranged, but they hadn't played a part in his life for years. He was nevertheless surprised to find himself telephoning his mother to say that he had left the seminary. She expressed no curiosity other than to say, 'I see,' her tone suggesting he had at least come to his senses. She asked what he was doing, and he said, 'Finding my feet, I suppose.' She implied that at least normal service had been resumed. The conversation left Parker feeling, as usual, that he had no knack for everyday exchanges.

He couldn't have known that his mother was wondering whether to voice her suspicion that his father had other men in his life, not women as she had once thought. The thing was, she didn't mind particularly. It wasn't that she hated her husband; she even enjoyed his tortured state, a result of his inability to come clean. He had, with age and loss of looks, become increasingly miserable, and she fed off that. About her son, she didn't know what to think, other than him being a lost soul, a state for which she had little sympathy because she regarded life as mineral and material.

They agreed to meet at the old BBC Television Centre in the top-floor restaurant, an anachronism which still had waitress service. His mother had worked for years in light entertainment. Their lunch was an almost deliberate non-event: the cool greeting of two people among a room full of professionals going about their business; discussion over the menu, with her recommendations taken; a celebration of sorts offered, with her having a glass of wine when normally she didn't at lunch; he stuck to mineral water.

The room was dominated by the presence of Jimmy Savile, with his peroxide hair, string vest and Day-Glo tracksuit. Parker watched him eating alone with the attitude of a man who didn't wish to be disturbed, while showing off in a way designed to make him the centre of attention.

The man was aggressively eccentric – the yodel, the guys-and-gals disc jockey catchphrases, tracksuits long before they were fashionable (ease of access), the gold jewellery and big cigar – in a calculated way that projected onto everything. Stories abounded, yet he continued to hide in plain sight, the lifelong bachelor who spoke openly about being a Jack-the-lad who had never come close to marrying (too busy 'living the business') and described sex as 'like going to the bathroom, and like what they say about policemen, never there when you want one.'

His mother had her back to Savile, and Parker didn't point him out, even though they had worked together. He

73

remembered her once saying that there was nothing light about light entertainment.

'It's nice to see you,' she said, and he almost believed her. Her hair was different, he said. 'Yes, I think better shorter.' She pointed out that she had lost weight. Parker had noticed but hadn't thought to comment (in fact, undiagnosed cancer). She had taken up a fitness programme and running, she said. Running! Running from what? Parker wondered, thinking of himself.

It was like having his childhood compressed into the space of an hour: the meaningless back and forth, his mother's fear of silence, the wariness of any confrontation. Parker said he was doing odd jobs for a strange but interesting man who was convalescing with broken wrists. He could see her thinking he was trying to make it sound more interesting than it was. And so it went, with his mother's effortless defensiveness controlling the situation.

In terms of conversations never had, Parker was close to chucking a brick by mentioning what Father Roper had done to him at school. In Savile, he saw something of the priest, which frightened him; two brazen men getting away with it. His old school had a website now, but had no mention of Roper. Searching within the wider order, Parker also found nothing, which was strange because it was thorough on whereabouts and obituaries. Perhaps the man had left the monastery; without its protection, Roper might be easier to confront – what Vod would call 'a pathetic old geezer, hanging around sweet shops'.

His mother in return was about to say, 'There's something you should know about your father.'

Neither revelation occurred because they were approached by Savile, who knew her well enough to join them and hijack the show. He was waving a large unlit cigar, which he pretended to smoke, kissed Parker's mother's hand with a wink and an aside to Parker, saying, 'She always was one of the saucy ones.'

Parker was surprised to see his mother simper. He supposed it was the man's fame. He had called her Jocelyn when her name was Joyce, which she didn't correct.

Savile kept up a seamless monologue, a pretence of conversation that brooked no interruption, however many questions he asked. 'And how's life treating you? Marvellous, gal, I can see!'

Parker was introduced as her son, followed by Savile's double take, announcing, 'She doesn't look half old enough,' followed by asking if she had been underage when she'd had him. He said he was keeping trim, always busy, but with plenty of time for the ladies. He turned to Parker's mother and asked, 'Now then, what shall you and I be doing in the lift on the way down?'

It was all done in such a crass way that it was impossible to take offence, as though the man were making a mockery of the sort of polite conversation Parker and his mother had wasted their lunch having. It would have been even more cringeworthy were it not for the granite hardness of the man's humourless eyes.

Savile looked at his chunky bracelet wristwatch and said, 'Time waits for no man and nor does the Director General, as it happens. Great to see you, doll.'

He joined his hands as though in prayer and bowed separately to Parker and his mother.

'You want to get something for that skin, son,' he said in a not unkind way that only underlined his indifference. Once his back was turned, Parker could see that they were forgotten.

His mother muttered, 'Everyone hates the man, but no one stands up to him.'

Parker told Robinson about the encounter, not expecting a connection to be made.

'Yes, Jimbo is familiar to us,' Robinson said. 'I have it on good authority that he has an arrangement at Stoke Mandeville hospital that lets him spend time alone in the morgue.'

What Parker wasn't expecting and Robinson seemed amused to admit was, 'My old man has an accountant named Halliday, with an office in the Holloway Road, near where that Telstar fellow had his studio. Halliday ended up fixing it for Jim, a lot of charity stuff.'

There was a further surprise when Robinson said, 'Both my old man and Savile have papal knighthoods, so they must have done *something* right.'

Parker said he had never thought of Robinson's father as a Catholic.

'A left-footer?' mused Robinson. 'Not as far as I know. Then how did he get a gong from the Pope? He probably bought it with a hefty donation in exchange for his so-called good works. Opens all sorts of doors.'

There was always the thrill of the quick pick-up, usually around the aptly named Queens Terrace. Parker's father, as did other men working for the BBC, used his marriage, home and family as cover for relentless sexual activity. Dominic Parker preferred shooting his wad free of female complications. While the pretence of conformity took a huge effort, the purpose of his al fresco cruising was blunt and to the point. All that remained was negotiating the how of it, usually the mutual wank. For the rough stuff and the leather, there was

The Coleherne Arms on Old Brompton Road, with the risk of being spotted (he was a face on telly, and sailing close to the wind was integral to the thrill). Appearing before the camera, he had learned how to compartmentalise (talking to the microphone while being fed instructions via an earpiece), so it wasn't that difficult to separate his life. He worked at first in current affairs, so named, the joke went, for the department's reputation for adultery (lots of paid travel). His wife had followed her mother, Katharina Fischer, into the World Service, before transferring to BBC Light Entertainment, that clubbable but bitchy enclave with high rates of depression and deviancy.

Dominic equated women with social aspiration; sex with men was an excuse for slumming compared to the tedious social rituals of feminine pursuit. Hunting men came easily in terms of cocksure impulse and furtive agenda. His great last love was nondescript, his choice of wife being more impressive than his taste in men – perhaps not so surprising as marriage was the more considered decision, and her role, not that she knew it, was to provide cover. The edifice needed to appear well-constructed. To be true to himself, he had to betray, and always the fear and thrill of exposure, with perhaps the relief of no longer having to pretend, and even a voluptuousness to the prospect of disgrace, with rent-boy scandals and blackmail only a whisper away.

Parker knew nothing of his father's other life. The little surviving evidence lay in several 'Christmas tree' files at the BBC, which was an assiduous snooper. Dominic's dossier included reports of his suspected leanings, noted his ability to rub people up the wrong way and being a possible target for extortion.

A secret MI5 report on high-profile staff noted suspected

links to MI6, and an aggressive interviewing style that had made powerful enemies of influential politicians, including one known 'pansy' with a reputation for being vindictive. The dossier concluded that he remained a valuable staff member, probably knew too much about what really went on, which might turn him into a whistleblower were he thrown out. Verdict: manageable on the inside, dangerous on the outside.

Despite the BBC's reputation for social liberalness and a cosy family atmosphere, its cult of informing wasn't far behind that of East Germany, but the organisation was careful to guard its information rather than sully its reputation by exposing scandals of those who were the organisation's public face. Even at junior levels, it was understood that ingrained into the culture were two maxims: 'Don't rock the boat' and 'No speaking out of turn'. Besides, there was the stressful schedule of getting the product out, which drove everything and excused short memories.

Dominic's transfer to senior management in Music and Arts was recommended, and reluctantly agreed to by him, on the grounds that he had upset too many politicians; the BBC was both mindful and craven when it came to governments and negotiating its often fragile independence.

Parker hadn't paid much attention to his parents while he was growing up. They hadn't been around much to pay attention to. He was aware of his father being older. His mother was thirty-three when he was born, his father eleven years older. Parker knew he had appeared on television in the late 1960s. He wasn't sure exactly what either of them did other than complain about workload and change for the worse. Like a lot of grown-up business, it wasn't of great interest to a child. He did remember asking if his father could arrange for him to be on *Jim'll Fix It*, to be told: absolutely not. He recalled the sharpness of the response, but put that down to it being his fault for asking.

The daily skein of their existence he struggled to remember. There was little sense of parental authority. An atmosphere of casual, frictionless tolerance prevailed, but he grew up not quite sure what role he fulfilled for either parent. Meals were often not taken together, with Parker being given supper early, 'so he could watch television' (*The Fast Show*, *Father Ted*), which really meant that they didn't have to put up with his company. When they did dine together, it was to the accompaniment of radio concerts or light entertainment. A strange sense of anachronism hung over the house.

Much later, Parker's mother told him there had been a child lost prior to him. As for the secrets she kept, it was not a miscarriage, as she'd told him, but an abortion following an accidental pregnancy, because at that stage she believed a child would get in the way of a career in which she considered herself ambitious and promotable.

The decision to have Parker came about when her professional options were reduced after she was bullied by a man brought in to head her department, attentive at first (because he wanted an affair), then hostile. She was reprimanded for a production error involving a chat show guest being taken to the wrong location, for which she was blamed when it wasn't her fault. She was also investigated over her expenses claims and found wanting when everyone got away with fiddling them. After that, her career moved neither forward nor backward. Stuck, she grew bitter (and drank more).

As for Parker's so-called normal childhood, there were anomalies. His mother had grown up speaking German with her mother, and in his early years she spoke enough with him for him to understand; this to the annoyance of his father, who could not see the point. At an early age, Parker decided that his life didn't unfold in the way people's did in stories, where there was an organising principle to what was being told. He didn't think of himself in terms of who or what. He'd had a difficult birth, as his mother kept reminding him, and he wondered if that was the cause of a reluctance to confront or engage. Always a bit of dreamer, it was said of him; not that he saw that, either. He regarded himself as unimaginative, other than creating elaborate hiding spaces in his mind and an imaginary sister, conjured up before he learned about his mother's miscarriage. He attributed to his fantasy sibling a wild and fanciful ability to make up stories out of anything; not that these were shared with him. Had he known about his father's secret life, would he have felt any less out of step, would it have explained his sense of growing up in the shadow of something? Probably not. The shadow was already there.

His parents coped, or at least it seemed they did. They complained but never rowed, at least not within his hearing. The conversation around his childhood was invariably grown-up, but when he tried to join in he was either ignored or momentarily indulged. Then it would shift up a gear and become like trying to follow a language he didn't understand. Thinking about it tired him, like writing school essays or feeling as though he were swimming uphill.

Finding himself aged almost twelve at a school run by Roman Catholic monks came as a complete shock. He remembered it happening soon after he had decided to give up on his parents. This was trumped by the extraordinary decision (as far as he was concerned) to pack him off to board at a Benedictine priory. The implications of his father's lapsed Catholicism and his own baptism had never been issues to

80

which he had given any thought. His religious instruction had been perfunctory. A First Confession and First communion had been his mother's doing, even though she wasn't Catholic, so he blamed her too, which was not quite fair as it had only been done to get him into the local Roman Catholic primary school, which was by far the best in the area.

His father's decision seemed to have nothing to do with any religious persuasion (church attendance minimal and religion not talked about). He could afford the fees ('Just') and believed enough remained of the English class system for a private education to be an advantage. Parker was told he had not helped himself by failing his Eleven Plus exam, which would condemn him to a rough local secondary school, so after discussing the matter with his mother (though not with him), his father announced that he had managed to get him into the Junior House (ages 11–13) of St Ambrose College.

The prospect of a boys' school run by monks struck Parker as horribly medieval, and he wondered what he had done to deserve such a punishment. It would be the start of a loop, on constant replay, outside time: 'Come in and shut the door.'

Outside that door, a red light shone, warning that no one should enter.

While they waited for the light to go green outside the recording studio, Molly Fitzgerald said to Katharina Fischer, 'There's someone I want you to meet. We're thinking of doing a series of religious broadcasts.'

'Religious broadcasts?'

'As a way of drawing attention to what's going on. We have a tame priest, Father Anton, Austrian, salt of the earth. I want you to work with him.'

'But I am not religious.'

'All the more reason. The plan is to start on All Saints' Day, so better crack on.'

Katharina was given a stack of folders and told, 'Last summer, we learned from the Warsaw underground that tens of thousands of Jews were being gassed in a secret death centre. Now it seems the business has moved to a huge labour camp and extermination is being carried out in a working environment. Summarise what you find in these files. We're being passed considerable amounts of information from the camp underground. I want to know its history, broad strokes, with names and so on, as quick as you can.'

The scale of the project shocked her. A huge slave colony; grotesque medical experiments in the name of scientific progress; a fantastic contempt for life; murder on a clinical, unimaginable scale; all on the edge of an ancient town with a medieval castle, and a garrison posting with staff wives and their children going to local schools.

She wrote: 'The camp was established in 1940 in a former Polish cavalry barracks with 7,000 mostly Polish prisoners. In 1941, construction of a second camp for 100,000 Russian war prisoners was begun at a nearby abandoned hamlet. This has since become a centre for deported international Jews, many of whom are gassed on arrival. Deportees, believing that they will be resettled, turn up with the permitted fifty kilos of luggage. This is confiscated and placed in store, but with the volume of traffic it is often left lying around for staff to treat like a rummage sale. Organised theft is said to account for a huge increase of sales to the Swiss jewellery market.'

Molly introduced her to Father Anton, a simple priest of peasant stock wearing a coarse habit and sandals. Her first impression was that he looked too young to be up to the job.

However earthly his physical appearance with its potato head, he seemed otherwise entirely unworldly.

Molly said, 'Father Anton hasn't yet read your report, so perhaps you can tell him the situation as it stands.'

'Auschwitz is a high-security zone that's off-limits to outsiders,' Katharina began. 'Until now, it has managed its own internal discipline.'

'Very much like the Roman Catholic Church, wouldn't you say, Father Anton?' Molly asked breezily.

'Of course. Himmler models his SS on the Jesuits.'

Katharina wondered if he was sharper than he looked as she went on. 'The camp underground reports that corruption has reached such levels that an external SS prosecuting judge by the name of Morgen has been sent in.'

Katharina didn't mention her discovery that Morgen's assistant had the same name as her childhood friend, August Schlegel. She wondered if it could possibly be him.

'What do we have on Morgen?' Molly asked.

'A known troubleshooter with a history of rocking the boat,' Katharina replied.

'How does a man square investigating corruption against a backdrop of mass murder?'

Father Anton answered. 'That falls outside his remit. The gassings are sanctioned, if not officially ordered. There will be no paper trail. Morgen will be there to clear out the barrel's rotten apples. But Reichsführer Himmler is a cautious, timid man and will be reluctant to accept anything that shows the SS in a bad light, so he will be watching closely.'

Katharina realised she had underestimated him.

'Any more on Morgen?' Molly asked.

'His investigations tend to end up blocked from what we know. He exposed a big black-market racket in Warsaw in

1942, until Himmler decided he was getting too close to favourites he wished to protect.'

'Any names for these favourites?' asked Molly.

'Hermann Fegelein, an SS cavalryman, currently Himmler's liaison officer at Hitler's headquarters.'

Father Anton said, 'And reputed to be Himmler's spy in the Chancellery.'

'Spy?' echoed Molly.

'They all spy on each other. In certain circles, Fegelein claims to be part of an organised resistance movement putting out peace feelers, not unconnected to Himmler's ambition to take over now that Hitler is considered no longer up to the job.'

'How do you know all this?' Katharina asked.

'The Church has a very clear idea of who its enemies are, and the confessional is a very secure way of passing on information.'

'Yes, but how do we introduce a religious angle into the broadcasts?' Molly asked.

'You could take the Ten Commandments. Thou shalt not kill . . .' Katharina suggested.

Father Anton nodded.

'We know about theft in the camp,' said Katharina. 'Thou shalt not steal. As for covetousness, there is that huge store of confiscated prisoner belongings they call Canada.'

'Canada?' asked Molly.

'Symbolising the land of plenty. The commandant's wife is known to be an avid shopper there.'

'Can we know this for sure?' asked Molly.

'The wife employs prisoners in her house as domestics, cooks, gardeners, seamstresses. They are observant and pass on information to the camp underground. It's said the wife is very friendly with the commandant's immediate boss in Berlin and sends him gifts because she is nothing if not ambitious on behalf of her husband, who needs protecting because Himmler is thinking of firing him.'

'Reason?' asked Molly.

'Rampant corruption and too many prisoner escapes.'

Christ the Redeemer was decided on as the name of the station. Father Anton asked Katharina to attend his first reading rehearsal. The delivery was cruder than what she had imagined and wasn't how the man really was. She could see he wasn't happy, so she pointed out that radio was an intimate medium.

'I don't mean you're shouting, but it sounds like you're trying too hard.'

'I was thinking of a popular seventeenth-century priest who was the imperial court preacher in Vienna. He addressed his congregation as a homespun man of the people and attacked privilege in informal and coarse ways. Given the sarcasm I have heard in other broadcasts, I presumed this was what was wanted.'

'Dialling down' was one of the unit's common expressions; she told him he should be more himself.

'You mean, don't preach. It would help if we could get the right music to set the mood.'

They went to the gramophone library and settled on Bach.

'Then I introduce the station and say a prayer,' he said, 'followed by sacred music – a Gregorian chant, perhaps. And then the talk. I will speak in my own vernacular, which says I am but a simple priest.'

The sincerity of the first broadcast brought tears to Katharina's eyes, despite which she couldn't decide whether

Father Anton was driven by simple goodness or was a consummate performer.

She wondered if he wasn't more Jesuitical than he let on when he subsequently suggested that word should be spread that the Christ the Redeemer station was secretly operated by the Vatican as evidence of the Pope's condemnation of the Nazi regime. This struck Katharina as mischievous, because the Pope had been especially careful not to voice the slightest opinion on the matter.

Penetration

'Bless me, Father, for I have sinned.'

Parker's sin seemed to take on a physical manifestation. His skin had started to crack, flare and peel, with painful red blotches that were impossible not to scratch, leaving him lacerated.

He didn't know what he might confess, other than choosing a priest with a reputation for being fair and friendly. Father Damien was one of the younger ones, with a cowlick of hair, and was indulged by the boys because he could distinguish between techno and rave. Part of the reason Parker had chosen him was because Father Damien suffered from acne.

The curtain in the confessional meant he couldn't see the man. He reminded himself that he was addressing God through the priest, and God's forgiveness was infinite and whatever was said remained sacrosanct.

Confession was usually a fabricated affair – a few venal sins mumbled like they were part of a shopping list: admissions of lying (fibbing in doing so because he did not remember any), then what were known as impure thoughts, which covered a multitude of sins.

This time, he asked if he could take communion if he was in a state of mortal sin.

Father Damien asked if there was anything he needed to confess. Parker fell silent. He wanted to say what had happened, but lied instead that he had been tempted to steal and asked if that was a mortal sin.

'Not unless you did.'

Parker remained silent.

Father Damien asked testily, 'Well, did you?'

'No, Father.'

He was given three Hail Marys for his penance and absolved of his sins, Father Damien telling him, 'Go now and sin no more.'

Parker had first come to the attention of Father Roper, headmaster of Junior House, halfway through the term before, his first, which had passed more or less in a state of shock, with the rough discovery of dormitory life after having his own bedroom at home; finding himself in an ugly uniform; the braying herd mentality; the confusing geography of the school and frantic searches for the right classroom; vile food, which had to be finished; a life of religious salvation where the stakes suddenly seemed a lot higher.

He was told to report by one of the prefects. Father Roper held his sessions at six o'clock, dealing with cases of discipline. Parker waited outside in what by day was a secretary's office. The red light by Roper's door was on, forbidding entry, and Parker wondered fearfully what he might have done wrong. When the door at last opened, a boy he knew by sight shot out, puce-faced, with his hands clasped under his arms.

The first words Father Roper addressed to him, standing on the threshold, were, 'Come in and shut the door.'

He was a tall, spare man, clean-shaven as monks had to be, with close-cropped hair. He wore round-framed spectacles and was generally feared despite an air of bonhomie. The monks wore dog collars and long black tunics, referred to by the boys as filthy habits, and they were collectively known as crows. Parker was told to sit. The chair was next to Father Roper's desk. The curtains were drawn. The room smelled of pipe tobacco and furniture polish. It was the first time Parker had been in it.

Father Roper announced, 'If you can't trust yourself, who can you trust?'

Parker had no idea what the man was talking about.

'Erskine said you copied his mathematics homework. Unfortunately, you repeated his one error, which was how it came to the master's attention.'

Parker could see no point in saying it had been the other way round. He was quite good at maths, and Erskine had been sitting next to him. He experienced incredulity and paralysis: the dank intimacy of authority's hand and, in terms of later jeopardy, souls in the balance and damnation.

'Of course, I must beat you for your own good,' said Father Roper.

He showed Parker what he called a ferula.

'Whalebone covered with leather. I smack your hands with it. Or there's the cane, six of the best to your backside. Your choice.'

Parker stared dumbly at the instruments, incapable of answering, other than to bleat, 'It's not fair, sir.'

He resolved to make no mention of the matter to Erskine, thinking he was being brave.

'Fair isn't for you to say, boy. Take the cane. Two extra strokes will teach you what's fair. Stand up and take your trousers down. You can keep the underpants on. Do you understand? Now, bend over.'

The fourth stroke made him cry out. The sixth drew blood, and the last two caused him to wet himself.

After the beating, Father Roper seemed to find reason to take an interest in Parker's welfare. He was regularly called in and lectured in a friendly way about realising his potential; it was the school's job to see that every boy achieved his best.

The smell of that stale, stuffy room with its permanently closed windows clung to him down the years. At first, Father Roper seemed to treat him as though he were an adult, encouraging him to talk about himself and how he saw the future, about which Parker had very little to say as he was still bewildered at finding himself in such a place.

'Well, plenty of time to decide,' he remembered being told, as well as being warned of the attentions of other boys.

'These can be difficult years at your age. Show me your hand. Not the left, the right.'

Parker held it out, deeply confused as Father Roper grasped his fingers. His hand trembled. For a brief moment, he thought the priest was muddling him with Jesus and looking for signs of Christ's stigmata, which they had just been told about in Religious Instruction.

'A good healthy lifeline,' was all Father Roper said, taking a long time to let go.

Father Anton's next homily asked listeners to imagine the temptation of untold riches in a netherworld of disease and squalor where tens of thousands were forced to sleep like animals in converted horse stables.

'Let us turn to the commandant's wife, who tends to her

roses and complains about the ash that falls on them. She is a compulsive shopper in the store known as Canada.'

Katharina listened as he continued, focused and bereft, standing at his lectern. He seemed not to be reading but reciting from some inner self.

'There exists,' he continued, 'the dirty miracle of shopping, a short walk from the gassings. The lucky prisoners, usually young women saved by their looks, who work as sorters in Canada are always arrayed in the finest clothes, which they change as they wish, their hair coiffured like they have walked out of a Paris salon. Each time a wealthy transport comes, they say, "Oh, this underwear, these shoes and all these eats! All I can say is: Canada!" The bliss of ownership begins to affect them like hashish. Perhaps this is also a form of oblivion, like the alcoholism of the SS.'

Father Anton was drenched in sweat by the time he finished. He stood for a long time before crossing himself, giving Katharina an intense look she couldn't read.

They were assigned to a small room at the top of the stairs with a distant view of an old graveyard. Father Anton was an assiduous maker of tea, which followed a precise pattern. He didn't talk much. Katharina didn't either but compared to him she felt like a chatterbox. At noon each day, he broke off to say the Angelus.

Katharina fell half in love, probably because his calling placed him out of bounds. Nothing was said but their gestures spoke for them. She thought this dangerous innocence was perhaps a response to the horror they were dealing with.

Colleagues seemed not to care about what was going on in Auschwitz, and Katharina was aware that theirs was seen as an unpopular job, lacking the element of gamesmanship that was relished. Jews were one of those subjects that remained ignored, other than casual references to them being pushy and vulgar; what Lady Monica would call 'trade'. That she and Father Anton were German and Austrian now seemed to count against them. Molly's Irishness was always regarded as borderline; by English standards, being married to a Hungarian was considered dangerously cosmopolitan.

They told Molly they wanted to call out the worst of the camp's staff, starting with a senior interrogator, who was only twenty-three.

'A lot of them are frighteningly young,' said Katharina. 'He's lame and walks with a stick.'

'Which he uses to hit people,' interjected Father Anton.

'A bit of a peacock, so everyone knows who he is. Struts around in mufti and a hunting hat,' Katharina said.

'Is that enough?' Molly asked.

Father Anton said, 'We have his medical report.'

'His actual record?' Molly asked, surprised.

'From the camp underground.'

As Katharina watched Father Anton record his next session, she thought how accomplished he was becoming. The tone was regretful yet intimate as she listened to him chide the young man. 'Let us examine your symptoms: stomach pains, insomnia and high anxiety, which under the circumstances we can understand. After drastic weight loss, you now weigh only fifty-nine kilograms, still a lot more than your starving prisoners. But the prognosis is not good. Your physicians attribute a psychosomatic cause to your complaints.' Father Anton paused for effect. 'Perhaps, my dear fellow, it is because you are in the wrong job.'

His performance reassured her that they might have an audience after all. The Calais crowd, with their daily broadcasts, music requests and disc jockeys, behaved like it had a huge following. Their staff swanned around like stars and threw the best parties. At the most recent, Katharina had witnessed the extraordinary sight of Father Anton dancing the conga.

She congratulated him after the broadcast, but he was not consoled, saying, 'We do what we can, but the killing goes on.'

They went to Molly and suggested that the names of several of the worst offenders, including the commandant, be given to the BBC to broadcast in connection with the crimes involved.

'I don't see why not,' she said, 'but it's a subject the BBC is nervous about.'

Katharina never found out what strings Molly pulled and was surprised when the BBC published the names in a stilted broadcast that sounded as though the reader was holding a peg to his nose.

Some weeks later, Molly told them, 'I think you can congratulate yourselves. The commandant has been kicked upstairs, probably after being named by the BBC.'

She said the official reason given was the camp's new corporate identity.

'How do you give a death camp such an identity?' asked Katharina.

'I know, but with long-standing boundary disputes resolved the region is fully open to new investment opportunities. A more accommodating front than what the commandant stood for was needed.'

'Boundary disputes!' exclaimed Father Anton.

'They have been arguing for years about who owns what,' Molly said, then added, apparently as an afterthought, 'Auschwitz has its own telephone area code.'

'It would, as part of the general German exchange,' Katharina said.

'2258. With a large switchboard and its own garrison directory, which we happen to have a copy of.'

Molly produced it from a drawer.

Father Anton looked at her. 'Are you thinking what I am thinking? It would be impossible. There are no lines to Germany from here.'

'But there are from Switzerland,' Molly said and announced breezily that she was about to go to Zurich.

'What for?' asked Katharina.

'Oh, this and that, including meeting my errant husband. He's concerned that Germany will make a move against his native Hungary before too long.'

'How's your German?' Katharina asked.

'Good enough to talk a man into bed.' Molly apologised to Father Anton. 'In a manner of speaking. I thought I might try to talk to Morgen.'

'Out of the blue?' asked Katharina.

Molly tapped the directory. 'He's in the book with a telephone extension number.'

Katharina said, 'If nothing else, it will spook the man. What do we want from him?'

'In terms of his future neck, he might find it useful to have an outside line.' Molly laughed. 'It's the fashionable thing now they're getting jittery. Hermann Fegelein – the man with the peace feelers – is sniffing around Zurich too.'

Molly returned a week later and announced that it was as they had said: general switchboard, a listed telephone extension, and at her second attempt Morgen had picked up.

'I was so surprised I nearly hung up out of nerves.'

Katharina doubted that. Molly was just making the most of her story.

'I told him I worked for an English jewellery firm in Zurich, hence my accent, and valuables had come to our attention of possible interest to him because they were probably stolen. Morgen took his time replying and I thought he was about to cut me off, so I said I was calling on behalf of neutral observers interested in his investigation.'

'Did he buy that?' asked Katharina.

'Well, he didn't hang up. I mentioned I was in discussion with Hermann Fegelein about the future of Germany, which got his attention.'

'Did you meet Fegelein?' Katharina asked.

'Ran into him, let's say. Not difficult, as he hangs out at the Hotel Baur. They all do. Nothing but the best for our Hermann.'

A daisy chain was being threaded by her diplomat husband between Allied parties and so-called progressive Germans.

'Fegelein plays the game, but he's easy to read,' Molly said. 'Lashings of dubious charm, fancies himself a womaniser, a lot of knee-patting and sitting on the political fence waiting to see which way it plays out.'

Katharina wondered how much Molly was telling and whether her role was more that of *femme fatale*. When Molly arched an eyebrow, it seemed as though she had read her thoughts.

She went on, 'I told Morgen I knew he had previously investigated Fegelein for corruption, so I was interested in his opinion. Morgen advised me not to touch him.'

'What's your impression of Morgen?' Katharina asked.

'Tenacious, unimaginative. Speaks with a ponderous

drawl and a lot of throat-clearing, which was good for me as it gave me time to note down what he said. He described the commandant as a monosyllabic man who says they have been handed an enormously difficult task and not everyone has the guts for it.'

Father Anton interrupted. 'Typical German self-pity, all about the sentimental tragedy of the perpetrator. Paints himself as the victim. We can use that.'

Molly referred to her notes. 'Morgen more or less said that in every army in the world a military guardroom is distinguished by a spartan simplicity. He demanded a full inspection upon arrival, and the one he was shown was more like a hotel, with colourful couches on which glassy-eyed SS men drowsed. There was a giant stove, at which four or five girls were baking potato cakes. They were obviously Jewish, all pretty and not wearing prison uniforms but normal, even coquettish, dresses. No one took any notice of him or the accompanying adjutant, who explained that the men had had a hard night dispatching several transports. He told Morgen that if no doctor was present they sped up disembarkation by inviting the newly arrived to select themselves by politely telling them that the camp was several kilometres away and whoever felt too sick or weak to walk could make use of the transport provided. Whereupon there was a stampede for the vehicles.'

The beatings started in earnest at the beginning of Parker's second term. He was not one of those who could talk his way out of trouble, and he found himself being regularly thrashed by Father Roper for all kinds of non-existent transgressions: inappropriate behaviour on the games field, kicking a football in the wrong direction, dropping litter (which he admitted to). Because the man stood for authority, Parker never thought of him in any other way. Bruising from the last caning was often evident when he was summoned for the next. He found he could take a beating, but Father Roper was expert at transferring blame, with a theological dimension to the whole charade, as though whatever was going on occurred at a level beyond Parker's comprehension. Closer to, there was the manky odour of the man, a clamminess of touch, bad breath and the monk's habit smelling of stale sweat and tobacco.

Parker would see Father Roper going about his business in school as though nothing had happened. He had no terms of reference. Might what was being done to him be a mysterious initiation that was part of a common secret experience? There was no one he could ask. Or tell. He didn't have the words to begin to formulate an objection.

The secrecy of the confessional and the show of religious observance further mocked him as he saw the monstrance being held up in Mass. He supposed he should stop taking communion, but carried on going. He knew suicide was a mortal sin, so when he considered hurling himself from the bell tower it only compounded his own lack of worth, which silenced him even further.

'Go now and sin no more.'

'Come in and shut the door.'

'Tripe, I would say,' Katharina told Molly, who had come back from Switzerland with a thin file and asked for her opinion.

'I thought it all sounded rather Edgar Wallace,' Molly agreed.

'Quite. Private clinic, three mysterious hooded bigwigs. Top-secret facial surgery performed. The men leave, one said to be Hitler, on a submarine from Bremerhaven, the clinic burns down and the staff all perish. The clinic did burn down, I checked, but even so. It's what the boys call bollocks. Where did you get this?'

Molly smirked. 'Passed on by dear Hermann Fegelein as an example of his bona fides.'

They were joined by Father Anton with his ever-present cup of tea and two for them.

'And who's doing Adolf's job for him now?' Molly asked.

Katharina said, with a straight face, 'We've had no reports of a regime change.'

That set them both giggling.

'One of the man's doubles, we can only suppose,' Molly said.

Father Anton, unable to understand their levity, announced ponderously, 'We know Stalin is thought to use them, for fear of assassination and so on, and Churchill is said to as well.'

Molly sniggered. 'There's a report from before the war that a double was sent to open a new autobahn and because of a cock-up the man himself turned up as well, to general hilarity, including the Führer's.'

By then, they could barely contain themselves.

Katharina said, 'The clinic that performed the recent operations is also said to have created four Hitler doubles.'

Composing herself, Molly asked, 'And Adolf's whereabouts now?'

'Retired to the Vatican, studying for the priesthood.'

That set them off again. Katharina expected Father Anton to laugh as she had when she'd read it, but he remained serious.

'The Vatican, of course, has the status and diplomatic immunity of a sovereign nation.'

Katharina, trying to keep a straight face, said, 'The surgeon was supposed to have been asked to give his mystery clients exaggerated Semitic features. I can't see that when the man's destination is the Vatican, unless someone has a very warped sense of humour.'

Molly agreed. 'This is pure mischief.'

'The report also claims Hitler has been appointed curator of the Vatican art archive, a post far above his humble rank as a novice, making him responsible for a collection worth millions and putting him in a position to receive priceless artwork looted by the Nazis.'

Molly said, 'Since we make up porkies for a living, it looks like someone is having a joke at our expense.'

'And Fegelein's motive?' asked Katharina.

'Joker in the pack, I'll be bound, although he's not known for a sense of humour, for which I can vouch. Willing to pass stuff on, perhaps to see if we're gullible enough to swallow it and broadcast.'

'And to slander the Vatican,' added Father Anton, who took the idea more seriously than they did. He thought it not impossible that Hitler had experienced a Damascene conversion after the defeat at Stalingrad.

'He sees himself as an artist, perhaps feels his vision has been betrayed by those incapable of realising it.'

'But the Vatican?' insisted Katharina.

'It could be argued it is the understandable desire of a man who regards himself as spiritual to seek a life of contemplation after considering his work against the Jews almost done, and perhaps not unappreciated by the Vatican, which is no friend of theirs.'

'Are you saying the man is redeemable?' asked Katharina.

'As are we all,' said Father Anton morosely.

Molly said, 'I don't know why we're laughing. The man's work is evidently *not* done. There's now the matter of Hungary's Jews since the SS took over. Contacts in Budapest tell us that none other than the former commandant of Auschwitz is hanging around the Majestic Hotel discussing deportations. What's more, he will return as overall garrison commander, with the task of handling delivery at their end.'

Later, Molly told Katharina that links between Hitler and the Vatican might be more established than was supposed.

'A militant clergy in Allied Croatia persecutes Jews. In Hungary, part of an equally aggressive Church backed antisemitic legislation. I know through my husband that back-channel negotiations were going on before the war, and the Vatican agreed Rome would remain silent on German political matters in exchange for persecution of the Church being stopped and it continuing to receive a large financial subsidy from the government. The arrangement involved quashing over seven thousand cases against Catholic priests accused of financial and sexual crimes.'

'Seven thousand!' exclaimed Katharina.

'I expect they're exaggerating, but the Church has a lot to thank Hitler for. He has eliminated the Bolshevist atheist threat for the moment.'

As Katharina left, Molly said, 'I think better not to share this with Father Anton. He takes too much on his shoulders.'

One beautiful summer morning not long afterwards, Molly announced, 'Morgen's back!'

Katharina remembered hearing a cuckoo outside as she said it.

'Or at least his deputy is,' Molly said.

Schlegel, Katharina supposed to herself.

Molly went on. 'Apparently they're trying to reopen the investigation into the commandant since his return and are looking for a female prisoner, possibly Jewish, who was his mistress.'

'Racial defilement, as they call it.'

'On top of which, he got her pregnant and no one can find the woman. Mostly they're got rid of when that happens.'

Father Anton wasn't at the meeting. Katharina had noticed Molly getting impatient with him. He seemed more downcast, as though his spiritual side was irreparably scarred. He had confessed to Katharina that he felt as though he was in danger of losing God's presence.

'Anyway,' Molly said, 'see if you can find out more about this woman. Thou shalt not commit adultery, and all that. Talking of the man's wife, take a look at this. She is evidently past caring.'

It was a handwritten letter on headed notepaper stating it was from the wife of the garrison commandant. Katharina wondered aloud if it was a fake.

Molly shrugged. 'The camp underground said it managed to get its hands on it via the post office.'

Katharina read, 'Dear Luise, sorry you could not be with us. Schilling was just splendid. Sat next to Brigitte, and she wore the most beautiful fur coat I have ever seen and the necklace she wore was fit for an empress. She told me she shops in Canada and that my husband is aware of it. So sad he could not be with us, for he received another shipment that night and all had to be processed by early morning, for there is another on the way. I don't know how much they will be sending. It is a good job, but they are working him to the bone.'

'Not much you can add to that,' Molly said bleakly. 'I would like to see the bitch shamed. Dig up what you can on the other woman.'

'Not much' was the answer. The underground had gone very quiet, apart from confirming the contents of the letter concerning the rushed deportations from Hungary.

In terms of things she would rather not know, Katharina learned that a new rail spur now took trains directly into the camp, with an unloading ramp adjacent to the new purpose-built gas chambers. Furthermore, the whole operation was being reported as a cynical exercise in economics, and the SS, which had built them, had occupied Hungary primarily to avail themselves of more Jews to gas because the four death factories, completed only the year before, remained underused and had yet to justify their cost.

Katharina reported back to Molly about the mistress.

'All I've managed to dig up looks like an old story.'

'Maybe there's more than one woman.'

'This one worked for the commandant's wife the year before last, and according to female staff her husband had a big crush. It seems she was treated more or less as an equal.'

'Therefore not Jewish.'

'She wouldn't have got a job there if she was. Said to be Austrian.'

'Regarded as German, then.'

'Still part of the master race. They get all the best jobs.'

'And if you're Greek, you probably don't stand much of a chance. Do we know what happened to her?'

'Apparently starved to death after getting pregnant. I presume she died.'

'Does she have a name?' asked Molly.

'Hidell or Hodys. And up to a point very chummy with

102

the commandant and his wife, because they threw a birthday party for her.'

'Do you buy that?'

Katharina nodded. 'Staff report a fairly thorough picture of life in the house, down to the colour of the tiles in the bathrooms.'

"Which are?' Molly asked.

'White in one, green in the other. And the commandant and his wife don't sleep together.'

'I would distrust anyone with a green bathroom. Perhaps the woman was well-bred and the wife's a social climber. Garrison life must be pretty ghastly – bored wives, social constraints, companionship in exile. Lots of repression and staring out of windows. It all sounds quite Ibsen, or is it Strindberg?'

The pressure of getting the programmes out was taking its toll. On a short break, the boredom of which was harder to handle than the confinement of endless work, Katharina was taken to the Savoy for drinks by Miss Herbert, who was accompanied by a man half her size who had been a jockey before the war. Katharina stared in disbelief at the drunken liveliness and sexual electricity. She apologised for being poor company and left early, to the evident relief of Miss Herbert and her tiny companion.

Years later, long after the events related here, Parker watched a Netflix drama series about Britain's secret black propaganda war against the Nazis and wondered if a minor character (a German female refugee, second-tier love interest) was based partly on his grandmother. The show was offered as a racy alternative to the more familiar Bletchley decoding war.

The young woman's part was beefed up far more than the sketchy account told to him by his grandmother. Some details matched – a rackety, upper-class English family, a stud, stables and grooms, all much grander than her version, which amounted to little more than anecdote. In the dramatised version, her straightforward application to stay as a refugee is beset with complications, until in a light-bulb moment her employer announces, 'Getting you hitched is the answer,' followed by an arranged and unconsummated marriage to a man of local distinction referred to as one of their 'bugger' friends. Parker was sure that hadn't been the case with his grandmother. The audience is reminded that homosexuality was then illegal with a subplot involving charges against the grooms for 'unnatural practices', conducted in part out of spite because of their Irish neutrality. As with such series, hours and hours had to be filled, and although the woman's story took up little screen time, there was a sense of inflating her meagre material so that, unlike in life, everything was 'explained'.

Parker's decision to study for the priesthood was based on crippling shyness and a fear of the outside world. Even if God were a hoax, the idea had served for millennia, and he persuaded himself of the advantages of a cloistered life. His senior school years had passed as though submerged in a bathysphere. His social mixing was poor. He tried fantasising over girls with no real understanding of what he was fantasising about or how he would react when they found out he was damaged goods. Parker wondered if he would be better off without all that. Sometimes at night he lay awake in the dormitory after the others had gone to sleep, touching himself, petrified, thinking of a shooting star hurtling through black space.

He had been left emotionally eviscerated by Father Roper, a period of eleven weeks and two days – he had counted them off – ending as suddenly as it had begun after his skin flared up, as though his body were articulating what he could not. It left him wondering if he shouldn't be grateful for it turning the man off, but it was the start of a lifelong curse. He avoided looking at photographs of himself taken before and was excused from official school photos, which left his passage through that institution unrecorded.

He viewed the affliction as his punishment. It left him deeply divided. He feared he had been set on a path.

Having been singled out – to which there had been an intense, hard malleability, however paralysing – Parker could only observe as Roper moved on. His memories were of his own horrible uniqueness and whether something about him had made Roper's choice inevitable; and always the recurring fear that even in his blighted state he might be recalled.

Doctors offered no solution. At the senior school, he was called Freddy Krueger, sometimes to his face. 'Hey, Freddy!' His parents gave up on him as a useless case and became even more inexplicably busy with work. Friends' children were all going to university. When it came to leaving, Parker in effect didn't, staying on by telling the headmaster he thought he had perhaps been called to serve God. He was a good dissembler when it came to believing. Over the years, he became dutiful in his religious observance as a distraction from the inner conflict. He served at sung High Mass, perhaps because his affliction left him little option but to join the God squad or work in a leper colony. The latter had been suggested by another boy during a class with the careers' master, a man spectacularly devoid of ideas. 'Do you think Parker should go and work in a leper colony, sir?'

By then, he had got used to the endless teasing, which he suspected was fuelled by insecurity. He knew he made other boys awkward and saw that the question had been asked less to embarrass him than to expose the useless master, who failed to see that the joke was on him.

Recruitment into Holy Orders was practically non-existent by then. The year he went in, one other boy from Hong Kong joined, a soft, pudgy lad. Parker suspected the monastery couldn't afford to be choosy. He completed his trial period and found he didn't miss anything, certainly not his parents, who had greeted his announcement of intending to become a priest with a mixture of relief and disbelief. If they ever suspected anything was wrong, they had not bothered to ask. Parker sensed their marriage was in crisis, but as they didn't ask about him, he didn't ask about them.

He took his vows despite his suspicion that his vocation was about remaining in the prison of his choice. He looked up and prayed to God to deliver him from his arrested state while the Devil tempted him with fantasies of crushing Roper.

Did he believe in God? He believed he believed, which was not the same.

Part of his thinking concerned Father Roper's discomfort at being aware of his having joined the community and being there as a reminder and possible accuser. Haunted as he was, Parker saw it as his turn to haunt the man, if only from a distance. He had barely seen Father Roper after the junior school. Parker's seminary was at a sister abbey in Yorkshire. Once, during a joint religious retreat, he passed Roper in the corridor and the years fell away and he was rewarded by Roper's startled look, though nothing could be said because the retreat was conditioned by a rule of silence, but seeing Roper's surprise – and fear – was enough for the moment.

Once Father Roper had done with his twelve-year-old body, Parker sought to suppress all feeling. Routine. Bells. Class. More bells. In the senior school, his one escape was joining the film society, sitting in the dark, being shown worlds outside his own. During the holidays, he watched a lot of television, finding some comfort in its escapism. Because of his skin, he had asked his father to write to ask if he could be excused school games. It was the last time he asked his father to do anything for him. The real reason was to avoid the communal showers because he feared he might be drawn to other boys' nakedness. His academic standards slipped from being seen as bright to being considered thick. He suffered panic attacks and told no one. He had to listen to his father berate him for a lack of effort. When he moved on to the senior school his performance remained barely that of an also-ran.

Time ceased to feel linear. It rushed, zig-zagged or barely crawled, while the flashbacks to Father Roper's room were a constant flicker in his head. He grew familiar with the toad squatting in his soul, Roper's malignant gift. Given the unlikelihood of it being evicted, there was always a chance it might devour him.

As for what he had suppressed, there were two incidents when he had tried to tell, more out of despair than courage. In their last session, as Father Roper started fiddling with himself, Parker had asked tearfully if the man would hear his confession. Roper said, 'Not now,' but soon gave up on himself and asked, 'What should you want to confess?' He regarded him queerly. Not that Parker could put it into words, but the man seemed gripped by a combination of ecstatic excitement and dread.

Parker said, 'I don't know if it is a sin or not.'

'Tell me, so I can decide.'

Parker said nothing, though it was obvious he meant what was happening between them.

As Father Roper guided Parker's hand up his habit to grasp the stiff member, he said, 'If you are shown something by God's representative in trust, that trust must be respected. It is not for you to understand but to obey. Now, kneel down, say an act of contrition and I will absolve you of your sins.'

Whether because of the condition of his skin or his pathetic attempt to confess, Parker was never summoned again. He left with his hand sticky from the man's ejaculation.

Two boys were expelled from the senior school after being found in bed together. Parker wondered if he shouldn't be expelled too. The idea was almost attractive. But where would he go? The thought of another school was terrifying. He was barely coping as it was. He feared being found out because disgrace would turn him into even more of a reviled object. Worst would be his parents knowing and the shame of having to account for himself. He revised that to it probably never being discussed, so it would become part of a greater silence.

He eventually screwed up the courage to confess to Father Damien again, partly because he had stopped taking communion and was asked why by an older boy. Seeing his tongue-tied state, the boy looked at him suggestively and said, 'A mutual wank's not a mortal sin.'

The first time, he had lost his nerve and said he had been tempted to steal. The second occasion was a repeat of the first, until Parker blurted that he had been interfered with.

He heard the priest's sharp intake of breath.

'Interfered with how?'

'I have been touched.'

'Touched how?'

'Down there.'

'Was this something you agreed to?'

'No, Father.'

'By another boy?'

'No, Father.'

'Did this happen at home?'

'No, Father.'

Father Damien was reluctant to ask by whom, if not a boy or at home. He said instead, 'If it was not with your consent, then you are not to blame. Was there any encouragement on your part?'

'No, Father.'

'This is a very serious accusation. Will you give me a name?'

'I cannot, Father,' he said, meaning he knew he wouldn't be believed. He was overwhelmed by hopelessness.

Father Damien said, 'I recommend you do not place yourself in a situation where it might happen again.'

'It has stopped, Father. It was Father Roper.'

It was as though the toad had spat out the name. Another sharp intake of breath from the other side of the curtain.

'You do realise what you are saying?'

Parker could tell the priest didn't believe him, which probably meant he thought him either mentally unbalanced or a troublemaker. He left the confessional in a state of confusion after Father Damien implied it was up to the perpetrator to bring the matter to God's attention and otherwise Parker was more or less telling tales.

The twist he hadn't been expecting occurred when he was approached subsequently by Father Damien, who appeared friendly if embarrassed. It was the end of school break, and he had the impression that the priest had been looking for him. They were standing outside, and the bell was ringing.

Father Damien said, 'That incident you referred to, can you tell me any more?'

Parker said he would rather not.

'We are talking about a senior staff member. It is a serious allegation. How were you interfered with?'

Parker stared at the ground, aware of scratching his face. He wondered what anyone watching might think they were talking about as he said, 'He touched me down there, in front and behind.'

'Did you do anything in return?'

'He asked me to touch him.'

'Which you did.' It wasn't a question.

'I was told to do as I was told.'

Father Damien said, 'I need to take this further for your own protection, but I can't unless you repeat the name outside the confessional.'

Parker saw only trouble and said he couldn't and anyway it had stopped.

'There might be others.'

'I still can't say, sir.'

It would be his word against Father Roper's. He would be accused of making it all up because of his skin and his failure to keep up. Sometimes even he almost didn't believe what had happened in the nightmare of that room.

A few days later, he was summoned to see Father Roper. Father Damien was waiting with another priest he didn't know. Father Damien introduced him as the Provincial Rector of the Order, who would talk to him about what had happened. Parker's immediate fear was that Father Damien had broken the sanctity of the confessional and informed Father Roper of Parker's accusations, which would be thrown out, leading to more punishment.

After that, Father Damien left and never spoke to Parker again. What amounted to an interrogation began. Father Roper said nothing. He appeared almost friendly, not avoiding eye contact; if anything, staring as though daring him.

The rector wanted to know every aspect of Parker's sexual history. Had he started to masturbate? Parker struggled to answer. He was asked whether he had done anything like it with other boys. Did he have sexual fantasies about other boys? Had he had sexual contact with any member of his family? The questions came thick and fast. He broke down, and Father Roper smirked.

Parker was having flashbacks to the start of the ritual beatings and the weird dependence that developed as Father Roper talked openly about temptation and damnation; then the progression from these thrashings to the man standing behind, pleasuring himself unseen beneath his habit; then the hand on the buttock, his head held down, turned sideways, the penis rubbed in his buttock cleft and the buggery, its passage eased with spit; it hurt, a lot; the only thing to be thankful for was it was always over almost as soon as it started. Then afterwards, the talk as though nothing had happened, the most chilling moment when the man said, 'In this room, you can call me Timothy.' Parker was too frightened to contemplate it. The sentence haunted him, for its excruciating attempt at an emotional intimacy. What troubled him most was his brief glimpse of the real man, trapped in anguish and loneliness, which was enough, even at the time, to be able to identify with him. He came to associate that forlorn utterance with the despair of the forsaken in the De Profundis. The session ended as always with another homily, a talking down as it were, waiting for the room to return to normal. Parker, burning with shame, sensed that the priest was both exultant and mortified, in contrast to his own pitiful state; he noticed that someone had pissed on the parquet floor, which must have been him, though he had no memory of doing so; the size of the puddle stood in marked contrast to Father Roper's dribble of desire.

The rector broke off his questioning and told Parker not to be upset. He and Father Roper left the room. When they returned, the rector was friendlier. He talked about how the school would deal with the matter. Parker was given strict instructions not to talk to anyone, including his parents.

Father Roper asked, 'Are you still unable to name this person?'

Parker looked directly at him and said, 'Nobody would believe me, sir.'

Father Roper appeared both disconcerted and pleased at that, and Parker experienced a moment of what he supposed was triumph, thinking that Father Roper knew it was within his power to name him, even if he didn't. Only afterwards did he see how his silence compounded the devilish pact between them.

He was told he was free to go. The rector thanked him for attending, but the unstated implication was that without a name he was wasting their time. Parker was left more desolate than ever, however much he tried telling himself that the whole business of physical penetration was absurd and meaningless. He had been a vessel, a lump of meat. If he meant nothing to the priest, he should try not to take it personally and instead blame his selection on misfortune. He brooded endlessly on the impersonal nature of these transactions and the talks afterwards, which were almost as traumatic with their abrupt resumption of normal service, like someone had just switched channels.

His report for his last term in the junior school was dismal enough for his father to write a letter of complaint. Parker had had to endure all his shortcomings being read aloud.

Father Roper wrote back, 'I think it fair to say the school has done a great deal for your son in the last two years. It is not for our lack of trying that he has failed to find his feet. I suspect he struggles with his skin affliction, and I know he has talked to the school matron about it. I have every confidence he will adjust to life in the senior school and make a success of things. Life is full of late developers.'

Katharina started to smell alcohol on Father Anton's breath early in the day. She persuaded herself it was communion wine from saying Mass each morning in his room. But the smell persisted and when he started to appear hungover and unshaven she wondered how much he was drinking.

Molly said to Katharina, 'I want you to meet someone.'

It involved a short journey in a car with a driver and blacked-out windows. Molly told Katharina to sit with her in the back so they could talk.

'The man claims to be an SS deserter,' she said. 'Not many of those; a cavalryman, by name of Kitzler, who says he was Hermann Fegelein's adjutant.'

Katharina asked the obvious question. 'Do you think he's a plant?'

Molly gestured equivocally. 'Claims he is part of a resistance movement and Fegelein is its leader. Apart from the pleasure of your company, I thought you should come in case my German misses something.'

They were taken to an internment centre that looked like it had once been a nursing home; there, they were escorted under guard to a windowless room.

Katharina had expected a tall, blond Teutonic type rather than a bright-eyed, rosy-cheeked young man with a high-pitched voice, who even in flannel slacks looked as though he were wearing riding britches. For all his fresh, boyish air, he barely acknowledged them, telling them he wasn't there to talk to women.

Molly sat, provocatively crossed and uncrossed her legs and finally said, 'Start singing or we parachute you back to Germany. I hardly need point out that desertion is a capital offence.'

Kitzler shrugged and answered with what Katharina recognised was Berlin slang; otherwise she would not have guessed where he was from.

Molly asked if he was aware of Judge Morgen's investigation into Fegelein's black market activities in Warsaw in 1942.

Kitzler sniffed. 'Brigadier Fegelein is no common criminal. His wife is sister to the Führer's mistress.'

Molly snorted. 'Yes, that shop girl. I can't see the sister being much of a catch.'

She mentioned that she had met Fegelein.

'And talked to Morgen, too,' she added.

Kitzler appeared disconcerted at that. Molly looked to Katharina to take over.

She said sweetly, 'If you feel you have been wronged, then help us get rid of those who betrayed you.'

Kitzler recited stiffly, 'The patriotic ideals of the SS have been traduced by an unworthy leadership, which has clothed its worst hangmen, sadists and gaolers in the uniform of the noblest elite of German youth, thereby soiling its good name throughout the world.'

Molly applauded ironically and said, 'Then help us wipe it out. Or we think about the parachute.' She glanced at her watch. 'We could have you back tonight.'

Kitzler resorted to Berlin slang again, saying, 'Stand around the coffin and join in the crying.'

Molly said, 'I think you're making up this resistance nonsense to distract from the fact that your brigade put thousands of Russian civilians to the sword. Shall we talk about that?'

Kitzler remained huffily silent, apart from saying he had been promised an interview with a senior officer.

'That's us,' said Molly.

Thinking that their background gave them something in common and Kitzler looked the sporty type, Katharina asked conversationally if he played tennis. He treated the question as though it were stupid.

Katharina persisted. 'I used to play in Berlin.' She named the club.

'Yes, the SS used to play competitions with them.'

That much was true, Katherina knew.

'We had a very good Russian player who gave me lessons,' she went on. 'He said at my level I just had to return the ball and wait for the other player's mistake.'

'The Russian coach, yes, I beat him.'

Katharina doubted that but let it go. She said, 'If we are now both on the same side, wouldn't it be better if we started returning the ball?'

The remark was met with a humourless laugh but it seemed to do the trick. Perhaps the man thought he was hitting winners.

He began with a sneer. 'That investigation in Warsaw conducted by that silly ass Morgen got completely the wrong end of the stick. The black market operation was cover for our real work.'

'What? Rounding up Jews?' Molly asked sarcastically.

'Well, that too, those were our orders,' Kitzler replied pompously. 'Our real purpose was to help arm the Polish underground.'

Even the unshakeable Molly looked surprised at that. 'How so?'

'To supply their guerrilla army with captured Soviet munitions. These were stored in SS dumps, and we could get hold of them without them being missed. We were also able to help free Polish resistance men from prison.' He added, as though it were perfectly obvious, 'We both hold Jews and Soviets to be the common enemy. We also smuggled Poles into Sweden pretending they were Gestapo agents.'

'How come you're here, then?' asked Molly, again sarcastic.

Kitzler scowled. 'I was betrayed and imprisoned by the Gestapo. But despite a reputation for big ears that hear everything, they have tiny brains and are bribable has-beens. It was easy to get me out, and the Poles returned the favour by smuggling me to Sweden. In Stockholm, they introduced me to British Intelligence.'

'And here you are,' said Molly, her tone implying that she didn't believe a word of it.

To their astonishment, Kitzler's story checked out, according to Polish underground sources.

Molly said, 'I still can't decide whether he has been sent as an infiltrator. Either way, you can bet he remains a die-hard Nazi.'

Katharina said, 'Kitzler means "tickler". Perhaps the name is more of a giveaway than it looks.'

Molly laughed at that and said, 'It also means clitoris. Would you like to go to bed?'

Katharina was surprised by the pass, as she had never considered their relationship in such terms, and thought: Why not? They were both a bit drunk. Unlike her little cubicle, Molly had her own room. It was the first time Katharina had been to bed with anyone, and she asked Molly to be gentle.

'You're a fast learner,' she was pleased to be told and wondered if Father Anton noticed any change in her.

Molly's religious upbringing hadn't affected her sexual appetite. One of the advantages of a Dublin convent boarding school was they learned the pleasures of the hairbrush early, she told Katharina, and, if anything, the doubly forbidden sin of doing it with a woman added to the thrill. 'And no worries about getting pregnant.'

They were in bed when Molly told her that Kitzler had been overheard talking freely about an imminent plot to kill Hitler.

Katharina wondered if this counted as pillow talk or whether Molly would have mentioned it otherwise.

Molly said, 'If they gossip like that here, they'll be doing the same there. As such, it's bound to fail.'

It did.

First, it was said that Hitler was dead, then he wasn't. The army had taken over, then it hadn't; order was restored, and the Führer would broadcast to the world that he was alive. The basics were done by the end of the night, the ringleaders arrested and shot, but for them the fallout lasted days. Given the underhand, interventionist nature of their work, they weren't sure how to react. They all got sucked into panicky meetings. Katharina suggested running with the Hitler doubles story as a way of sowing further discord, but she was laughed at.

'They're getting complacent,' Molly said afterwards. She and Katharina drafted a script for a programme cobbled together in response to German accusations of a British plot using a bomb of British manufacture. They countered that Hitler was too much of a useful idiot for them to want to kill him. They named Hermann Fegelein among the 'lickspittle lackeys' who were hushing up the facts in a fog of sycophantic optimism.

'Serves Hermann right,' said Molly. 'By the way, it's now being said he was in the room when the bomb went off and fortunate to survive.'

Katharina thought about that. 'Which rather suggests he knew nothing, or he would have made his excuses.'

They worked all hours. Speculation on the aftermath was by no means straightforward with all the conflicting information, including one report that it hadn't even been Hitler in the room but a double. Katharina's stolen nights with Molly became shorter, and her main memory of that hectic period was a fear of getting caught sneaking in and out of Molly's room.

They quizzed Kitzler again. Molly laughed at his claims to be a deserter, dismissed his resistance group as a fantasy and said he'd been sent to give them the runaround.

Kitzler held his ground.

'The extraordinary fact is it took place at all,' he said, 'given the shower that organised it. Hermann and I are involved in a much more sophisticated game.'

'To do with?' Molly asked sceptically.

'Back-channel negotiations with the Western Allies for

when Reichsführer Himmler takes over and we fight the war that should be being fought.'

Molly nodded impatiently. 'Yes, yes, everyone ganging up to bash the Russians.'

'Unlike you, we are serious,' Kitzler said.

A few days later, when Molly announced, 'Kitzler's dead, hanged himself in his cell,' Katharina was surprised she wasn't more surprised.

It left her wondering how much Molly was telling. She found a new decisiveness in herself when it came to exploring the delights of Molly's body. She associated it with an emerging toughness she noticed in her accepting without qualm that Kitzler had been got rid of. That Molly might have taken part in the decision made her, perversely, only more desirable.

It also left her wondering whether she was being physically kept in the same way the commandant's mistress had been. In occasional bursts of exhilaration, she thought of the affair as unique and sweetly piquant for its clandestine nature. In her more frequent low periods, she came to see it as mundane and probably inevitable, given their virtual captivity, their pressure-cooker existence and Molly's sexual adventuring. She couldn't decide how serious Molly was about her. For herself, she suspected she was using their stolen nights as a way of blocking what was going on with Father Anton. He was drinking more. Some days, he didn't show up at all. Once she knocked on his door because she was worried and found him passed out with vomit down his habit. He in return volunteered nothing. She sensed he was damaged and damaging himself. Their work being about other people's dirty secrets didn't encourage personal confiding. She in turn said nothing of this to Molly. She came to believe that she was just as conditioned by where she worked as the Germans they

119

were calling to account. What she hadn't expected was for the affair to throw up such conflicting emotions, which she put down to the relief of frustration after the suppression of any interior life for the last three years.

She didn't know whether her being with Molly contributed to Father Anton's drinking because he had guessed, however careful they were to avoid tell-tale signs during the working day. When Katharina was depressed, which was increasingly often, she came to regard it as a hellish triangle and wondered if she and Molly should break it off.

Before she could, Molly told her, 'I have to join my husband. He needs me in Berlin.'

Katharina supposed it was hush-hush but knew she wouldn't get a straight answer if she asked.

Molly was gone within forty-eight hours. Their farewell was rueful and matter-of-fact. As they had hidden their feelings for each other from others, now Molly distanced herself, shaking hands with her in front of others. It took Katharina several days to realise she was heartbroken.

She and Father Anton laboured on. The atmosphere grew strained. Katharina wrote a script about the commandant's affair, but she was never happy with it. What was adultery in such a context? It seemed to trivialise everything else that was going on. She found it difficult to paint a convincing picture of the strange, fractured world through which this enigmatic woman drifted, or to decide whether she was a manipulator or victim, or what kind of survival tactics were necessary. Katharina suspected that in the woman's place she would have done whatever was required to get by.

She could see that Father Anton was uncomfortable with the material.

'Just read it!' she snapped.

She was mortified when she broke down sobbing in his arms, saying she was so lonely. She pulled herself together and apologised.

That moment changed everything. They started getting drunk together – morose, relentless binges. He continued to say Mass daily, blindly hungover. One Sunday he asked if Katharina would help serve. When they got to the communion wine, they gave up and carried on drinking.

They managed to pull themselves together enough for him to record Katharina's script the next day. That was abandoned halfway through when he complained of being too ill to continue.

That evening they drank even more heavily and he announced he wanted to renounce his vow of chastity.

'It is my most earnest desire that you assist me.'

Part of her thought she should, partly to spite Molly, not that Molly would know. Father Anton deserved to be released. Another part of her said it would be a disaster and there was the fear of getting pregnant.

She wondered if the commandant and his mistress had had what Molly called 'good sex'.

By then they were very drunk. After some excruciating fumbling she kissed him using her tongue as Molly had taught. She must have passed out because she woke to find Father Anton lying across her, weeping silently, and realised she had lost her virginity during her blackout. They went back to drinking as though nothing had happened.

He was found by one of the cleaners, dead in the bath after consuming a bottle of whisky and cutting his wrists. He left no note.

The Church refused to bury him. Katharina arranged for his cremation, for which she was allowed out. She was the only mourner. She told the funeral director she wanted nothing read aloud. As the electric whir of the conveyor belt started up, she felt faint. As she watched the flames consume the cheap wooden coffin, she passed out. When she came to, it was finished and the funeral director was fanning her face. He offered to fetch a glass of water. The pathetic curtains in front of the oven had been drawn again. The man returned with the water and asked suggestively whether she would like to come and lie down.

Konrad Morgen, July 1944

Theft in Auschwitz was so blatant, anarchic and universal that our investigation over the autumn and winter of 1943 can be considered no more than a limited success. We did what we could, which was not nearly enough, because departments that otherwise fought like cats and dogs were united against us as naive meddlers who 'didn't know the score'. True, to a point: I had not gone there expecting to find a deadly civil war being waged. This bitter dispute, which tore the garrison apart, was about the endless unresolved argument over the iron fist of prisoner discipline versus reform for the sake of economic efficiency. That such a hellhole had a reformist movement was almost beyond comprehension.

In the middle stood the hapless, compromised commandant, with little real authority and, like the rest, eaten up by power. After he was moved on, before we could press corruption charges, one cynic announced that there was a new word going round, called 'hope'.

Reforms turned out to be not worth the paper they were written on. It was all very well for a dynamic executive in Berlin to point to things from a distance, but on the ground I have never encountered anywhere so demoralised by drunkenness, mutual hatred and self-loathing. Even the monsters were reduced to howling fits.

When all our evidence went up in flames in December 1943 (arson, so-called), our business was in effect finished. Accompanied by the sound of closing ranks, we were left no option but to depart with our tails between our legs.

Reichsführer Himmler subsequently informed me, with his trademark smirk, that too much was invested both economically and in its 'appointed task' for the garrison to have its dirty laundry aired.

The appointed task trumped every venality; it was always the same defence with the crooks, that helping themselves was a perk of the job. The universal excuse was, 'Anything I do on planet Auschwitz doesn't count on planet Earth.'

When my deputy Schlegel alerted me to the commandant's return in the spring of 1944, I was no more than mildly curious. I had been warned against further interference, though I had told Schlegel to stay in touch with the place, as he had contacts with the underground, medical clerks mostly, who worked for doctors keen to end corrupt practices that they saw as interfering with their reforms.

These doctors were often tortured gentlemen with tunnel vision, capable of looking the other way while it was their duty to improve prisoner healthcare to maintain the workforce. As for their other task, selecting those fit for work on the disembarkation ramp, they preferred to see that in terms of those they saved.

I told Schlegel I was not optimistic about pursuing the commandant, as the case was technically closed.

'Unless an entirely different charge can be brought,' he ventured.

Neither of us could think what that might entail until he telephoned in a state of excitement after receiving what he called an extraordinary piece of news.

'The commandant has a mistress,' he said.

'Most of them do. A prisoner, I presume, but what makes her special?'

'A Polish prisoner doctor recently carried out an abortion on his order. The woman, identified only as H., was sixteen weeks pregnant; her whereabouts are currently unknown.'

I told him to spare no effort in finding her. Even so, I thought nothing would come of it. In a place that size, it would be like looking for a needle in a haystack.

In one of those moments that takes place in a distant echo chamber, Eric Burdon, lead singer with what used to be called a British beat and blues combo, The Animals, known for their 1960s' hits 'The House of the Rising Sun', 'Don't Let Me Be Misunderstood' and 'We Gotta Get out of This Place', was by the 1980s touring a lot in West Germany. He happened to be travelling alone, after missing his flight with the band from London, and was in transit at Frankfurt. A man always at home in the departure lounge, he was waiting in the bar, observing two men sitting along from him, both large, which he was not, and imposing, which he was. One was English and seemed to recognise him, the other German, who spoke okay English. Eric would often tell people about the men's conversation, which he listened to, fascinated.

Many years later, Robinson offered Parker his version of how he had chanced across Morgen while waiting for a connecting flight to West Berlin; in those days, you couldn't fly direct from outside Germany. The man next to him was also travelling alone and as the flight was delayed suggested they adjourn to the bar.

Robinson did indeed recognise Eric Burdon, who declared on the plane, where they were by chance seated next to each other and carried on drinking, that singing had been his saviour through a wild life on and off the road, Jordanian deserts, Spanish islands, German prisons (dope bust), Caribbean tax scams, fame, wine, women and all the drugs under the sun.

While Eric would forget about his solo encounter with Robinson, he remembered the conversation in the bar because the German said he had been in the SS as a prosecuting judge, which impressed Eric because he hadn't known that the SS had any sort of equivalent to internal affairs.

Eric was intrigued, as he had been born in the war and had his own take, declaring to Robinson on the plane that if he thought UFOs would come and save him, don't, because the Nazis had invented them. Robinson let that pass, but he saw how Eric was bound to be interested by what he had overheard: how the German had an incredible story about the prisoner mistress of the commandant of Auschwitz, and things there were very different from what everyone had been told. Millions of prisoners starved and died, but some lived like kings and queens. Eric was hooked because, being rock and roll, he was always suspicious of any official version.

Furthermore, the German believed that Hitler hadn't died in the bunker or, if he had, events were in no way like what everyone had been told. The German said only four men in the world really knew what had happened. Two were probably dead, the other was a former colleague, for whom he was still looking years later, and the fourth Eric couldn't remember.

Robinson's recollection of his meeting with Morgen was slightly different as told to Parker. He omitted any mention of the commandant's mistress or the claim about only four people in the world knowing the true story about Hitler's end.

'A heavyset man, quite nondescript and slow, but amiable enough,' Robinson reported to Parker about Morgen. 'A big drinker too. He made a joke about his name, "Guten Morgen, Herr Morgen," which he recited for my benefit and thought hugely amusing. Herr Morgen told me how after the war he was forced to work for the Russians.'

Morgen had enough English to tell Robinson that beggars can't be choosers. He related how Stalin was obsessed about Hitler not being dead, and Morgen was ordered to question the official version provided by the British, claiming Hitler and his mistress had killed themselves.

'The British Intelligence officer responsible went on to make a living out of it forever after. He was the idiot who later authenticated the fake Hitler diaries.'

Robinson told Morgen he was familiar with the name. The man taught at Oxford and wrote for newspapers. Morgen grew excited. He said Robinson knowing about him must explain why he had decided to tell the story, which was not something he was in the habit of doing.

As a result of what he found out, Morgen had never quite believed that Hitler had shot himself as claimed. To paraphrase his imperfect English: the suicide pact with his new bride, champagne followed by death, all sentimental nonsense, appropriate in a novelettish way, but did any of it happen?

Morgen told Robinson he suspected the couple, or maybe just one of them, had fled.

Their flight was called. 'There is more,' said Morgen, 'but that will have to wait for another time.'

'Interesting story,' Robinson told Parker. 'We sat apart on the flight. When we were waiting for our luggage, he seemed to have forgotten who I was. He must have carried on drinking, because he was very drunk by then, me moderately so. I retrieved my case, left him waiting and never saw him again. As far as Hitler stories are concerned, we know the world is full of such bullshit, but Herr Morgen was oddly convincing, possessed, even. That fellow who sang with The Animals was on the same flight, a Geordie, also drinking.'

After the death of Father Anton, Katharina experienced a numbness she supposed was grief. Her leave, taken more often, was spent picking up men in London hotels, usually the Savoy, where more than enough passing through were willing to ply her with free drinks. She said she was from Zurich, rather than admitting to being German. At first, she just drank until she was barely capable, then took to going upstairs with the men or to cheap hotels where what she remembered most was the receptionists' bored tolerance. Some men were unable to perform and they lay in awkward silence before going their separate ways. Once or twice, she had vague memories of self-pitying excuses and wondered if she should feel sorry for them or herself. One night, she was shaken awake by a policeman after passing out on a bench in the Embankment gardens. She held conversations in her head with Father Anton.

After his death, she was assigned to the Soldatensender Calais section. The war was as good as won, and the general mood was larks and drunken outbursts.

They started getting high-grade gossip from the heart of

the Chancellery: how Hitler was a drugged-up husk who had abandoned any military strategy in favour of playing with architectural models for his great new capital that would never be built. They listed the drugs with which his physician was injecting him and how they had reduced him to a trembling dotard.

Katharina presumed the source was Molly, as a result of bedding Hermann Fegelein, who was mentioned in the broadcasts as one of the leaders of a decadent, hedonistic court intent on pleasuring itself as everything went to pot. Listeners were told of 'popsies' being brought in to amuse a jaded Führer; of the boisterous hijinks of the blonde young wife of the Foreign Ministry's representative at Hitler's headquarters and how she had showed her prowess as a barber by soaping and shaving Fegelein, who was always introduced as being married to the sister of Hitler's secret mistress, the frivolous Eva Braun. That Molly was physically sharing with Fegelein what she'd once done with her left Katharina feeling soiled. She wondered sourly if Molly was as eager in bed with Fegelein as she had been with her.

One of the men she took up with during her London sojourns was Evelyn Robinson. They were in the Savoy. Evelyn was drinking alone. Katharina watched him and rather than wait to be approached went up and said she was looking for a man, which got his attention. She didn't mean it like that, she said (though she did; it was obvious they would end up in bed). They had a drink while she waited for her non-existent date and when she said it looked like she had been stood up, he announced, 'I'm more of a slummer myself. Let's go to the Fitzroy or the Wheatsheaf.'

They stayed several days in a Charlotte Street hotel, eating hangover breakfasts in greasy cafés in preparation for the drinking that started at opening time with a stout to settle the stomach. When the pubs closed for the afternoon, Evelyn knew of members' clubs or private addresses where they could carry on, or they would go back to the hotel. The affair was good for her confidence, she decided, telling herself that she might be quite good in bed with men after all.

She was surprised when it was time to leave that he suggested they stay in touch. He proposed using the Fitzroy as a poste restante as others did.

Some weeks later, she didn't know whether to tell him she was pregnant. She wrote in the end, in the expectation of being ignored, so was surprised when he sought her out and showed himself to be less of a cad than she'd thought, saying that he worried about being a father because he'd had a brother born with spina bifida who died, so there might be a risk to her child. Katharina didn't know whether to believe that, but understood he wasn't keen. He admitted to being quite flush thanks to selling this and that on the black market and said he knew a man in Harley Street. She felt bad for the child she wouldn't have. Perhaps without Evelyn's gesture she would have gone through with the pregnancy, though she had never given a thought to children. She blamed herself for Father Anton's death. Had it been a boy, she would have named it after him; then she hated herself for being sentimental. During the abortion, she saw Father Anton consumed in flames and the commandant's mistress, on her back, spreadeagled and strangely faceless, making it impossible to tell if she was a witness to sexual congress or if, like her, the woman was having her womb scraped. Katharina's experience was more unpleasant for the leering doctor, who asked afterwards if she fancied a drink.

It poured for the best part of a week. A biblical rain filled the gutters and fell hard on the pavement, soaking Parker's shoes. In a charity shop, he saw a book on the history of corporal punishment. The first time, he ignored it. The second time, it was still there. He picked it up and put it back without opening it. Instead, he bought a big umbrella and a black suit, which had an Italian designer label, for ten quid.

The third time, he took the book off the shelf and read: 'Fear is the first step of knowledge and understanding. Beating can mould the mind as well as the body, can instil morality and help students learn and remember their previous mistakes, and teach them obedience.'

The fourth time, he bought it and had to endure the ribald banter of the two old girls at the till, wondering if he was one for corrective treatment. '50p,' the other said, 'and worth every penny, dear.'

He thought more about Father Roper and decided that in moments of self-examination he must have known he was trapped. He surmised his interfering with boys had less to do with sexual preference than power and control, which did not as such fit the psychiatric definition of paedophilia. Nor did Parker believe that Roper would have been attracted to boys in the outside world, but within the enclosed community they were what was to hand. Roper probably wouldn't have interfered with girls, given the chance. Boys were physically familiar, an extension of himself, no mystery or surprises.

Roper's desire was a product of extreme frustration and a growing resentment of superiors telling him what to do (as he ordered others), leading to nihilism and alienation from the institution to which he had dedicated his life. His soul grew curdled. Vanity perhaps, and again Parker was right: Roper

130

identified with Christ's despair at the ninth hour on the cross: 'My God, my God, why hast thou forsaken me?'

They had been warned of the temptations of seeking physical solace, though not overtly, as spiritual guidance on sex was almost non-existent. Suppression of desire and frustrated communal energy best expressed itself in the ridiculous dressing up of religious ceremony that verged on camp. Its other outlet lay in climbing the greasy pole to be nearer to God, a worldly process of jostling and backstabbing. It let Roper cover his tracks: the higher he rose, the more he could protect himself. Tradition was on his side: the Church managed its own discipline in-house, with any culprit foolish enough to get caught dealt with by removal to a backwater to contemplate his exile with the appropriate humility.

The stink of funk was everywhere. Priests feared the bishops, the bishops feared Rome. Fear bound the system. The loneliness of the vocation affected them all, the non-sex of everything (even a virgin birth, for Christ's sake!), resulting in mutual suspicion. Which one had scratched on a toilet wall: Why does God hate cunt? In one respect, the bonds held. Neither bishop nor priest feared the laity; certainly not children.

By the time Parker left the seminary, priestly abuse was an open scandal. Far from his own case being isolated, he came to see how such offences were commonplace – rife, even. He had been part of a conveyor belt. Even when he came to understand that Roper's urges were the product of a system founded on the eradication of desire, creating its own fault lines, he did not forgive.

During his time in the seminary, Parker had become uncomfortably aware that he too might be tempted to seek relief from mortification of the flesh. Roper infiltrated under

131

the guise of authority, whereas Parker supposed he would be one of the soft ones, venerating the object of affection, telling himself that the boy would not be harmed by sexual acts, at least not overly, unless he was breached, which Parker would draw the line at.

There was a sickness to these reveries: he could imagine himself in the role of the boy (in pursuit of himself, as it were). For Roper, the experience would have been the thrill, the cure for loneliness, the secret drive otherwise neutered to the point of deadness. Punishment and sadism formed the core of his excitement. The bigger crime was that the education of minors was entrusted to such men.

There is that moment in Westerns where figures gather on the skyline as the threat is revealed. Parker felt like that in those drenched days. Vod and Robinson seemed less substantial than ghosts from the past.

He wore his new second-hand suit most days. He grew less self-conscious about his skin as he realised its effect on others was more about embarrassment at their own inappropriate reaction rather than anything to do with him.

Whether he was growing more adventurous or in the grip of existential despair, he fell into the habit of standing in the rain looking at properties for sale in estate agents' windows, wondering about the meaning of home. As he was evidently too young to afford a mortgage, he said he was looking on behalf of rich elderly relatives living abroad. The properties he chose were upmarket. Perhaps his time in the seminary had given him a certain gravitas, because he was surprised to find himself taken seriously by pushy, unquestioning young agents desperate for a sale. Or maybe he was a better liar than he'd thought.

Parker asked Vod where he might buy a cane. If Vod thought the request strange, he didn't say. Parker said he'd read that thrashing a cushion was a good way of getting rid of aggression, realising for the first time that his rage had no outlet and drove him as much as guilt and shame.

Vod had an unquestioning logic, so Parker was not wholly surprised when he found himself being taken to Soho to what turned out to be a sex shop. He felt less embarrassed than he might have done, because Vod took charge with a proprietorial air and the woman in the shop served them with worldly indulgence. Vod announced they needed a cane because they were putting on a play.

'As a prop.'

Vod, as usual, performed like a man about to be recognised, which he wasn't. Parker looked at mysterious sex gadgets. Their display seemed both harmless and pitiful, but not furtive in the manner of Roper. Vod asked no questions about why Parker might want a cane beyond what he had been told.

The cane lay unused in Parker's room apart from whacking a pillow to no great satisfaction. He supposed it was a prop, after all, but what kind he couldn't decide. Or perhaps it was a marker for some future action, the first flicker of considering himself an avenging angel.

Strangers On a Train

'Assignment Berlin,' Parker was told by Robinson, who claimed he wasn't up to the journey himself. 'Vod isn't capable of the job. Passport?'

There had been French holidays with his parents, so yes.

Robinson went on, 'About time you started to see the world. A woman there has an interesting sounding cache, but don't commit until after you have consulted me.'

'Cache?'

'Goods for sale. Brokering for Russian collectors and English rock stars with more money than sense. Himmler's official motor car, sold that once. The pistol with which Dr Goebbels shot himself – oh, I know, how does one know? – but it was monogrammed. Art once owned by Göring, a Venus by Jacopo de' Barbari, if I remember. The man's general taste was surprisingly mediocre, considering what he had the pick of. There's even a market for footage showing the July 1944 conspirators being hanged with piano wire.'

Parker pulled a face.

'Me neither, but some are willing to part with a fortune for the privilege. Quite a lot of filmed executions generally.

Not savoury, but in a fool's market … High-class private Hollywood porn was popular in its day, especially with the Japanese, for reasons best known to them. Hardcore home movies made by big stars, shot on 35mm and lit by tame cameramen working at the weekend, showing Joan Crawford fucking for real in *Torture Me with Your Finger*. I once had footage of a big star naked in the desert, off his head on drugs and tossing off into a ten-gallon hat. Made his reputation as part of the hippie counterculture; turned out to be a lifelong Republican voter.' Robinson looked at Parker. 'People usually ask who. You don't.'

Parker was back in the room with Roper.

Robinson went on. 'Had footage of director John Huston masturbating a monkey. Robert Mitchum told me the first time they met Huston was doing just that, so maybe it was the same occasion. You look sceptical. I can see I have a point to prove.'

He had Vod drive them down to the Thames. Robinson smartened himself up with a recently laundered suit, needing help with his buttons and shoelaces. Their destination was a huge moored cruising yacht. Robinson told Vod to wait, saying, 'They're not ready for you yet.'

Vod smirked as though he had passed some sort of test.

The Russians on the boat were expecting them. There was a gathering of sorts, not quite a party, though drinks and canapés were served on deck by uniformed flunkies. Robinson, surveying the scene, in a whispered aside to Parker, announced, 'The whole boat is off its head on cocaine … Ah, Michail!'

A short, intense young man was approaching. He bear-hugged Robinson, who was twice his size.

'Effendi! You came!'

'When did I not for you, dear heart.' Robinson held up his plastered hands. 'Even with broken bones.'

'How come?' Michail enquired, more from politeness than curiosity.

Robinson said, 'Crucifixion,' which Michail fell for, before uneasily laughing it off.

Mikhail wore what Parker suspected was incredibly expensive white sportswear with gold trainers that looked like they had been inflated with a pump. A huge watch dangled from his wrist. Parker noticed a discreet tattoo between thumb and forefinger.

Most of the men on deck were older, in smart casuals, and despite being evidently rich sat around looking insecure. The women were young, tall, all beautiful and statuesque, sleekly turned out, holding champagne flutes from which they didn't drink. The only exception was a dumpy woman, also young, who introduced herself as Sasha, Michail's sister, to the evident annoyance of her brother. Several bulky men in tight suits Parker supposed were security. The mood seemed tense for what was meant to be a relaxed gathering, not that Parker knew anything about parties. Michail was either so up himself or cool enough not to remark on Parker's skin.

'Come,' he said, including Parker, 'let's go inside and leave this riffraff.' He dropped his voice. 'All hangers-on with advanced degrees in sycophancy. I tell you, my friends, the travails of being rich.'

'Stratospherically so,' said Robinson. Michail gave an exaggerated high laugh, showing surprisingly bad teeth, then nodded at one of the suited men, who followed them into a lounge that more resembled a stateroom, all marble and gold.

Michail asked Robinson, 'How's your spot of bother?'

'What bother would that be?' Robinson deadpanned.

'You English, so inscrutable.' He turned to Parker. 'Cheated a rival of mine. Absconded with funds.' He spoke fast and fluently, with a flat American accent.

Robinson looked theatrically miffed. 'Says who? The books were in order.'

'I believe you, thousands wouldn't,' Michail said with a wink at Parker, who gathered that this was something of a running joke, as Robinson didn't appear to take it seriously, even when Michail asked, 'Is there still a price on your head?'

They were invited to sit on enormous sofas and drinks were served. Parker asked for mineral water. Robinson and Michail drank champagne. Odd-looking snacks were offered. Michail said, 'Whelks and pork scratchings, which appeal to my simple tastes.'

He had the grace to laugh at himself. Robinson tucked in as Michail asked, 'What business do we have?'

Parker thought him like an actor; always the pause before the delivery.

'First refusal on what might be of interest,' mumbled Robinson with his mouth full, 'though of course authenticity needs to be established. Mr Parker here will do that. Good German and a student of the period.'

Which was news to Parker.

Michail addressed him in German, asking how come he spoke it.

Parker answered in German that Robinson was flattering him. He had some because he had learned it from his mother.

Michail said, 'Everyone speaks English anyway.' He turned back to Robinson and asked, 'First refusal?'

'Original documents by an SS judge, including a report for the Russians after the war, about what really went on in the last days in Hitler's bunker. Written, as it happens, by a man I met once. Other papers by him, including an account of a female prisoner who had an affair with the commandant of Auschwitz. He knocked her up and tried to have her starved to death.'

'Of interest,' said Michail. 'But be careful. I had a buyer, a Mr Smith, who purchased on my behalf drawings by a rabbi in Auschwitz, depicting life in the camp. I found out these were fakes from Ukraine. It infuriates me that people make money out of this.'

Michail gave Robinson an arch look and told him to go on.

'Home movies by the commandant of Auschwitz. Kiddies running around. Easy enough to verify. The woman I deal with in Berlin is trustworthy. Known her for years. Worked in the film industry, mainly for an enfant terrible, long dead. Never met the fellow, but I had dealings with his producer in Cannes, who was using a film advance to buy a raft of cocaine.'

Robinson shrugged at the way of the world. Parker suspected that Michail was eager for such lowlife details.

'Too risky, I told him,' Robinson said, with a moue of regret. 'The next item I'm not sure whether even to mention. It's being floated without any evidence to support it. The seller is being cagey. I don't even know at what remove we are.'

'Try me,' said Michail.

'The Nazis were assiduous recorders. We see film of mass shootings in the east and so on. The holy grail, so to speak, would be film of the unfilmable, again so to speak, shot for the purpose of scientific study. Whether the footage is of individual tests or some sort of mass occasion ... ' He let the sentence hang unfinished. 'I am inclined to be sceptical, though it is possible such film has emerged from some long-lost archive, but celluloid doesn't store well.'

Michail turned his wrist. 'What we know of the Germans, anything is possible, but why not turn it over to the authorities?'

'Who would want it? It would remove all doubt, lay to rest the theory that none of it happened. They would have to live with the guilt all over again. The last thing they want is proof. The Krauts are rehabilitated these days, nicer than they were. I've always got on with them. How about you?'

'We have long memories, even my generation,' Michail said.

'Well, you've a lot to remember. I am of the school that prefers to let bygones be bygones.' Robinson laughed mirthlessly. 'I suspect someone is looking to score. There may be a look-see fee upfront. Are you on for that?'

'Let's see what emerges.'

'Quite. At the same time, they're offering footage of experiments involving prisoners in freezing tanks, followed by the benefit of coital revival – on instructions from Himmler, whose pet theory it was.'

Robinson raised an eyebrow. Michail's eyes glistened.

Robinson said, 'Between us, I would say the item really on offer is the freezing stuff, with some other bits chucked in, and the so-called prime item is being dangled to talk up the price of the rest, which will be agreed and overcharged to establish the buyer's bona fides. Or gullibility. After which, there will be a complication and the prime item will suddenly be off the table and the buyer will be left with something he has overpaid for in his eagerness to get his hands on the other material.'

'A con?'

'Not exactly. Sharp practice. As we know, this is a largely under-the-table world. I say this now so you don't think later that I've cheated you. Which you tell everyone I am capable of.'

Parker arrived in Berlin early in the evening, disorientated by its foreignness as he negotiated the S-Bahn to Zoo Station. The S-Bahn ran on an elevated track, overlooking the backs of buildings and streets where everything appeared strangely colourless.

He was booked into a modern box on Kantstrasse, with a clean, functional room. He was aware of not going to see where his grandmother had lived when he probably should have, as Fasanenstrasse was only a short walk away. Instead, he lay down in a state of exhaustion.

Because of how events unfolded, he would think a lot about his grandmother. She had always been a rather ostracised figure while he was growing up, on account of her 'problem'.

He knew little about her except that she had worked for the BBC World Service and lived in a pedestrian terrace with doll-like houses near Tottenham Court Road. He visited occasionally once he was old enough, mainly because he sensed that his parents would disapprove of his being there.

His arrival involved the same ritual: him ringing the bell and her calling out, 'Door's open!' because she couldn't be bothered to get up and answer. The door gave direct access to the living room. When he asked if it was safe to leave it unlocked, she said, 'There's nothing worth stealing, and I have nothing to hide. Make tea if you want. I'll stick to my poison.'

Katharina Fischer drank gin. If Parker was going to tell anyone about what Father Roper had done, it would have been his grandmother. He thought of her as someone who had kept her secrets, starting with never naming his mother's father.

Once, she remarked that he seemed troubled. He said nothing; the moment passed. She in turn didn't invite questions. There never seemed to be anyone in her life. She admitted that her routine was structured around her drinking.

'Quite disciplined, you know.'

She asked if Parker had read Nabokov. He hadn't. She said he should, and not just because the man had once given her tennis lessons. Most days they watched television, usually *Blockbusters*.

If Parker didn't share his secret, his grandmother offered one of her own on the last occasion he saw her. She appeared drunk when she normally didn't and started singing off-key.

'"We'll Meet Again",' she said. 'Vera Lynn, from the war.'

Again unusual for her, she got up and started searching in a secretaire with a drop-down desktop and an intriguing array of cubby holes and drawers. She gave up, then remembered whatever she was looking for was elsewhere and rummaged through a drawer of a mahogany tallboy, before asking, 'Do you ever wonder about your grandfather?'

'Only that no one ever talks about him.' Parker thought his answer rather grown-up.

She was holding a small snapshot.

'That's him,' she said, handing him the photograph.

Parker was looking at a young man sitting in a dark space, smiling guardedly at whomever was taking the picture. It was in faded colour and showed prematurely white hair. Both the subject and the photograph looked utterly remote.

His grandmother sat down and said, 'His name was

August Schlegel. I knew him as a child in Berlin. He was the first boy who kissed me, as a matter of fact, and I happened to run into him again after the war, in Hanover of all places.'

She seemed to be reciting for her own benefit more than his, hearing the words out loud.

'He became quite important in post-war Germany. His name isn't Schlegel now.'

Parker was confused, thinking that women changed their names when they married but he wasn't sure why a man would. He looked at the photograph again. His grandfather was notable because of the hair, but otherwise appeared almost deliberately unremarkable, a man in a dark jacket and a loosened tie sitting at a table with a glass. He asked if she had taken it.

'No, dear, he gave it to me.'

They sat in silence until she said, 'I would prefer you keep this between us. After all this time, it's of no consequence to your mother. In some ways, it's easier to skip a generation. Tell her after I am gone if you must, but I don't think it's important.'

Parker felt obscurely flattered by his grandmother leap-frogging his mother to share with him.

'We all have different lives,' she went on. 'Let's call it our secret. Is there anything you want to tell me in return?'

Parker was silenced by Roper standing behind his grand-mother's chair, finger to his lips.

'In Hanover?' he asked instead.

'Went to see a chap called Evelyn. We'd had a bit of a fling, just up the road from here. He'd had a bad war. The strain of flying all those night raids. He was thinking of marrying me, but we both knew he wasn't the type.'

Katharina Fischer made no mention to Parker of Father Anton. Of her subsequent affair with August Schlegel, she concluded that it was because she'd felt guilty about abandoning her homeland and not being there to suffer with her compatriots. He represented a connection to her childhood and the attraction of the forbidden. He regularly hit her, which she accepted as her punishment for what she had done to Father Anton.

She did tell Parker that during her time in Hanover August had said he wanted to travel, implying that she was invited. He reckoned tourism would become a big business as sun-worshipping Germans became desperate to get away. The war had given them a taste for it. Lots of places they wouldn't be welcome, but there was still Spain and Portugal.

'We met annually for ten years, a fortnight in the same parador north of Barcelona. After the last holiday, I found I was pregnant.'

She didn't mention that she had been pregnant once before, by Evelyn Robinson. She had once or twice received postcards from him. One read: 'Find myself in Hanover, of all dumps, which by the look of it we must have flattened several times over. Fond memories of our brief encounter.'

The war had ended almost without her noticing until her unit was abruptly disbanded. She wandered around London like someone let out of prison. She hung around Charlotte Street with a hard-drinking Bohemian crowd and continued to seek obliteration in casual sex, though many of the men struck her as anything but casual. One, a future famous artist, left bite marks on her breast. By then, she was working in Selfridges' millinery department and living in Rathbone Street, within walking distance. The war had ended, but it didn't feel like it.

With Parker, she confined herself to saying, 'When August said he didn't want the child, I decided to have it anyway. He said I was on my own then, which I accepted. I think it was his way of breaking it off. He had acquired a vacuous wife and was probably tiring of our arrangement. So I became a single mother with no more Spanish holidays. We never saw each other again. He gave me money to buy this house, which he could well afford, which meant your mother was raised in a degree of comfort. He also insisted I didn't say who he was, which I have respected until now.'

She told him the photograph was his to keep. Parker was gauchely effusive in his thanks, in the way people are when given something they don't particularly want. What would he do with it? To whom would he show it? Certainly not his mother. What earthly use was it to him, a picture of a man who had played no part in his life?

Before he left, she said, sounding almost offhand, 'He was a Nazi, of course, which is probably why I never mentioned him.'

What kind of Nazi? Parker wanted to ask, instead of staring at his feet.

She said, 'I was never sure how much to believe what he said, which was never much, apart from a couple of occasions when he got very drunk and started going on about how he was in Hitler's bunker at the end. He got angry when I laughed and said I didn't believe him. We were both drunk, I suppose.'

Parker knew enough to know the bunker was where Hitler had killed himself. His first reaction was to be obscurely thrilled at the thought of a relative standing so close to history. Perhaps the man was more interesting than he looked.

His grandmother said, 'I wouldn't get too excited. I thought his claims extravagant. He told me he'd once had a pistol belonging to Hitler and gave it away. Another time, he boasted that he had hidden Hitler's ashes. What do you think?'

'About knowing Hitler?'

'In general.'

'It's quite a story.'

'I think you will find that is what it was, just a story.' She went back to watching television, leaving Parker to wonder why she had chosen to tell him. He felt a first resentment stirring. On top of the secret of Roper, it felt like an additional burden.

Eventually she said, 'I have a feeling you and your grandfather might meet one day. I can't think why.'

Nor could Parker.

'Perhaps you could give him back the photograph. It's the only personal souvenir he gave me. A mysterious, difficult man, yet quite dull, if that makes sense.'

As he walked back to Tottenham Court Road, Parker wondered how much of a Nazi August Schlegel had been. He told himself he should feel encouraged by her confiding and resolved to share his secret about Father Roper. He went back a few days later, wanting to ask what he might do to break the deafening silence. He felt sometimes that there were two of him: one who just about kept his head above water, the other submerged.

He rang the bell as usual. She didn't call out, as she normally did. The door was open, the television was on – *Blockbusters*, at which his grandmother, sitting in her armchair, sightlessly stared. One of the last things she must have done was make a cup of tea, which stood stone-cold on the table beside her while the host congratulated a young contestant.

Evelyn Robinson and August Schlegel, then calling himself by another name, met on a train to Hanover in the dusty, bomb-damaged summer of 1945. Both were around the same age. Schlegel was tall, thin and preternaturally pale. Perhaps in deference to their Russian conquerors, he was reading a copy of *The Idiot*, which starts on a train, as he remarked later to Evelyn, who asked which of them was the idiot. Schlegel learned early that Robinson liked to have his jokes laughed at.

Years later, when Parker watched Alfred Hitchcock's adaptation of Patricia Highsmith's *Strangers on a Train*, he decided he preferred the book, which got under the skin more. It left him wondering about timing.

Had August Schlegel been delayed, which he nearly was, and caught a later train, he and Evelyn Robinson would never have met.

They found themselves thrown together on old rolling stock that rattled along and was subject to frequent delays. The carriage was crowded with exhausted, hungry and often bad-tempered passengers and whiny children. Many had to stand in the corridor, but towards the end of their journey they had the compartment to themselves. Evelyn was wearing the uniform of an RAF Military Police officer. He looked old beyond his years, chain smoking, with a wasted boyishness that Schlegel suspected harboured a fabulous nihilism. Schlegel asked in English if he could scrounge a cigarette. Evelyn asked how come he spoke 'the lingo'. Because his mother was English, came the laconic reply.

The question of Schlegel's war was bound to come up, but the other man just smoked and stared out of the dirty window, as if making up his mind about something, while

146

Schlegel thought about the journey that had brought him there when he could have got out on a boat from Genoa to Buenos Aires.

When their train at last arrived, after interminable delays, Evelyn said, 'How about a drink, old boy? I'm parched.'

Hanover's wartime ruins rather reminded August Schlegel of a child's nursery after an enormous tantrum. There was something both childlike and ancient about the survivors. As for Evelyn, whose eyes became infused with blackness when he was drunk, he suspected a man on the make. At the end of their first night of drinking, Evelyn announced that he wanted a woman. They were in one of the few good hotels still standing, since requisitioned. Evelyn's uniform got them rooms. Schlegel was asked his profession. Diplomatic attaché, he stated; rather than war criminal.

Women hung around the lobby, regular bourgeois, many of them widows, Schlegel suspected, offering sexual services for payment or a decent meal. He found a woman for himself, decided he didn't want her after all and paid her off. She seemed nice enough for him to feel sorry. The woman felt rejected when she should have been relieved.

Whether Evelyn believed the story about him being an attaché, Schlegel couldn't tell. As for his professional status, it wasn't a time when the word 'job' defined anything. He now seemed to be working for American Intelligence, with false papers that gave his name as August Tieck; though how much he trusted the Americans was another matter. But he felt secure enough as no one knew who he was. He had cropped his white hair to a stubble, dyed it and grown a moustache so he bore little resemblance to old photographs, few of which, if any, still existed. His suit was about decent, the shirt collar and cuffs a bit frayed, shoes passable, if in need of a shine. Compared to most, he looked smart.

They carried on drinking the next day. Evelyn said, 'Cheerio!' or, 'Down the hatch!' or once or twice, 'Bombs away!'

They fell in with each other, talking about this and that, and how to turn what Evelyn called a shilling.

On the third day of drinking, Schlegel said, 'I might stay a while,' meaning that it seemed as good a place as any to go to ground.

'Be my guest,' said Evelyn. 'Cheers!'

On Evelyn's recommendation, Schlegel got himself hired by the RAF as an interpreter, which gave him access to the barracks' NAAFI canteen, where he could buy cheap cigarettes to sell on at fifteen times the price.

Twenty cartons a month no one bothered about; a hundred a week and you might get asked whether you really were such a heavy smoker. Four packets of cigarettes would hire you an entire orchestra for an evening.

Evelyn said, 'I'm an advocate of quiet money, preferably fronted by another party.'

As all-day drinking was common among troops, discipline often non-existent, fraternisation illegal but barely enforceable, Schlegel agreed to look for a suitable outlet. He decided on a bar calling itself The Havana, in a basement not far from what had once been the centre, not that you could tell from its flattened state. The joint reminded him of pre-war underground jazz clubs in Berlin: barrels for tables, candles and not enough chairs. The owner was a one-armed young man who had grown his hair long in an effort to distance himself from what had gone before.

Schlegel and Evelyn paid The Havana a visit. A few people

were there, but even so the place was a dive. Evelyn was wearing civilians. They spoke to the long-haired man and Schlegel translated.

Evelyn said, 'It would make my job easier if there was a place to which I could turn a blind eye, where Fräulein Helga could enjoy herself, be bought drinks by friendly young soldiers and improve her English.'

The man showed a bit of spark when he rejected the offer on behalf of girls consorting with what he called the enemy.

'Grow up, for God's sake!' Evelyn said. 'Fuck the old order. We're here to screw your women, drink all your booze and teach you democracy, which we'll do in exchange for shipping a lot of business through your rathole. Fifteen per cent of your take will ensure you don't get raided by the Military Police.'

Evelyn shipped in a load of cheap Spanish brandy, known as Franco's Revenge. The boys went berserk on it. To calm things down, Schlegel dug up a local trio, which hadn't been able to play proper jazz for years. He paid them two packets of cigarettes an evening, which was generous, and they soon drew a crowd.

Over that dusty summer and autumn, August Schlegel counted his money and watched the broken-backed parade emerge blinking into the daylight, bearing no resemblance to the serried ranks and regimented order of before. Requisitioned houses, improvised afternoon brothels, schoolgirls smelling of urine and crow-like nuns doing good works summed up the bled-dry, postwar exhaustion, its psychosis and misogyny – a fine line between consent, coercion and emotional impoverishment – which with drink could take on a cheesy sentimentality, often a preface to violence.

Hollywood movies started to be shown, featuring tough, laconic men and radiant women with superior dentistry, dealing coolly with whatever existential crisis they faced while the audience thought: those cars, those milkshakes, those diners, the open road, the way women smoke!

Evelyn turned up one evening with a tall young woman whom he introduced as Kate. She and Schlegel shook hands and she gave her full name as Katherina Fischer, which was an awkward moment for him as he had been introduced as August Tieck.

Both men were drunk. It seemed to Katharina that everyone in Hanover was on a bender. She hadn't known what to expect, certainly not someone she suspected was August Schlegel.

Evelyn hadn't told Schlegel much other than someone from England was coming and she was Swiss. Schlegel supposed the ugly duckling he'd once known could have blossomed into this attractive woman, though she didn't sound like she was from Switzerland. Her arrival shook him more than he cared to admit, just when he was starting to think no one knew who he was.

Katharina had seen the newsreels showing the bomb devastation and now found a jungle. Nature made its own intervention: vegetation covered ruins, bushes grew in bomb craters and in streets that weren't completely buried a purple flowering rosebay willow herb flourished. She wasn't sure why she had come or why Evelyn had asked, other than sending her a postcard to say money was to be made, he needed German speakers and he had thought of her, 'as always with affection'. To the victor the spoils: they dined and drank well; her not so comfortably. Being back in Germany felt as though she were collaborating. She both despised and felt sorry for her compatriots. The men tended to be self-pitying, while most women proved commendably resilient.

The affair with Evelyn resumed, but Katharina suspected that outside of war they were both struggling. Evelyn was drinking more; she was trying to drink less. Schlegel was drunk most of the time but held his drink better than Evelyn, whose charm was wearing thin, or rather becoming more pronounced, perhaps as a way of covering his shot nerves. Sometimes he woke in the night with what he called the 'screaming abdabs', and she would have to hold him and suspected he needed mothering.

She noted the easy bond between Evelyn and his friend, less complicated than with her. It left her wondering if she wasn't a front for the real love affair going on between them, physical or not. She supposed it had to do with wartime male camaraderie and the anticlimax of peace redefining what was permitted. Perhaps because of their patronising manner, she did her best to make both men fall in love with her, projecting herself as a fatuous male fantasy – impulsive, coquettish – to flatter their perceived masculine nobility. She was reminded of this years later when she went alone to see a matinée of *Jules et Jim*, whose love triangle captured the febrile quality of that contrived episode in Hanover, one of the least romantic places she had ever been.

Most nights they dined together, sometimes in the Officers' Mess, more often in a restaurant Schlegel patronised which served passable food, before adjourning to The Havana for long drinking sessions, in which Katharina's good intentions went out of the window. It was what the boys did. Usually,

151

it reduced Evelyn to a brooding presence while his friend grew more attentive. He had good manners, kept it light and topped up her glass. He chatted easily. He wasn't a businessman by choice, he said, but financial security seemed a sensible goal these days. They slipped in and out of German, which left Evelyn feeling excluded and tetchy.

They were in bed after an evening during which Evelyn had been largely silent when she suggested sex might cheer him up, at which he shrugged.

She said, 'You can't expect your friend and I not to talk if you sulk. Are you in love with him?'

He didn't seem thrown by the question. He considered and said, 'Men are easier on the whole, if that answers your question.'

'What do you mean?'

'It's just about the sex.'

'And it's not with me?' she asked.

'Men don't get pregnant.'

'Touché.'

She was surprised not to be more angry. She changed the subject and asked where he saw himself in a year's time.

'Hard to say when I never expected to survive. Sometimes I think I didn't.'

'What are you talking about?'

'That this is all a dream and I will wake up in flames. Anyway, you're doing a pretty good job of making us both fall in love with you.'

The three of them were picnicking on the banks of the River Leine one Saturday afternoon, drinking bottled beer with two fräuleins whose names Katharina had already forgotten. One had padded her brassiere. The other had bad skin and asked her to ask Evelyn if he could get her some cream from the barracks' chemist. Evelyn said, 'For you, dear heart, anything.'

Katharina was surprised that he later remembered, because she didn't associate him with small acts of kindness.

'Here's a thing,' Evelyn said. He was reading a week-old *Sunday Express*. 'Some bright spark has worked out it'll take until 1960 for ten trains a day, pulling fifty wagons, to clear Berlin's rubble. Same bright spark calculates German rubble amounts to 400 million cubic metres, which is the equivalent of the whole of Britain being covered to a height of several feet.'

They drank all day and ended up in The Havana with a bottle of whisky under the table to supplement the beer. They caroused and fornicated in the backroom until dawn, by when they were all reeling. Katharina had a vague memory – no more than a squirming blur – of fooling around with both men, who were fucking the fräuleins, and a clearer one of her kissing and fingering the one with the padded brassiere, which the woman refused to take off. She woke in a terrible state, unable to remember if she'd fucked one or both or neither of the men; some things were better forgotten or at least not remembered, other than someone, she thought one of the girls, giving her a shuddering orgasm. The episode left her with a feeling of grubbiness, and if the men remembered any more than she did they weren't saying. The matter was never referred to and it didn't happen again.

Evelyn's *Sunday Express* story gave Schlegel his epiphany. The racketeering was in danger of getting out of hand because of what Evelyn called the hangover of violence. Trained German fighting men – what was left of them – were bored with peace and trying to make ends meet. The economy was controlled by the black market. Rival gangs required enforcers. Score-settling took away the bitterness of defeat. Everyone carried weapons, resulting in drunken shoot-outs. One night when Evelyn was on duty, Katharina and Schlegel fell in with an old soldier in a bar who was given to prolonged bouts of delirium tremens and while staring at his shaking hand told them that the only thing he was truly ashamed of was shooting a monkey in Belize in the 1930s and how the monkey lay crying as it died, its face all screwed up with fear.

Later the same evening, in The Havana, the owner asked to speak to Schlegel in the back. He said a Yank had turned up in a big American car and told him from now on he was working for him. The Yank was new in town and came accompanied by a gang of ex-SS thugs, and drugs were now part of the deal. Katharina, fed up of waiting, drifted into the back, and Schlegel laughed as he said to her, 'You're not supposed to hear any of this.'

She told him it sounded like it was time to move on. He agreed. He had funds in Switzerland, explained away as an inheritance 'from an aunt in Zurich' and said, 'The thing they'll be doing for years is building.'

'What do you know about construction?' she asked reasonably.

'That's not the point. Millions will go missing in rebuilding Germany. Money is endlessly fluid if treated with respect.'

She wondered what he was getting himself into.

Evelyn, who had his own plans for expansion, was a willing partner. They set about forming limited companies. Schlegel cultivated a town planner with gambling debts, who introduced him to contractors, who suggested he made a practice of underbidding in exchange for guaranteed sub-contracting work. The tricks of the trade were learned and applied, and no one cared. Schlegel invested his Swiss francs in plant and equipment. Katharina helped, sending out false invoices with inflated labour and material costs, billing for skilled labour that wasn't, charging rental fees for equipment owned, invoicing for unperformed work and so on.

When she next passed The Havana, civilian police were swarming all over. One officer told her there had been a gun battle and several men were dead, including the owner.

At ten o'clock the following morning, Parker presented himself at an address on Eisenacher Strasse, a twenty-minute walk from his hotel. It took him past postcard landmarks – the church with its preserved bomb-damaged spire and the large KDW department store – to a long side street with a gay bar that didn't bother to disguise what it was, which came as a shock after England, where Parker had seen nothing like it. His destination was a large stucco building from the Wilhelmine period with a communal front door and a broad staircase with sisal carpet and brass runners that took him to a first-floor landing about the size of half a tennis court.

He would have a stronger recollection of those common parts than of the large apartment on whose threshold he stood. What was about to happen was more like a series of ambushes than any regular unfolding of events. Afterwards, he thought of the pattern as like a mosaic or a sequence of rooms, some of them hostile, in which time and memory collided.

A rail-thin woman of around sixty with an extremely lined face answered. Parker's German wasn't tested, because she had good English. She introduced herself as Frau Trauner (the name on the bell) and said that Parker was younger than she was expecting. She made a point of ignoring his appearance, as though she thought it typical of Robinson to send a freak.

She led the way down a long corridor to a big, partly shuttered room with shelves of books on cinema. A projector with film threaded through it stood in front of a portable screen.

Seeing Parker looking at the books, she asked if he was interested in the history of film.

'Catching up,' he said.

She pointed towards a cardboard filing box on a polished mahogany table, said she had calls to make and left.

Parker sat and addressed the contents of the box, which contained three documents.

The first was a ring-bound file titled *Bericht über den Tod von A. Hitler, Dezember 1945. K. Morgen.*

The coarse old paper was browned at the edges. The ring binders were rusty. The document smelled musty and looked as though it had lain unread for years. The pages were unnumbered. He supposed there were about thirty-five. They were typed, single-spaced and densely paragraphed. Much of the content appeared technical. In one section, the word 'Zahnspange' kept recurring. Parker looked it up in a pocket dictionary he had thought to bring: dental bridge.

He supposed the document would appeal to Robinson, as he had met its author.

The two other files, also by Morgen, were titled *Addendum to the Testimony of E. H., January 1945* and *Testimony of A. Schlegel, November 1944*. Parker was surprised both were in English.

His first thought was that 'A. Schlegel' must be a namesake rather than his grandfather. Skimming through the documents he wasn't so sure. The name recurred, and he was left with an uncanny feeling that he was being presented with unwelcome evidence of his family's past. He heard Father Roper say, 'Come in and shut the door.'

The Schlegel dossier was only a few pages and started grippingly enough: 'Because we have worked together and I regard you as a friend, I wish to give this statement of events so extraordinary that few will be inclined to believe them, and also because I may not live to repeat them.'

Before Parker could read on, Frau Trauner returned. He asked what she knew about the documents.

'They are what they are. For you to decide.'

'Is there a price?'

'Of course,' she said, looking at him as though Robinson had sent a cretin.

'I mean, what is the price?'

'We can discuss that once interest has been expressed.'

Parker gestured at the projector, presuming it was the footage he had been sent to view.

Trauner said, 'You understand that discretion is required. The seller insists the sale remains private. '

Parker was starting to feel a fool. He pointed at the projector again and said, 'Perhaps we could ... ', asking himself whether he had the stomach for it.

Frau Trauner gave a mirthless peal of laughter. 'You will have to go to the Hotel Adlon for the film in question. I suggest you take a taxi, then come back afterwards.'

She paused, considering, then pointed at the projector. 'I was going to show you this anyway, knowing how Mr Robinson used to deal in such material. It's one of Rainer's trifles, shot just before he died, perhaps the last thing he ever did. 35mm. Very graphic. No sound. Pricey, though.'

Halfway through, he had to ask quickly to be excused and

threw up violently in a washroom basin before he had time to reach the toilet.

What upset him most was the drugged ecstasy on both men's faces and the sheer body worship, as though such an act could be associated with pleasure. At one point, a third man with a mop of greasy hair, a wispy moustache and a round Slavic face appeared in front of the camera and stared very close and hard into the lens, then grinned.

'Oh, Rainer,' Frau Trauner said indulgently as Parker rushed to find a lavatory.

If she was puzzled by his abrupt departure, she gave no sign of it on his return. The projector was off. Parker wasn't sure how long he had been gone. It had seemed to take an age to clear the sink.

'I would rather not sell,' she said matter-of-factly, 'but I am somewhat hard up at the moment. I am sure Mr Robinson will be discreet.' She peered at him and asked without concern or curiosity, 'Why are you crying?'

Parker knew he was weeping in front of altogether the wrong woman and thought of the admission he should have made to his grandmother years before.

Frau Trauner carried on as though nothing had happened, announcing briskly, 'Tell Mr Robinson I would be looking for ten thousand, pounds not euros.'

Angered by her coldness, he asked sharply, 'What about the other films and so forth?'

'Go to the Adlon. Regarding terms, there may be other interested parties and it will go to sealed bids. Given the nature of some of the material, are you sure you are up for it?'

It was said quite nastily. He rather wished he could thrash the woman with his cane.

One day when Evelyn was working, Katharina suggested she and 'Tieck' (she had started putting his name in quotation marks) walk by the river, where she said, 'I think you're hiding in plain sight.'

Schlegel, strolling, hands in pockets, looked disconcerted. 'Plain sight?'

'You recognised me when we met. You recoiled at the mention of my name, hardly noticeable, but you did. Now you are someone else.'

'Someone else?'

'You don't have to repeat everything I say. Tieck translated Shakespeare. Are you a descendant?'

'Not as far as I know.'

'Tieck's co-translator was August Schlegel.'

'Ah, yes.'

'I once knew someone by that name.'

'Then you're no more Swiss than I am.'

They stopped and stared at each other, a wordless exchange and a half-smile from him.

'He kissed me once,' she said.

She tilted her head and they kissed, chastely. Katharina surprised herself by laughing.

'Funny,' she said, 'some of the things I know about you. I'm not supposed to say, but your name – or rather Schlegel's – came up in connection with a judicial investigation. We knew quite a lot by then. He worked with a man named Morgen.'

Schlegel paled.

Katharina said, 'Oh, don't worry, I am not going to shop you. I expect you'll tell me you were just doing your job.'

Schlegel remained silent. Katharina asked, 'Are we talking about the same person?'

'Probably.'

'What did he do that's so terrible he had to change his name?'

'To be honest, I don't know, other than someone put me on a list of war criminals.'

She said, 'Your name was broadcast in connection to Auschwitz, so you know.'

'Broadcast?'

'Fake radio stations pretending to be German. We got up to all sorts.'

After that, they barely mentioned the war. Katharina didn't know what to make of Schlegel, other than her attachment based on an accidental bond of childhood. That first slippery kiss had remained a more or less constant companion since. Now there was the relief of speaking German rather than English, which she had always regarded as a defensive language whose unspoken meanings were hard to breach unless born to it. At the same time, she was homesick for somewhere that wasn't home. However wary she was of the English, they did at least get on with things, even if it was only with their drinking.

She supposed she and Schlegel would have an affair. She quite fancied whispering guttural instructions in his ear in German, telling him what she wanted.

Parker presented himself at the Adlon's reception, gave the room number and was told to go up.

No one answered when he knocked. He checked he had the right room. The endless corridor made them all look the same. He was still in a state of shock from the film. He had stared at people in the street and the crowded lobby and wondered what they got up to in private.

He knocked again to no answer. He tried the door. It was

open. He stuck his head in and asked if anyone was there. Silence. The room was a suite. He tentatively wandered around, calling out with some trepidation: movies told him that prowling around unfamiliar spaces could end badly. He told himself not to be stupid, but he felt as though his head was clamped in a vice. He heard the swish of Roper's cane and flinched, waiting for the strike. The bedroom was empty, the bed unmade. He knocked on the bathroom door, reasoning that he was spooking himself. He remembered the shock of finding his grandmother, peaceful in her armchair but very dead. He supposed he must have telephoned one of his parents. He recalled standing outside waiting for the ambulance, which came quickly because the hospital was just up the road.

The bathroom was empty, apart from a pornographic magazine left open on top of the lavatory, showing a full-bosomed, naked woman with her legs spread, fondling herself in a pantomime of ecstasy. Parker averted his eyes. He smelled Roper's presence and felt as though he was standing on a high ledge, dizzy and about to topple. He had to sit on the edge of the bath to steady himself. The woman in the photograph seemed to wink at him.

Why was no one there? Why had someone left a magazine like that? Parker composed himself and returned to the main room, where he found a man standing alone, who asked where he had been.

Parker said no one had answered and he'd had to use the bathroom. He had no idea how the man had materialised and sensed he wasn't staying there. He wondered whether to point out that he had found porn in the bathroom in case the man thought it belonged to him.

He looked at him properly: probably about ten years older

than he was, not tall or tough exactly, but a disconcerting presence in his combat trousers and leather jacket. From his accent, he guessed he wasn't German. Polish, perhaps, or Russian.

The man just said, 'Passport.'

Parker, trying to make light of what seemed to be on the brink of a threatening situation, said, 'Just as well I have it with me. No one said they needed identity.'

The man checked it, glanced at him, handed it back and told him to wait, and with that he left as mysteriously as he had appeared.

No one came. Twenty minutes, then thirty. Parker couldn't stop thinking about the two men in the film. He became convinced that someone else was in the suite, hiding or watching him. Feeling stupid, he checked the bedroom cupboards. They were empty. Whoever had booked the room wasn't staying there. He had a feeling that the bed had recently been used to fuck. He checked, and there was semen on the sheets. He had another dizzy spell and perhaps even blacked out, because the next thing he knew it was dark outside and everything looked smashed to smithereens. He could just about make out a woman in a wheelchair, wearing what looked like a fur coat. The man pushing her was tall, with a hat.

He must have blanked out again, because when he next looked it was daylight. He supposed he must be experiencing a severe psychotic reaction to the film, which kept flashing though his head, along with images of Roper going about his business. One time when he looked up, Roper was fiddling under his manky habit, no older than before and with a superior look on his face as he said, 'Shall we kneel and pray together?' Another time, he saw a tall young man in

162

the bedroom and realised from his white hair that it must be his grandfather. His grandmother had said he had been in Berlin. At first he thought the man was alone; then saw that he was standing pressed against a woman, who started grunting gutturally. When Parker realised what was going on, he screwed his eyes shut and pressed his hands against his ears, thinking he might scream. He supposed he was having some kind of flashback, as he did with Roper, but this extended beyond his own past. When he next looked, they were gone, and he was uncomfortably aroused and wanted badly to masturbate. He got as far as the bathroom, avoided looking at himself in the mirror, yet he could see a reflection, a beautiful red-headed woman putting on lipstick and the man standing behind her watching was the same as in the photograph his grandmother had given him. Parker pulled himself together. He wondered about the exact nature of the footage he was there to see and had the strongest premonition that he would learn about it one day, not yet, and it would involve the man in the mirror.

'Fuck,' he said to himself aloud. He wanted no more of any of it. Roper he was almost used to dealing with, but not this other man, whom he viewed as an intrusive and possibly malevolent figure. He cursed his grandmother for ever having given him the photograph.

In terms of the history of rooms and walls with ears, the Adlon knew more than Parker. The man and the woman – August Schlegel and Molly Fitzgerald, once intimate with Parker's grandmother – had played their part in an endgame decades before, taking time out for what amounted to an anti-erotic fuck, to be added to all those other joyless chance encounters the hotel had witnessed. A little later, Schlegel found himself back in the same hotel, at the bitter end, with another woman, in contradiction to what history told.

Parker was driven from the room less by impatience than a feeling that he had to get out. He didn't know why, but he asked at the desk in whose name the room was booked, to be told a Mr Robinson, which left him in even more turmoil.

He returned to Eisenacher Strasse and explained what had happened – or rather not happened – at which Frau Trauner regarded him as though he was wasting her time.

'You should have waited,' she said.

'What is Robinson's game?' he asked. 'I thought he was in the market to buy. Yet the seller's room is booked in his name.'

'Of course,' she said, adopting the tone of someone addressing a backward child. 'He would have been required to book the room on the seller's behalf. I expect Mr Robinson is representing several parties.

'Why does he need me?'

'To establish that the material exists.'

'But no one showed up.'

'Maybe they got cold feet or were bluffing, or they didn't like the look of you. You're hard to take seriously, under the circumstances.'

She went off to answer a telephone call, came back after a minute and said, 'You were followed.'

Parker couldn't think what to say except, 'Who was watching to see if I was being followed?'

'You are dealing with careful people, Mr Parker. There are serious deniers who would prefer that such material was destroyed, preferably without paying for it.'

Parker didn't know what she was on about.

'The alt-right,' she offered. 'Or, on the other hand, Israeli

Intelligence. Who most of all would want that material exposed? The Jews. Perhaps it's not for you.'

Parker decided she had at least provided an answer to something he had often asked himself: whether he was watching the world, or the world was watching him. He knew now: he was being watched. Part of him had always thought so, being invisibly checked on and judged according to how he reacted.

After complaining of too little to do during the day, Katharina was invited to join Evelyn in his jeep on what he called his 'rounds'. These had less to do with official policing than the collection of envelopes from bars, shops, cafés and garages. Evelyn bought and sold anything: old tyres, bicycles, cars, lingerie, scrap metal, gasoline, the ubiquitous cigarettes.

He got her to place a classified advertisement in a local newspaper asking ex-soldiers or their families to come to a given hotel. The advertisement made the initiative seem like part of an official programme, ending with a stern warning that it was against the law to have in one's possession anything with a swastika on it.

Katharina was surprised by the numbers that turned up sniffing an opportunity. They were given generous amounts of beer while she explained the situation and Evelyn sat back looking pleased with himself and smart in his starched summer uniform. All banned items would be requisitioned as part of an amnesty, with financial renumeration. People came with so many bags that Evelyn ended up offering a collection service, cash on delivery; a pittance, under the circumstances. Sometimes Katharina went with him. They started with a jeep before graduating to a removal van.

She was astonished by the sheer volume gathered, sacks and sacks of helmets, daggers, medals, guns, flags and uniforms, with everything from Afrika Korps to camouflaged snow wear. Several motorcycles and sidecars made it into the storeroom, which expanded to a warehouse to accommodate army trucks, dignitaries' cars, even a couple of light aircraft and pieces of field artillery. Because her invisible war had been conducted over the airwaves, Katharina was in awe of this accumulated evidence of its physical manifestation.

A ton and more of ephemera was collected: postcards, stamps, letters, old currency, stationery, photograph albums, reels of cine film, official letters and the detritus of an abandoned bureaucracy.

Evelyn had a host of young local women making inventories of everything, however insignificant: headed Ministry of Housing notepaper, several hundred sheets; six women's swastika-embroidered cotton handkerchiefs.

Katharina came across photographs that should never have been taken. She knew about the mass shootings in the east because of her wartime work, but it was a shock to see private photographs showing them, neatly stuck into albums, interspersed with pictures of recreational activities like beer drinking and naked swimming.

She asked Evelyn what he was going to do with it all and was told he might ship it back home because one day it would be worth a fortune. He said he was in the process of negotiating for Himmler's official car, a Wanderer W11/1.

Katharina wondered if he was right about its future worth. From what she could see, everyone wanted to forget the war.

She said, 'It's like Ali Baba's cave in here.'

She didn't say, 'You've enough to start your own war.'

Years later, when she told Parker about August Schlegel, it

was Evelyn Robinson and this image of negative profligacy that came to mind, perhaps because to her it was this show of the war's spoils that Schlegel represented, rather than the crooked, shiny new future he was constructing out of the rubble of Hanover.

As it was, her stay was interrupted by a postcard from Miss Herbert, with whom she had stayed in touch, offering her a job in the BBC European Service.

As he was leaving Berlin, Parker was more or less bundled into a car outside his hotel and driven off with his case by two men with big necks, one of whom sat in the back with him. For them, it seemed like business as usual. The best explanation Parker could come up with was that he was being taken off to meet the seller of the film.

He was surprised when after only a couple of minutes they drew up outside another hotel, where he was taken up to a room in which a woman and a man stood waiting. It took him a moment to recognise the suited security guard from Michail's boat and the sister, Sasha, who stood confidently with hands on hips. Her face was strong, though in no way beautiful. The short body looked as though it didn't belong to the head. Jet-black hair was worn like a helmet, a different colour and cut to when Parker had last seen her. She was expensively but tastelessly dressed in a studded orange leather outfit with enormous padded shoulders and a calf-length skirt. She was also – extraordinarily to Parker's mind – wearing Doc Martens, which had been popular in his youth. He'd had a pair, of which his father had disapproved because of their skinhead associations.

Parker told Sasha that no one had showed up for his appointment, so he had no idea what was going on. He presumed it was she who'd had him followed, thus blowing any chance of a deal.

She asked what he had discussed with Robinson.

'He told me to inspect and report back, though he did say he was sceptical about any sale of film.'

'Unless it is Mr Robinson who is pulling the wool over *your* eyes.'

He said he didn't understand.

'Film or not, he will be taking retainers from other clients, not just Michail, in spite of promising his exclusive services, as his intention is to cheat them all.'

Parker wasn't sure where that left him other than as Robinson's dupe. It wasn't as though he had a clue what he was doing. Was Frau Trauner an accomplice to the deceit? Was Robinson masterminding the operation to see who turned up? He had, after all, admitted to Michail the possibility of someone doing just that.

Seemingly as an afterthought, Sasha said, 'I didn't know you were gay.'

Parker shook his head.

'You went to a gay bar last night.'

Parker supposed he must have been followed.

'The one in Eisenacher Strasse,' Sasha prompted. 'Famous.'

Why had he gone? Out of curiosity more than any personal interest; he supposed he wanted to see if he could find further evidence of the sort of sexual abandon he had glimpsed in the film, but he'd found nothing other than it was there and was godless, with only a handful of customers. He exchanged banalities with a barman, who said it would liven up later. He resisted the urge to get wildly drunk and cause a scene. He had no interest in being picked up by a man or vice versa. Deciding it was a tourist trap, he left and outside found himself being embraced by a thin white guy who greeted him effusively after apparently recognising him. Parker supposed this was an attempt at a pick-up. He wondered whether he minded, until what must have been a sixth sense (because he was in no way streetwise) told him that the man was after his wallet. Parker shoved him off. The man, who addressed him in broken English, was unabashed and suggested a drink. When Parker walked away, the man tagged along, saying he would show him a good time. Parker, uncharacteristically, told him to fuck off, which the man eventually did, not that Parker noticed until he looked back and saw him embracing another stranger.

Sasha said, 'Tell Mr Robinson I am not as soft as my brother. Mr Robinson has taken a substantial upfront fee to negotiate on his behalf.'

Parker wasn't surprised: a fool and his money were easily parted.

Sasha went on. 'Michail will no doubt be strung along, more money will be demanded and paid, then pouf! The whole thing will vanish. Michail will shrug it off because he's too rich to care and has an inexplicable soft spot for Mr Robinson, so much so that I suspect Mr Robinson has found a way to blackmail my dear brother, which, given his record, wouldn't be difficult. Ask yourself, why should Mr Robinson choose a lamb like you unless it was to run you in circles?'

On the train back to London, Parker had plenty of time to think about Sasha's parting warning. She had told him to pass on to Robinson that while she thanked him for past introductions, she wasn't naive.

She'd concluded, 'Perhaps because so much of our activity is extracurricular, he thinks we are not in a position to complain. We know there are some he annoyed sufficiently over that Russian Western film business – from which he milked millions, and it lies unseen and unfinished – who are keen to engage Mr Robinson in frank discussion when they find him. Tell him to think twice before adding me to the list. Are we clear?'

The night before, Parker had phoned Robinson late, probably sounding deranged, saying that he wasn't sure what he was getting into.

'Suddenly I find my grandfather is involved, and I even think I see him sometimes.'

He had to explain that Schlegel was his grandfather and how he, his grandmother and Robinson's father all knew each other, and now Schlegel's name kept cropping up in Morgen's documents.

Robinson sounded more indulgent than surprised. In fact, he was thinking ahead, having immediately made the connection between August Schlegel and what Morgen had once told him about a colleague of his being in Hitler's bunker at the very end. Thinking the Morgen documents might be useful after all, he told Parker that he would arrange for Trauner to deliver them to his hotel.

'Let the lazy bitch get off her skinny arse for a change.'

Later, he would complain about the cost. 'Expensive at half that.'

He suspected Trauner had made a point of screwing him because he had shown no interest in her film. Let her stew; he knew she would come down to three grand, because she was nothing like as tough a negotiator as she liked to think.

When Parker asked about the other stuff, Robinson said, 'Fuck that. I can string Michail along until the cows come home. Let him wait, he'll only want it more.'

170

Parker, still in a state of confusion, was about to ring off when Robinson said, 'You sound distressed, dear boy.'

'I didn't expect to stumble across my grandfather here.'

Robinson sounded philosophical. Amused, even.

'It's probably just the malfate.'

'Malfate?'

'Through coincidence, there are people we shouldn't have met, but it's inevitable, like they're waiting for us.'

'Malfate?' repeated Parker, thinking of Schlegel. 'But I've never met the man.'

'It doesn't matter. It is what is written. We're all written. The choice you make has already been made for you. You are merely the executor of that decision.'

'August Schlegel?' Robinson wondered aloud as he hung up, thinking that the man would be interesting to talk to, were he still alive, because his story would be worth a fortune.

Konrad Morgen and the Testimony of A. Schlegel

I have known August Schlegel since 1943, when we worked in financial investigations in Berlin. In November 1944, he wished to make a sworn testament so that a record exists of treasonable activities involving Party Secretary Bormann. Schlegel feared that 'knowing too much' rendered him expendable. He hoped the document's existence, held by a third party, might serve to negotiate his survival. Failing that, I was to bring it to the attention of an appropriate authority.

Schlegel was somewhat unhinged at the time, probably drunk and suffering from a persecution complex. He maintained Bormann had altered his record so he would be sought as a war criminal, should he survive. He admitted to witnessing round-ups and civilian shootings in the east over the

171

summer of 1941 as a Gestapo 'official observer' but took no active part. Bormann, he claimed, had revised his war record to make him out to have been a unit commander responsible for thousands of shootings.

On the traumatic effect of witnessing those events of 1941, he is quite clear: it turned his hair white overnight. Schlegel remains a troubled young man, to the extent of remarking how disturbed he is by his growing callousness and a belief that there are no mitigating circumstances.

He declared that he had worked for Party Secretary Bormann on financial operations that were partly official, partly under the table.

The official business was a result of a secret meeting in Strasbourg in August 1944, where Bormann's personal representative (in fact, Schlegel's father, Anton) informed the assembled industrialists that government export controls would be lifted immediately. This was to be done before the end of the war, which was considered lost.

A word of explanation is needed on the role of Schlegel's father, Anton, who played a significant deep-cover role in the above. In the 1920s and '30s, he was closely involved in the financial affairs of the Party and was an intimate of Martin Bormann, then relatively junior but a rising star. Anton Schlegel was responsible for the transfer of substantial funds away from the prying eyes of German tax officials to Switzerland. Only Bormann and Anton Schlegel knew the exact whereabouts of these secret accounts.

For many years, Anton Schlegel was believed dead, a victim of the purge of 1934, only to resurface a decade later, physically much altered and calling himself Anton Tieck. He sold his services to Bormann, who needed his old partner's expertise in financial evasion for his grand exercise in capital flight.

Over 750 companies were set up following the meeting: 112 in Spain, 58 in Portugal, 35 in Turkey, 98 in Argentina, 214 in Switzerland and 233 in other countries.

August Schlegel states: 'These firms are capable of generating an annual income of 30 million US dollars, all of it available to the cause of the next Reich. Whereas Himmler and the SS hold that Germany should negotiate an anti-Soviet pact with the United States, Bormann favours economic migration. Transporting these assets involves underground routes leading from all over Germany to Switzerland or Rome and after that by sea to South America.'

As well as these clandestine initiatives, Schlegel says he was involved in treasonable negotiations on behalf of Party Secretary Bormann, who arranged Vatican diplomatic papers that let him pass freely in and out of Switzerland.

Schlegel states, 'These meetings were with American OSS Intelligence regarding joint operations to remove further assets to safety. US agent Dulles knows the German financial market because he was a Wall Street lawyer before the war, investing in the Third Reich on behalf of US clients. I have proof of this long-standing association, a photograph showing my stepfather, a banker, with Bormann and Dulles, taken before the United States entered the war at the end of 1941. It is now obvious that the association continued after that.'

Parker thought to himself after reading the document on the train back from Berlin: And this man was my grandfather!

It left him contemplating whether what had happened to him at the hands of Father Roper was punishment for the sins of the fathers. Perhaps it was their scars that he had inherited. He didn't know whether to mourn for himself or for them.

Parker turned to the dossier on the commandant's

mistress, not expecting to find Schlegel's name again – on the first page – and asked himself what he was being dragged into. As he read on, he experienced a feeling of clammy familiarity. His and the woman's story both had authority's penetration in common.

Addendum to the Testimony of E.H.

I first met H. in the autumn of 1944 while she was recovering in an orthopaedic clinic in Munich where children with amputated limbs and wounded soldiers were cared for by Catholic sisters who wore shapeless bonnets and looked like scarecrows.

Schlegel warned me that he considered her in every respect remarkable, charming, educated, cagey but artful. She was still very sick, recovering from an abortion performed that summer by a Polish prisoner doctor when she was sixteen weeks pregnant, as well as having contracted tuberculosis of the hip. Yet it is incredible, after what she has gone through, that her looks and character have not suffered. I immediately saw why the commandant was smitten. But, as Schlegel reminded me, she was a convicted political criminal, sentenced in 1930 to two-and-a-half years in Hamm on a charge indicating an intended form of political assassination 'planned carefully and insidiously, e.g. by poison'. She had pharmaceutical training. Her otherwise sparse record has her born in Vienna in 1903, married and divorced. According to Schlegel, the relatively trivial offence that brought her to Auschwitz involved minor fraud over misuse of a Party badge and a ten-month sentence.

On the first day we were both unwell and got nowhere. H. was unwilling to discuss the commandant. At 5pm I went to bed exhausted and woke up just as exhausted at 9.30am. The föhn, that ill wind associated with psychosis, was blowing, and I wondered aloud if it had any bearing on our edginess.

Schlegel had confiscated and forwarded the commandant's arrest books, which listed admissions into the punishment block, discharges and deaths where applicable. I suggested we start by looking at these, as H. was a rare witness to what went on there, having been detained under the commandant's arrest for eight months from October 1942.

Her recall was badly affected by her experience, but by showing her the names in the books I was able to prompt her.

She said twice weekly clear-outs and executions took place in the yard; they were known as 'house cleaning' and done to reduce overcrowding. These were ad hoc and nothing to do with official cases, where the death penalty was authorised by a visiting judge. No one was exempt, with many chosen on whim. From her cell overlooking the execution yard, H. saw as many as fifty prisoners being shot at any one time. The men were naked and stood in rows facing the black execution wall; women were allowed to keep on their panties.

She was nearly shot herself. She was sick at the time and was woken and told to get ready. With ten or so men, some in chains, she was put at the front as the only woman and marched down the camp alley to an alternative execution site near the former administrative buildings. There they were met by Grabner, security chief of the universally feared Political Department. Seeing H., he made everyone go back and later told her that the episode had been a practical joke on the part of the man who had called her out.

What on earth to make of such a 'joke'? Why might she have been selected in the first place, and why would Grabner

175

rescue her? I suspected I knew. Schlegel reported that Grabner and the commandant were consumed by mutual loathing and at constant loggerheads. But upon asking H. if she thought the commandant was responsible for the order, which was then thwarted by Grabner, she grew upset and said that he had always looked after her best interests.

Grabner, a fitness fanatic, was, it should be said, barely capable of stringing a sentence together. After being caught red-handed by Schlegel with stolen goods and arrested, he warned that H. had made up the affair and her real relationship with the commandant was mercenary. As the man was by then looking to save his skin, Schlegel was disinclined to believe him.

H. grew calmer, following the lists with her finger. She paused when she recognised names and was able to state that the record was consistently faulty: often entries had no cross marking a death when she knew the person was dead.

Women reported to have died from natural causes were in fact killed by lethal injection. These were administered by a medical orderly known to all as Injection Heini, a man with a strange walk and a face like a monkey. Once, H. saw him inject four mothers and their babes-in-arms. Otherwise he came every fortnight to what she called the 'school'. Asked what school, she couldn't remember, though it was where prisoners were paraded for Heini to make his selections.

False death certificates were issued. Aneurysm and heart failure were the commonest given causes. H. knew because her detention work involved distributing the dead person's personal effects, and the certificates passed through her hands. Part of her job involved writing letters of condolence to relatives, offering to send them the ashes!

The lists contained the names of men in her corridor who

176

had been starved to death in standing cells. One was supposed to have driven to the women's camp to take away a load of corpses and used the opportunity to meet a woman. H. pointed out his low prisoner number, indicating that he was among the original gang of thirty German hardened criminals handpicked by the commandant to run the prison. H. said how rare it was for such a senior prisoner to be so severely treated for a relatively minor offence, when generally they lived like lords.

She grew distraught recalling the agony of listening all night to the starving men complaining of thirst. One, begging for mercy, was told he would die like a dog. The arrests officer, one of the most sadistic of the guards, tried to placate her with cigarettes, but she suspected he was fishing to see if the men had told her anything. She experienced great anxiety after their deaths, still hearing their voices in her head.

H. elsewhere saw the same arrests officer kill another prisoner, whose name she could not remember, with 'a single blow to the stomach or near the heart'. She was being bandaged by a Polish prisoner doctor when she saw this happen next door.

She also recalled how, shortly after her own arrest, she witnessed Heini inject six German female prisoner supervisors. This was after a riot at a women's sub-camp, where German women had beaten nearly a hundred Jewish women to death. The SS, keen to hush things up, insisted that no one would be punished because the dead were 'only Jews'. Six ringleaders gave themselves up and told H. 'the whole story': how the male prisoner in charge of the punishment section had incited them to kill the Jews, and how SS guards pitched in.

H. reported the women being cheerful because they were getting job transfers to the petrochemical factory. Instead, they were finished off at five or six one morning by Heini. H.

could confirm this because she was in the next room, again receiving medical treatment, being bandaged. She later heard that the block chief responsible for the riot was released after temporary arrest.

She remembered the name of the prisoner she had seen the arrests officer kill when she came across his name in the book – another with a low number, in charge of the garrison abattoir, whose death was listed as 'suicide by poison'. When I asked if it could have been an injection rather than a blow as recalled, she answered it hardly mattered; the wretch was dead either way.

I noted separately that the man had been arrested with two others for gold and jewellery theft. The second, another block senior, had also died under suspicious circumstances, 'committing suicide' by hanging himself in his cell. The third, Franz Fichtinger, who worked in the leather depot, survived.

H. later rather extraordinarily referred to Fichtinger as her fiancé but made no mention of his name at this time.

She added, 'Neither have I found in the book the names of three men from the clothes depot Canada, who were arrested in April or May 1943 and shot.'

She said these cases were widely discussed as a 'purely SS matter'.

Later, she qualified that by adding that only large-scale shady deals involving so many senior prisoners would cause the SS to take action. 'I can tell you this because everyone was saying things had got so out of hand that the SS feared being compromised by their own involvement.'

H.'s confinement was very different from her life of privilege before her fall. She was in the first transport of 999 women to be taken into the camp in March 1942. A lot of SS men turned

178

up to gawp. Most of the women were uneducated dregs, criminals or asocials and were grouped accordingly. H. was among the very few political prisoners, held to be of higher standing and prioritised. The commandant and the head of employment asked if any were typists or had qualifications. H. gave her profession as a drugstore assistant and seamstress. A doctor wanted her for the hospital. (I was aware of this man as a practitioner of lethal injections.) He didn't get her. On the commandant's instructions, she was assigned her own room (almost unheard of, she admitted) and soon after was taken to his house to be interviewed by his wife, was shown a carpet in the hall and was asked if she could mend it.

After taking the job, she saw the commandant coming and going. He told her it was probably not proper for him to employ a political prisoner, but until then his wife had had a limited choice of female domestic staff, let alone German speakers. I can add that H. spoke more elegant German than the wife.

The work included two tapestries, a tapestry cushion in silk, a car rug and various blankets.

H. sewed and ate alone in a room with a radio. She was separately served the same food as the commandant, who came home for lunch: soup, entrée, meat, vegetables, pastries or cakes, fruit salad and coffee. She compared it to the menu of a big hotel in peacetime and mentioned that she had travelled widely, to Abyssinia, Africa, Palestine and Italy.

Her confinement appeared so civilised compared to normal prisoner conditions that I wondered aloud if she was daring me to believe her. She merely said that the commandant did all he could to make her detention lighter. She had shared her first room with three others until he she was given her own. When I pointed out that she had claimed to have

179

had one from the start, she asked sharply if I wanted her to continue.

The privileges went on. Her own furniture and carpets. A cook and a maid for her personal needs. A weekend pass let her move freely about the town and stay overnight in outside staff buildings. She was accorded informal privileges. The commandant caught her smoking, which was forbidden, and when she tried to hide the cigarette, he told her not to bother.

When I repeated that this all sounded quite incredible, she said I was free to check with the commandant's deputy who had arranged it.

I asked if the commandant had at that point expressed any personal interest. (How pompous I sounded.) No, and it hadn't occurred to her. It was fellow prisoners who first commented on his crush. She admitted to having an easy, almost informal relationship with the man.

'He talked of business but laughed at the same time in a particular way. I answered in the same way because I must confess that I liked the man.'

On the subject of his wife and their lavish standard of living, H. would only say, 'Where the commandant or his wife secured this amazing quantity of material or clothes, I don't know, as the commandant's wife went very plainly dressed, one could say almost *too* plainly dressed.'

Otherwise H. avoided any comment on the woman, other than to say that she'd liked working in the house as far as keeping up the 'entrance lists' allowed her the time. Then, 'On my birthday, a special party was organised for me in the commandant's garden. The people in the camp believed at first that we were related.'

It was her thirty-ninth.

When I again expressed astonishment, she didn't think it so remarkable. The commandant's wife indulged her staff and made a point of knowing when they had birthdays.

Only later did she note that her fall had in fact begun the month before. The wife was out. H. was working alone by the radio when, without a word, the commandant came and kissed her.

She made it sound rather like some tawdry romantic novel. Later, she revised her statement, saying that without the kiss she would have served her time and gone her way. As it was, she ran off and locked herself in the lavatory. Whatever the attraction between them, she had done nothing to encourage it. She thereupon made herself scarce by reporting sick and avoided working in the house, although she said the commandant succeeded time and again in finding her. No mention was made of the kiss, but he remained keen that good relations were maintained between H. and his wife. He sent an adjutant to tell her that as she was free on Sundays she should bathe, have her hair done, put on her best dress and call on his wife.

This social arrangement lasted into the autumn – perhaps ten to fifteen visits in all – by which time plans were underway for her release. In September, she was told she would be posted to a hospital on the eastern front, but she talked her way out of that, blaming her nerves, and wangled a job as a pharmacist in the garrison. She was sent for training in the prisoner hospital in the new camp. Her escort that evening was Injection Heini; it was the first time they'd met. Finding conditions there as dire as everyone had warned, H. remained forceful enough to kick up a fuss, refusing to work with Jews and saying she didn't require training. She was allowed her way and spent her preparatory month back in the garrison, schooling a prisoner nurse.

When H. turned up for her Sunday visit at the beginning of October, she was told that the commandant was in hospital after a riding accident and that his wife needed to be with him. She thought nothing of it until her works supervisor announced that she was being sent to the women's penal colony for having violated 'her terms of employment in the commandant's house'.

She wrote separate letters to the commandant, his wife and their cook, begging them to clear up what must surely be a terrible misunderstanding. She insisted she had done nothing wrong and begged them to take no account of any rumours and do something to help.

'As an answer, the next day, on 16 October at 1.30pm, I was transferred to the commandant's arrest.'

This on the day of her intended release was the cruellest blow. Her arresting officer, the woman in charge of employment of female prisoners, told the guard: 'This one won't be coming back.'

The threat was not matched by H.'s privileged confinement that included her own room, a bed with a mattress, being allowed to smoke and read, and even a cat for company.

She wrote two or three times more to the commandant without any reply. Grabner, head of camp security, sometimes came to see her.

'He told me my case depended directly upon the commandant. I was all right. And then he would laugh.' His laughter, she decided, meant he knew something she didn't.

The next morning, H. without any preliminaries stated, 'According to my recollection, on 16 December 1942 at about 11pm, I was asleep when suddenly the commandant appeared. I hadn't heard him open my cell and was very frightened. It was dark, and I thought some evil was afoot. At first, I believed it was an SS man or a prisoner.'

H. said she knew of occasions when women's cells had been opened at night so prisoners and SS men could have intercourse.

She lay in the dark, fearing the worst, until she heard a 'Pssst!' and a torch was switched on, lighting his face.

'I exclaimed, "Herr Kommandant!"'

They were silent until H. composed herself to ask what was wrong.

He spoke for the first time to say, 'You are coming out.' She asked, 'Now, at once?', fearing she was about to be executed.

He said once more, 'Pssst! Be very quiet. We'll talk it over.'

With that, he sat at the foot of her bed. She reminded him that she had written and asked why she was under arrest.

He asked if she was all right, hadn't he done everything to improve her conditions, and did she need anything?

'Then he moved up and tried to kiss me. I pushed him away and must have made some noise, because he warned me again to be quiet, nobody knew he was there. I asked if anyone had seen him.'

He told her he had come through the garden gate and unlocked the cell himself.

H. complained that her release had been arranged and she should be working in the garrison hospital. He said he would look into it, because he had been ill, and this was his first time back and he had come straight to her.

'I asked why he had come at night when he could see me during the day. I was still afraid. He told me not to worry; I was under his protection, and he had come alone to talk without being disturbed. He asked why I was always so reserved. I told him it was because he was a respected married man. He repeated not to worry, he knew what he was doing, then he became somewhat sweeter and tried to kiss me again.'

H. remained anxious, listening and glancing at the door, which was open. She could not believe he had come alone, because he would not be allowed to go unescorted in the prison compound at night. She insisted he leave.

'He told me I should "think about it" and he would come back. I said, "But please not at night." He left, closing the door very quietly, and I heard his departing footsteps. I did not hear the outer gate close or the front door. These were always locked at night.'

What of this garden gate? I wasn't aware of the punishment block having one. It sounded more like an open sesame in a fairy tale.

Most significant seemed to be the commandant's admission of having been ill for two months, corresponding more to Schlegel's report of a rumoured nervous breakdown through pressure of work than to any riding accident. He certainly wasn't behaving like a man in any right frame of mind: the *pssst!* of a pantomime villain; his renewed interest in her out of the blue, six months after a kiss, which had been their only physical contact; the risk of coming to her cell at night; the apparition revealed by the shining torch, which must have made him appear grotesque – all making H.'s account more like one of those dreams where the apparent waking is part of the continuing dream; or the start of a sick fantasy.

In fact, it was I who suggested the date of 16 December, as the commandant's arrests book showed twenty-two Polish prisoners apprehended that day in a move against the camp underground. They would have given him a reason to be

184

in the punishment block late at night and to use that as an excuse to visit, perhaps on impulse.

Two nights later, he came again. H. said, 'He asked if I had made a decision. I said, "No, I don't want to." All I wanted was to be released.'

He said he had arranged a nice room for her in a beautiful house. To her question of when, he answered it would be very soon. They talked for two hours. He asked about her life and family situation, which were not in her records. He again made advances. She resisted, saying the door was open. He told her nobody would come. She didn't let that influence her, and he left in a temper.

The next day, she was moved to a cell where the door could be opened from the inside. I asked if this involved a transfer to the commandant's office in the garrison with cells in the basement which he could visit whenever. A cell was a cell, was all she said. She did add that the commandant had access to his office through a private gate in his garden wall, across the road; this at least explains the previous puzzling reference.

He came some days later, again at night. H. said, 'He asked if he should go away. I said no. Then he came to me in bed, and we had sexual intercourse.'

He returned after some days and this time undressed completely and was nearly caught when the cells were inspected after a fire alarm went off. He crouched naked in the corner while H. covered his uniform under her bedding and pretended to sleep. The cell light went on, the duty officer checked through the Judas hole, the light went off. The commandant dressed but soon returned, saying too much was going on outside; a building was on fire.

I could find no record of any fire in the garrison over the

Christmas period of 1942, though I knew very well that there had been one a year later, on the night of 7 December 1943, opposite the commandant's office, which destroyed all my investigation's evidence – an act of arson that was officially blamed on 'undetermined causes'.

H. stated, 'All in all, we had four or five nights of sexual intercourse. His interest in me did not seem to wane.'

When she brought up the subject of her release, he told her to be patient. Nervous about their situation, she asked what would happen to her if he was discovered. He advised her to say that a prisoner had been with her. He was sure there were good-looking senior ones who took an interest.

'I replied that I didn't know any. He asked what I had going with the prisoner Fichtinger. Were we having an affair? I said Fichtinger had written to me, and I'd answered telling him not to pester me as he was not my type.'

He nevertheless insisted she name him should anyone ask. She did not want to, but he thought if she did nothing would happen to her. At that, he took a sheet from his notebook and by the light of his torch made her write that she was acquainted with the prisoner Franz Fichtinger.

That night, he accidentally left behind a leather glove strap, which she kept as a souvenir, indicating, I dare say, a sentimental attachment.

The commandant stated that he would return.

Parker instinctively understood H.'s inability to connect events – the jagged timescale, the before and after, her fall, her jumbled memory and a fractured account that mirrored his own inability to make sense of what had happened to him. He could relate perfectly to a life of flashbacks, lack of context in a recognisable institution, closing ranks, one hopeless situation after another in a place where survival depended on keeping one's eyes fixed on the ground and ghosting oneself.

Only much later did he question these men's stories and the roles within them of troublesome and troubled women, who never quite fitted or were seen in their own right. There was Valerie Robinson and his grandmother (and what of his virtually absent mother?), but none more so than H.

H. waited in vain for the commandant's return. At the beginning of February, she suffered a severe attack of what she thought was a recurring gallstone problem. This was confirmed by a male Polish prisoner nurse named Stossel. After a second attack with terrible vomiting, she was seen by Dering, the chief prisoner doctor, who told her the previous diagnosis was incorrect because, 'You are pregnant.'

She refused to say who the father was and begged Dering to help, because pregnancy was punishable by death. The next day, a bunker janitor slipped her two medicines. The first gave her terrible pains so she threw the second away. Dering did not return.

Early one morning when she was finishing washing she was fetched by an arresting officer and allowed only to put on a shift before being taken without explanation to one of the standing cells, a small, dark hole with room enough only to kneel.

She had to remain there all the time. However much she asked, she was not told the reason.

'I became terribly afraid and started crying, which resulted in buckets of cold water being thrown over me. I cried so terribly because a dead body was in the cell, which I could feel in the darkness. I was taken out of there and put into

187

the next one. As I continued crying, more buckets of water were thrown. At first, I received normal food rations. After that, I only got bread and coffee and every fourth day some cooked food.'

H. went on: 'For nine weeks, I had no possibility to wash, and the last seventeen days there was no using the WC. I had to do this in my cell.'

She was called an 'old cow' and a 'hysterical goat', and surprise was expressed that she was still alive.

She could hear the pleas of one of the men being starved, begging to be spared, only to be told, 'You will die, you dog.' Following that, H. said, 'I had to vomit and felt better afterwards.'

I wondered at the accuracy of her figures in such a timeless space – 'nine', 'seventeen', recited almost as though part of a litany – but I could see how much she was affected by the memory.

If the punishment was without reason, her release was too. Around April or May, she was moved to an ordinary cell, and she asked the woman in the next one how to manage an abortion.

'She told me to get hold of a long needle to open the ovary and put green soap inside. I managed to be brought these, and with the aid of a mirror tried and lost a lot of blood without any result.'

Nothing happened after that until the end of June. During a big clear-out, H. was told to stand in the corridor for execution. This was after the commandant and Grabner had reviewed prisoner cases, leading to fifty-five being shot.

'I was standing there when Grabner saw me and said, "For heaven's sake, that is Nora," and sent me back.'

Her last-minute reprieve she could not explain, other

than her belief that the commandant remained her protector. Whereupon she was transferred to the women's penal colony at Budy and told she would have 'all the advantages by special order of the commandant'. Her immediate problem was dealt with. 'I got into the hospital, where I received something which managed the abortion.' After being allowed to recover in bed for a week or two, she was given a supervisory job.

With the termination, her position was annulled, her history unwritten; she was lucky to be alive.

Reading H.'s account, Parker thought about August Schlegel's testimony and how both resembled a Pandora's Box. Why was he being exposed to that past, almost as though it was being given to him? What was he meant to do with it? He felt as though he was being recruited in some way.

'Mr Parker?'

He looked up to see a stranger. Parker supposed he had to do with Sasha or someone connected with selling the film. He was neat and of conventional appearance, with tamed hair, blue suit, tie and raincoat. Parker supposed him around fifty or so. Only the moustache seemed an affectation, as though the man were trying too hard to appear respectable in an old-fashioned way.

'It so happens – fortuitously, it seems – I am travelling to Brussels,' the man went on, as if that explained everything. 'So I thought I would jump the gun, so to speak. Do you mind if I join you? Frau Trauner said you would be on the train and told me you were quite distinctive in appearance.'

Parker could see that the man was going to sit, invited or not.

'My name is Mr Smith,' he said. Parker wondered if it was. 'I believe you have certain items for sale. I follow the market.'

189

'What market?' Parker asked stupidly, wondering what Robinson would make of the man. When they subsequently discussed him, Robinson thought he sounded like a parody, but (unlike Parker at the time) he remembered that a Mr Smith had sold Michail fake artefacts.

Mr Smith told Parker his reason for going to Brussels was because he was a member of the European Parliament. He had been in Berlin on business and only heard about certain items being for sale late the previous night.

Heard how? Parker wondered to himself.

Mr Smith answered without being asked, saying he was familiar with Frau Trauner and they talked from time to time about whether she had anything of interest.

'I rather reprimanded her because she should have alerted me. That said, I suppose she isn't to blame because she doesn't really know who I am. Where did you go to school?'

Parker told him. Mr Smith said he had gone to Dulwich, and Parker supposed he was being subjected to an example of English oneupmanship until the man said, 'But my mother was German, so I was "Kraut boy".'

Parker wondered where this was going.

'I am interested in the home movies,' Mr Smith said.

It took Parker a moment to gather that he meant the ones shot by the commandant.

'Do you have them with you?' Mr Smith raised his eyes to the case on the overhead luggage rack. Parker said he didn't. He didn't say he hadn't seen them.

'A pity,' said Mr Smith. 'And the Morgen documents?

Parker pointed to what he was reading.

Mr Smith asked, 'Perhaps you would allow me a shufti.'

Parker couldn't think of a reason not to.

Mr Smith reached into his briefcase and produced a pair

of white cotton gloves, saying that one never knew when an occasion might arise for handling rare documents. Parker self-consciously wiped his palms on his trousers before handing over the papers.

'I've done a speed-reading course,' Mr Smith announced.

The remark seemed typical of the man's prissy manner. He wore half-moon glasses to read and occasionally made notes with a propelling pencil on a little yellow pad. Parker saw he had handwriting even smaller than his own.

Not a very fast speed-reading course, Parker was thinking as Mr Smith finished and said, 'Disappointing, I must say. The Schlegel document is of little interest.'

Parker decided not to mention that the man was probably his grandfather. Mr Smith was starting to get on his nerves.

Mr Smith said, 'Unfortunately, the Hodys document is the wrong one.'

'It's the only one I know of.'

'No, there are several translated versions.'

'Why translated?'

'You don't know?' Mr Smith asked, surprised.

'I have no idea.'

'After the war, Morgen was dealing with the Americans. He was SS, so probably in an effort to save his neck, he made out that he was one of the *good* Germans. You see the translation of the original testament reproduced quite often, usually just the section covering the affair. It is very rough, questionable and largely incoherent. This version is Morgen's subsequent write-up, cleaned up for the Americans.'

'Cleaned up?'

Mr Smith ignored the question. 'I see that this document is supposedly signed by Morgen. It must be possible to find other examples of his signature to check, but it isn't what I'd hoped. I was expecting the unexpurgated text.'

Parker was hoping the man would go away, but he seemed to have only just started.

'Unexpurgated?'

'Morgen is said to have written, shall we say, an even more private account, to the extent of it being pornographic.'

Parker said he found that hard to believe.

Mr Smith said, 'Some say the whole story was cooked up by Morgen in a failed attempt to bring down the commandant.'

Parker suspected it was one of those cases that could be argued endlessly, and Mr Smith was capable of going on and on.

'It was only ever her word against the commandant's,' Mr Smith declared. 'He never spoke of the affair, except once, under questionable circumstances.'

Parker wondered about Mr Smith and his prurient interest.

'To a young American Intelligence officer,' Mr Smith explained. 'After his arrest, the commandant told an English army psychiatrist that he'd led a normal family life with ordinary marital relations, but sex never played a great part and he wasn't interested in affairs. He repeated as much to the American, but added that when his marriage broke down, he had found a camp inmate, who asked no questions.'

Mr Smith looked expectantly at Parker, who asked doubtfully, 'Are you suggesting that the admission was planted?'

'Think about it. US Intelligence knew of the testimony, as it had done the translation. Such a document would have been regarded as sensational, and this single reference exposes the man's hypocrisy. One is bound to deduce that the Americans were responsible for its insertion. Oh, don't worry,

I am not trying to make a case for the commandant, quite the opposite.'

Parker was coming to see how any account – of anything, perhaps even his own story – was endlessly revisable. He had always believed that the past was set in stone, yet as he sat there he wondered if his own could be derailed by some unforeseen intervention.

'You see,' said Mr Smith, 'I am the man's grandson.'

'Excuse me?' asked Parker, though he had heard quite clearly. He asked himself how this man, who behaved like a combination of the Ancient Mariner and an English caricature of the kind later adopted by Nigel Farage (also Dulwich-educated), could be who he claimed. He wondered if his credulity was being tested and if Mr Smith's unsolicited appearance might even be an elaborate practical joke on the part of Robinson.

Mr Smith was nevertheless convincing in his declaration that he was the son of the commandant's youngest daughter. Her older sister, he threw in, had modelled for the fashion house Balenciaga in Spain. Later, Parker saw how such incongruous details gave his account its heft.

His mother had married a British Army officer in 1965 when Germany was still under military occupation. As a boy, he had moved around until sent to English boarding schools.

'The sick joke was that my father was more Nazi than Nazi. He didn't like Jews, and when I became friendly with one, he gave me a right good hiding. It's why I don't drink. He hit me and my mother after he'd had a few. My mother never told my father about the past, just that her father had died in the war. When I was fifteen, she swore me to secrecy. She couldn't bear to carry the burden alone. There I was, a normal English schoolboy, so imagine my devastation on being told that this monster was my grandfather. At first, I was too shocked to do anything, until drawn by morbid curiosity I started reading, reading, reading. The war had nothing to do with me, but because of who I am it came to haunt me. I have dedicated my life to Holocaust education and reconciliation. I am an honorary Jew. My motto is "Never Forget".'

There was no stopping the man.

'My mother was the baby of the family, but she inherited plenty of accounts from her brothers and sisters about how they had grown up in a garden paradise. I sat for hours making recordings of her talking about her life. She would cry a lot and say how she felt guilty about something of which she had no memory, as is the case with me. My grandmother was a cold fish, according to her. When she came in a room, it felt like being in a freezer. My mother was one of five children and spent her first year or so in a large villa within the camp perimeter. The footage I am interested in was taken during the war with a 9mm cine camera, which my grandfather was given by Heinrich Himmler. I am told it shows the older children frolicking and swimming in the pool built by prisoners, featuring the garrison and its crematorium chimney in the background. There was a high wall and a large garden, beautifully maintained, with a summer house and a huge adjoining vegetable allotment. My mother didn't know anything about my grandfather until 1963, when a newspaper article appeared with a photograph of him and the family. I think that moment was pivotal in her decision to get out of Germany. She married my father within eighteen months.'

'Didn't he recognise the commandant's name?' Parker asked.

'She'd changed it, which was easy enough as so many certificates had been lost in the war.'

Back in London, Robinson asked Parker, 'Do you believe him?'

'Why would he make something like that up?'

'Quite, though people make up the strangest things. But it's interesting that he started out wanting to buy, then all of a sudden has stuff to sell.'

'Yes, watercolours done by the commandant, given to him by his mother.'

'Did he say why he's selling?'

'He has a foundation and is raising funds to finish a Holocaust film.'

'I'm not getting involved in any film.'

'He spoke knowledgeably about Lanzmann's documentary *Shoah* and his spat with Godard over misrepresentation.'

'Enlighten me, dear heart.'

'The two filmmakers had a public argument. Godard complained that *Shoah* showed nothing other than verbal testimony. Mr Smith says he has a letter from Mr Godard endorsing his film. He says he will bring it.'

'He's coming here?'

'He asked, and I thought you should meet him as he'll be in London.'

After her release from detention in June 1943, H. became anonymous in the camp system: three months as a janitor, then in charge of a kitchen, with no more talk of pharmacy work or release.

The commandant was moved on at the end of the year, which she didn't mention. She had nothing to fear until 8 May 1944, when he returned. This brought about a hectic final period of irreconcilable account, as though all props of understanding had been removed. Whereas the calendar of the arrest books had acted as an aide memoire, the solitary date H. now offered was 12 July when she was due a transfer to Dachau, with the cryptic observation: 'About the fears which I had in connection with my transfer, I spoke to my fiancé, the already mentioned Fichtinger, who advised not to mention the commandant's name under any circumstances.'

A degree of protection appears to have been offered, in that H. volunteered, 'I was careful enough to put myself under psychiatric care for a period of six weeks.'

I refrained from saying that I found it hard to believe that any such treatment was available for prisoners' mental welfare. Nor did H. say how such protection was gained, though it merited a certificate from a Polish prisoner doctor!

After that, she fell ill with tuberculosis and was sent to the women's infirmary, where she caught typhus, which caused over a thousand fatalities in the month of June. On the day of her transfer, she was still in hospital when a major clear-out took place, after which only six were left, five old Jewish women and H., who was told she would be placed in solitary confinement until her transfer, the date for which had anyway passed.

H. said, 'When I refused, an order came from the commandant that I should be admitted to the medical block in the garrison.'

When I pointed out that her being in a position to argue terms suggested she still had leverage, she said, not really, because the medical block refused to take her and she was told she would be sent instead to Birkenau for gassing (the first time the place or the method was mentioned).

She was rescued – 'in the nick of time' – only because Schlegel, who was searching in vain for her, learned from the camp underground that she was on a list of those who were 'going up the chimney', and he managed to intervene as she was about to be taken off in a vehicle with several Jewish women.

Schlegel believed the commandant was responsible for the order, so he didn't know what to make of H.'s assertion that she had been in correspondence with the man about not being admitted to the medical block. The commandant claimed not to have received any letters, but later sent a go-between and cordial relations were resumed. 'I was asked to state any special wishes I had about food,' she said. 'I was allowed to write a list. I did so, and it was signed for agreement by the commandant.'

That such an exchange about dietary requirements could occur at this stage seems utterly bizarre, unless it was a case of the commandant trying to appear accommodating, after learning that Schlegel now had her in protective custody.

H. nevertheless persisted that the commandant remained her benefactor. Her attitude transcended criticism or accusation, as if to say what if – in other circumstances, other times. Her tolerance seems to be a mechanism, suggesting that in a tale of such wild irregularity he remained a fixed point.

She was bedridden when a last meeting took place between her and the commandant, by all accounts the first time they'd met since he left her cell promising to return eighteen months before. The occasion was instigated by Schlegel to see if, in his words, anyone could make head or tail of the matter.

After composing herself, H. told me, 'I was asked what enabled me to say that the commandant knew who was with me in the dungeon. I laughed, and the commandant said this was quite unclear to him.'

I asked what she meant by 'knew who was with me'. Was that a reference to Fichtinger, previously discussed by them? She said no mention was made of him, but the commandant 'got rather excited and put his hand on the bed to steady himself. He confirmed also that I had behaved very decently and had to be kept in the dungeon for my own protection.'

He said he had no idea why she had been kept in that 'little hole' in the first place – in fact, blamed her for not having drawn it to his attention! Schlegel said they sounded like actors in different plays.

I decided that the puzzling sentence about knowing who was in the cell with her could be made to make sense with the removal of 'knew who'. Perhaps what she had meant to say was: 'I was asked what enabled me to say that the commandant was with me in the dungeon.'

Then it made perfect sense; no wonder the man had had to steady himself.

Of this final meeting, H. forlornly concluded, 'When I was told in January 1943 that the commandant had refused my release from camp on account of very bad behaviour, I did not have any answer for that.'

When it fell, many years later, to Robinson and Parker to do the detective work that Morgen had failed to address, Robinson offered, 'Morgen's infatuation.'

That was a bit rich coming from him, as H. had planted herself in his psyche, representing exactly what he didn't know; probably the allure of death. She became twinned in his mind with Valerie Robinson. Robinson drove himself half-crazy trying to picture what they had looked like: two women with no visible record in a century when most people left a trace. Blurred images of the two slid together and, still blurred, became one. Their stories had unfolded in parallel and mysterious circumstances. He thought both deserved better than two unimaginative plods as chroniclers.

The malevolence into which H. had been pitched seemed to haunt a strange, jagged correspondence that had started between Robinson and Vod.

Vod's latest email read: 'The werewolf probably committed the first murders out of despair, because the heads he talked at didn't hear him, which he smashed by making a hole in them, as a way of having a relationship with another.'

Robinson, using a dictaphone, replied to Vod's answer machine. 'The butcher is blind to the fact that he is almost suffocating from his unfulfilled needs, which is why he passes on to his apprentice the blows he once received from his master.'

Robinson thought: Which the master and which the apprentice?

He dreamed of a nurse injecting him and woke sweating, thinking how the observations H. had given Morgen, however happenstance, were not those of someone who knew by chance.

Robinson told Parker that he remained sceptical about the whole affair.

'How likely is it that a woman in her fortieth year would conceive in a place where nearly all women ceased to menstruate, let alone that any foetus could survive such starvation?'

Parker thought to himself: Rooms into which I do not want

to go. It was but a step from Roper's study to H.'s standing cell, like in a series of dreams, resembling cubism or an Escher drawing in false perspective.

'One thing you can guarantee is that the woman always seemed to end up with her own room,' Robinson said. 'And one wonders about the place's internal postal system, with all that writing of letters, even prisoners writing to prisoners.'

Other than thinking that it came down to rooms, Parker was anyway distracted by then, after two plain-clothes detectives came round. They looked like a stand-up double act – one short, one tall – or car salesmen, or something dreamt up by Vod. When Parker answered the door and they said who they were, he supposed they were there for Robinson.

'Mr Parker?' the short one asked, showing his identity card.

They were there about theft from properties for sale. Parker's name was on the list of houses visited.

Parker, at a loss, asked, 'What theft?'

'Valuables. Jewellery. Watches.'

Parker shook his head. Neither man appeared much interested in investigating pilfering from people who could afford the loss. They both looked the sort to help themselves, given half a chance.

Upstairs, Robinson considered: If the German experience was rational thinking applied to a grand vision of the irrational, H.'s testament worked in counterpoint, where a proper understanding lay in what remained unsaid.

Downstairs, Parker thought to himself: Dozens must have visited the properties with a view to buying.

He said, 'It doesn't seem very bright, if you are going to do that, to give an actual home address. Anyway, the people I am looking on behalf of have changed their minds since one of them got cancer.'

He sensed that they believed he had done it and didn't care, beyond warning him not to waste their time.

He went back upstairs, shaken. He had thought of the stuff as trinkets and souvenirs, not valuables. He wasn't even aware of lifting anything, not until finding it in his pocket much later, asking himself: How on earth did that get there?

Robinson looked up.

'You look like a man having a bad dream.'

'Two coppers investigating a robbery, wanting to know if anyone had seen anything.'

Robinson grunted. 'Always the three monkeys. Hear nothing, see nothing, say nothing. What are we to make of Hodys? She remains frustratingly vague.'

Parker was relieved by the distraction.

'She knew the commandant, worked for his wife and led a privileged existence, all that seems clear. It falls apart after that. H. could offer no reason for her starvation, let alone her arrest.'

Robinson said, 'And no explanation is given for the commandant breaking off the relationship when she expected him to return.'

'It was Christmas. Maybe the wife and children were away, which left him with time on his hands.'

'Even so, I suspect he wasn't responsible for her punishment,' Robinson said. 'The man was flaky when it came to affairs of the heart, getting her to write a note saying it was someone else, promising, and delivering nothing.'

'Are you saying the wife found out?'

'Perhaps he coughed up about H. being knocked up. A lot of ifs, but if the man had had a nervous breakdown, did he have the affair when not in his right mind, then all of a dither spilled the beans to wifey? She was pregnant, too, as it happened.'

Parker hadn't known.

Robinson said, 'Wikipedia. Did the maths. At any rate, a daughter popped out nine months later, making him responsible for two pregnancies – almost operatic – one embryo starved, while the other grew fat on extra milk rations.'

Mr Smith's mother, according to the man, Parker thought to himself.

It made sense: the commandant confessed, and the unforgiving wife insisted on the woman being starved.

With all the contradictions surrounding H., they concluded that perhaps a better key to any understanding lay in splitting and fragmentation, which left them asking how much of her splintered account was made up of recurring tropes, repeat punishments and more men than just the commandant using her.

Robinson said, 'There's no reason she was exempt from being exploited by others.'

Grabner had been investigated for prisoner affairs, another SS man was charged with sexual race defilement, and a third had arranged for his Polish mistress to disappear after she became an embarrassment.

Robinson said, 'H. wouldn't have had any say beyond treating such men as strategic to her survival. If women were passed around like chattels, to say that she was up for grabs is only to show how rare it was in the context of such historical anonymity for one female prisoner to be singled out for so much attention.'

Parker thought, given such ease of death, that H. had

proved remarkably resilient; a nuisance and a survivor, afloat on unfathomable currents of intrigue.

They turned to Morgen's conclusion.

I had been naive in my questioning. Given that the affair was the point of her statement, other areas I chose to ignore by not asking two simple questions: who was she really, and what did she do beyond what she had told?

I had cast H. in a passive role until I checked various names in the garrison directory.

One such man mentioned had approved her transfer from the prisoner hospital after she refused to work there. I had supposed he was part of the medical or employment departments. But no; he was in charge of property administration, whose function was the cataloguing and reuse of confiscated prisoner clothing and valuables.

H. and I had a difficult final session in which I asked if she was willing to answer off the record. 'What?' she asked, wary but resigned.

What was her other job, referred to just once as the 'entrance lists'?

H. stared at me equably and said, 'I manipulated the situation as there was only one rule, thou shalt not get caught.'

The other job involved working in Canada.

'Where I was known as Diamond Nora,' she added wryly.

So named because she was employed in the jewellery section. I asked if she had been there from the start.

'Not at all. I was well cared for in the commandant's house, but after that kiss I couldn't carry on there for fear of the wife.'

My next question was whether her meetings with the wife had served any purpose other than social.

She shrugged and said, 'I spoke with the commandant and said I didn't want anyone compromised and there must be another way. He thought about that and said he should introduce me to Herr Grönke.'

Grönke was a former prisoner, one of the original gang of thirty, who after his release returned as a civilian to run the leather depot and operate as the commandant's fixer.

H. said, 'He came round as often as twice a day to the house with what were known as sweeteners – presents for the family, fashion accessories and fabrics. He took the wife riding in his carriage. He said goodnight to the children.'

H. went on. 'I was introduced to him at my party. I said that the commandant's wife had expressed an interest in jewellery. Grönke took the bait, and I was transferred to Canada.'

'When you said the commandant talked to you of business, was this what you discussed?' I asked.

'What else?' she answered reasonably. 'He would come to the store. It put our relationship on a more equal footing. Showing him things his wife might like let me work around his infatuation.'

'And your meetings with his wife, was that his idea?'

'I suggested it would be more practical if I brought samples to the house. I was keen to remain on the right side of her, because she could be vindictive. He was desperate to placate her. I don't remember him being present on Sundays. He was socially awkward. So I came and we sat in the summerhouse and I showed her stuff. "Oh, that one looks best on you!" She was easy to please and eager to be liked, although she once asked sharply why I was no longer working in the house when she was always saying what a good job I did. She confided in me, saying how their sex life had gone to pot. Perhaps she turned against me because she thought I had betrayed her confidence when I hadn't.'

I asked if the Canada business was the real reason for her arrest, and was that the 'great disobedience' mentioned by the commandant in their last meeting?

'They lost their nerve and made out it was personal rather than a huge racket about which people were starting to talk. One reason to sleep with the man, apart from hoping it would secure my release, was to spite his wife, who I am sure was behind my arrest, probably because she suspected an affair or had been told there was one when there wasn't.'

'And all along she and her husband were part of the bigger racket.'

'By then there was so much wholesale looting, with people being bought off or threatened. The attitude was that one may as well when so much went to waste.'

She once overheard talk between several internees, whose names she said she did not know, about hiding places they had with some SS men, where they stashed foreign currency, gold and silver to take with them after the evacuation of the camp. As for what got chucked away, H. said, 'I saw them burn great hills of valuables, textiles, clothes, suitcases, furs, leather goods and boots. Two barracks full to the ceiling had lain neglected, and after the rats were done everything had to be burned.'

At the very end, she announced, 'The psychiatric certificate issued by the Polish doctor as well as my written diaries about everything that happened are in the possession of Fichtinger.'

Written diaries! I suggested retrieving these as evidence. H. laughed at that and said she couldn't see how it was a realistic possibility.

I asked about the exact nature of her relationship with Fichtinger. She didn't say, other than that he'd looked after her. But with that she perhaps unwittingly revealed the threads connecting all levels. The closeness of Grönke, the commandant and Fichtinger, who worked for Grönke and had written H. a love letter, suggested that they were all in the same gang and H. was as much a part of it as any of them: the contact between Grönke's end of the operation and the commandant's wife; 'Oh, that one looks best on you.'

I thanked her for her frankness and said I would make no mention of these activities. I did not admit my fear that our efforts would get me nowhere as the case reached far beyond Auschwitz to higher echelons in Berlin.

I left depressed at being powerless to stand up fully for this unfortunate woman. If no one is there to push the case forward, everything will get bogged down. Who will look out for her when I am no longer in charge? Only her enemies. And maybe she will suffer one day for having given me her trust. A hint of that came as we finished. She was in despair, and I could offer nothing but my goodwill. What was that to a woman who has been disappointed so often? After our awkward parting, I experienced deep remorse at having used and abandoned her, as had others.

It was Parker who said, 'Morgen refers to an abortion prior to H.'s rescue in July 1944.'

'Oh, I see,' said Robinson. 'A whole year later than by H.'s reckoning.'

Parker didn't know what to make of that.

Robinson grunted and said, 'Multiplication. Maybe she was starved twice and there were two abortions.'

Parker shook his head. 'The pregnancy was put at sixteen weeks. Four months, and the commandant didn't return until May.'

Robinson thought about that. 'He could've been back and forth. The wife had refused to follow him to Berlin because of the air raids and stayed with the children.' He shrugged. 'Everything seems to have its shadow. Two jobs. The seamstress and Diamond Nora. Two pregnancies. Two abortions.'

'Why not admit to both?'

'H. had lost the plot by then!' Robinson exclaimed. 'Anyway, how do you satisfactorily explain resuming the affair after everything she had said?'

'Then did the whole thing happen a year later than she remembered? She reported a fire, of which Morgen could find no record in December 1942, but there was the big one in 1943 when his evidence went up in flames.'

'One can suppose. The commandant had been sacked by then, but his fifth child was only a few weeks old. Paternity leave, perhaps they had such a thing.' After brooding, Robinson said, 'I fear it gets worse.'

'How?'

'A lot was kept off the table until Morgen asked. Diamond Nora, for instance. She had presented herself as a domestic mouse, albeit a well-treated one, essentially a pet, rather than a mover and a shaker.'

Parker was thinking about H. being in a position to negotiate, even after her fall. From the beginning, her privileges indicated someone at the top of the prisoner hierarchy.

'Either she had the commandant's protection or she had influence in her own right.'

'You don't get called Diamond Nora for nothing,' Robinson said. 'Even with her punishers, there was a degree of familiarity: "For heaven's sake, that is Nora" – Grabner.'

They batted it back and forth until Robinson summarised. 'Prisoner survival depended on cooperation and coercion. Gossip and information were potential lifelines.'

'Passing things on.'

'Say Grabner attached a price to his protection in exchange for her life.'

They found themselves questioning H.'s account of the penal colony riot, which had puzzled Parker. It didn't need to be there. Morgen had not asked, and she had no need to mention it.

Robinson said, 'I rather wonder at the point other than to finger Injection Heini, who is more than fingered elsewhere.'

They had assumed that the SS offer of job transfers to the ringleaders was a ploy and they were going to kill them all along.

Robinson said, 'Unless the SS learned something that led to a change of mind.'

'As a result of information passed on.'

'By the charming older woman who befriended the women, and they told her "the whole story".' Robinson sighed. 'Well, there you are. See where a close textural reading gets you. I don't wish to trash the woman's reputation. I am sure we all would have done the same. Dog eat dog. No point in sitting in judgement.'

'We have no evidence,' said Parker, who was in two minds about dragging H. through the mud.

'Oh, I know, speculation,' said Robinson, 'but H. was isolated and vulnerable after her arrest. She had been abandoned by the commandant. She tells of being well cared for. Perhaps the deal with Grabner was in exchange for her privileges: anything you pick up, tell me. It would have been quite casual. They were on first name terms.'

They sat in silence, neither wanting to end up where they had, until Robinson began thinking aloud about H.'s convenient whereabouts, chancing to see this or that, being bandaged, seeing Heini off four mothers and their babies; always *there*. This staging was at its most improbable when she was able to report the executions after the riot – because again, quite by chance, she was being bandaged next door. She gave the time as five or six in the morning.

Robinson exclaimed, 'As if it was likely that general surgery was being held at that time!'

He asked Parker if they had any information on the conditions surrounding killing by lethal injection, even though he was fairly sure of the answer. Parker dug up some huge tome and reported that there was a standard practice involving uniformed orderlies, private rooms, screens and medical procedure.

'I thought so,' said Robinson. 'Given that, how did she manage to see what she did?'

He examined Parker's book for several minutes, put it down and said, 'I offer this with the greatest reluctance: *unless it was part of her job.*'

The book noted that prisoners with medical training often carried out or helped with lethal injections. One such named by H. was easily checked: the medical assistant Stossel, a Polish prisoner, who had failed to note that she was pregnant. He was also known, according to the book, to administer lethal injections on behalf of the SS.

'Do we give her the benefit of the doubt?' asked Robinson. 'Considering her pre-war charge of an intended political assassination by poison? She had the training. She knew Injection Heini – whom she had no need to mention – compromising her perhaps more than she let on.'

He looked at Parker, who said, 'She wasn't clear about timescale or what the "school" was.'

'Unless she was referring to before her arrest and her training in September 1942, when she first mentions Heini. Do we draw the wretched conclusion that she was recruited as Heini's assistant and carried on working with him afterwards? Was being bandaged her way of saying that she was the one preparing the syringes, which was why she could report as she did?'

Parker wondered if Morgen had guessed as much and chosen to ignore it. What if Grabner were right and the relationship with the commandant had been mercenary all along? Had H. inflated his infatuation into an affair in exchange for Schlegel's witness protection? On her part, it would have been another survival tactic, giving Morgen what he needed to hear.

Robinson was in no doubt that H. had been starved, but so were others at the same time on charges of theft and smuggling. Had that been the reason for her punishment? There was no real sense in her account of her carrying a child during her solitary confinement, other than to mention it as an afterthought.

'Maybe this is a story of phantoms and unreliable narrators.'

Not unlike like ours, Parker thought to himself. 'But there's an independent witness,' he pointed out. 'The female prisoner doctor reported performing an abortion on H. in the summer of 1944.'

'Throwing into question the whole timeframe. But was this woman any more reliable? People were gunning for the commandant, the place was in turmoil after Morgen started turning it upside-down. Maybe this doctor was part of a plot to nail the commandant, as her report let Morgen reopen his case.'

The more Robinson unpicked what he thought of as H.'s patient stitching, the more he saw a strange dance of death, but a dance nevertheless.

What had the commandant seen as he gazed longingly through the doorway at her quietly sewing; a Vermeer, perhaps? Thin, dark, watchful? Robinson failed to square the modest seamstress, who ran away on being kissed, with the hip-rolling burlesque of Diamond Nora; voluptuous, blonde, zaftig. He didn't doubt the man's infatuation. Did she represent a fatal temptation of female submission and louche independence: too much woman, not enough little woman? And if an affair *had* happened, in a world of splitting others to preserve the self, perhaps the dangerous attraction to the tempted husband was the woman's embodiment of both. The contradiction had to be punished – and only when her spirit was caged, and he had painted himself into a corner, could he have his way with her. A pretty shabby piece of stage management. A garden gate. A trick cell door that opened from the inside. Scraping boots. A Judas peephole. A notebook and flashlight. Furtive whispers. A lost glove strap. Desperate acts in the dark. False promises. Fire and clamour offstage. The hopelessness of a man starting to realise that actions have consequences. Repercussion hangs heavy.

It turned the taking of H. into the desperate act of a man who knew that without Auschwitz he was nothing. Identifying the boundaries of the camp with those of his own ego transformed her nocturnal cell into the black hole at the centre of everything.

Borderlines

W hat August Schlegel didn't tell Morgen was that in the final months of the war, his cover for Bormann's clandestine work involved travelling, usually not far from the Swiss border, attending summary court sessions condemning shirkers and malingerers to be hanged.

Courts consisted of a resident judge, a local political leader and a visiting officer to check procedure. 'That's you,' said Bormann. 'Anyone not prepared to fight for his country, who stabs it in the back in its gravest hour, must fall to the executioner.'

For a moment, Schlegel thought Bormann meant him.

He was given a car and a rota. It amounted to a lot of driving, flying visits and cheap lodgings where he drank himself into a stupor.

He sat hungover in a succession of courtrooms that stank of cowardice and defeat. A succession of men (they were nearly all men) staggered in, holding up their trousers because belts and braces had been removed, and looking stunned as though they had already seen themselves beyond death.

There were three verdicts: guilty, exoneration or transfer to a regular court. 'Two and three you can discount,' Bormann said. Once, in the case of a woman, Schlegel argued for mercy and was outvoted. He avoided looking at the woman, young and pretty, as she was taken away.

Hearings lasted between five and ten minutes. Defence was pointless because the verdict was a foregone conclusion. The judges were weaselly jobsworths, the third official usually of retirement age or younger and missing a limb.

As many as fifteen to twenty cases were heard in less than a couple of hours, including a morning break, during which the three of them stood around, not voicing any opinion. Even the weather was not a safe topic. When one judge declared it a bit unsettled, Schlegel watched him backtrack, realising what he had said. They laughed, nervously, and went back to dish out arbitrary terror to a country in its death throes.

Just as Schlegel participated in wholesale hangings *pour encourager les autres*, he half-expected to find himself strung up at any moment for his own treasonable activities whenever he slipped into Switzerland at weekends.

The Yankee spy Allen Dulles was a bluff and genial show-off with an academic manner, fond of the inclusive, 'You will, of course, remember ... ' whether one did or not. He had a twinkle in his eye that went dead in unguarded moments. He was a pipe smoker, fiddling, tamping, probing, whose one joke was, 'I don't know what that fellow Magritte was on about. I can assure you, this *is* a pipe. Come and have a drink.'

Over Scotch and an open fire, Dulles casually boasted of having a mistress, and said he was using to pump 'her quack, a man by the name of Jung' for his assessment of Hitler.

'As a political realist, I am nevertheless intrigued by the man's mystical reading,' Dulles said. 'Jung considers Hitler to be a medicine man. By which I mean he rules by magic rather than conventional political leadership.' Schlegel noted how Dulles had appropriated Jung's argument.

'A complicated arrangement of masks makes him more like a robot,' he went on. 'Or a mask of a robot, or the double of a person, given to hiding in order not to disturb the mechanism.'

Dulles chucked another log on the fire and asked, 'What do you make of that?'

He was clearly not interested in any answer, and Schlegel wondered what Jung would make of Dulles and what the mistress saw in the man, who struck him as dankly puritanical despite the show of bonhomie.

Schlegel was what Americans called the bagman, passing on documentation that Bormann regarded as too sensitive for telecommunication. They were getting the money out, mostly to Switzerland, but also to the Vatican Bank in Rome, where, according to Dulles, a young chap named Angleton was doing a first-class job.

Dulles regarded intelligence work as a clubbable business to be conducted in first-class hotels, in Basel where he lived and in Zurich where he hobnobbed with German industrialists and bankers, conversing in German that wasn't as good as he thought.

Dulles' preferred Zurich hotel was the Baur. Even though Bormann was moving millions, Schlegel's budget was measly, and he was reduced to staying in pensions. By day, citizens went about the almost unrecognisable pursuit of ordinary business, and of an evening, cafés and bars were full. Bormann grumbled at the size of Schlegel's drinks bill despite him being expected to entertain at the highest level.

'Get the fucking Americans to pay,' was Bormann's response.

Dulles still had vast sums of American clients' money tied up in the German market from before the war and he told Schlegel, 'You understand, it's in my interest to see nothing happens to that. Do you play tennis?'

Schlegel did, a bit. Dulles insisted they have a game.

'I am sure the hotel can find you a set of whites.'

Dulles played in long flannels and, although middle-aged and not fit, his competitiveness, positioning and shot placement gave him the edge. Dulles hardly broke sweat, wafting at the ball with careless ease, appearing unbothered about winning when he was desperate to. As he tired, he asked Schlegel if he could serve underarm. When one of Schlegel's shots beat him, Dulles shouted, 'Out!' Schlegel protested. A puff of chalk said it was on the line. When Dulles approached the net to confirm that the ball was out – implying a lack of respect for his word – Schlegel realised it wasn't about tennis. Dulles was telling him to play by his rules.

Schlegel was introduced to Jim Angleton, the young Intelligence officer from Rome. He had a gaunt face like an El Greco, a poetic, melancholy air and impeccable manners, chain-smoked and was so softly spoken that Schlegel had to strain to hear. Most of the time, it sounded as though Angleton was conducting a monologue with himself. He liked to be addressed by his military rank, which was not necessary on that occasion, he told Schlegel, as he was wearing mufti, an exceptionally well-cut suit with waistcoat, which he boasted was from London's Savile Row.

Dulles had told Schlegel, 'Jim's the exception that proves the rule when it comes to never trusting a man who dresses too well. Quite the Jim Dandy, mentally and sartorially.'

Dulles had also told him Angleton was half-Mexican. He

said 'beaner', and Schlegel had to ask. Angleton was on a flying visit, Dulles added, vaguely.

They sat in a private room off the bar in the Baur with an electric buzzer to summon a waiter. Both Americans drank one Scotch after another with no visible sign of inebriation, as they aired their concerns about what might happen once the war was won.

Angleton was worried about Italy.

'The docks are likely to end up under Commie control. I know cardinals in Rome who fear they might have to abandon the Vatican and go into exile. They dread a repeat of the Avignon Papacy.' He sipped his drink and threw in the dates. '1309 to 1376. Isn't that right?' he asked, turning to Dulles.

'You're the scholar,' Dulles said genially. 'Not that Avignon is safe from the godless hordes. Territories now held by Germany will go red – Poland and the whole of the east, the Balkans down to and including Greece. Italy, France possibly and even Germany itself.'

Angleton had a half-smile, almost a smirk, as though he regarded Schlegel as a specimen for his amusement. Never had Schlegel met two men so self-satisfied. They projected openness but gave nothing away, leaving him feeling like a novice with two skilled poker players. Angleton made a point of acting the protégé, being witty for the senior man's sake. Both made a point of treating Schlegel as an equal when it was clear that neither thought he was. He supposed it was some sort of trick. The Americans claimed to be classless when they weren't. These two were walking advertisements for privilege and entitlement. Angleton claimed the friendship of Ezra Pound, 'The poet, you know.'

Because he had been raised in Italy, Angleton reckoned he

had more of an understanding of Europe than most Yanks, and he had gone to an English public school.

'Quite a minor one,' he said disparagingly. 'They taught Latin declensions and how to address an envelope correctly, but not much else.'

Schlegel wondered why he was there, other than to applaud the two men's performance, before he realised that it was a sales pitch. First, there was talk of Germany doing a deal with 'us Yanks'. Dulles' eyes took on the gleam of a fanatic.

'That chap Himmler is supposed to be reasonable.'

Schlegel caught a look between the two men that he couldn't decipher.

'There's something else,' Dulles said. 'The thing is, we're a bit strapped for cash.' He looked around genially. 'So we thought we would rob a train.'

The two men greeted the remark with a great deal of mirth, then Angleton said, 'With your help.'

If Mr Smith was surprised on his visit by the mess that confronted him in the house, he showed no sign of it. Robinson appeared accommodating and enquired with politeness about the reason for Mr Smith's dedication to his subject.

'I saw a shift to the right spreading all over the globe and how people worldwide were beginning to ignore it all again,' he said.

'Do you have Mr Godard's letter approving your film?' Robinson asked.

'I thought I had it here in London, but it must be in Brussels after all.'

'And the watercolours?'

'I have photographs.' He produced an envelope and passed it across. 'They are signed and dated.'

'How much?'

'Ten thousand for the lot.'

Robinson counted. 'So a thousand each. I can't see it.'

'Hitler's sell for four times that.'

'You can also pick them up for a couple of hundred.'

'As an alternative, I was thinking of a straight swap for the commandant's home movies.'

'Can you show us some of the film you're making?' asked Robinson. 'So we can see.'

'Yes, of course. I'll bring a DVD next time.' Mr Smith looked around. 'I see you have plenty of equipment on which to show it. My plan is to burn the commandant's movies after watching them. As an act of exorcism and in repentance for all the books they burned. It will feature in the film. Perhaps we will do it in the garden where they were filmed. The villa still stands – now owned by a Polish couple. Many people don't know about the secret escape tunnel built by my grandfather. A prisoner who worked there told me my grandfather would make the family practise using the tunnel at least once a week. The current management don't like to publicise this because they're worried that neo-Nazis will turn the place into a shrine. Prisoners still alive remember my aunts and uncles when they were children.' Mr Smith looked tearful for a moment. 'I do not hide how proud I am to share with these survivors. Somehow I manage to connect with them. I wear a Star of David necklace I was given by one of them.'

He undid a shirt button and showed it, holding it in front of his tie. He appeared quite overwhelmed. Robinson stared at the ceiling. Parker didn't know what to think.

At last, Mr Smith said, 'There is still so much hostility. In Israel, rumours circulate that I am selling items, but it is only so I can finance the film, which is dedicated to them. You will hear stories of me being a confidence trickster who uses my family notoriety to exploit and steal from elderly survivors. The last time I was in Tel Aviv, Customs held me for three hours for questioning.'

Robinson asked, 'Do they know whose grandson you are?'

'I make no secret of it without advertising the fact. I am not asking for anyone's pity. I am telling you this so you know, and I swear on all those who died that I have never cheated anyone.'

'A Russian I know says otherwise,' said Robinson.

'Just what I am saying. I know who you mean. I was exploited by him. The items were genuine. He said otherwise, which was his excuse not to make the balance of payment. I heard he sold them for a handsome profit.'

'What is it that you really have to sell?' asked Robinson. 'Besides some indifferent watercolours. I might be interested, but not at the price.'

Mr Smith produced another envelope and passed over more photographs.

Robinson looked at them. 'A ring and a pair of leather gloves, both with what I presume are the commandant's initials. So?'

'If you have those and the Morgen document Mr Parker showed me, as well as locating Morgen's unexpurgated text, you would have quite a package.'

'I don't see how,' said Robinson.

'Hodys has a cult following but there is no ephemera, giving her even more rarity value.'

Robinson remained unconvinced. Mr Smith pointed to the photographs.

'The commandant gave her the gloves and the ring.'

'Says who?'

'My mother told me the story, passed on by her mother,

about how when she was pregnant with my mother the commandant had a longstanding affair with a female prisoner who became pregnant at the same time.'

'You said before that there was no affair,' said Parker.

'It was *said* there was no affair, which is not the same.'

'We are talking about the same woman?' Robinson asked impatiently.

'Of course. My grandmother told my mother about it after her father was dead, as a way of distancing her from his memory. When my grandmother found out about the affair, she called Himmler and told him to deal with it. The commandant was in the hospital at the time. H. was placed in solitary confinement prior to being taken to the gas chambers, but then my grandfather returned and ordered her to be brought back. She said Dr Clauberg, a Nazi doctor who experimented on Jewish women, carried out the abortion.'

Parker said, 'Morgen has it being done by a Polish woman prisoner doctor.'

'Unless there were two abortions,' Robinson added.

'Yes and no,' said Mr Smith. 'Two pregnancies, one abortion. I spent hours looking through archival information, which is how I found that she was impregnated *twice* by him. The second time, she was sent to Ravensbrück camp but somehow managed to escape to Vienna.'

Parker said, 'No, she went to Munich.'

Mr Smith grew strident. 'First there, where she was questioned by Morgen, who then had her transferred to Ravensbrück.'

'Are you saying she was pregnant when she left the camp?' Parker asked. 'Morgen dates an abortion in the summer of 1944, just before she left.'

'Why should we believe him more than anyone else? I

know because I located a man who was H.'s neighbour in Vienna. He confirmed that she did indeed arrive pregnant. After she gave birth, she disappeared overnight, so it's possible that another of my grandfather's children is out there somewhere. H. died in 1964. The point is, the gloves and the ring were given to her by the commandant.'

Robinson said, 'A bit of a stretch. How do you know?'

Mr Smith nodded in earnest agreement. 'I would say the same but I succeeded in finding Hodys' estate. It was located in a storeroom of the executor of her will in Vienna.'

Parker no longer knew what to believe. He certainly had not expected any sequel. He couldn't decide whether Mr Smith was driven to chase the truth, however improbable, or actually believed whatever he was saying because it inflated his image of himself.

Mr Smith continued, still nodding. 'Inside a box, we found these gloves, uniforms and the initialled ring, made of gold taken from the teeth of Jewish prisoners. There are 153 grams of gold in the ring. If you consider that the average person had between one and five grams worth of gold fillings in their mouth, a lot of Jews died to make that ring.'

Robinson sighed. 'Well, you are a long way ahead on this. Let's say, given your dedication, you locate the so-called unexpurgated version, then we'll talk again.'

Mr Smith looked crushed but put on a brave face, saying, 'Yes, I should have thought of that. I have one or two leads.'

After he had gone, Robinson asked Parker, 'What did you make of that?'

'Apart from everyone else saying an abortion was performed before she left?'

'Did you believe any of it?'

221

'Why lie?'

'He does inherited guilt quite well, I will give him that. Maybe he is who he says he is, or he's just another grifter.' Robinson gave a bellow of laughter and said, 'Maybe both. I know a conman when I see one. Look at Mr Smith's books, and I expect you will find a large mountain of personal debt. I would say he's trying to tap us for money to finish a film that doesn't exist. We've all done that.'

'I haven't,' protested Parker.

'You will. Did you check whether we do, in fact, have any member of the European Parliament named Smith?'

Parker looked and found that there were two. One was a woman. Entries for British members had photographs, and Parker found himself looking at their Mr Smith, so he was at least telling the truth about something.

Still in a state of turmoil after Berlin, Parker took to visiting the church in Quex Road, off the bottom of the High Road, sitting in a pew watching the few mostly elderly women coming in to light votive candles and pray. What he was waiting for he couldn't say, other than probably spoiling for a fight.

He turned up once when the priest arrived to hear confession. The man was elderly, kindly-looking and probably clueless, so Parker joined the short queue. When his turn came, he asked how to find human love as a manifestation of God's love because sex screwed it up and the relationship between sex and money was a consequence of inhibited sexuality and a crippled capacity for love.

The only advice he was given was to pray harder for enlightenment.

Parker asked how he should conduct himself when human

beings were made to need each other but still hadn't learned how to live together.

He suspected the priest wasn't as naive as he looked and perhaps even enjoyed their game to the point of handing out the heftiest penances, especially after Parker confessed to being assailed by homicidal thoughts. The priest asked the circumstances, and Parker said a man of the cloth had once abused his position in an unforgivable way. He enjoyed putting the priest on the spot, as it was quite clear to what he was referring. Vengeance was the Lord's was the best the man could come up with.

'If not murder,' Parker went on, 'then is the desire to inflict physical pain a mortal sin?'

'Do you wish to inflict pain?'

'What of the man who thrashed me and more in the name of authority, does that count as a sin?'

The priest had no answer.

The closest Parker came to an actual confession was when he said, 'I fear my erratic behaviour is distracting me from what I should be dedicating myself to.'

'Which is what?' asked the priest.

'Serving the beast.' He had meant to say, 'Serving the past.' Parker asked, 'Is there much else the Church has kept silent about?'

The priest rallied and said, 'It would be naive to presume that the Holy See can be transparent when its existence is founded on the essential Mysteries.'

He advised him to contemplate humility, then asked, 'What is it that you seek?'

'What your Church preaches against: revenge, humiliation. I don't believe the Lord will do that on my behalf.'

The priest sighed. 'I cannot absolve you unless you make a full act of contrition.'

Parker rejected that, saying, 'We all know sin is the condition, not the exception, so what's the point?'

Robinson fell into a fretful mood and announced, 'I waste my time watching stupid programmes about family trees. I never gave a fuck about family, but since breaking my wrists I find I'm at least curious. The missing father, his sister, the mother with a shot memory, and an identical twin brother who died at birth, me Elvis to his Jesse.'

Parker didn't know about the twin. It made sense in that part of Robinson always seemed incomplete.

Of his father, Robinson said, 'He seems to be calling himself Slattery now. Marble floors, large terraces, azure skies, an elderly but elegant couple.'

'What are you talking about?'

'An old television foreign property programme I happened to watch.'

He dug the tape out and showed Parker an episode featuring a couple inspecting several apartments in Split, Croatia, with a sea view stipulated.

'Mr and Mrs Slattery, so-called,' Robinson said.

The man kept in the background. He wore slacks and a floral shirt. He had kept his figure and his hair and looked younger than Parker had pictured and nothing like the actor Trevor Howard.

Robinson said, 'He gives his job as construction, retired. Lets her do the talking. Looks quite at ease, but going along and indulging her, wouldn't you say?'

'On what grounds is this your old man?' Parker asked.

Robinson shrugged and said, 'Frau Trauner says you were taken ill.'

When Parker didn't say anything, Robinson shrugged again.

'Probably something you ate.'

'What else did she say?'

'That your trip to the Adlon was a waste of time. As for Sasha, she's meddling. She and her brother hate each other. She's a lesbian, of course, probably spies for Israeli Intelligence.' Robinson pointed at the screen and asked, 'Is that my old man, what do you think?'

'I have no idea what he looks like.'

'Always had a head of hair. Runs in the family.' Robinson pointed to the woman and said, 'Funny thing, the last time I visited my mother while you were away – Vod took me, since you didn't ask – usually she just sits drooling and can't remember anything from two minutes before and watches racing on telly, but this time she suddenly announced that the old man had had an affair in Kenya with a woman working on a Hollywood film shot there in the 1950s. Pitch her back and the past is more or less intact, however much the present is lost as it happens.'

'Kenya? You said he was in the Met.'

'Special Branch, recruited out of the Met. Kenya was a colony in those days. HMG and all that, liaising with Military Intelligence, fighting the fuzzy wuzzies. Beatrice was the woman's name, according to my mother. A Belfast girl. The old man was in and out of Belfast in the 1970s, so perhaps they were still an item. Can't be many Hollywood films made in Kenya.'

The film Robinson was talking about was *Something of Value* (1957), with Rock Hudson and Sidney Poitier – racial tension, colonial conflict – an Anglo-American co-production. The only credits Parker found didn't list lesser personnel. But Beatrice was easy enough to trace with a telephone call to the film technicians' union.

225

He lied to a friendly young woman, saying he was trying to find a long-lost friend of a recently departed relative to invite her to the funeral, but he only had her first name. Again, he was impressed by his plausibility on the telephone. She offered to find out and asked him to call back at the end of the afternoon, when she told him there was only one Beatrice. She'd done continuity work, and the Hudson film was among her credits. Last name Slattery.

'Ah,' said Parker, 'that sounds right.'

'She must be long-retired, and I have no idea if the address and telephone number are the same.'

The address sounded vaguely familiar; Parker couldn't think why.

The number was discontinued. The address led him to the same short street in which his grandmother had lived, to a house on the other side whose shutters were closed. No one answered when he rang the bell. His grandmother's house still looked the same, and he wondered who lived there now.

He was struck by the improbability of her ending up opposite the mistress of a man with whom she'd had an affair.

Robinson said, 'It's how the fates conspire, and we are but their playthings. It must explain why I hired you. It certainly wasn't for efficiency or qualifications.'

When Robinson next wondered aloud about looking for his father, Parker thought it was probably to do with money, because it came after he announced, 'I need to find a mill in a hurry.'

He sent Parker off to the newsagent to buy lottery tickets and scratch cards. Robinson's finances were a mystery to Parker. He said he thought Robinson was rich.

'To a point, dear heart. Short-term cashflow problem.'

'They want to *what*?' asked an incredulous Bormann.

'Rob a train,' said Schlegel.

'This isn't the Wild West.'

'That's exactly what they think it is.'

Bormann asked why they should want to.

'For the sake of the future, they say.'

Dulles had pointed out that he and Angleton wore spectacles because they were short-sighted. 'But not when it comes to the political map. We can't just go home again once this is over. We'll need an equivalent to the FBI for foreign affairs, recruiting at a higher intellectual level than their flatfoots.'

Dulles believed that such an agency would eventually be created and he would run it.

'But for now we'll have nothing, because our Intelligence Services will be closed down. We need a budget for operations until Washington comes to its senses.'

Bormann turned out to be more equable than Schlegel was expecting.

'Why not? Give them a train from Hungary, then it's not our money. But are they up to the job?'

'They say they have tough guys who can help out.'

Schlegel had to put up with Angleton lecturing him about the history of the American train robbery, with gangs graduating from bank raids, using their civil war guerrilla skills to make off with the loot. Angleton went on about how he was a fan of Westerns.

He said, 'We'll have to lose some of the guards by uncoupling the rear vans in a siding before derailing the train in a remote spot, with the likelihood of gunplay involving the remaining guards.'

He was childish in his enthusiasm.

What Angleton referred to as his 'heist' was nothing of the sort. The train, after passing from Hungary into Austria, would stop at an appointed spot beyond the border with trucks waiting to transfer two wagonloads of bullion.

Which was exactly what happened – unlike another gold train, which took three months to travel barely a hundred miles, its journey hampered by the battles raging around it and ten unsuccessful robbery attempts (nine of them by rogue elements of the SS), which Hungarian soldiers detailed to protect the train's cargo successfully fought off.

As a native speaker, Schlegel was required to sign off the delivery; typical German thoroughness. The contents of the freight cars were carefully recorded, numbered and classified. Schlegel duly received a fat copy like a huge auction catalogue, itemising five tons of gold, vast amounts of diamonds and pearls, 1,250 paintings, 5,000 Persian rugs, over 850 cases of silverware, seventeen bundles of walking sticks with silver handles, fine porcelain, rare stamps, coin collections, furs, watches, alarm clocks, cameras, topcoats, typewriters and silk underwear.

The Americans would help themselves to the gold. Dulles dismissed the rest, saying it wasn't a rummage sale and he didn't need alarm clocks, at which Angleton hooted.

Schlegel drove himself to the meeting point, thirty minutes from the pick-up. Swathes of countryside remained untouched by the war, whose only single reminder was the thrum of a huge American bomber fleet high overhead.

Schlegel did his best not to think about anything these days and was rarely surprised, but he had been when he recently ran into Hermann Fegelein in the lobby of Zurich's Baur Hotel. Fegelein was in mufti (a cravat and what looked like an English sports jacket). He made out that he was there for social reasons and introduced Schlegel to a very attractive Irish woman, Molly Fitzgerald.

Dulles walked past and didn't react when Fegelein inclined his head. Schlegel realised he must also be secretly meeting with Dulles, who appeared to be holding open shop. He wondered if there was anyone the man wasn't talking to.

'And you're here because?' Fegelein enquired.

'Spot of leave,' Schlegel said, trying to sound casual. 'Running a few errands for my stepfather.'

'Banker fellow, owns racehorses.'

'That's the one.'

Schlegel wondered about the Irish woman. Later, he saw her sitting by herself and went over, curious. He asked in English how she knew Fegelein. She said they'd run across each other at the hotel some time before.

'Amusing and charming,' she said, not as though she believed it. She congratulated Schlegel on his English.

'No love lost between you two,' she observed.

'Professional rivalry.'

The woman was very beautiful, he thought to himself, then said, 'I hear this place is overrun with American spies.'

She laughed. 'They're not backward about coming forward.'

Schlegel ardently wished to sit down and warn her what a shit Fegelein was, but he sensed she already knew that.

'Are you a spy, too?' he asked, flirting.

She laughed again. 'In the house of love, maybe,' she replied, holding his eye.

Schlegel couldn't decide if she was making a pass. The moment was broken by Fegelein hurrying over, saying, 'We're late.'

Molly smiled as she left. Fegelein ignored him.

Schlegel reported this to Bormann, making no mention of the Irish woman, saying he believed Fegelein was meeting with Dulles.

Bormann said, 'Dulles hobnobbing with Fegelein is not on our agenda.'

Bormann had a way of looking at people as though questioning their very existence while seeming like a man who couldn't quite believe his luck. It was done in a pleasant, almost bovine way, as though to say that any human endeavour was futile.

Angleton, dressed in an SS officer's uniform, gave Schlegel a flippant half-salute with a raised palm. Darkness had fallen, and they were gathered in a big walled courtyard in an abandoned schloss. Several trucks were parked and a couple of dozen men milled around, also wearing SS uniforms. Fires had been lit against the cold. The men talked loudly in English and were eating American rations. None appeared remotely German. They looked American, specifically Italian-American.

Schlegel didn't know that they were Mafia or that their services had already been used to protect New York's docks from sabotage and to assist as liaison officers after the 1943 invasion of Sicily. That night marked the start of a fruitful collaboration with Angleton, an axis that would still be in place in 1963 for the shooting of John Fitzgerald Kennedy.

To Angleton, it made perfect sense that espionage and the underworld, each with their strict codes of honour, should co-exist as poetic interpretations of a flawed world. It is not known if the Jewish mobster Meyer Lansky, the Michelangelo of money laundering, was privy to that night's events, but he and Angleton became familiar, and Lansky certainly profited from the haul. Follow the money: Angleton would know about the brown-bag cash (two million) delivered by Lansky to President Harry Truman, his price for supporting the founding of the state of Israel. Angleton would know about the millions distributed via the Vatican in black (rather than brown) bags to stop the Communists winning the 1948 election. There would be fun and games using slush funds from the money train to blackmail that old hypocrite and declared homo-hater J. Edgar Hoover with dirty snap-shots of him sucking his boyfriend's dick, in exchange for Hoover dropping FBI opposition to founding a new Central Intelligence Agency. The fun of working with Lansky's tech-nical boys who'd grabbed the Hoover snaps. The fun of being 'No-knock Angleton', walking into Dulles' office to show him Hoover with a mouthful of his boyfriend and explaining proudly, 'It's called a fish-eye lens.' Lansky was genial, tell-ing Angleton, 'Deep down, Jim, I think you are just another Mexican bandit.'

They found the train waiting; a long, darkened silhouette, huffing steam. Once Schlegel had signed off the paperwork, the trucks would back up so the goods could be loaded di-rectly as each crate was checked off. No talking. If any of the men was addressed, Schlegel would take care of it.

He dealt with a corpulent young officer whom he found sitting waiting in the open doorway of the appointed wagon. He was smoking a cigarette, his meaty legs dangling over the edge.

Everyone else seemed to have made themselves scarce.

Angleton paraded around, occasionally coming to peer as Schlegel checked off each crate. It was cold enough for their

231

breath to show. Angleton nearly blew the operation when he produced a packet of Lucky Strikes and offered one to the officer. Schlegel intervened to say, 'American cigarettes,' as if to suggest what was so unusual about that, given the amount of loot on the train. The young officer, smoking his cigarette, seemed to grow wary, and Schlegel feared a trap, saw the doors of the guards' vans opening and machine guns mowing them down. But nothing happened and he left without waiting for the rest, his part of the job done.

Parker's next prompt was an old song on the radio, 'Going Back', a wistful, soppy ballad despite the woman singing believing it. Because of that, he telephoned his old school and asked if he could be sent a copy of the current journal.

It was as he remembered: society reports, a couple of pages of photographs of identikit sports teams, a photograph of an art exhibition and so on. A list of old boys' achievements, family births, engagements, marriages and deaths. His former confessor, Father Damien, was now headmaster of the junior school. There were various missions abroad, some in Africa and one in the United States, but, as on the school website, Parker found no mention of Father Roper. So where was he?

He wore his black suit. He inserted his cane into his big black umbrella so it was hardly visible. He had no idea why, unless it was to thrash anyone in sight until he was overpowered and taken away. He felt like one of those lone assassins who considered himself sane and everyone else dismissed as crazy. He told himself that he felt calm.

It was term time. A security hut now stood at the gates. Parker said he had an appointment with Father Damien.

A call was made. He was told they had no note of any

232

meeting. He insisted. 'I am an old boy. It's about a charity donation.' The security guard couldn't care either way and waved him through.

Bells, uniformed boys rushing down corridors, the din of break time. Parker, pitched back, half-expected to encounter his younger self, wan and wraithlike.

The secretary, a woman he didn't know, sat in the outer office. He asked, 'Would it be possible to have a word with Father Damien?'

'You're the one with no appointment?' the woman asked sharply.

Parker said he'd happened to be passing. He wanted to give his regards to Father Damien and discuss making a large donation. It didn't look like he was going to get anywhere – the woman was clearly used to guarding the man's kennel – when Father Damien walked in on his way to his study. He regarded Parker askance, with a shock of recognition.

Parker watched him go through the show of exasperation of a busy man struggling to remain polite, then, 'I suppose you had better come in. I am afraid I can't give you much time.'

The study was Father Roper's old one, same furniture, same big desk, the visitor's chair next to it, the heavy curtains, parquet floor and a lot of dark brown. The same red light was still outside.

Parker was grudgingly invited to sit.

Father Damien asked, 'How have you been keeping? When did you leave? It must be some time ago.'

Parker said, 'I went into the seminary for a year.'

'Yes, of course you did.'

The conversation petered out until Parker, laying his umbrella on the floor, said, 'I am inquiring about Father Roper.

There's something I want to give him, but there's no record of his current whereabouts.'

'He's in Rome,' said Father Damien.

'Rome?'

'We have a college there. He's attached to the Institute for the Works of Religion, better known as the Vatican Bank.'

'There's no mention in the school journal.'

'I can't think why not. It must be an oversight.'

'I suppose I could write to him there.'

'About what?'

'We both know what happened.'

Father Damien said carefully, 'That was discussed with you, I believe.'

'Yes. You were there. Nothing was done.'

'That's not what I mean. Don't you remember?'

'Only too well.'

'I mean the psychological report. Didn't anyone talk to you about that?'

Parker had no idea what the man was on about.

'Oh, I see,' Father Damien said. He sighed and stood reluctantly.

'Things were very different then. Give me a minute and I will see if we still have it.'

He was gone a lot longer than a minute. Parker looked around the room and began to freak out. He got up, produced the cane and flexed it, whacked the back of the chair a couple of times, gave up, put the cane away and sat down, embarrassed.

Father Damien returned at last, looking flustered and carrying a thin folder.

'Did no one discuss this with you?'

Parker asked, 'Is that my actual report? Why do you still have it?'

'Reports of psychological disturbance are kept for the record. The dead corridors of bureaucracy, I suppose. It would all be online now.' Father Damien flicked through the short report. 'It was based on a questionnaire you did.'

Parker started to sweat. He had no memory of any such occasion. He recalled answering a few questions for the matron about his skin condition, as she was puzzled by its late onset. Perhaps her questioning had been more extensive than he remembered. Was he getting that muddled with the interview with Roper and the rector where notes were taken but he had no idea how long the interview had gone on? Had he suppressed that in a way he had failed to blank the experience with Father Roper?

Parker asked if he could see the report.

Father Damien handed it over and said, 'This was discussed with you at the time.'

'Not that I remember.'

'You may have forgotten. It must have been a troubling period.'

Parker had to read it twice for its implications to sink in.

He was being told he had made everything up: submitted a false claim where his refusal to name was taken for evidence that any actual accusation would be exposed as fantasy.

The report concluded: 'The boy's claim of sexual abuse was almost certainly conjured up as an explanation for the disturbing outbreak of psoriasis, which is a physical condition with no history of being psychosomatic.'

Parker said, 'Breathtaking, really.'

It left him questioning his own judgement. He carried on less certainly. 'First, not true. And second, this report was not shared with me, nor was any counselling offered.'

'I don't know what to say, other than that things are different now.'

'No more beatings, for a start.'

'It was, looking back, a barbaric practice.'

'There is no note of whether my beatings contributed to any psychological disturbance.'

'As I said, we are a very different community now.'

'Yes, I expect you rely on mental cruelty these days.'

He asked if the red light was on outside.

Father Damien looked momentarily puzzled, then said, 'Oh, we don't use that anymore.'

Parker picked up the cane which was lying next to the umbrella. He struck it hard against Father Roper's old desk and again experienced the sensation of flipping out.

He had no idea what he was going to do, other than produce the cane as a threat. He saw Father Damien's lack of meaningful apology. When he looked again, it was Father Roper sitting there, with the same half-smirk. He whipped the cane one way, then the other, across his face, listening to its pleasing hiss as it cut through the air and the thwack as it made contact with flesh and bone, the second time drawing a line of blood. Parker didn't know how many times he thrashed him. He left the priest hiccoughing and half-sobbing, and travelled home in a state of shock, contemplating how the psychological report had unwritten him and whether he had been twisted enough to have made the whole thing up.

Of course someone was making it up; Parker knew that much. We all lead parallel lives to the ones ostensibly led, he knew that too; which were the realer? Fantasies of denial, fever dreams and blind refusal to read the writing on the wall; it was ever thus.

In an effort to think about anything but himself, he came to regard his situation in terms of the riddle of Hodys, where any facts presented were just one reading, not necessarily accurate. What you show or don't show; what is left out.

The Hodys material was an embellishment of a story that was possibly fabricated in the first place, which in the end only compounded the mystery, because no definitive version could be determined; as with Valerie Robinson.

It left Parker wondering whether women were the eternal mystery and God had in fact created Eve before Adam, and if everything thereafter was male vengeance. He also asked himself how much it was within his right to speculate on questionable historical narratives.

Apart from a few lone voices, no one ever talked about life in Auschwitz, only death, which made H.'s contrary account of privilege and fall so strange.

Parker came across an interview in which Jean-Luc Godard talked of an unrealised film in macabre terms of solution: 'How to get a two-metre body into a fifty-centimetre truck? How to dispose of ten tons of arms and legs in a three-ton truck? How to burn a hundred women with only gasoline enough for ten? One would also have to show the typists typing out lists of everything. What would be unbearable would not be the horror aroused by such scenes, but, on the contrary, their perfectly normal and human aspect.'

Parker followed up the mention of Allen Dulles in August Schlegel's testament and disappeared down another rabbit hole, where he ran smack into an obsession of Vod's: the death of President John F. Kennedy.

Vod said he was trying to write about Kennedy's so-called assassin, Lee Harvey Oswald.

'One of life's great drifters, perhaps the ultimate drifter, or the patsy in the frame. Drift and conspiracy are seen as polar opposites, yet around Oswald they coalesce, which is perhaps why the mystery will never be solved.'

Vod and Parker went to the National Film Theatre to see Oliver Stone's *JFK*. Afterwards, as they walked along the Embankment, Vod surprised Parker by reciting, word- and accent-perfect, a speech by Donald Sutherland playing a deep throat, X, about the how and the who being just a guessing game for the public to prevent them from asking why Kennedy was really killed, to whose advantage, and who had the power to cover it up.

Parker was impressed by Vod's recall. Vod shrugged. 'I always was a quick study. The thing about Oswald, I am aware of not offering any redemption, but redemption and closure seem just as much fictions as religion, which is civilisation's greatest act of creative imagination and its greatest hoax.'

It was a mild night and high tide. Moonlit water slapped against the embankment wall as strolling couples wandered past, stabbing Parker in the heart.

'Most of the time,' Vod said, 'I don't know if I am playing myself or someone else. In terms of a fictional character looking at himself, there's Christopher in *The Sopranos*, with the paradox of him bemoaning a lack of direction when the actor is both being directed and delivering lines. Like me, Christopher is trying to write a script. Do you know *The Sopranos*?'

Parker said he preferred movies.

'Your choice, I respect that. Anyway, Christopher goes on,' – Vod adopted a nasal New Jersey twang – 'to say that every character has an arc, they start out somewhere and do something, then something gets done back, and that's called their arc.' Vod paused to light a cigarette. 'I've taken up smoking. Again. I wish I knew what my fucking arc was. Any idea of yours?'

Not a clue, Parker thought to himself. It left him wondering whether his psoriasis was psychosomatic after all, despite what the school report claimed, in which case a therapeutic cure was technically possible, except that Father Roper conditioned his every thought and made any conventional resolution impossible.

He was about to say, 'If I have learned nothing else, it is that institutional abuse is the great fault line of civilisation and is not pointed out nearly enough.'

Instead, he asked, 'What of Allen Dulles? X mentions him in the film. I think my grandfather knew him.'

Vod looked impressed but his curiosity didn't extend to asking, and Parker realised that Vod was lost in a world of his own.

'Doyen of the CIA, secrets taken to the grave. When it came to who whacked Jack – another stupendous fiction – Dulles knew where the bodies were buried, because he had put a lot of them there. Looked at as a parlour game, as X suggests – who, where and with what, before we even get to motive – Dulles' name recurs over and over. The CIA already had form with regime change abroad and the assassination of foreign heads of state, so why not bring it on home? Did the murderous synchronicity of Dulles being a virtual rhyme for Dallas ever cross the man's mind as he laughed up his sleeve? Who do *you* think killed Kennedy?'

Parker had no idea, beyond thinking that Dulles made sense. These things usually turned out to be close to home. It was brother Cain, rather than a second cousin, who had killed Abel.

Vod said, 'I like that. Maybe I will use it. The most interesting theory I came across was that it was the Vatican.'

'But Kennedy was one of theirs. A Catholic.'

'I know, but I came across an obscure text purporting to be a transcript of tapes made by Dulles' sidekick and number two, James Jesus Angleton.'

Parker was unaware of the connection between Angleton and August Schlegel.

'A paranoid dandy,' said Vod, 'so I can identify. A man who knew all the secrets. He was supposed to have recorded solo tapes at the end of his life spilling the beans while on a fishing trip in Lapland. Only a transcript available. Fake? Who knows, but Robinson has been looking for the actual tapes for years.'

They were halfway across Hungerford Bridge.

Vod said, 'I shall recite. As I told you, I am a quick study and I know the text by heart.'

He stopped and composed himself, coughed and adopted a soft, persuasive mid-Western accent, declaring, 'Let's run with the idea that the Vatican cardinals had most to gain from seeing JFK whacked. An Otto Preminger picture, big and bombastic and not for the faint-hearted, but why should I, a man so dedicated to secrecy, suddenly 'fess up? A man whose son grew up believing his father worked for the post office, which I did in a way, because we ran an illegal mail-opening service! Or maybe I just want to dump a barrel load on the fuckers that fired me. As for my Rosebud moment, I am not talking about a sled, so let us venture into the wilderness of mirrors. How deep do the secrets go? The American juice is paranoia, oil, hysteria and the unrequited. The McCarthy witch-hunts became inseparable to my mind from the tenor of Presley's voice. Heartache and hysteria, the corollary

240

of cool. Mary Pinchot Meyer wound up shot dead on a Washington tow path. Big scandal to hush. My own Presley preference was for 'I Forgot to Remember to Forget'. Much to talk about, because Mary was doing it with Jack-rabbit Jack. Mr Hoover, head of the Bureau, reported that Mr Kennedy was no fan of foreplay. On and off in jig time. The knockabout romantic antics of JFUCK came to resemble bad farce, especially in the case of Mary, who was not only turning the President on to sex. They took LSD together, for Chrissakes! Hello! Security! Some say Mary's big mistake was turning the Prez on to peace; Yoko Ono to JFK's John Lennon *avant la lettre*. Detente. Pally with the Reds. Arms treaties. Cold War thaw. Back channels, you name 'em. Get out of Vietnam. Giving it all away. Anathema to any Cold Warrior worth his spuds. Jack had already forced Allen Dulles to fall on his sword after the Bay of Pigs and promised to smash the CIA into a thousand pieces. One of Jack's sexual peccadillos was a Red in the bed, whom we had down as an East German spy. Hello! Security! And those gunslinger Israelis wanted to expose Jack's scandalous sex life via the French gutter press because they were pissed off, as the Brits say, that he was not about to let them have nuclear capability and was sending in the weapons inspectors. Listen carefully, it gets complicated.'

Vod had drawn a small crowd, curious about what was going on. Vod waved his hand in appreciation and continued.

'Some say I was the one giving the Israelis the scientific information they needed to make said bomb. Some say I was in Israeli pockets since, oooh, about 1945. While it is a given of counterintelligence that it should have nothing to do with active operations, questions were asked as to why I, as its head, was running not only the Israeli desk but also the Vatican. To which I can only reply, Heh! Heh! Que sera, sera.

Some say the Israelis had me blackmailed from the beginning because they knew about the Nazis we'd made disappear after the war using Vatican ratlines. As for the dark arts of Machiavelli, none proved more adept than those slinky cardinals. Okay. The Vat had no choice if the Izzies were about to expose the world's number two Roman Catholic after the Pope as an extramarital humper of Olympic standards, so they turned him into a martyr. Mafia gunmen, easy. Hello, our old friend the grassy knoll. Am I telling it right here, or is this another of those feint right, go left dodges? To tell the truth, I no longer remember.'

By the time Vod was done, the small audience had moved on, apart from one elderly woman who pressed 50p into his hand. Vod stared at the coin before pocketing it, saying, 'It's hard sometimes for the sake of entertainment not to indulge in false suspense and cut to the chase.'

It was the weekend after the bullion robbery, and August Schlegel's initial assessment of Andrey Turkul was cautious. He had returned to Zurich to be told that Allen Dulles was indisposed. He didn't know if this was an excuse not to see him now that Dulles had his loot.

Andrey Turkul was a superior Russian of early middle-age, mysterious and elegant, with lustrous russet hair worn swept back. Schlegel was staying at his usual pension. As Turkul was the only other guest, they took breakfast together at his suggestion. He spoke several languages and said he felt like a rest from German, so they settled on English. He introduced himself as 'a travelling salesman', said with irony. He was talkative and Schlegel wasn't expected to contribute, though it dawned on him that the man wasn't staying there by chance.

Turkul was one of those exiled Russian aristocrats who floated on the international scene. By his account, he had seen more action than most, having been a White Army general who had led his troops in battle against the Reds. Forced to flee, he claimed to have lived variously in Berlin, Paris and Rome, always caught up in the stew of émigré post-revolutionary Russian politics.

'Not altogether willingly,' he said. 'It can be a deadly business with so many spies, traitors and double dealers. One is a target simply for what one is and must be careful. Here, for instance, is a hotbed of cosmopolitan intrigue.'

Until then, Schlegel had taken the man for international flotsam and a bit too full of himself. His manners and feminine air made his stories about mortal combat hard to believe, and Schlegel wondered if he was homosexual, though he failed to ask himself why a homosexual should not be brave.

Turkul pushed his empty boiled egg aside and smoothed the tablecloth as though preparing his next move.

'I take it you are aware of the American Dulles.'

Eye contact, which Schlegel failed to hold as he started to think that he might be being played.

'What of it?' He tried to sound unconcerned.

Turkul looked around. 'Not that walls have ears, but the conversation I have in mind is more suited to a stroll.'

They wandered by the picture-postcard lake on a cloudless morning. At first, Turkul offered little other than idle gossip. Like most such men familiar with the back corridors of international relations, he could drop names with aplomb.

Turkul at last said, 'You might be able to pass on a message to Mr Dulles.'

Schlegel was disconcerted by how much Turkul knew,

which left him questioning whether the Bormann-Dulles channel was that secure.

He countered by saying, 'He's ill, or maybe he just doesn't want to see me.'

Turkul frowned. 'That makes two of us. I'm told Mr Dulles regards me as an amateur opportunist. On the other hand, everyone will soon be changing partners, and I would like to mark his card.'

Why me? Schlegel asked himself.

The other man went on. 'There's an Irish woman, a free floater, reputed to be one of Dulles' lovers. Dulles brags in private about how he is talking to everyone. The point of espionage is: when does one become indiscreet? After all, it's a mixture of discretion and indiscretion, wouldn't you say?'

Schlegel waited for Turkul to continue.

'I was told I should contact you.'

That was when Schlegel came to realise that, in contrast to all the bloody fighting going on, he was caught up in what more resembled a minuet, defined by gestures, hints and controlled moves, that could still end badly in a dark alley. He wondered what Molly Fitzpatrick's role was, apart from horizontal.

'What do you have in mind?' he asked.

'To sell intelligence to whomever is anti-Soviet. I have a network of agents behind enemy lines providing first-class information to your man Gehlen and his very capable Eastern Army Intelligence Service.' Turkul stopped to address Schlegel directly. 'Thanks to your technology, we have burst transmitters to convey information. Mr Dulles appears to have an old-fashioned preference for couriers. I am based in Rome, where we have excellent relations with the Vatican, with whom we share a hatred of the godless Communists.

It is a connection Mr Dulles would like to cultivate, but alas, what can I do if he won't see me?'

They walked on. Turkul continued. 'It would be to Mr Dulles' advantage if he widened his options. It's not just about money.'

Schlegel wondered if Turkul had heard about the gold train.

'Of course, talking of money,' Turkul went on, 'Bormann is in the business of capital flight and Dulles is part of it.'

Schlegel, again alarmed by how much Turkul knew, said nothing.

'And Herr Himmler is courting Dulles on the separate matter of conditional surrender. But there is a split in the two initiatives, and that is?'

'I have no idea.'

'Timing. Herr Himmler is looking for a quick solution, the better to further his leadership ambitions. Herr Bormann needs longer to get the money out, which means the war must be fought to its bitter end.'

Schlegel supposed that made sense, though Bormann hadn't mentioned it.

Turkul said, 'Let me entertain you with another story, that a last stand will be made in the mountains of Bavaria. All baloney. Bormann is behind that to buy time.'

As their walk neared its end, Turkul said, 'I think you should report our little talk to Herr Bormann. Isn't that who you answer to?'

Schlegel was rattled. 'To tell him what?'

'That he is overlooking a vital aspect, which I am keen to discuss with Mr Dulles, except that he is too obtuse to listen. In short, my agents who provide Gehlen with his intelligence will soon be looking for another employer.'

Schlegel told Bormann what Turkul had in mind, and Bormann ran with the idea as though he had just thought of it himself.

'I am well aware that Mr Dulles fears he will not have an Intelligence Service after the war. Now he has robbed his gold train, he has the money to buy one. Go back and tell him we'll sell him ours. Anything else?'

'Turkul thought rumours of a German redoubt might have something to do with you.'

Bormann laughed. 'True or not, you can persuade Mr Dulles of that while you are about it.'

Bormann looked pleased with himself.

'I will telephone and arrange for you to meet Dulles tomorrow morning. For breakfast. Bright and early. The Americans like their breakfast.'

It meant Schlegel had to drive through the night. He filled the car and added a couple of jerry cans of petrol.

He hurried to get to the Baur on time, only to find a message saying Dulles would be late. Schlegel booked a room, thinking hang the cost, Bormann could pay. He tidied himself up, then went to the hotel barber and was at least presentable. Still no sign of Dulles, so he told the desk to say he was in the breakfast room.

There, the world appeared normal, almost. The smell of proper coffee and fresh bread helped, as did a pretty waitress wearing black with a white apron, who poured his coffee while Schlegel admired the turn of her wrist. He was sitting more or less where he would over sixty years later, at the end of his life, to find himself confronted by Parker.

Dulles breezed in without apologising and annoyed Schlegel by helping himself to his bread rolls. Because of the others in the room, they were forced to make small talk, which Dulles didn't have much of.

Schlegel reluctantly cut short his breakfast, and they adjourned to the private bar room where they had met with Angleton. Dulles said he wasn't used to being summoned and this had better be good.

Ten minutes later, after several nips from a hip flask, he was sunniness itself as he announced, 'I am glad you brought this up, son. What's on the table?'

'Any number of secret anti-communist organisations. Ukrainian nationalists, Romania's Iron Guard, the Croatian Ustashe, the Vanagi of Latvia, Vlassov's army of Soviet defectors and what's left of General Bór-Komorowski's Polish home army.'

'Quite an address book,' said Dulles. Schlegel saw how eager he was for it. 'Anything else while we're about it?'

Schlegel informed him that fanatical Nazi werewolves were gathering in the mountains for a rearguard action.

Dulles duly reported this, whereupon an indecisive American command stalled its advance on Berlin, delaying the war's end and achieving Bormann's aim. It left Schlegel marvelling at how easy deception was sometimes. On the matter of the Gehlen network, he was sure blind eyes would be turned all the way to Washington. Dulles brokered exactly that deal, being one of just seven American officials involved. Nothing stated whether the acquisition was ratified by any legal or political authority, or whether anyone discussed with the White House the implications of hiring a Nazi spy network. Probably not, because the cold war that Dulles wanted was central to the deal.

What no one knew was that Andrey Turkul had been working for the Soviets all along, a consummate double agent, never exposed. Via Bormann, he sold Dulles a compromised network, which had been deeply penetrated, leaving

Russian Intelligence to control much of what went on after 1945.

Had James Angleton's vaunted methodology when it came to counterintelligence amounted to more than swagger, he might have paid more attention to Soviet practice, a continuation of the Czarist model of setting up false resistance groups and recruiting into them. Penetration of many anticommunist groups was therefore a given, because Soviet agents had created them in the first place.

Schlegel saw Dulles only once more after that, in the same private bar under very different circumstances, when Bormann sent him to deliver a warning to an angry, sweating Dulles, whose eyes popped at what he was hearing.

He interrupted to say, 'I won't be told what the fuck to do by a young whippersnapper.'

Schlegel said he wasn't telling, he was relaying what he had been told.

Bormann's message was blunt. Dulles was behaving against their mutual interests by continuing to try to broker a peace deal. Dulles was to desist from any such negotiations with other parties, namely Himmler and Fegelein. He was to refer only to Bormann, with whom he now had an exclusive arrangement. Otherwise the story of Dulles' gold train would find its way into the London *Times*.

Dulles blustered, denying any such negotiations.

Schlegel said, 'Herr Bormann has proof to the contrary. Hermann Fegelein is a loudmouth. There are assets still to be got out. If the war is brought to a premature conclusion through your efforts, Herr Bormann warns you to look over your shoulder, as there are plenty of what you Americans call "hitmen".'

Bormann hadn't actually said that, but Schlegel was enjoying Dulles' discomfort.

Dulles stood, fists clenched like he was trying to be some Hemingway tough guy, and said, 'I don't take threats, boy.'

Schlegel saw Dulles was afraid and would never forgive him for that. Dulles took a step forward so they were toe-to-toe.

Dulles said, 'You should take care leaving town, son. I have plenty of men too.'

Without thinking, Schlegel socked Dulles in the solar plexus and drove his knee up into the groin, wondering when the man had last been hit, if ever. The air swooshed out of him as he collapsed to the floor and lay on the carpet groaning, while Schlegel stood thinking: It serves you right for cheating at tennis. The man's sense of entitlement irked him. Time to get out; he suspected Dulles was ruthless enough to have him killed for humiliating him.

Schlegel immediately drove back to Munich, filling up on the way from a jerry can, which left his hands reeking of petrol. It was a beautiful winter's day with clear, sharp skies, at odds with his mood. He told himself he should have stayed in Switzerland and gone to the mountains and sat out the rest of the war, which could only be a matter of weeks.

Konrad Morgen's war ended in Breslau, where he served as a court judge on routine cases until caught up in a Russian tank offensive and imprisoned by the Czechs. He was arrested wearing his SS uniform. Where others were executed, he persuaded his captors that he was a harmless cog in the legal department.

When the Russians turned up, he feared they would shoot him out of hand but, after being roughed up, he was taken to an old school classroom with the remains of the last arithmetic lesson still on the blackboard, made to sit at a child's desk and treated with contempt and curiosity by two educated young Russian officers with good German, who paced around with unfastened holsters and decided he was perhaps more useful alive for what he could tell them about the internal workings of the SS.

He was put out to graze in a remote holding camp in a forest, where he kept his own counsel while they decided what to do with him.

At some point in the autumn, he was sent with others under armed escort to Special Camp Number Seven, previously Sachsenhausen concentration camp outside Berlin. As they travelled in covered trucks, Morgen saw nothing of the city's devastation. Camp Seven was now a holding centre for tens of thousands of lower- and middle-ranking ministry and public officials, but also SS and concentration camp guards. Morgen again kept his trap shut, because the place was no doubt riddled with informers.

He supposed it was around October – the leaves had fallen, and it was getting cold – when he found himself being questioned by a Russian officer with a stubbled head and beard to match. He didn't give his name; Morgen presumed counterintelligence. He spoke ungrammatical German, which Morgen resisted correcting, looked about thirty and had an open, friendly face. Morgen supposed the man was there to soften him up. He was offered a cigarette, which left him dizzy; he hadn't smoked in a long time. The Russian, whom Morgen thought of as Sergei, had the air of someone not quite sharing a joke.

He also turned out to be well-informed: he knew how Morgen had pursued cases of SS corruption in Warsaw and several concentration camps; how he had a reputation for insubordination; how after six months' detention in 1942, he had been packed off to fight on the eastern front for another six months.

'In winter, wearing a summer uniform,' Morgen added.

He thought it diplomatic to praise the Russians as good fighters. They had wiped out his company several times over. He said nothing about how barbaric they were and did his best to appear a good loser.

'Then, after six months on the front line,' Sergei said, 'you were recalled to financial investigations, despite your reputation as a troublemaker.'

'I would argue I had merely been trying to do my job, which others stopped me from doing.'

Sergei waited for his explanation.

'The SS punished its members who broke the rules, but many got away with murder, literally in some cases. After returning home, I resolved to do what I could. I had seen a lot of brave young men die on the pittance of army pay while others sat around at home stuffing their pockets.'

Sergei produced a pipe, went through the ritual of preparing it, lit up, sat back and said, 'I can offer a choice.'

Morgen, thinking he wasn't in a position to be given one, asked carefully, 'Between?'

'Be sent to Russia or perform "a certain investigation" here, as one of the enemy who understands the system. Dogged. No stone unturned. I believe you were known as the Bloodhound.'

The first he'd heard. The man's next question surprised him.

'Do you believe Hitler is dead?'

Morgen was alert to what sounded like a loaded question.

251

'That's what is being said.'

He left a lot of space between the words.

'Not my question.'

Morgen said that his circumstances made it hard for him to keep up with the news.

Sergei seemed to find that funny before saying, 'A press conference is being held in Berlin tomorrow by the British to announce their findings on Hitler. I can arrange for you to attend.'

'Why, when I know nothing?'

Sergei frowned, annoyed at being questioned. 'Fresh eyes and ears, not one of us. How's your English?'

'No better than so-so,' said Morgen.

'I am sure they will have simultaneous translation.'

Early next morning, before daylight, he was driven into town by a severe, intimidatingly tall young woman with bad skin whom Sergei had introduced as a political adviser. His watchdog, Morgen supposed. She held the rank of major. He knew that because Sergei had said he would be accompanied by one. Morgen's surprise must have shown when a woman walked in, because after that he was treated with contempt. Again, no name was given. Morgen decided to call her Natasha. She spoke sound German with a strong accent.

He was sent to a camp barber for a shave and haircut, then given what was no doubt a dead man's suit, with sleeves that were too short. A scrappy-looking press card showed he worked for a Russian army German-language newspaper produced for the local population.

Natasha drove them in a draughty jeep, expertly double-declutching, and was as forthcoming as a deaf mute. Morgen was speechless as it was: in the emerging slate-grey light, what had looked more or less normal when he was last there now resembled the ruins of Pompeii. Natasha stared ahead, unmoved, as if to say they deserved nothing less.

Their destination was the British press headquarters at the Hotel-am-Zoo on the Kurfürstendamm. Inside, a crowd gathered in a conference hall that smelled of furniture polish, cigarettes and sweat. Morgen looked around – a hundred or so international reporters, a lot of loud Americans, photographers with flash cameras and a heavy military presence of all Allied denominations. His only thought was they were all free men and behaved like it. The mood was like a theatre audience waiting for the curtain to go up, both tense and casual. Simultaneous translation was available via headphones, but not in German.

A young English major entered, sat at a table at the head of the room and introduced himself. There were complaints that people couldn't hear, and a technician fiddled with a microphone until it worked. Not the most auspicious start, thought Morgen.

As it was, he found he could more or less follow what was said, having picked up enough English from studying international law in The Hague before the war.

The academic-looking, bespectacled major was everything Germans admired about the British, being clear, to the point and a little ironic. The major announced that, on the evidence available, based on eyewitness accounts, he was able to state – as conclusively as possible in the absence of any bodies (said meaningfully in the direction of the Soviet contingent) – that Adolf Hitler and his female companion, Eva Braun, had died on the afternoon of 30 April 1945, between 2 and 3.30pm, in a bunker beneath the Reich Chancellery. Hitler had shot himself in the mouth;

Braun took a cyanide capsule. Both bodies were immediately burned and buried.

The statement lasted a few minutes. There was nothing in the way of proof, from what Morgen could see. It was more like a news bulletin stating what had happened. The mood was sceptical. The major was asked by one American newspaperman if he was aware of the Russian view on Hitler's death. The major said he understood they were inclined to think he was still alive. Morgen noticed several Russian uniforms nodding.

A question was raised about whether the body was in fact Hitler's, rather than a double. The major was emphatic that there would have been no time for that, plus Hitler's physical condition put him in no fit state to escape. He raised an eyebrow as he drolly pointed out to laughter that the woman would hardly have agreed to a suicide pact with a substitute.

Hitler and women, Schlegel thought to himself as he stood next to the Führer's mistress in the man's fancy, barely used Munich apartment in Prinzregentenplatz. It was February, 1945, and the war still had a little over two months to run. They were in the room that had belonged to his late niece, Geli, which had been preserved as a shrine since she'd shot herself, aged twenty-three, in tragic circumstances in 1931, using her uncle's pistol. At least, that was the story the woman standing next to him believed.

The scandal had threatened to destroy Hitler's leadership and nearly broke the man. Bormann effectively hushed it up, despite rumours of incestuous, unnatural sexual acts and Hitler being in the apartment at the time of the girl's death. The only proof that he wasn't was the alibi of a speeding ticket, which Schlegel knew had been arranged by Bormann and fixed by the future head of the Gestapo.

According to a woman Schlegel had met the year before, who had known both niece and mistress, Braun was jealous of Geli because she was everything she wasn't: vivacious, impetuous and probably better in bed.

Schlegel hadn't expected to find the woman at the apartment, as she was generally hidden away in the Führer's mountain retreat at Berchtesgaden. He was there to fetch a package from the housekeeper for delivery to Bormann. He had no idea what; more errand boy than bagman. Given that Hitler hadn't lived there in years, the housekeeper ruled the roost. After a frosty welcome, he was ushered into a large front room overlooking a square and told to wait in a way that suggested the woman was in no hurry to serve his needs. No refreshment was offered. The furniture was covered with dust sheets.

The room, done out in impeccable interior designer's taste, was like a stage set, with a solid if unimaginative library that looked as though it had been assembled to show that its owner was well-read.

After ten minutes of waiting, Schlegel was about to search for the housekeeper when he heard the front door open, followed by the sound of a woman's heels. She walked into the room and stopped in surprise.

Schlegel stood and said, 'I'm just waiting for the housekeeper to fetch me something.' He added her name, 'Fräulein Braun,' wondering how she would react.

'Do I know you?' she asked.

He said they had met briefly the year before, but she showed no sign of remembering.

'That day at the races,' he said. 'Hermann Fegelein was

there with your sister.' He didn't say that the man had been more than usually obnoxious and everyone had been pissed.

Braun said, 'A day at the races? Hard to imagine that now.'

They stood awkwardly until Schlegel said, 'Don't let me stop you.'

Braun looked around until she found a key in a shallow dish.

'Do you know about his niece, the one who shot herself?' she asked.

He restricted himself to saying, 'I have heard.'

Braun said, 'Perhaps you can check the room with me. It gives me the creeps. It has been kept just as it was. There should always be fresh flowers on his instructions. I suspect that lazy cow of a housekeeper doesn't bother.'

Braun was right about the flowers. Long-dead. The curtains were drawn, the atmosphere oppressive. However vivacious its owner, the room said nothing about her. Schlegel presumed the indifferent watercolour on the wall was by her uncle.

It was strange standing there, as he was one of the very few who knew what had really happened. What he didn't know, however, was that Geli, a spontaneous and physically generous young woman, had fucked his father, who had made an exception for her because on the whole he preferred his own sex.

Whatever; the room had kept its secrets.

They returned to the reception, and Schlegel was surprised when Fräulein Braun began weeping. She quickly dabbed her eyes, stuffed the handkerchief up her sleeve and sniffed theatrically.

Schlegel wasn't sure whether to show concern or say nothing.

They were interrupted by the housekeeper. She had a small leather holdall for Schlegel, who wondered what was in it.

She inclined her head coolly in the direction of Braun. Schlegel was aware of a palpable animosity.

Braun haughtily announced, 'The Chief has bigger things on his mind than your duty to replace the flowers in his niece's room. It's not as though it's the first time.' Braun turned to Schlegel and announced, 'As we're both here, shall we have some tea before we leave?'

Schlegel doubted they would have much to talk about, but as she clearly wanted to boss the servant, he agreed.

She turned out to be quite easy, chatting on with little need of prompting. She said she had recently celebrated a birthday in Berlin. 'Don't ask which.'

She told him anyway, and Schlegel obliged by reassuring her that she looked nothing like thirty-three.

'I won't live long,' she went on, as though discussing something quite inconsequential. 'I get this heart flutter. I fainted once and remember thinking, "Well, that's curtains!"'

Schlegel laughed politely. If nothing else, he was well brought up.

'Shall I be mother?' Braun asked rhetorically when the tea arrived, then ordered the housekeeper to pour it, which was done with ill grace while Braun produced an envelope from her handbag and held it out to the woman.

'It's a list of certain possessions of ours here which we want putting in safe-keeping. Better delivered in person, so you can't blame the postal service and say you didn't get it.'

With that, Braun gave the woman a nod of dismissal.

As they drank their tea, Braun sometimes seemed momentarily puzzled, accompanied by sudden starts that left Schlegel wondering if she was on medication.

He asked if she intended to stay in Munich long.

'The Chief says I'm in the way in Berlin and he worries

about me and air raids. I wanted to bring the dogs back anyway – Negus and Stasi, such delightful creatures, Scottish terriers, you must meet them – and to have a second birthday party with family and friends, but that had to be put off for two days because of an air raid. Bloody RAF murderers! The Chief gave me the most beautiful pendant of topaz surrounded by diamonds. I say "gave", he probably had someone choose it for him because he's far too busy to go shopping! Do you think a woman should stick by her man?'

'You mean, go back to Berlin?'

'I like you already, you understand what I am on about. What's in the bag?'

'I've no idea. Party Secretary Bormann asked for it.'

Perhaps his tone betrayed his dislike of the man, because she volunteered, 'I can't stand him.' She didn't say 'either', but she may as well have done. 'Of course, he says the right thing in his diary – the Chief in radiant mood on the evening of my birthday, and me looking all the time for dancing partners.'

Complaining about Bormann was safe enough. They all did.

'Do you read the diary?' he asked when it was obvious she did.

'Everyone does! He knows we do, which is why he leaves it around. Bormann doesn't want me there. He made sure my sister and I were on that bloody midnight milk train back here three days after my birthday. He forbids me to return, although the Chief promises we'll spend Easter together. What are your plans?'

'Return to Berlin, I suppose.'

'Shall we take a peek?' she suggested mischievously, pointing at the bag.

He wondered at her calculated spontaneity. Perhaps she

was trying to be like the niece. She opened it and peered inside.

'A lot of sealed papers and two pistols,' she said.

Braun produced a gold-plated Walther.

'Rather vulgar, don't you think? I know he thought so. Given for his fiftieth birthday. Why should he want it now? Anyway, how are you getting to Berlin? Do you have a car?'

He did.

'Can I cadge a lift, do you suppose? I know the Chief really wants me there. There's no one else he can trust.'

Braun produced a packet of cigarettes and lit up, saying, 'We're not supposed to, but he's not coming back and that housekeeper woman can complain all she likes. My sister complains too. I was smoking in Berlin after dinner. The Chief had excused himself, and she got annoyed when I sprayed the room with Chanel to hide the smell. She thought I was being extravagant. She was in a funny mood generally. She had been forced to flee the Russian advance and arrived with nothing but a small suitcase after three sleepless days and nights on a packed train. Have you heard that British propaganda station which pretends to be German? Everyone listens to it.'

'The Calais station?'

'That's the one. They broadcast stuff that can only have come from inside the Chancellery, including rumours of a Russian spy at a very senior level, maybe even "in the kennel outside his master's door". No wonder Bormann's beside himself.'

For whatever reason, Fräulein Braun decided she could be indiscreet.

'You said you know Hermann,' she said casually.

'Doesn't everyone? He's married to your other sister.'

Braun pulled a face. 'And recently found in bed with a chambermaid. Bormann was left working overtime to hush that one up! Hermann's also bedding an Irish woman in Berlin.'

'Molly Fitzgerald?'

'Have you met?' Braun appeared impressed that Schlegel was able to keep up his end.

'We were introduced,' he said.

Braun sighed. 'It's all so impossible. The Chief is surrounded by traitors, which is why I must be there. I worry so about his health. What would you do?'

'In terms of going back?'

'Oh, I know. There's so much bomb damage. But I am painting a gloomy picture. I am not a defeatist. Far from it! Last time wasn't so bad. I had my hairdresser and dressmaker, there were walkies for Negus and Stasi, and dining alone with the Chief. We had Christmas and New Year together, when he accepted champagne for the toast. But I had a row with my sister after she accused me of being in denial.'

Braun flicked ash onto her saucer.

'She thinks I have airs and graces, when I was only trying to put her at her ease. I arranged for her to have the Adlon suite I'd had before moving into the Chancellery. She complained about that too. She said I was treating her like a society friend staying for the weekend rather than a political refugee. I ask you! That's what she called herself. That was the evening I fainted. I told her she wasn't the only one suffering from nerves. Then the woman had the gall to say she'd had a dream where she saw me on a pyre, smiling but surrounded by rats, then a wall of flame hid me from sight.'

Braun wrote her telephone number in a pocket diary, tore out the page, handed it over and said, 'Call me. It is our duty to be with the Führer. I know you won't let me down.'

Robinson surprised Parker when, after days of indolence, he announced, 'I have a job for you.'

It involved cataloguing a rich man's library, a Russian oligarch whose young wife had literary pretensions.

Robinson said, 'She's being advised by a high-end book dealer friend of mine to collect English modern firsts, which of course he is able to flog her. He is also in a position to offer bookish, student types to catalogue the library. That now includes you. My dealer friend says it'll take a couple of hours to explain what the job entails.'

Oleg Yashnikov was among the richest of the rich. All Parker knew, as instructed by Robinson, was that if the billionaire made an appearance, which was by no means guaranteed, given his yachts and an international property portfolio, Parker was to give him an envelope.

'Directly,' said Robinson. 'Not to any third party. If this fortuitous encounter takes place, tell friend Oleg that the item is for private sale, no middleman, via the number provided.'

The man's home in Kensington was the size of an embassy. But a house is still a house, thought Parker: four walls and a roof; up to a point. He wasn't shown the sauna, the gym, the squash court, the swimming pool, the cinema or the safe rooms. He was put to work in little more than an upstairs cupboard. The part of the library he was cataloguing consisted of every novel long- and shortlisted for the Booker Prize; all copies mint, preferably signed. Parker was given white gloves like those worn by Mr Smith. Each book had to be indexed on a library card and itemised separately on a computer. Sometimes he could hear children playing elsewhere in the house. The main noise was of construction deep below ground.

He was told by a man who said he was a butler but looked

more like security that he was to talk to no one; no mobile calls; and not to comment to anyone outside on either the surroundings or his employer. He said the room was 'under observation', though Parker failed to spot any camera. He was expected to bring his own sandwiches, which had to be eaten in a small kitchen in a separate adjacent apartment. A kettle, skimmed milk and instant coffee were provided, which he was forbidden to drink while cataloguing. There were cheap novelty mugs and no biscuits. Nothing like the meals given to H. in the commandant's house, Parker thought sourly to himself.

He saw none of the house's principals, only the butler. He also had to work with the blinds down to protect the books from direct sunlight.

He was in the kitchen eating his sandwich when a scruffy man walked in and made himself an instant coffee. Parker thought he was a builder. It took him a while to realise that the unshaven man wearing tracksuit bottoms, crocs and a grubby hoodie was Yashnikov. Anonymous and harmless was his impression; boyish in manner, though easily forty.

Parker addressed the man, who appeared not unfriendly, and said he had been asked to give him something. After reciting his little speech, he handed over the envelope, which was a small, regular-sized one of the sort used for letter writing. He pointed to the telephone number on the front of the envelope, which Yashnikov took without comment, making no attempt to open it.

No one answered the door when Parker turned up for work the next morning, or the morning after. He supposed that Yashnikov had decamped to one of his other properties or a yacht. After that, he didn't bother going back.

Robinson said, 'It looks like you've been fired.'

Parker wasn't privy to Robinson's next move, which was to have Vod drive him down to Michail's boat, where he found Michail bored with his Xbox and cocaine.

Robinson said, 'I have my doubts about the Berlin package. I am afraid we were led on.'

'"We"?'

'The Morgen documents are authentic, but I have decided to keep them.'

'I heard they were yours all along,' said Michail enigmatically.

Robinson ignored that and said, 'I am here because something else has just come on the market. I have come straight to you. First refusal.'

'It had better be good,' said Michail, doing a line of coke without offering.

'It is. None bigger. On his fiftieth birthday, in 1939, Hitler received a gold 7.65mm Walther PP from Carl Walther, the German gunsmith. The weapon is heavily engraved and embellished. Across the white ivory grip, "AH" is inscribed. Walther most probably presented the gift in person, as Hitler had armed much of his army with Walther semi-automatics to replace the old Luger. To you, one million quid.'

Michail said, 'Well, at least you're not trying to sell me Eva Braun's knickers, as someone recently did.'

'Interested?' asked Robinson, aware of sounding needy. 'Others will be.'

Michail said, 'The problem is, a lot of fake material is coming from Bulgaria, Poland, Ukraine and even Pakistan. Some of it is done so well, it is difficult to tell. On the other hand, much of it is not and is so ridiculous that it amuses me to buy it. A desk statue of a hippopotamus behind a fence, for instance, surrounded by swastikas. What the hell is a hippo doing on a Nazi piece? It's so kitsch, there's no sense to it. So, what is the provenance of your item? Bulgaria?'

Robinson didn't say it was Poland or that he'd had a copy made to sell to David Bowie, who had lost interest by the time it was ready. He had decided to pass off the replica as authentic because he still had the original. Besides, any buyer would be unlikely to broadcast the purchase.

He didn't tell Michail that he was strapped for the million.

He didn't admit that Berlin had amounted to a fishing trip. Not putting the gun on the table immediately was an old selling trick: we've this and that, and then: oh, look! This has just come in.

In answer to Michail's question about the gun's provenance, Robinson said, 'Rock solid. Given to my father by a man who was in Hitler's bunker and left with it.'

'Why would he want to sell a lifelong souvenir?'

'Medical bills.'

'First refusal?'

'That's what I said.'

'Not what Oleg tells me.'

'Oleg?'

'Yashnikov.'

Robinson shrugged ruefully. 'A game to see if I could reach him, nothing more. Hardly first refusal, as I knew he wouldn't buy it, but establishing the connection is useful, as I believe he rather welcomes such initiatives.'

Michail added, 'Oleg says the real problem with buying from you is that you've insulted and cheated friends of his.'

'Not that I am aware.'

'I also happen to know you need at least a million to keep those long-suffering Russians quiet over the business of that film. Would these be the friends Oleg is talking about? He may even have passed on the number you gave him, so I would advise you to change it. Dealing with me, at least you know that these same people are no friends of mine, so I am not insulted. Except I am, because you offered me first refusal.'

Michail's tone remained reasonable, as though he was willing to accommodate Robinson's waywardness.

'I would have given you the money,' Michail went on, 'if you had asked as a favour instead of trying to sell me what I suspect is a fake. A million means nothing to me. But sorry, no deal.'

Refusing to be fobbed off, Robinson said, 'I suggest you meet those in question, and they can confirm the story. I need to find them, but I will do that at my own expense, of course.'

'Are you saying you don't know where your own father is?' Michail asked, incredulous.

'We English lack the close family ties of you Russians.'

Michail started cutting another line. 'My sister advises me not to deal with you. Usually I don't listen, though she may be right.'

'Believe me, it will be worth it.'

After leaving Braun, Schlegel checked into a cheap hotel and booked a call to Bormann's secretary, who told him to return to Berlin with the holdall. It can wait, he thought, and fell into an exhausted sleep until he was woken by air raid sirens. He went downstairs and followed the crowd to the nearest shelter. The bombing was mostly elsewhere, apart from a few closer explosions which released a fine concrete dust that settled on them like ash. The ceiling lights – a green, sickly glow – blinked on and off before deciding to stay on. People looked careworn beyond belief, apart from one couple rutting under their coats in a corner while a young mother covered her child's eyes. The sound of weeping and a case of hysterics drove the couple to harder thrusting. Schlegel went and grabbed the man's collar and told him children were present. The man grunted and rolled off, while the woman gave him a hard, lascivious stare as she carried on working at herself, and Schlegel found himself desperately tempted.

Nothing was worse than dying with a crowd of strangers, so he left. The sky was ablaze. He heard the solid cascade of a building collapse a street or so away. The immediate surroundings appeared surreally intact, with a fog of dust and a single tree on fire and a shower of flaming debris. Part of him felt like just walking to see where he ended up. Instead, he went back to his bed and fell into the deepest sleep, from which even as he slept he half-hoped he might never wake.

The next morning, he found the telephone downstairs was still working and called Fräulein Braun's number. A maid eventually answered and went to fetch her. Braun didn't sound sure who he was, then said with artificial brightness, 'Yes, of course!'

Was she still interested in a lift, he asked, wondering why he was bothering.

'Today? I am about to have my hair done.'

Schlegel thought he would probably save himself a lot of trouble by hanging up.

'Why don't you come around two?' she said. 'I'll give you the address.'

The thing was, it turned out he no longer had a car, other than a burnt husk. As nothing else in the street had been touched, he wondered if it was vandals. He had heard of juvenile delinquents using air raids as an excuse to cause all sorts of damage before being packed off to fight. Given the age boys were being conscripted these days, the kids who had wrecked his car were probably about twelve.

A train was out of the question, as he found out at the station. He called the airport and was told no flights. He supposed he could get Bormann to pull strings, but he preferred not to. He knew he would end up in Berlin; he just wasn't going to make it easy for himself.

For want of anything better, he presented himself at Fräulein Braun's address, a secluded villa in a quiet, undamaged part of town, within walking distance of the Führer's apartment.

Braun was fetched by the maid. She came down and breathlessly announced that she was nowhere near ready.

Schlegel inanely complimented her on her new perm and set.

'Oh, thank you,' she said coyly, touching it, while Schlegel wondered how many people had died during their brief exchange.

'I came to say I no longer have a car. Thanks to the RAF.'

She looked at him aghast, shook her fist and exclaimed, 'The utter bastards!'

At that, she sat in a heap on the hall floor and started crying.

'What am I to do?' she asked.

'There must be a way,' Schlegel said, wondering if he could spin this out. The woman was bound to eat well. He'd heard she drank only champagne. The house was large enough to have spare bedrooms. God forbid that he would want to fuck the woman or vice versa. There were limits! He presumed that apart from Adolf she was a virgin; maybe even still was, given stories about the man's lack of performance.

Putting on his best voice, he said, 'Do you think I could

have a cup of tea? I'm parched. Then we could put our heads together and see what we can come up with.'

Over tea, cake and sandwiches, served as though the world was still perfectly normal, he asked, thinking of the Führer's fleet of vehicles, if there weren't any she could use, at which she perked up and said, 'There's my old car – well, not that old, from before the war. In mothballs. Daimler-Benz should still have it.'

Schlegel made the call to the managing director and said he had been ordered by the highest authority to escort a close associate of the Führer to Berlin; a matter of urgency.

Daimler-Benz took its duties seriously. A car was dispatched to collect them. The boot was hardly large enough to accommodate Fräulein Braun's luggage. She took an age saying goodbye to her two terriers, promising to return soon, and Schlegel had to pretend to make a fuss over them both.

A meeting took place in the manager's office. Yes, the car was in storage. Schlegel presumed he would drive, but the manager pointed out that he wasn't insured ('Given the importance of your passenger') and Fräulein Braun's former driver was available.

She said, 'He would probably prefer driving me instead of being thrown into battle at any moment,' which was when Schlegel realised that the woman had more of a mind of her own than she let on.

The manager said, 'I recommend the car be sprayed grey to make it look more like a Wehrmacht vehicle.'

Fräulein Braun asked, 'Do we have time for that?'

The manager assured her it would dry within an hour or so, and anyway it would be wise to wait until after dark. In the meantime, she could rest in the boardroom.

Upon departure, they were presented with two travelling rugs as a gift from the company. The manager snapped off a stiff salute and wished them a safe journey without looking hopeful about it. The driver said under normal circumstances the trip would take seven or eight hours but in present conditions more like fifteen.

Schlegel was going to sit in front when Fräulein Braun asked him to keep her company. They sat in the back under their rugs, and she was silent, smoking one cigarette after another. At her suggestion, they shared champagne, drinking from the bottle, again saying little. She apologised for it being warm. Usually, there was a picnic freezer.

'I must have left it in the mountains. It's one of the problems of having two homes. I'd be happy with just one.'

She asked where he lived.

'Berlin,' he said. 'The last time I looked.'

She seemed amused by the remark. They were both a bit tipsy. Just as Schlegel was beginning not to care about what might happen to them, she shuddered and asked if he'd seen the dead cow in the road.

'Lying on its back with its legs in the air, poor thing.'

He looked out of the window and saw only pitch black and wondered if she was making it up.

When she fell asleep against his shoulder, lightly snoring, he didn't know whether to try to move her. She still had a burning cigarette in her hand, which he managed to remove and stub out without waking her.

Robinson woke in the night, thinking, not sure to whom or what he was referring: You're in another fucking dimension here, pally. There are people who arrange this. Brazen. Absurd. *Quelle genre de voyous sont-ils?* Men of limited imagination who nevertheless concoct bizarre scenarios, weird deaths, strange exhibits.

They were attacked shortly after dawn by a British fighter on a long straight stretch. It came in so low that Schlegel thought it would rip the roof off the car. Two lines of tracer bullets stitched the road, somehow missing them. Schlegel watched the plane streak ahead until it was a dot before banking. Fräulein Braun appeared a lot cooler than he was, apart from grabbing his hand. There was no question of outrunning the aircraft. The countryside was open, with nowhere to pull over. He scanned the skies, saw nothing and hoped the pilot had found something else to terrorise. Then there it was again, a low speck on the horizon, approaching from behind at several times their speed, with Schlegel thinking none of them would live to see the plane's victory roll. He watched the bullets smash into the road, getting closer. Again, they missed; he realised the pilot must be playing with them. On the third attack, just as they were about to be carved up, everything grew darker as they passed into what Schlegel realised, as he saw the bullets splinter tree trunks, was a wood.

They pulled over and listened to the plane disappear. Fräulein Braun, still clutching his hand, said she needed to pee, at which they both giggled while the driver kept a straight face, saying he thought it was safe to get out.

Schlegel and the driver stood by the road while Fräulein Braun disappeared into the trees. Better to lay up somewhere, the driver suggested, and wait until dark.

When Fräulein Braun returned, it was the driver's turn to stretch his legs. Schlegel told her what they'd just discussed, and she said, 'No, I'll take my chances. If it isn't meant to be, so be it.' She even seemed quite excited. 'You can't believe how dull life is, always waiting, preparing for his return in the unlikelihood of that happening.' She gave a harsh laugh and said, 'My boyfriend's not going to win the war. I've had plenty of time to consider my options. If I am alone in the mountains when the end comes, Bormann or Himmler will have me shot rather than be paraded as a trophy. Last December, there was a hard bombing in Munich, and I had my jewellery in the shelter and remember thinking, "I don't need this anymore".'

Schlegel said in a friendly way, 'You're not exactly travelling light.'

She laughed again and said, 'Standards have to be maintained.'

The driver appeared among the trees on his way back.

Fräulein Braun gripped Schlegel's arm and asked, 'Can I trust you?'

Not a question he wanted to hear, but he nodded.

'You see,' she said, facing him, 'I mean to go down in history.'

As the driver joined them, Schlegel was left to wonder what on earth she had in mind.

Despite detours, they arrived at the end of the day without further mishap. Braun suggested they enter the Chancellery separately to avoid Bormann blaming Schlegel for her being there.

All Bormann asked as Schlegel handed over the holdall was, 'How the fuck did that woman get here?', to which he said that he'd heard a chauffeur drove her. As Bormann didn't know about the fate of his car, Schlegel said he'd driven himself as far as the outskirts of Berlin, where he had hit a pothole and the big end went. After that, he'd hitched a lift, then taken the bus. He thought Bormann probably knew the truth, but he did not comment, other than to say, 'Find out who's the source of the leaks here. I don't mind when that fucking Soldatensender Calais broadcasts idle Chancellery tittle-tattle, but when they start pointing their finger at me, saying there's a Russian spy in the house, I want the man's guts for garters.'

Morgen couldn't see what he was supposed to report after the major's verdict on Hitler and Braun's deaths. Back in Camp Seven, Sergei took him to a separate high-security compound, where he was given a room with a bed, a desk and a chair. The table was covered with documents and newspaper cuttings. Some were in English, for which he was given a dictionary.

'All yours,' Sergei said.

'Do you actually want me to disprove the British theory?'

'Start by not trusting it,' Sergei suggested.

'What is the Soviet position?'

Sergei shrugged to say he didn't know, when Morgen was sure he did.

Morgen's unasked question was: How much help are you going to give me? It was like being expected to sit an examination without knowing what the real subject was. He suspected Sergei didn't care about Hitler as such, being caught up in a political endgame and the start of a propaganda war.

Natasha turned up from time to time with more papers, some in Russian, for which she gave verbal translations while Morgen took notes. As there was only one chair, she stood by the window and smoked, refusing to engage. When Morgen suggested it would help to have some sense of acquaintance if they were to work together, she snapped, 'I don't talk to pigs.'

The day-to-day of it as the world tried to mend passed him by. His main memories were of a lack of identity to anything, including the central riddle he was supposed to address, as well as his own questionable worth. Whatever he had once been, he no longer was; but who he was now and to whom he belonged, he could not say.

That political games were afoot appeared to be confirmed by a Russian newspaper story claiming that Hitler and his mistress were living in a castle in Westphalia.

'Is this true?' Morgen asked Natasha.

'It's what it says.'

Morgen suspected Russian mischief, implying British complicity because Westphalia was in its zone.

The Russians had also issued a statement denying that the bodies of Hitler and Braun had been found, in spite of initial reports to the contrary. However, 'irrefutable proof' existed that, shortly before the end, a light aircraft had left the Tiergarten at dawn flying in the direction of Hamburg. Three men and a woman were on board. It was also established that a large submarine had left Hamburg before the arrival of the British forces, onto which the aircraft passengers had embarked, including the woman.

Morgen thought it looked as though the practical British had produced their report to scotch that story and numerous other Hitler sightings over the summer.

A German translation and update of the major's press conference was published. Written with the clarity of an English debating society, it established that a farewell ceremony had taken place, with handshakes all round, before the couple retired, while the high priests and acolytes waited outside. A single shot was heard. Hitler and Braun were found in peaceful repose on the sofa, united in death by a single bullet and a potassium cyanide capsule.

The problem was the British were not consistent. The

most significant witness the major had was Hitler's transport officer, who had already been interviewed by America's *Life* magazine, of all things! He declared for the benefit of a breathless readership that Braun had shot herself through the heart, not taken poison as the major had it, and Hitler had shot himself in the head, not the mouth as claimed by the major.

Another problem was the quality of the major's other witnesses. Four were lowly police guards and one was female, secretary to Martin Bormann. None had access to the Führer, yet all stated that the couple's farewell to staff was conducted with dignity, after which they had retired to consummate their relationship in death. A widely seen photograph of the bloodstained sofa on which they'd ended their lives had been also published in *Life* magazine.

Morgen remained thrown by the insistence on Braun being there. He'd thought her vain and superficial, not at all the type to show up for the last act. Sometimes he asked himself whether her stated presence was to contrive a sentimental ending, with her chosen to symbolise the sacrifice of Germania or some such nonsense.

Morgen asked for Sergei and told him, 'I need to see the bunker and know what any Germans you are holding have to say.'

He was sure the Russians had them.

Sergei said, 'You were asked to assess the facts given.'

'Without fuller access, these are just playground games. Do you want to know the truth?'

'The truth can be dangerous,' Sergei recited pompously. Then, 'Permission takes time.'

Morgen was still in bed when Natasha turned up before daylight and watched him dress. When he was done, she slapped him hard across the face. Perhaps she felt he was inconveniencing her by making her drive him into town after being told he could inspect the bunker. That was the only reason he could come up with, other than her disliking him and being able to do as she pleased.

The bunker didn't tell him much more than the photographic spreads in *Life* magazine taken after its evacuation, which showed its upper space and claustrophobic lower level. They were given torches because the electricity no longer worked. A dozen of them were down there. Apart from Natasha, he had no idea who the rest were beyond Russian men in uniform. Going underground was like a descent into Hades. The atmosphere was fetid and as heavy as lead. The only sound was the drip of leaking pipes. The floor was covered with a film of scummy water. The weak beam of Morgen's torch showed a mess of litter, strewn papers and empty beer and schnapps bottles. The stink of shit was enough to make him gag; toilets were blocked and overflowing. The total squalor was at odds with accounts of the controlled, self-conscious deaths of the doomed lovebirds. It was like being in death's antechamber. Morgen was poking around when he saw two barely discernible shapes approach down the corridor. For a second, he thought they were the Führer and his woman returned to haunt him. He stepped into a room to let them pass and could just make out a female Russian guard and a stumbling man with his arms handcuffed behind his back. He followed and joined them as the man was presented to Natasha, who ordered him to state who he was. He said he was Hitler's valet, Linge.

Torches were shone in his face, and the man stared around, looking like he'd had the senses beaten out of him.

'Let's start with the bedrooms,' suggested Natasha.

Morgen tagged along. Linge mumbled that the first room was Hitler's. It was dominated by a huge empty safe – as tall as a man – which stood at the end of a single cot. Morgen noted blood on the mattress and the edge of the bed and wondered if anyone had considered that.

The torch beams scanning the room were like a pathetic parody of all those nocturnal rallies with their extravagant light shows; no one on the podium now, just a rifled safe with its door hanging open, revealing nothing, and a discarded bottle of Dewar's whisky on the floor.

The other bedroom, also with a single bed, accessed by a narrow little corridor, showed signs of feminine occupation.

Linge told them that the room had belonged to the Führer's companion in death.

He led them back out to what he called the map room, where he said his Führer had told him to come in and shut the door before entrusting him with the disposal of his and his companion's bodies, making sure that no one recognised them after death.

'When was this?' Natasha asked. 'And don't refer to him as your Führer.'

Linge winced, fearing he was about to be hit. 'I remember checking the time,' he said ponderously. 'It was 3.50pm.'

Not consistent with the English major's timings, Morgen noted.

The order came moments before Hitler shot himself and no one else was present, according to Linge, who had then fled, not wanting to hear the fatal shot of a man he had served for ten years.

Morgen saw the Russians look at each other in disbelief.

Linge went on. 'Yet I returned and noted a whiff of smoke coming from under the door, no noise, no crack of a pistol.'

Natasha lost patience and exclaimed, 'A likely story!' She pointed. 'A door that is fireproof and soundproof.'

Linge hung his head, jabbering incoherently.

Natasha asked, 'What of the Braun woman?'

Linge looked as though he had no idea what she was talking about.

'Hitler referred to two bodies. What did you do next?'

'Found a blanket to hide his face.'

'Others report seeing the face.'

'Perhaps it didn't, then, the blanket, I mean, hide the face. My mind was on serving my master's last wishes. Fräulein Braun might have been there.'

'They were found together,' Natasha added testily. 'Do you suppose she was hiding in a cupboard when you spoke to him? Then what?'

'We took the bodies up to the garden and burned them with gasoline.'

'So by then Fräulein Braun was restored to the picture,' Natasha announced to general amusement.

'My responsibility was to my master.'

'Who is the "we" who went up to the garden?'

Linge shook his head as his memory failed. 'All I recall,' he eventually managed, 'was that ten or so paid their respects. The end was very near. Your army was at the gates. Hitler was recognisable by his black trousers sticking out from under the blanket and Fräulein Braun by her blue dress, which was one of his favourites.'

Linge crossed himself.

Natasha said, 'Enough of your nonsense. By any other account, Hitler didn't die in the map room.'

'It's hard to remember,' whined Linge. 'There was no sense of time down here, nothing to tell night from day. It was a

277

big surprise to go upstairs and find it still light. It truly was Götterdämmerung.'

And no doubt they were all beyond drunk, Morgen thought to himself.

They went back to Hitler's living quarters, where Natasha said, 'What are we to believe – your pathetic whiff of smoke or what others say happened here?'

The sound of her laughter in the bunker was one of the most unsettling things Morgen had ever heard. She spoke to the quivering Linge, saying, 'Either we shoot you on the spot or take you back to the map room so you can die in what is, according to you, the same glorious death chamber as your master.'

Morgen had no doubt that she was serious.

Linge, panic-stricken, struggled through a show of remembering. 'Maybe the map room was earlier, yes, it must have been this door where I saw the smoke.'

Morgen was surprised he was sticking to that story. Linge pointed to the sofa, closed his eyes and recited, as though describing the picture in his head.

'Seated together in death, the Führer slumped forward but upright, with a small hole in his right temple. A trickle of blood running slowly down his cheek. Fräulein Braun was peacefully at rest beside him.'

Morgen looked around. The dried blood on the blue and white velvet sofa seemed inconsistent with Linge's trickle. If the man had shot himself in the mouth, as the major had it, blood and brains would be all over the wall. It looked as though the British had not conducted any proper tests. Morgen wondered if the Russians had.

There was no stopping Linge as he warmed to his performance.

'I remember now, the only sign of upset was a blue Dresden vase that had been filled that morning with tulips and white narcissi from the greenhouse. It had tipped over, spilling water on Braun's blue chiffon dress, near the thigh, and had fallen to the carpet unbroken.'

Linge, ever the valet, had picked it up, examined it for cracks, replaced the flowers and set it back on the table.

Morgen supposed this touching detail was the closest the man would admit to the room being redressed after whatever had been found: a tasteful tableau to be passed on for others to share and remember.

With that, they broke up. Morgen climbed the stairs slowly, thinking how – after being exposed to such a suffocating underworld – if he went up too quickly, he might be exposed to the mental equivalent of a diver's bends.

Hair of the Dog

P arker was familiar with the facts of Hitler's death because he had seen *Downfall*. Watching it again (several copies were available in a local charity shop), he was surprised by how much conformed to the version published by the British major after the war.

Downfall held no surprises. Seen through the eyes of an ingenue – Hitler's secretary, Junge – it featured a cast of female acolytes and uniformed men of little character deferring to Bruno Ganz's scenery-chewing Hitler.

After Morgen's report, Parker didn't think of what he saw as anything that had actually happened. It wasn't Visconti's *The Damned*, which caught the stench of moral decay. *Downfall*'s humourlessness invited others to laugh, including parodies with the English subtitles jokily rewritten to have Hitler ranting about anything but the matter in hand, including his gaming account being banned from Xbox Live.

Downfall lurched towards its inevitable end with drunken rowdiness, a stooped and shaking Hitler screeching at his officers and sentimental towards the women, none with any sign of interior lives, raising questions about that whole weird troglodyte existence. Braun complained about the shortness of her leash but gave no indication of what she saw in the man or why she was there. She was attractive in a fragile way and liked a party, but no psychological understanding of her was offered beyond deference to the events related, as though the filmmakers wanted to treat the subject with the decorum noted by the original witnesses, which was among the first things Morgen had questioned.

The deaths of Hitler and Braun occurred off-screen. Much time was given to the documented end of the Goebbels children as they were 'painlessly' poisoned after sedation, with sheets drawn over their heads to expose dead little toes.

After Hitler's death, the film went on and on. The escaping women looked very war chic disguised in men's uniforms and scuttle helmets. The end was rank sentimentality: a young boy (the future!) was befriended by Junge, a bicycle was found and they rode into the bright sunlight of peace.

It seemed easier to laze around watching DVDs than the slow business of translating Morgen's text with frequent reference to the dictionary. Covering the same ground and made much earlier by the Austrian director G. W. Pabst, *The Last Ten Days* (1955) was far surer. Pabst's minimalist bunker, with its poorly rendered concrete, was both realistic and stylised – labyrinth, warren, hellhole and deranged head space, shot in stark black and white. Pabst had made films since the silent days (*Pandora's Box* with Louise Brooks), had done Brecht (*The Threepenny Opera*) and even worked for Dr Goebbels, so knew of what he spoke, knew how these people spoke, recognised the right amount of swagger and the double bind of initiative and obedience driven by Hitler's hysteria. Beady observation turned *The Last Ten Days* into a film about manners, and an interpretation of those manners, more than *Downfall*'s animated waxworks. The atmosphere was simultaneously claustrophobic and agoraphobic, with little by way of life outside, other than a street hanging and U-Bahn stations, used as emergency hospitals, awaiting the deluge; grotesque interludes that sent the film scuttling back underground.

The skewed madness seemed entirely logical, nightmarish (because illogical) and inevitable. Everything had been played out already, leaving little room for false drama: larger than life, but also terribly reduced, with the camera managing a conjuring trick of perspective, showing Hitler's head sometimes the size of a watermelon and elsewhere as tiny as a shrunken Peruvian skull.

Parker knew that Hitler was usually seen as an excuse for actors to shout, but Albin Skoda ranted more effectively, being less certain, more betrayed, more divided, more medicated, more Austrian (which the actor was, like Hitler, whereas Ganz was Swiss). His one long internal monologue with puppet gestures out of sync with the voiceover split the man, telling Parker everything he needed to know about Hitler, drugs (he is shown getting his shots), the ups and downs (oh, those downs) and madness. The performance was allowed to verge on the grotesquely comic while understanding that there was nothing funny about it.

The soldiers around Hitler seemed to understand the uniforms they were wearing, when to salute with nonchalance and when to give it the full snap, presumably because many of the actors had been in the military, the film having been made only ten years after the war. (On the business of how to salute, Parker noted *The High Bright Sun*, another DVD acquired from a charity shop, about the British army in Cyprus, in which actors who had done National Service understood the nuances of the salute.)

Pabst hired Hitler's secretary Junge as technical consultant. *Downfall* was based on the same woman's memoirs, yet the two films couldn't have been more different, starting with a direction specific to Pabst (and what was direction about other than directing?). The philosophy was more Brechtian, as shown by a discussion between two extremely drunk officers: the futility of all human endeavour. Parker had seen Pabst's version of *The Threepenny Opera* at the NFT after coming out of the seminary, an atheistic piece which accorded to his unbelieving mood, as in Brecht's line, 'Human aspiration only makes me smile.'

The Last Ten Days featured lots of telecommunications (teleprinters, switchboards) and an increasing sense of being cut off: meaningless maps, all moral compass lost, with which Parker could identify. Its B-movie feel, avoiding the expensive but half-hearted action pieces of *Downfall*, suited the progression from companionable singalongs to sexual licence that climaxed with a drunken, crippled dance.

Skoda treated his Hitler as part of the ensemble, another performer there for the show, both together and alone, while presenting a complex portrait. The marriage scene – a matter of simple record in *Downfall* – becomes an essay in humiliation and social embarrassment, as in: what on earth am I doing? How did we get here? The actor's face shows that it is not really about marriage at all, certainly not one to be consummated, but the price being extracted by the woman for going along with him, a meaningless ritual that serves only as a portal to death.

Parker thought the story might as well be told in terms of the selective reality of its props and details: Ferragamo shoes (Braun's, reportedly worn for her death), birthday parties, lacklustre weddings, a surfeit of exclamations, damp concrete, fetid atmosphere, surreptitious smoking, a considerable wine cellar, six noisy Goebbels brats, four tiny new puppies (the last recorded photograph taken in the bunker) and, at the bitter end, their poisoned mother Blondi, with the litter also killed, still pressing against their mother's cold teats. The dog was dispatched because Goebbels was worried that the cyanide might be past its use-by date. Secretary Junge said that after Hitler had seen his dead dog, 'His face was like his own death mask. He locked himself in his room without a word.'

'I want to poison a dog,' Morgen told Sergei.

'What?'

'Hitler's dog was, as a test.'

'What will that show?' Sergei asked.

'That death by cyanide is a messier business than anyone's saying.'

A German doctor was in attendance, but Sergei ordered Morgen to administer the dose. Morgen wondered for a moment about taking it himself. He had to hold the mutt's jaws clamped shut as it ground its teeth and looked at him with beseeching, terrified eyes. Not quick or painless. It seemed to go on forever.

When the cur was at last still, it had messily voided itself and the room stank. Morgen asked the doctor to explain what they had just seen.

'Convulsions, dramatic thrashings, gasping for air. In humans, what is called opisthotonos, when the head and spine are forcibly extended backwards, is not uncommon, plus trismus, in which the jaw muscles clamp to produce a rictus grin. The body ends in total collapse.'

Morgen said, 'After what we have just seen, there is no way Braun would have not ended up in a heap on the floor.'

'Frothing at the mouth and shitting herself,' added the doctor with what sounded like relish.

Morgen thought to himself: Not one witness is credible.

Parker asked Robinson, 'Have you ever come across any reference to photographs being taken in the bunker?'

'Not that I've ever heard. Why do you ask?'

'Because Braun sent a picture of the dog's four newborn puppies to her best friend to pass on to her pregnant sister, with the message that the one marked with an arrow was for her.'

Robinson grunted. 'Interesting to know what else was on the roll. Führer happy snaps! Braun would have had a camera. She fancied herself. She had been a photographer's assistant. There were loads of pictures she took in the mountains and colour cine footage. Photos in the bunker? I don't see why not. There was little else to do down there. But there has never been a squeak on the market about any such product.'

Braun pointed the camera at Schlegel.

'Say "Ameisenscheiße".'

Schlegel dutifully did, showing his teeth while she took his photograph. They were sitting drinking at the time, fairly sloshed.

He asked, 'Are you allowed to? Security and all that.'

In common areas, signs forbade photography.

'If I'm careful, who's going to stop me?'

She developed the film in her room. A red silk scarf dimmed the light sufficiently to avoid overexposure.

It was the same photograph Katharina Fischer had given Parker, who examined it again and saw a haunted-looking

285

young man, older than but not so dissimilar to himself, apart from the prematurely white hair in need of a cut and an uneasy smile as he sat in an enclosed, low-lit, windowless space, looking warily at the camera.

It had taken Parker until then to realise the when and where of it: his grandfather, photographed in all likelihood by Eva Braun in the bunker, proof beyond doubt that he was there.

Hitler's obese doctor, Morell, to Schlegel: 'You might want one of these for when the time comes.' It was a cyanide phial. 'On the house. Plenty to go round.'

The mood below ground was heavily medicated: a cocktail of cheap stimulants and anti-depressants, and when there were no more pills, alcohol combined with energy drinks. It wasn't as though most of them had much to do. A terrific ennui clung to everything, which became a grand piece of anti-theatre.

The once charismatic Führer was a reduced to a flatulent, drooling, food-stained wreck, capable only of crazed mood swings, none of it quite real in any accepted sense of the term; a lot was hearsay, for no one saw him much. The raving madman was talked up by some, while others reported him as blank; heroin, had they known.

Morell, in exchange for having enough booze poured down his gullet, would entertain the listener, in this case Schlegel, with the full cornucopia of his master's medication: dexedrine, pervatin, cocaine, prozymen, ultraseptyl and anti-gas pills, as well as that wonder drug which reduced his master to inert bliss; in other words, said Bormann, would 'shut him up'.

Bormann, who could hold his drink, was drunk most

of the time, as were they all, playing cards for matchsticks, either gin rummy or Go Fish (Bormann, Schlegel, Fräulein Braun and Bormann's secretary Krüger, who ostentatiously fiddled with him under the table to distract him into losing, with him saying, 'This is such a hard hand to play' to general mirth). Goebbels made a show of being the loyal family man, but still with time to give the switchboard operator a knee-trembler; and she had fucked almost everyone. The uniforms started to look stupid as the men began to shrink inside them. A palpable funk added to the general stink of shit – the burrow where the animal goes to die; only a matter of time.

Morgen feared the worst when Natasha came to his quarters and announced that Sergei had been 'transferred'.

Never had the word sounded more loaded.

Morgen presumed he would be next, packed off to a gulag or worse. Russian purges were marked by an almost childish vindictiveness.

Natasha's manner seemed strangely uncertain for a change, so Morgen took a gamble and said, 'I want to see the forensic reports.'

He watched her frown. He found her furrowed brow attractive, which made him laugh, perhaps because it was the sort of detail that had been missing from his life for months.

She asked what was funny.

'The ridiculousness of the situation. I can't speak for you, but I think we are both in difficult positions.'

If the Russians were anything like the Germans, each department would have its own shadow with lethal rivalries, making finding the right path in any situation perilous. The Gestapo had been slow to punish its ranks. He expected the Russians were not.

He said, 'I believe the British are being credulous. Perhaps it suits them to draw a line. If bodies were found by the Russians, as originally stated, and autopsies performed – which I believe they were – why withhold the results?'

Morgen suspected Stalin, for whatever reason, had persuaded himself that Hitler was alive after all, otherwise why force the army to hold a press conference to deny deaths that had been previously announced?

'What do you care?' Natasha asked.

What was interesting about the question was it was the first time she had asked anything personal.

'Let's say I have always liked detective stories.'

Even so, he was surprised when the next day she drove him to a mostly intact hospital on the north-east outskirts, where they questioned a matronly woman in a white coat who was visibly afraid of Natasha's uniform. The woman wore thin, rimless glasses to consult her files, smoothing the pages with nervous hands.

Natasha seemed to become friendlier when dealing with death. The woman stated that she was Major Marantz, an anatomical pathologist.

Autopsies had first been done on Dr Goebbels, who had shot himself; a female corpse, also shot, thought to be his wife; and their six children, all poisoned in the bunker while lodging with their parents.

'The children's autopsies were straightforward,' Marantz said. 'Their bodies were found dead in bed. Goebbels, in spite of being burned, was identified by his still-intact metal leg brace and short stature. The only question was over the identity of the woman. On the grounds of expensive dentistry, she was assumed to be the wife and mother, but without proper records that couldn't be proved.'

Natasha had to translate, and it sometimes seemed questionable to Morgen, because her translation was often a lot shorter than the statement.

His transcript of Marantz's interview read: 'On 3 May, a body in the vicinity of the Chancellery thought to be Hitler was found in an empty water tank, along with many others. This was taken to be a case of mistaken identity when two further bodies – a man and a woman burned beyond recognition – were found buried in a crater, along with two dogs. Post-mortems were conducted (Documents 12 and 13). The woman was 150cm tall, aged between 30 and 40, with a shrapnel wound to the chest, sustained while alive because haemorrhaging had occurred. Glass splinters in the mouth indicated that a cyanide phial had been taken.'

Morgen asked, 'How fatal was the wound?'

'Terminal.'

'So this woman who was supposed to have died indoors chose to commit suicide with a handy cyanide capsule after being fatally injured by shrapnel?'

Marantz looked at them and said nothing.

Morgen went on. 'Despite fatal injuries to the thorax, the stated cause of death was cyanide.'

'That's what the report says.'

'Did you write the report?' he asked.

'I carried out the dissections.'

'The bodies were identified as Hitler and Braun.'

'Yes.'

'Based on?'

'Dental records. They are the only way to identify such damaged corpses.'

'"Dental records"?' echoed Natasha.

'The dental practice in question was still open.'

'When?'

'9 May.'

'Where?'

'Kurfürstendamm.'

'Lucky for you that normal service was resumed so quickly.'

Morgen thought it sounded almost as though the records had been waiting for someone to show up, as in: 'Oh, you need dental records for identification. Here they are, with technicians on hand to discuss them!'

In Braun's case, two identical dental bridges had been made for her sometime before. The one in the mouth of the female corpse matched the spare that was found in the Chancellery.

'Indicating that the corpse was Braun's?' Natasha asked.

Marantz nodded.

'What about the male corpse?'

'The three dental plates were Hitler's. The largest upper plate corresponded to records showing that the bridge had previously been sawn off in surgery.'

'Was any reason given?'

'Because of problems with an abscess underneath,' Marantz said. 'The same bridge was then reinserted. Dental x-rays taken at the time show that the severed edge of the bridge matched the one found.'

Natasha asked, 'And the given cause of death?'

Marantz stated, after consulting the file, though it was obvious that she knew the answer, 'As with the female corpse, there was a strong smell of cyanide about the body and the remains of a cyanide phial was found in the oral cavity.'

'Any gunshot wound?'

'No, but part of the back of the skull was missing.'

'Missing as in *lost*?' Morgen asked, incredulous.

'It was considered irrelevant to a diagnosis of death by cyanide.'

Natasha said, 'The officers of SMERSH who conducted the investigation have since been shown to have behaved precipitously and acted with far too much indulgence to the Fritzes.'

Marantz stared at her hands. If she distanced herself, she risked being accused of incompetence and political unreliability. If she now questioned the report, she could face punishment for not having spoken up earlier.

She rather cleverly offered a combination, saying it had been considered paramount to close the case and inconsistencies noted by her were overruled.

She said, 'The evidence was deemed sufficient for identification.'

'So the issue was who rather than how,' Natasha said.

'Yes.'

'And your thoughts now? Start with the woman.'

'I noted that the teeth had extensive decay and many were missing. Braun's dental record showed a much fuller set in good condition. There were other inconsistencies.'

Morgen asked, 'Did anyone note that a dental plate is a detachable item?'

Marantz waited a long time before answering. 'One such inconsistency was that Braun didn't need a plate, given the condition of her teeth.'

Natasha interrupted to ask, 'Are you telling us the plate was made solely for post-mortem identification?'

'Well, it did serve that purpose, I see that now.'

Natasha said, 'To be clear, had the plate been inserted in another mouth and matched the dental records, then the body could be assumed to be Braun's.'

Marantz didn't commit herself other than to open her hand to say that might be so.

'Inconsistencies,' Natasha repeated sternly.

Marantz gathered herself and went on. 'Forensic tests carried out on all six Goebbels children established beyond doubt cyanide poisoning.'

She trailed off, not sure how to continue.

Natasha prompted. 'You presumably carried out the same tests in Documents 12 and 13.'

'Yes, but the organs contained no trace of cyanide residue.'

'Meaning?' asked Morgen, baffled.

'Whatever they died from wasn't cyanide.'

'But the report states a strong smell of cyanide on both bodies,' Morgen said.

'If potassium cyanide is placed in the mouth, the smell will remain even after burning.'

'Introduced into the mouth after death, is that what you are saying?' Morgen asked.

Marantz answered, 'The glass splinters found were not consistent with the gnashing of teeth in extremis – they more resembled a single crushing of the phial to suggest suicide by cyanide.'

'Did none of this strike anyone as questionable?' he asked.

'They were concerned only that the dental records matched what they had.'

'Did you say so at the time?'

'No one was particularly interested in the woman. We were barely aware of who she was.'

Again, Morgen wondered if Braun had been in Berlin at all, and he asked, 'Could such a bridge have been made without her knowledge?'

Marantz answered, 'From a dental impression, probably.'

Natasha interrupted. 'Do you believe the male corpse was Hitler?'

'Yes. There was monorchism, which we'd had reports of.'

'Monorchism?'

'One testicle. The left was missing. The dental records were an exact match. Hitler had only five of his own teeth, all in the lower jaw. The others were metal, capped with porcelain. There were three plates altogether, all of which corresponded.'

Natasha asked sarcastically, 'Any more inconsistencies?'

Morgen thought that there were bound to be. The war had been over only a matter of days, and Berlin in chaos.

Marantz said, 'It was noted that the lower jaw had come loose and was unattached. But that's not impossible in a fire, which can destroy attaching ligaments. But fractures in the lower jaw made it probable that there had been recent tooth extraction.'

Natasha said, 'Meaning teeth had been removed so there were only five?'

Marantz sighed. 'Overall, I had no quarrel with the verdict.'

Natasha said, 'Unless you were dealing with a case of forensic fraud, which you failed to realise. Then what was the cause of the man's death, if not cyanide?'

Marantz paled, reluctant to commit herself, before carefully saying, 'I can't possibly say, based on a lack of evidence.'

Natasha snapped, 'You can say off the record, otherwise you will find yourself held for further questioning for withholding evidence.'

Morgen said, 'We are bound to ask if making it look like cyanide was to disguise the real cause of death.'

Marantz, looking miserable, repeated herself. 'I can't venture any medical opinion, as nothing is left to go on.'

Because of Natasha having to translate, Morgen couldn't be sure what exactly Marantz had said overall, whether he had missed something or Natasha had deliberately not passed it on, which left him asking himself: what is the story being told here? Who exactly is telling it, and to what end?

In Parker's mind, those last days in the bunker came to resemble a combination of soap opera and Buñuel's *The Exterminating Angel*, where party guests find themselves inexplicably unable to leave. The entrapped, distracted mood was caught in a letter written by Braun, dated 18 April, to her sister, complaining that her dressmaker was demanding 'thirty marks for my blue blouse, she's completely crazy, how can she have the face to charge thirty marks for such a trifle?'

The next day, she took her last walk in the Tiergarten and wrote to her best friend: 'As you can imagine, we're terribly short of sleep. But I'm so happy, especially at this moment, at being near him. Not a day passes without my being ordered to take refuge in the mountains, but so far I've always won.'

The little facts of life were set down by Bormann with exactitude, no detail too small; books borrowed, movies projected and always those meticulous lists of names. No alternative existed to contradict him. He made a careful record of those in the bunker – who came, when and why – one of the few documents recovered by the Soviets, raising doubts about its authenticity when it had probably been left on purpose, the point being that few of those named escaped the Russians.

Hitler's fifty-sixth birthday was on 20 April. Braun gave him a portrait of herself in a jewelled silver frame. After he retired for the evening, things livened up with a late-night party held upstairs in Braun's abandoned apartment, which

Bormann attended. There was a gramophone and only one record, 'Blood-red Roses Tell You of Happiness', played over and over. Braun was reported as dancing inexhaustibly. At the end, a heavy bombardment turned the sky red.

The next day, a general exodus took place. The women, including Braun, refused to leave, loyal to the last. Among those who went was Hitler's doctor, fired on the spot when a petulant Hitler screamed: 'Morell, get out of here! You're planning to knock me out and force me to leave Berlin! That's what you all want – but I'm not going!'

Morell's quarters were taken over by Magda Goebbels, who moved in with her children, of whom Braun complained in a letter, apologising for her distraction because 'G's six children are in the next room making an infernal racket.'

Hitler's medication was taken over by the resident surgeon Stumpfegger, a hulking giant and Bormann's drinking companion, commonly referred to as 'Stumpy'. Over the last days, this came down to endless fretting over the best way to commit suicide.

The end mood seemed less one of apocalypse than lethal banality, with fewer men and a staff of loyal and bewitched women, among them a cook whose menus included a last meal of pasta and tomato sauce.

That thin thread of narrative came down to what was said to have happened, but Parker found no mention anywhere of August Schlegel.

Morgen was arrested in the middle of the night, beaten and taken away with a hood over his head, thinking to himself that he needed a fast lesson in learning to take his punishment like a man. He had dished it out often enough with little thought for the consequences. After being driven for a long time, and further beatings, he found himself in a windowless cell with, of all men, Hitler's valet, Linge.

It took him longer than it should have done to work out that Natasha must be behind his arrest and was treating this punishment as a continuation of the investigation in the hope of him befriending Linge and getting him to admit to the charade and reveal the truth.

Linge was taken off for nine-hour interrogations, mostly at night, and was otherwise deprived of sleep, which didn't bother Morgen because he was able to rest while the man was gone, even though the light was left on all hours.

Linge was determined to stick to his story, which he shared with Morgen, putting a warning finger to his lips and looking upwards to suggest hidden microphones.

He announced, 'All this stupid questioning is because the Ivans want to mollify Stalin's phobia that the Führer might have outwitted him at the last.'

'How?'

Linge stonewalled, saying he could only report what he'd seen. He winked at Morgen. The wink became an irritating trope.

Sleep deprivation gave the man verbal diarrhoea – liquid, punch-drunk ramblings about what he had already told the Russians or rehearsing what he would say, interspersed with endless anecdotes about his master's greatness, which was marked by a genuine humility.

'What a shithole that bunker was!' Linge exclaimed. 'The Führer deserved better.'

Morgen asked about rumours of a double, and Linge said, 'Not that I heard, and I waited on the Führer hand and foot.'

'The Americans are saying the body wasn't his.'

'Pure fantasy, as you would expect from the Americans.

They are like children.' He laughed self-consciously, presumably for the microphones. 'I saw with my own eyes!'

Linge had worked on his story of the double suicide. Braun came and went like a faulty radio signal, but was there or thereabouts. Whereas his previous account had barely mentioned her, it was now full of snippets, such as how she had opted for poison after declaring that she wanted a beautiful corpse; how, even at the end, she was complaining about her dressmaker charging a small fortune.

Linge bolstered his version by assuming the role of the observant servant, deferring to others. These saccharine narratives were attributed to Hitler's secretary, Junge. How Braun, after a farewell embrace, had said, 'Give my love to Bavaria', and presented Junge with a silver-fox fur coat.

'She must have looked magnificent in that, making her getaway through the rubble of Berlin,' said Linge.

Linge had an eye for clothes in common with Junge, with whom he had discussed what Braun should wear for the wedding. 'One of her consort's favourites, a blue number with a scooped but decent neckline.'

Junge told him that she was upstairs helping feed the Goebbels children (fruit and ham sandwiches) when a shot rang out, so close that the eldest, nine-year-old Helmut shouted, 'Bang on target!'

Linge said he couldn't see how, because Junge wouldn't have been able to hear from where she said she was. He seemed to have forgotten his own inconsistencies. Linge respected her woman's eye for detail, how she pointed out what he hadn't noticed, how Junge – now an apparent witness to the death scene – noted that Braun had kicked off her buckskin shoes and pulled her feet up snugly under her lithe body, with her head resting comfortably on Hitler's shoulder.

Morgen saw that he wasn't going to get anything Linge wouldn't repeat to the Russians. Let them sort it out between them!

Cold, hunger and lack of proper sleep were starting to wear him down. He listened to Linge drone on, reciting the menus of state banquets, saying how the Führer wasn't the teetotaller of legend or even fully vegetarian, as they shared a liking for what Americans called hotdogs.

Sometimes Linge went into a paroxysm of rage about the unfairness of everything. Other times passed in weeping and despair before he rallied to pour forth a torrent of memories that sounded like more rehearsed performance.

'I remember someone asked why he used an army service pistol to shoot himself rather than one of his personal Walthers. At least it was an honourable death, the officer's way.'

And so on, round and round. The vision started to take on a life of its own. One day, in between drifting in and out of sleep, only to be woken by the guard rattling the cell bars, Linge said, 'They asked me again about the bullet hole and whether there were any traces of blood on the clothes. In fact, I had noticed a patch of blood on the right temple – a red dot – not exceeding the size of three stamps. I don't know if this was in reality a bullet hole – this stain could have been painted on.'

Morgen wondered whether the Russians had picked up on that, given that Linge insisted he had seen Hitler just after he shot himself, certainly before anyone could have doctored anything to resemble a bullet hole. Morgen had trouble picturing it: a red dot was quite a different size than three postage stamps.

Had Hitler not shot himself after all, then it was made to look as though he had?

This was nothing compared to what Linge told him next.

He gestured for Morgen to come and sit next to him on his cot and whispered, 'They will never crack me and never convict me, because only Bormann, Stumpfegger, Schlegel and I know the truth.'

'Schlegel?' Morgen asked, shaken.

As to what the real story was, Linge couldn't say, as he was sworn to secrecy. He smirked at Morgen and winked.

Schlegel saw Hitler once, shuffling alone down a corridor, looking lost. That said, the man gave him the rather charming, conspiratorial smile of one who believed he still had a card or two up his sleeve.

Schlegel wondered if the Führer knew about what Dr Goebbels called his 'script conferences'. Schlegel attended these on Bormann's insistence, probably to annoy Goebbels because he was seen as Bormann's man. The only others present were Bormann, when he could be bothered, and his secretary, Else Krüger.

The tiny doctor started by announcing, 'We have to get the ending right, give history good copy. I have sketched various scenarios.'

After he was finished, Krüger agreed that the proposal of a last-minute wedding was good.

'The woman's angle,' said Goebbels, nodding eagerly at her agreement. 'Moving on to what I call "the death pact",' he said, 'I have some reservations.'

Bormann looked bored. 'Yes, yes, a joint suicide, cultish, the couple entwined in death. What reservations?'

'He'll be up for it, but does she have the nerve? She made a mess of it when she tried to shoot herself when she was feeling neglected after the death of the Führer's beloved niece, Geli.'

'Yes, 1931. Attention-seeking,' said Bormann.

'Then the botched sleeping pills a couple of years later,' added Goebbels.

'Third time lucky,' Bormann said cheerfully.

'Any famous last words for him?' Goebbels asked facetiously.

'Geli, I would imagine,' said Bormann, quick to laugh at his joke, to which Goebbels snapped, 'She might have spared us all a lot of grief had she lived.'

'Or caused even more,' said Bormann tartly.

They moved on to the next part of what Goebbels was calling his masterplan.

'Muddy the waters! Complicate things! An alternative ending. The honourable death announced, then a hint of grand mischief,' he said, with his rictus grin. 'A sleight of hand, body doubles, forensic detail, abracadabra, the suggestion of a nick-of-time escape and the possibility that, Houdini-like, they might yet be alive ... and the legend lives on!'

Goebbels' every utterance was a tiresome exclamation.

'Meanwhile, the Führer's ashes will be conveyed as a holy relic to a sacred site, which will become a secret shrine for the Fourth Reich. That is the whole point of the exercise. Her ashes we probably needn't bother about.'

Somehow Braun found out. Schlegel suspected Bormann was using his secretary as a feed.

She insisted on attending the next meeting, telling Goebbels, 'As this is about the Führer, I insist on knowing what is going on.'

Bormann smirked. Goebbels summarised. Wedding. Suicide pact. Other bodies that could be shown to be hers and the Führer's.

300

'He won't agree to marry me anyway, and what is the point of this tomfoolery when the master and his wife are dead?' Braun asked reasonably.

Goebbels stared at the ceiling. 'Dental plates will be found corresponding to your records.'

'I still don't see the point, other than to test Russian medical efficiency,' said Fräulein Braun, again reasonably. 'Besides, I don't have a dental plate.'

Dr Goebbels showed his teeth and said, 'Dr Blaschke—'

'My dentist,' interrupted Braun.

'An appointment can be arranged for one to be made.'

'As I said, I don't need a plate.'

'For the purpose of identification, corresponding to the record.'

Goebbels was growing impatient, but Braun insisted on carrying on.

'Either the Russians will believe the bodies are those of the master and his wife, or they won't. Again, what is the point?'

'If they see through the subterfuge, they will believe that the Führer might have escaped after all! Which will set the cat among the pigeons!'

Braun found that funny, saying, 'Then why don't we cut the nonsense and take our leave? I know in the end I can persuade him to retreat to the mountains to fight another day.' Bormann raised his eyebrows at that as Braun went on. 'He never liked Berlin. He will sacrifice it to save his mountains.'

Schlegel watched her carefully. She'd clearly had something in mind before coming to Berlin, but then she shrugged and said, 'Someone had better make me an appointment. Even the dentist is better than being cooped up down here.'

Braun looked at Schlegel and flashed him something between a grimace and a smile as she stood to go, saying, 'And while someone is about it, they can book me a ticket on the next Lufthansa flight to Madrid.'

Goebbels believed she was serious until she, rather wittily in Schlegel's opinion, added an exclamation in the manner of the man being addressed, 'Oh, Josef, you never did have much of a sense of humour!'

Goebbels laughed extra loudly.

Thus, Schlegel thought to himself, Dr Goebbels' version of *Twilight of the Gods*, operatic nonsense, rewriting history before it was written.

Morgen's incarceration ended as suddenly as it had begun. He was returned to Camp Seven as though nothing had happened, to find himself back in his old room where he was debriefed by Sergei, who reappeared as mysteriously as he had vanished. Morgen was reminded of a weather house where one of two figures appeared depending on the forecast, and he wondered if Sergei and Natasha operated in a similar way.

Sergei asked about Linge. Morgen explained how he had been reminded of play rehearsals: after a lot of uncertainty, everyone had just about learned their lines, albeit with contradictions.

'To what end?'

'To conform to how they want the end to be remembered. Linge implied that Hitler might not have shot himself, but the scene was rearranged to make it look as though he had. But he insists he's dead.'

'And this report of Braun's body not being hers?

'It's my opinion she was never there.'

'Then where is she?'

'Dead or hiding, it hardly matters. The accounts of the end

are all very gemütlich. Linge was sketchy on Braun at first, but he now has her square in the picture.'

Sergei said, 'I personally have never heard of a single case where husband and wife commit suicide together using different methods.'

Morgen decided not to mention Linge reporting about Schlegel and the others. He would rather follow that up on his own if he ever got the chance.

Morgen missed Natasha but resisted asking. He sensed things had moved on. He asked Sergei what the latest thinking was on Hitler.

Sergei said, 'Reports have been submitted, a few heads have rolled. Your supposition that the man was both dead and alive went down well, as it was never seen as a case of either/or, more a question of position. Stalin is desperate to know what really happened, so I suspect evidence will soon be produced to show that the body known as Document 13 was shot after all. Anyway, the Americans are interested in you, and in the name of international cooperation we're sending you off to Zehlendorf, where they have much better canteens.'

There was no sting in the tail. That was that. Sergei parted with a warm, dry handshake and a hint of a smile, as if to say that Morgen was luckier than he knew being able to walk out alive into a cold world of anticlimax.

Bormann asked Schlegel, 'Well, Mr Detective, are you any further on with the business of that leak? Soldatensender Calais is still banging on about a Russian spy in the house.'

Schlegel hadn't done much about it, other than pull a couple of names out of the hat, including an unpopular adjutant who was known to dislike Bormann (as everyone did,

303

leaving Schlegel not short of future suspects). Mention of the adjutant's name was enough to have him transferred to active duty. But the leaks had continued.

The obvious suspect was Fegelein, which didn't require any great sleuthing powers. For a start, there was the Irish woman, Molly Fitzgerald, in Berlin according to Braun. Schlegel was sure Fitzgerald was milking Fegelein.

The only reason he hadn't mentioned this was because Bormann and Fegelein were huge drinking buddies and fellow cocksmen, sharing women. Besides, Fegelein had been absent for a while. He was said to be gathering a battalion to fight his way out of Berlin and continue resistance in Bavaria, where he would join his wife, who was about to deliver their firstborn.

Curious about Molly Fitzgerald, he went one evening to the Adlon, which was only a short walk away. The cold air cleared his head. The hotel remained open, operating in part as a military hospital, but still taking guests. Since he was last there, a huge ugly brick wall had been built in the lobby to protect the function rooms from flying debris. The hotel was surprisingly crowded with nervous groups getting sloshed. He asked at the desk if Molly Fitzgerald was staying and wasn't altogether surprised to find she was. He asked to leave a message and was told she was in her room. He spoke to her on the desk telephone, reminding her of their brief encounter in Zurich.

'Oh, I see,' she said, adding suggestively that she was about to go to bed but could meet him downstairs in ten minutes.

She took her time; a woman's prerogative, Schlegel shrugged to himself, then worried she might have slipped out the back. She eventually turned up, immaculately dressed and in control, ordering drinks, a dry martini for

304

her, insisting they sit in the lobby because she liked to watch the passers-by.

'What brings you here?' she asked.

Schlegel said he happened to be working round the corner, which seemed to amuse her. 'And you?' he asked.

Because of her husband. 'The Hungarian diplomat,' she said. 'Maybe I mentioned him. It's all getting rather hairy, isn't it?'

Thinking they might end up just having a social drink after all, Schlegel pulled himself together and asked, 'Have you seen Hermann?'

'Hermann?' It was obvious she knew who he meant.

'Fegelein. He owes me. Gambling debts.'

She asked, 'How did you know I was here?'

'I heard you were in Berlin, and you have a taste for first-class hotels.'

'Not many to choose from these days. I preferred the Kaiserhof, but alas, no more.'

Before he could go on, he was accosted by a voice behind him, announcing in English, 'August Schlegel! What on earth are you doing here?'

It was the dubious Irishman, Francis Alwynd, 'lecturer and lecher,' as he sometimes introduced himself. He stood there with his usual bemused air, looking like a man not sure how he came to be there. Alwynd usually wore sandals and corduroys, but he had on a thick tweed suit and looked like a man about to appear in court. Schlegel suspected he had come over only because he'd spotted him with a beautiful woman.

He introduced them, saying that Alwynd was a fellow countryman of hers. 'He teaches at the university.'

Molly, it turned out, knew he was a writer and had read

305

one of his books, *The Pigeon Loft*, saying, 'I wondered what had happened to you.'

Alwynd looked bashful. To take the wind out of the man's sails, Schlegel added, 'Francis has done quite a lot of broadcasting, too.'

'I wouldn't say that,' Alwynd muttered. 'Well, as a republican and a neutral. Can I get you two a drink?'

Alwynd was not a man known to pay for anything. He looked compromised and nervous. Schlegel supposed the Allies would have him down as a collaborator.

Schlegel said, 'Later, perhaps.'

Alwynd shuffled off. Schlegel presumed he was hoping to run into someone from the Foreign Ministry and attempt to wheedle his way out.

Molly asked, 'How do you know him?'

'Ran into each other at parties,' Schlegel offered and left it at that. He caught her eye and held it. If she was nervous, she hid it well. At least the interlude had concentrated his mind enough to address what he wanted to say.

'As for our mutual friend Hermann, I am sure his pillow talk has outlived its usefulness. It's too late now for any business with Dulles and the Americans.'

She cocked her head, waiting.

'If you tell me where he is, I'll make sure you're safe.' He watched her consider and added, 'I would say it's pretty obvious you are a spy.'

'It takes one to know one. Cheers!'

He said lightly, 'We could always have you shot. There's a lot of it going on.'

Given her stony reaction, he backtracked.

'Anyway, this conversation is probably academic. I hear Hermann's away.'

Molly got out a cigarette and took her time, expecting him to light it. He didn't have matches, and they were well past the stage of the hotel providing complimentary ones. She handed over her lighter, and he cupped the flame as she leaned into it, delicately balancing the cigarette, holding his eye.

He watched the end catch, snapped the lighter shut and handed it back. She took it with her free hand, brushing his so subtly that he couldn't tell if she was being suggestive.

As she blew smoke out of the side of her mouth, she said, 'Talking of going away.'

'Still in town?'

'Very much. At his apartment in Bleibtreustrasse.'

'Any plans to see him?'

'As you say, probably outlived his usefulness. Anyway, a plane's coming to pick him up, he says. Always a big talker, Hermann.'

She didn't know the number of the apartment, and he could see he wouldn't get any more out of her. He found he was unwilling to leave. Given the uncertainty of everything, transitions were always difficult. They slowly finished their drinks, talking about this and that – the hotel mainly.

'The service remains good,' Molly said. 'Lucky it's still open. But for how much longer . . . ?'

'Then I suppose it will be borscht on the menu.'

They both found that funnier than it was, and the atmosphere between them was suddenly febrile and electric.

The contrast with the bunker couldn't have been more marked: civilised drinks; the strained chatter that pretended everything still passed for normal; an attractive, sexually active woman; their speaking English, which seemed to bother nobody; a sense of last days and desperate couplings. Schlegel thought about the woman in the Munich bomb

307

shelter, fixing him with her lustful gaze, and was wondering whether to make a pass when Molly said, 'The beds are comfortable.'

He hadn't gone expecting anything. What was happening had nothing to do with seduction. She probably relished adventure and that extended to the bedroom.

He followed her upstairs, noting her tight skirt and slim ankles. She had flawless white skin, the sort that wouldn't tan. He wondered what her nipples were like. He never found out, as they barely undressed.

None of it had much to do with him, he thought afterwards. He was expertly used and discarded. No preliminaries, no kissing. She told him everyone had bad breath these days. When he tried fondling her, she said, 'There's no need for that. I'm ready.'

The woman could have been masturbating, given how little it involved him. She did it with her eyes shut, away somewhere else. She smelled of the same perfume as Braun. Whatever was going on in her head, Schlegel suspected it was to do with not having to fuck Hermann.

Afterwards she was friendlier, saying, 'Nothing like a good hotel room grind. Monkeys in the zoo. I hope we both get out of this alive.'

He stood uncertainly, not sure if he had satisfied her or whether he was supposed to offer dinner.

She seemed to read his thoughts. 'It's all right, off you go,' she said. 'We've done everything we need to.'

She at least sounded good humoured about it.

The air raid sirens started as he was leaving, and he hurried back to the bunker. In its sealed space, the sirens could no longer be heard. He ran into Fräulein Braun looking troubled.

'There's another raid,' he said rather meaninglessly.

'Why don't we have a drink, then?' she said. 'The chief's asleep.'

She sneaked him through their quarters, past his bedroom, like they were a couple of kids. Drinks were three bottles of champagne.

'Properly chilled this time,' she said, referring to the warm fizz they had drunk in the car.

As their relationship became more confidential (or desperate, depending on how one saw it), she took to inviting him regularly for these late-night sessions. They had to be done after the Führer announced that he was retiring, but it was never a guaranteed safe passage as the man was a notorious insomniac. Once Schlegel was surprised by the valet Linge, who bowed obsequiously and said nothing but must have reported to Bormann, who said, 'I hear you have become a listening post for Fräulein Braun. What's her current position?'

'Undecided.'

Bormann grunted. 'No shortage of champagne, I hear.'

Each time began with Braun offering yet another version of: my dream was that the Chief would marry me. At that point, the sniffles would start. 'If he did, it means I would have to stay and die with him, so he refuses, as I knew he would.'

With the quantities drunk, everything blurred and repeated. Schlegel was told over again how in the Führer's lucid moments he knew he was finished and insisted, 'Make the best you can of it. Get out and live your life. No one knows about you or us.'

'What can I do?' she asked repeatedly. 'I am treated as a nonentity. Even if by some miracle we get out, there is no future.'

She dithered between going and staying, dying beside her man or being reduced to a state of funk.

On another occasion, she announced that the Führer was apparently having a change of heart about marriage.

'In which case, I will have to stay and face the music.' She looked less than certain about that. 'I still dream of taking him away. Bormann is shipping tons of stuff to South America. We could live in the mountains. I would take care of him and ride.'

Schlegel remembered her making a case for herself with desperate conviction. 'Oh, I know I am written off as a decorative companion rather than a politically committed woman who won his affections, enjoyed a healthy sex life with him, sympathised with his politics and gave him psychological support, unlike that flibbertigibbet niece.'

He wondered about the healthy sex life, but who was he to say? Everyone's sex life is a mystery.

She remained jealous of any rivals, which invariably came up around the time they hit the third bottle; especially the promiscuous niece, who thirteen years after her death still cast a long shadow.

'I think the Chief was terribly hurt by that. He would have given Geli everything, but she was a bubblehead, only interested in shopping and him buying her things and paying for singing lessons when she could barely hold a tune.'

Braun went blank. Schlegel was by then familiar with her way of deflating.

'What do *you* want?' he asked.

'If only I knew!'

Schlegel listened to her go round in circles until she clenched her fist and exclaimed, 'He is so stubborn, but I will have my way!'

Schlegel asked if she had a plan after all.

She shrugged helplessly and started crying.

'He knows however much I love him, I am not ready to die. I tried killing myself twice and I'm not much good at it. But I want my name to be remembered with his.'

But nobody has the faintest idea who you are, Schlegel said to himself.

Parker often found himself thinking: if the English major was misled about the bunker, then the timing and method of Hitler's end was almost immaterial. Bormann had controlled the man's diary for years, which amounted to writing his life. He remained in constant attendance, detailing the trivia of each day when everyone else was saying the space-time continuum had collapsed, with everything eventually dominated by absence: no briefing sessions, no more fixed schedules, no more maps spread out on the table; doors wide open; nobody bothered with anything anymore.

Perhaps it was why *Downfall* worked as a fiction and one in which Bormann barely featured, as he would have wanted.

Parker was also struck by the English major's convenient discovery of key documents in the winter of 1945. By his account, after a lot of chasing around, Bormann's adjutant was traced to Bavaria, where he was working as a gardener. Following a tip-off about a suitcase belonging to him being hidden in a house in a quiet lakeside resort south of Munich, it was found and confiscated. A thorough search proved disappointing until a secret compartment was discovered.

This was starting to sound like bad spy fiction until it occurred to Parker that the major was being given the run-around. The secret compartment turned out to contain papers of huge political significance: Hitler's Last Will and

Testament, Goebbels' appendix to the testament and Hitler's wedding certificate, smuggled out of the bunker only 48 hours before the end.

Bormann's adjutant was subsequently arrested and confirmed many details which corresponded to what the English major had gathered from less well-placed sources.

Had the major been played? Parker thought he had, rather well. The Germans couldn't have hoped for a better choice: an arrogant, unimaginative and susceptible man who saw himself wrestling with an intellectual puzzle, not realising that a frame was being put around him: oh, look, here's a suitcase with a secret compartment we didn't want you to find! How clever to have hunted it down! It proves what we've been saying all along!

After Michail, Robinson went to ground; better safe than sorry and all that. He didn't want two gentleman callers like the last time, coming round to break his wrists. Just a warning, he was told then. He still had time before payday. There was something childish and indulgent about the Russian threats. They could be fobbed off up to a point. They never seemed in any hurry. When it came to revenge as a dish best eaten cold, they could make the Italians look impetuous. Robinson knew of long-forgotten cases where they had struck late and decisively.

He bunkered down for a few days in West Hampstead, staying with his wife and her kid in Dresden Close, off Lymington Road. The woman kept an orderly house, and he went for a bit of peace and quiet, which he got, mainly spent watching episodes of *Family Guy* with the boy. He could never decide whether the boy was his or not. They rubbed along well enough without Robinson ever being sure if the boy thought of him as a father.

Parker knew about Dresden Close, but it didn't occur to him that Robinson might be there. Among his occasional errands was the delivery of envelopes to the address. The first two times, the boy had answered and taken the envelope without comment. Parker supposed him about six or seven and noted a lazy eye, which gave him an almost feral look.

The third time, a strikingly attractive woman of around thirty came to the door, accepted the envelope and said in accented English, 'You don't look as bad as he said.'

He had asked Robinson about her and was told that she was from Romania and Robinson had married her to allow her to stay in the country; to fuck the Home Office more than anything. At a perfunctory registry office wedding, Robinson had insisted they play Simon and Garfunkel's 'Mrs Robinson', a song he detested, which nevertheless seemed to have found its place, as it amused his bride to be formally addressed as Mrs Robinson.

Parker, meanwhile, remained so immersed that it was only when he wanted to ask Robinson something he realised he wasn't there. He called Vod to see if he knew where he was.

'Gone to ground, I expect,' Vod said. 'He does that from time to time.'

'Do you know where?' Parker asked.

'Probably holed up in one of the crappy hotels his father owns in North London. I drove him to see Michail, and afterwards he told me to drop him off at Bank Station. A bit odd that, because as far as I know the man hasn't been on a tube in years.'

Parker continued to bury himself in his work, like a detective interpreter of past texts, until the whole cast ended up inhabiting the same dreamscape: August Schlegel, Braun,

Morgen, Molly Fitzgerald, H., the commandant, Father Roper, Robinson, Vod and all the nameless dead. H. he came to regard as an alter ego, because she was the most psychologically damaged. He and Robinson had put her in the role of informant and collaborator, which Parker suspected he would be, too, under the wrong circumstances.

He disregarded the present because he believed both it and he were infected by the past. He became distracted by every noise in the house as it creaked and groaned – pipes, radiators, floorboards, new cracks appearing in the walls. Sometimes he believed he could feel the building settling on its foundations, prior to collapsing.

He went running to break the spell, pounding the streets, or sat in the church in Quex Road without bothering to seek out the priest; all that struck him as pointless now.

Robinson, meanwhile, asked himself: what is the worst that can happen? The Russians might send a big van and take everything, including the film and editing equipment, and they might break his legs or worse if he were around. As for stringing them along, he had told them the funds had been diverted into the land grab around the Olympic site and they'd get a big future payday – the long money. He was doing them a favour, the film was unreleasable crap, but he wasn't sure how long the argument would hold.

After that, he moved to his mother's care home, which had guest rooms, and spent his afternoons with her watching racing on the television. Her not being able to remember anything left him wondering what was worth remembering anyway.

He made various calls, including several to Halliday, his old man's accountant. He wondered if his father knew that Halliday was a paedophile, because it was pretty obvious.

Eventually he got around to calling Vod, saying he needed to see a man about a dog, and told him to bring Parker.

As the Russians advanced, whole chunks of the city disappeared under their ceaseless pounding. Schlegel heard of one Soviet contingent fighting in historical costume after raiding the wardrobe department at Babelsberg Studios.

The drinking with Braun now ended with them passing out. The first time, Schlegel woke up and staggered off so blind drunk he could hardly see. After that, Braun set an alarm clock, saying, 'The others will be completely out of it, but it's probably better if we aren't found by that creepy valet, Linge, then people really will start to talk.'

Her room was in disarray when it was usually immaculate. Drawers were open, possessions lying around. Braun seemed unusually hyperactive.

She had lost a watch. 'A Lange & Söhne, engraved with my initials.' She had been given it by *him*, she said, with a desperate jerk of the head in the direction of the Führer's quarters.

They were on their second or third bottle, interspersed with sporadic, futile searches for the watch, when Braun announced in tears, 'I have agreed to go.'

'To leave?' He sounded stupid saying it.

'A plane will land in the Tiergarten and take me out.'

'Well, probably for the best,' Schlegel said, doubting if that would be the last of it. 'What made up your mind?'

'Is it made up?' she wailed. 'The Chief and I had another row. Marriage is out of the question. I told him I am, of course, willing to stay as his wife, to which he said what he wants most is for me to live and cherish his memory.'

'I am sure it's the right decision,' Schlegel said, sounding like a speak-your-weight machine. The glass in front of him was going in and out of focus.

'When do you go?' he asked.

'As soon as a plane can come. Goebbels wanted to put me on a flight to Madrid, but I made him agree it was on condition that I was taken to the mountains.'

She started fretting about how to say goodbye to 'her man'. Her shoulders slumped as she looked around the room and asked Schlegel to get down a suitcase from on top of the wardrobe, saying she wasn't tall enough without standing on a chair.

'I hate packing.'

As Schlegel was leaving, she took both his hands and pleaded, 'Swear on something for me. Make sure he comes to no harm, except on his own terms.'

Schlegel muttered some banality about how he was sure they would all look after his best interests.

She shook her head. 'No, they're sending me away so they can get rid of him. They're all plotting against him now. Himmler, Göring ... Goebbels and Bormann are no different. Swear you will look after him. He should at least be allowed to be the master of his own fate.'

Schlegel couldn't see what earthly difference he could make.

Schlegel was right about that not being the last of it, because Braun's destiny was decided by Hermann Fegelein after he telephoned to tell her he was getting out of Berlin and she should join him; the rest could go to hell.

Schlegel happened to be with Bormann when the conversation was reported by the switchboard, which was listening in. Bormann said there wasn't much he could do, because

316

Fegelein hadn't said where he was. Schlegel was struck by the extraordinary hunch that it was Bormann himself who was the source of the leaks. After all, he had initiated the contact with Dulles and the Americans. Perhaps it suited him to pass on information, true and false, to give himself credit with the men who would become the next masters.

Fuck Fegelein, Schlegel decided. He found one of the man's ADCs and asked which number Bleibtreustrasse. The man claimed not to know until he was told he could join the queue for those to be shot. Schlegel found three drunk policemen sitting around and ordered them to follow him. He requisitioned a vehicle from the motor pool after some haggling. 'State security!' he barked and got his way.

They saw nothing of the city in the fifteen-minute drive, other than the dim tunnel of night barely illuminated by the shrouded headlights and a sullen egg-yolk glow to the sky.

Fegelein answered the door with an unlit cigarette stuck in his mouth, clearly expecting someone else. He feigned nonchalance. He was very drunk and not in uniform, wearing a silk shirt and expensive-looking trousers with the braces hanging down.

'Not a good time,' he slurred. 'Urgent business for the Führer.'

Schlegel said it couldn't wait and herded Fegelein inside.

Molly Fitzgerald was sitting in an armchair with her legs crossed, and smoking a cigarette. She seemed amused by Schlegel's arrival, as though it made the situation more interesting.

Fegelein stood slack-faced, waiting for an explanation. The policemen looked embarrassed, thinking Schlegel had exceeded his brief. They were dealing with an SS general, after all.

A suitcase lay open on a table. A cursory inspection revealed jewellery and expensive watches, gold and silver coins, a huge amount of German marks and Swiss francs.

Fegelein said, 'Ask the Führer. It's on his instructions and all accounted for.'

One of the watches was a woman's Lange & Söhne. Schlegel saw the engraved initials 'EB'. He ordered one of the policemen to count the money and told Molly Fitzgerald to show him the rest of the apartment. She stubbed out her cigarette, looking nervous for the first time. Schlegel realised that his pistol was in his hand, unaware that he had drawn it. He followed her, inspecting the other rooms, which revealed a man in the process of clearing out. The bed was unmade. Schlegel pocketed the pistol and checked the window, which opened. It was a ground floor apartment.

He said, 'I'll tell them I've locked you in here while a search is made.'

Molly smirked and said, 'Hermann has trouble getting it up these days, so you know.'

Schlegel nodded towards the window and said, 'At least you're wearing flat heels.'

Molly smiled ruefully. 'At least give us a hand.'

He helped her out, and the last he saw of her she was crossing the yard. He went back and found the policeman still counting the money like he could barely add up.

Fegelein snapped, 'There's over a hundred thousand marks and three thousand Swiss francs. I am under orders to return to the mountains to carry on the fight.'

Wondering if the man was right after all, Schlegel almost lost his nerve as he said, 'I'm arresting you for deserting your post.'

Fegelein protested. 'Stop being an idiot!'

318

They sounded like bad actors in an even worse film.

Schlegel turned to the nearest policeman and said, 'Just handcuff him, for fuck's sake.'

One of the men asked about the woman.

Schlegel said, 'Forget her. She has diplomatic immunity.'

'Shouldn't we let her out?'

'I'm sure she'll find her own way in due course.'

Schlegel spent the next fifteen minutes listening to Fegelein whining in the car.

'You've got this all wrong. My wife's having a baby. Fräulein Braun's sister, in case you need reminding. The Führer will hit the roof.'

When that got him nowhere, he started wheedling. 'What say you drop me off and I'll pay you for the ride, fifty-fifty, between four of you, that's not bad, is it?'

Schlegel was sitting in front, with Fegelein behind in the middle. He glanced at the driver, who appeared interested by the offer.

Schlegel laughed and said, 'You can add attempted bribery to the charges.'

News of Fegelein's arrest was all over the bunker within five minutes. Braun sought Schlegel out to berate him, saying, 'He's family! The baby's due any day.'

Schlegel answered, 'He was with a woman. They didn't look like they were on their way to Bavaria.'

Braun stamped her foot. 'I can't leave now, not at all, not with this to sort out! Hermann's a rat, but he is my brother-in-law, and the baby can't be born an orphan.'

The crisis overrode any thought of her leaving.

Schlegel produced the Lange & Söhne and said, 'I believe this is yours.'

'Oh, bless you! Where was it?'

Schlegel feebly offered, 'It's back safe now,' wondering if she thought he might have stolen it. He said, without meaning to, 'Hermann had it,' and added that among the contents of his case he had found papers proving a conspiracy.

'Against the Führer?' she asked.

'Himmler's peace negotiations, proclaiming himself the Führer's successor.'

Braun insisted he go with her to Bormann's office. When he questioned his need to be there, she grasped his wrist and earnestly scanned his eyes. 'We are beyond trust now, and you may well betray me, but at least you will be a witness to my intentions.'

She announced to Bormann, 'Now we know that Hermann is a traitor, there can be no mercy. Family considerations no longer count.'

Bormann, taken aback by the woman's imperative, demanded, 'Have you talked to the Führer?'

'I know his thoughts. Besides, we're all aware that Hermann probably isn't even the father.'

Bormann smirked. Later, he told Schlegel that the sister was incapable of keeping her hands off men.

A bottle of rum stood on the desk. Bormann produced three small glasses, poured shots and said, 'A last toast to Hermann, then.'

Braun said, 'Make mine a double.'

Bormann laughed and filled her glass.

Braun said, 'To a common thief and adulterer.'

'Cheers!' said Bormann before turning to Schlegel. 'You take care of the man. You were responsible for his arrest, finish the job.'

There was no question of putting together a firing squad. Schlegel fetched the three arresting policemen, who were lolling around in a state of stupefaction, and collected a sub-machine gun from the armoury.

Fegelein was in no fit state to be properly shot, being more drunk than ever after being liberally supplied. He giggled as though he had one up on them. His cell reeked of piss and vomit. When Schlegel said he was to be executed and ordered him to stand, Fegelein refused and demanded a priest to give him the last rites.

Schlegel looked at the men. 'A priest?'

He supposed Fegelein was entitled to one. He sent one of the men off to make enquiries. Fegelein clasped Schlegel's legs and begged for mercy, a sight so unedifying that he almost felt sorry for the man. He kicked himself free and walked out, trying not to shake, followed by the other two. Fegelein was reduced to howling.

They stood in the empty corridor waiting for the return of the third policeman. The sound of running footsteps was followed by the sight of the Goebbels boy charging round the corner. He paused on hearing Fegelein's screeching, then ran up and stood listening, before delivering his verdict.

'A coward like that deserves to die like a dog.'

'Fuck off, son,' said one of the men, sounding not unfriendly.

The boy gave a smart salute and a 'Heil Hitler!' before running back the way he had come, as the policeman returned, shaking his head, to announce, 'What chance of finding a priest in hell?'

Schlegel ordered the men to take Fegelein out to the garden. The man had to be dragged, writhing and screaming, leaving a trail of urine. He messily shat himself, and at that the policemen dropped him and stood back waving their hands at the stink while Fegelein curled into a ball.

Schlegel handed the gun to one of the men, gestured to another and told him to grab one of Fegelein's wrists. He took the other, and they pulled him the rest of the way while the man screamed in a piercing falsetto.

Schlegel was supposed to read an order of military execution. Fegelein was meant to stand against a wall. There was no light to read by, and Fegelein was incapable of remaining upright and fell to his knees, dry retching and crawling in circles, mewling like a baby.

Schlegel retrieved the gun as Fegelein managed to kneel up, hands clasped in supplication, and more or less coherently rambled on about the child he would never see. He caught Schlegel's eye and said, 'How can you deny that child a father?'

Schlegel's finger was frozen on the trigger. One of the men pointed out that the safety catch was on. Two of them started laughing as Schlegel released the catch. The gun's kick surprised him, and it fired high into the wall. The men were laughing even harder. He dragged his aim down. Fegelein's mouth was a screaming 'O' as the top of his skull flew away, his face turned to red pulp and the impact threw him back. Even that wasn't enough. With half his head and face missing, Fegelein managed to struggle onto all fours.

Schlegel refused him the coup de grâce. He handed the gun to one of the policemen and said, 'Let him die in his own time and wait here until he does.'

With that, he left. The last he heard, Fegelein was still squealing.

'Where to, boss?' Vod asked Robinson.

Robinson didn't say. They were standing in the lobby of his mother's care home. If the night nurse was surprised by this impromptu nocturnal gathering, she showed no sign of it. Parker assumed she had been charmed by Robinson.

Vod looked around and asked, 'Thinking of moving in?'

Robinson grunted. 'Any port in a storm.'

He started by insisting on a detour through East London to the Olympic Games site, a flat, barren wasteland where teams of nightshift workers in yellow jackets laboured under arc lights. Robinson got out, and Parker watched him speak at length to a man wrapped in a heavy overcoat. An envelope was given to the man. Robinson got back in, complaining, 'Fucking Jesus, Japanese knotweed is costing eighty million quid to get rid of. Now, let's see that man about a dog.'

They drove on: the beat of the windscreen wipers as it started to rain, the smear of traffic film reducing visibility, half a tank of petrol. Robinson told Vod to find some music.

Vod turned off the motorway, and they drove east into the Fens, down flat roads as straight as an arrow until you decided they ran that way for ever and met a vicious dog-leg bend. 'Steady on,' said Vod as they slewed round a corner. He drove on full beam, not bothering to dip for the occasional car that trundled past, leading to flashed exchanges. The night landscape looked like an unfinished drawing: black sky bisected by the darker line of the land, canals as oily as sluggish mercury.

Schlegel decided that what tipped the ending was the news that Braun's beloved mountain retreat had been bombed after she had agreed to go, and her decision not to was because she had nowhere left, and she used Fegelein's arrest as her excuse to stay.

Nevertheless, her transformation was extraordinary after her brother-in-law's death.

A woman of resolve emerged, against any expectation.

323

Schlegel watched as she shaped her previous indecision into coherence.

Secret meetings were not so difficult by then, as they were all looking to save their skins. Braun took Schlegel to the boiler room on the upper level, where she told him, 'I am going to do what I have always been quite good at – make up a romantic story. I knew the Chief would reject marriage, but I want the world to know about our love.'

'What will you do?'

'Mourn him and cherish his memory as he asks. Our course is run. He is old and sick, and I know from experience that I am not one of life's carers. I can sell this to Goebbels at the drop of a hat. It will infuriate Bormann and the wretched Linge. Now we need to talk to Goebbels, and I want it witnessed.'

We? thought Schlegel to himself. It was as though Hitler had already ceased to exist.

Goebbels was in his room, drinking and trying to read a book. He had grown increasingly shifty in the last few days, no longer capable of believing his own hot air. Family life was cramping the man's style. The children moving in had been on the insistence of his wife, an hysteric who spent most of her time in a state of collapse, which left Goebbels with the kids on his hands.

'What can I do for you, dear lady?' he asked listlessly.

In an assured voice, Braun told him that she was tired of going along with things and it was time to defy the passive role ascribed to her and take charge.

She said, 'First, I insist that a wedding is shown to have taken place with a proper certificate.'

Goebbels went along, with an effort at enthusiasm.

'Yes! Yes! I will organise a tame official.'

'I am adamant that the Chief should not be seen to have

died alone. The death pact will be said to have taken place and the staff informed.'

'You mean, without it happening?'

Goebbels really did look like a man out of ideas.

'Just as the marriage won't happen but will be shown to have.'

'Yes, of course,' said Goebbels, slow to take on board what she was saying.

She went on, 'You then vouch for our deaths, and the rest will believe what they are told.'

'Yes. I suggest Linge, myself and Bormann. We can keep our mouths shut.'

'Why Linge? The man's as thick as two short planks.'

Goebbels threw back his head and tried to laugh, but nothing came out other than a strangled gargle. Eventually he managed, 'I can handle Linge and turn his stupidity to our advantage. What else?'

'The Chief will be cremated and his ashes given to me to take to the mountains.'

'I have said as much myself – the secret shrine for the future glory!'

Braun faltered before adding, 'If I make it.'

'Destiny will guide your hand,' said Goebbels fatuously. 'It's the perfect solution, as they won't be looking for a woman.'

'As for the rest,' she said, 'the two substitute bodies need to be prepared.'

Schlegel thought it rather brilliant how Braun proposed to write herself out of the story; in effect, controlling the endgame. One escapes, the other doesn't, with the substitute bodies indicating that they had both died. Whether she or any of them had a chance in hell of getting out was another matter. Goebbels looked relieved at being absolved of responsibility.

Braun said, 'I presume there are plans for an evacuation.'

'Of course,' said Goebbels.

Schlegel wondered about that. He was sure it would come down to *sauve qui peut*, with no concern for women and children.

Goebbels said, 'The route is west, ahead of the Russians.' He didn't sound sure about it.

Braun said, 'Of course, I can't be seen to be alive, but I will think about that and how best to take my chances.'

That night, a party to end all parties took place, which was about all Schlegel could remember when he came to in a toilet cubicle after God only knew how long. He was slumped on the floor, the seat digging into his face, dimly aware of what he eventually identified as warning klaxons, which he tried to ignore, except the noise hurt too much. Someone's birthday had been the excuse for everyone to get more legless than ever.

He had the vaguest recall of swirls of shouting, singing, dancing and shrill laughter, as well as a lot of vomiting and shameless public fucking, some of it simultaneous, with one woman on all fours spewing as she was taken from behind. He saw another totally drunk woman fondle an SS man's untrousered cock and being asked to 'Take one for the Fatherland, up the arse because it is no time for babies.' Condoms had run out. Schlegel had a blurred image of Braun drifting through with her camera, but he thought it was probably a dream.

He must have passed out again, because when he came to the klaxons had stopped. His watch was gone; lost playing cards, perhaps. His head felt like it was simultaneously being pounded by pneumatic drills and scraped with sandpaper. His hands shook. Someone had said they were all probably not far off seeing pink elephants; he had no idea who, but there were gales of mirth. At some point, Goebbels, as far gone as the rest, announced, 'I am floating.'

He had the haziest memory of being taken to Goebbels' room, where he was entrusted with the man's pistol. He couldn't think why until, ransacking his brains, he decided it might have had something to do with preventing Goebbels from shooting himself.

That was it; the little man had yapped on in his shrill way, 'To stop me writing my family into the tragedy, a tour de force which will have me blowing out my brains after poisoning the six children and shooting my wife as the finale to the whole magnificent opera. The last of the loyal will be told what to say. Do you have plans?'

Schlegel had no idea what he had answered; probably nothing, because he had spent most of the night in a state of stupefied observation, little of which he could now remember. Had he given the gun to someone else? He didn't have it about him. Perhaps, as with Braun, he had imagined the incident, because there seemed to be no difference between advanced intoxication and the dream state.

More than one party was going on that night, because at some point he had found himself with others in one of the rooms of the Führer's upstairs apartment, now in ruins, cold, eerie and lit by candlelight. A kitchen maid was marrying one of the drivers; whether it was an actual ceremony or a pretend wedding, he wasn't sure. The local bombardment made the proceedings almost inaudible, and they scuttled back below at the first opportunity, though a few stayed on for dancing, accompanied by an accordion and a violin.

Downstairs, a man who was past drunk was berating Bormann, telling him that the youth of a people of eighty million had bled to death on the battlefields of Europe while Bormann had enriched himself, feasted, robbed estates, swindled and oppressed. What had they died for? Not for the Fatherland, but for Bormann and his life of luxury and thirst for power. Bormann merely gave the man a good-natured smile and replied, 'My dear fellow, you don't have to be personal about it.'

Schlegel pulled himself together and staggered up. He was in the men's washroom. The corridors outside were deserted. Had the building been evacuated? Would he go around a corner to be confronted by trigger-happy Ivans?

The immediate rooms looked like they had been left in a hurry. He found no one until he stuck his head into Hitler's normally guarded quarters and saw the Führer slumped, passed out or dozing at his desk. Schlegel tiptoed backwards, only to be asked, 'Where is everyone?' He found himself being addressed for the first time by the man, a shrunken little old figure seemingly incapable of speech beyond a guttural mutter. He became transfixed by the sight of the Führer's arm, spasmodically pumping his closed fist forward, beating thin air. The words became clearer, emerging as a high-pitched whine. 'Treachery, treachery, a deserving doom for all who betrayed me. Devastation for the soft nation that threw away the chance of greatness I gave them.'

An army pistol lay on the desk, and Schlegel supposed he had interrupted the man as he was summoning the courage to shoot himself. But where was everyone?

For want of anything else to say, he mentioned that he was looking for Fräulein Braun.

Hitler snorted. 'Frau Hitler as she would prefer.' He

waved in the direction of the sitting room, then fell into a dull trance.

The door was closed. Schlegel knocked. There was no answer. The door wasn't locked. The room was dark. He felt around for a light switch. He feared he would be sick as vomit rose in his throat. At last, he found a switch. The faulty light blinked on and off. The room was deathly still. In between flashes of illumination, he made out Braun, twisted sideways on the sofa. He found a table lamp that worked and turned off the maddening light. The full picture revealed Braun, head thrown back, leaning dramatically against the side of the sofa, still holding her wrist, dripping blood onto the sofa arm. On the floor lay a cutthroat razor, presumably Hitler's. Braun groaned. Schlegel's first thought was that Hitler had tried to kill her, except the man appeared to be in no fit state to finish anyone off, even himself. She moaned again. There wasn't much blood. The cuts weren't deep enough, which was when he realised that she must have done it herself; yet another futile gesture, as on the two previous occasions. Gun, then pills and now a razor, and none had worked.

He checked the pulse, which was faint. He went to the bathroom and found a roll of bandage and applied what he hoped was enough of a tourniquet. God only knew why, but he thought she might be better off on a bed, so he carried her to Hitler's next door rather than negotiate the awkward narrow corridor to her room. He addressed the unconscious body, saying that he would seek help.

Hitler roused himself when he saw Schlegel on his way out and demanded, 'Where's the Geli gun? I asked Linge for it. The man's an idiot peasant. No one thinks he's overly bright, most of all me.'

Schlegel, sounding like a mad butler, announced that Fräulein Braun was indisposed.

Hitler shrugged. 'I told her that soon I will be with my darling Geli, the only one I loved, my sleeping princess.' He sniggered. 'She has always walked by my side.' He nodded in the direction of the sitting room. 'That one was always too much of an attention-seeker. Needy.'

Schlegel said, 'She cut her wrist.'

Hitler appeared resigned at that. He looked at Schlegel with watery, blank eyes. 'Get Bubi. He's the only one who understands.'

'Bubi?'

'Bormann.'

He dismissed Schlegel with a wave.

Schlegel searched more empty rooms until he found Goebbels curled up on his bed in a foetal ball; dead or alive, it hardly mattered, the man was in no position to do anything. An empty brandy bottle lay beside him.

He found some sentient, if very drunk, humans in Bormann's office, playing cards. As well as Bormann, there was Linge and the hulking surgeon Stumpfegger, who seemed to take up half the room.

Bormann demanded to know what the hell Schlegel was doing there. 'The area's sealed off and evacuated. You're supposed to be upstairs.'

Schlegel ignored that and said, 'Fräulein Braun has tried to kill herself.'

'Tried?' asked Bormann archly.

'She's still alive,' Schlegel answered.

'Can't she do anything right? And the Führer?'

'Still alive.'

Bormann sighed.

Stumpfegger was drinking whisky from what looked like a cracked urine-sample glass. A bottle of Dewar's stood in front of him.

Bormann said to him and Linge, 'Find out what's going on.'

Stumpfegger picked up the Dewar's and looked to Bormann for further instructions.

Bormann said, 'I suppose it is part of your Hippocratic oath to preserve life where possible.'

He sounded remarkably indifferent about it.

The two men went off.

Bormann said, 'You look like shit. Hair of the dog?'

He produced a bottle of schnapps and poured Schlegel a glass without asking. 'Down the hatch. What's going on with you?'

Schlegel told him what Hitler had said to Braun about joining Geli. He presumed it was why she had tried to kill herself.

Bormann showed no surprise. 'Tact never was the man's strong suit. A round of Go Fish to pass the time?'

Schlegel said that the Führer was asking for him.

'Let him wait,' Bormann said and started dealing.

It was after midnight when Parker, Robinson and Vod arrived at the same big shed as before. Despite the lateness of the hour, even more vehicles were parked outside. Inside was a demented Walpurgis Night that seemed to welcome rather than ward off evil spirits – fairground rides, loud music, candy floss, cage fights, human and animal, even a bullfight involving a dozy beast and a beefy farm boy waving a union jack that did nothing to bait the creature. Robinson went to find his man and Vod wandered off, leaving Parker contemplating hell. Someone asked if he was part of the 'freak show'. Vod came back with reports of children being auctioned and a disabled beauty contest. As usual, Parker couldn't tell if he was serious. Despite all the thumping action, everything appeared suspended until the bull charged and a roar went up. Parker told Vod that he would wait in the car. Vod said, 'It's only just kicking off. I'm going to play shove ha'penny.'

The man Robinson was seeing about a dog was his father's accountant, Halliday, to ask if some sort of loan could be arranged. His verdict after speaking to him was that he was 'fucking useless'. Halliday said that there were 'complications'.

Then: 'Your old man wants to see you.'

Robinson waited to be told where, thinking he had wasted his time.

'Now,' Halliday said. 'Follow me.'

They went through to the back and the huge storage area, beyond which lay another space that Robinson had never seen, the size of two tennis courts, in the middle of which stood what looked like a prefabricated holiday home, all wood and glass, laid out on astroturf. It was like finding himself in an Ideal Home exhibition.

Evelyn Robinson was sitting on a patio sofa, watching golf on a Euro sports channel and drinking Scotch.

Robinson's first thought was: So much older. Stick-thin.

'Hello, son,' Evelyn said without getting up. 'Looks like you've put on the weight I lost.'

Two peas in a pod, Robinson thought, no awkwardness or false cheer. How many years it had been he couldn't remember, but it was as though one of them had simply been down at the corner shop for all of five minutes.

Schlegel had no idea how much time passed before Linge and Stumpfegger returned; enough for several rounds of cards and drink. He became almost light-hearted under the circumstances, playing a children's game. Bormann behaved as though it were perfectly normal.

Stumpfegger announced that Braun was stable.

'Where's the Dewar's?' asked Bormann.

'Under the Führer's bed. I finished it.'

'There was over half a bottle left!' Bormann protested. He looked at Linge and asked, 'Is the Führer any nearer to making up his mind?'

Linge shook his head. Bormann said, 'I thought you were supposed to make it up for him. Isn't that your job?'

Bormann looked at Schlegel. 'Same old story. If you want anything done, don't ask any of this shower and do it yourself. Come with me.' He jerked his head at Linge and said, 'If it's left to him and his master, they just fudge it.'

Schlegel followed Bormann down the corridor, staring at the man's bull-like neck bulging over his collar. He walked with an easy, rolling gait, showing more swagger than when he was playing the deferential factotum.

'You might have to hold him down,' he said, and it finally dawned on Schlegel what was afoot, however much it had been staring him in the face.

Hitler's face lit up when Bormann walked in.

'Bubi! I knew you would come.'

'Hardly couldn't,' growled Bormann in a friendly manner. 'Just paying my respects to your missus. Spot of bother, I hear.'

Hitler acted like a child who secretly enjoyed being told off.

Schlegel followed Bormann into the bedroom. Bormann stared at the unconscious Braun before getting down on all fours and reaching for the bottle of Dewar's under the bed to check that it was empty.

They rejoined Hitler, who seemed to think it was one of his tea parties.

'Are we recording, Bubi?' he asked.

'Off the record this time, boss.'

They had the easy manner of an old couple wearing comfortable slippers.

Hitler turned to Schlegel and said, 'Bubi records my table talk for posterity. Sit down. We have time.'

He pointed to the pistol on the table and said, 'I asked for the Geli gun.'

Bormann said, 'I thought you might, Bubi. I took the liberty of having it fetched from your apartment. This young man here brought it.'

Hitler said in admiration, 'You think of everything.' He looked at Schlegel and asked, 'Do I know him?'

He turned away, distracted by Bormann producing the gun and putting it on the table.

Hitler asked, 'Are you sure it's the one?'

'Walther PPK 7.65, the very one. I also had him bring the golden gun in case you wanted to use that, but I would have to fetch it from the office.'

Hitler shook his head. 'No, too ostentatious.'

'I agree,' said Bormann.

Hitler turned to Schlegel and said, 'I find gold a bit Jewish, don't you?' He picked up the Walther and held the barrel against his temple, in his mouth and under his chin before putting it down and saying, 'I can't decide.'

Bormann said, 'Remember Röhm?'

'Ernst? My dearest friend. Whatever happened to him?'

'Shot on your orders,' Bormann said cheerfully. '1934.'

'Really?' said Hitler, as though he was hearing this for the first time, turning to Schlegel with a complicit shrug.

'He was offered a pistol,' Bormann continued, 'to take the officer's way.'

'Well, I should hope so,' said Hitler.

'Except he was in too much of a funk.'

'What happened?'

'They shoved it up his arse and fired.'

Hitler teetered between amusement and horror. 'Well, you wouldn't want that! I expect it was because he was a pederast.'

It was extraordinary to Schlegel how detached the man was, as though Röhm's death had had nothing to do with him.

Bormann said, 'Someone chalked on a wall SA 0-1 SS.'

Hitler giggled. 'That is funny. It was Operation Hummingbird until that show-off runt Goebbels decided to call it the Night of the Long Knives. No one was knifed from what I recall.' He turned to Schlegel, as though he were the only person who mattered at that moment. 'When I first came to Berlin and saw its luxury, I thought of myself as Christ driving the money-lenders from the temple. The persecuted Jews were to become the visible manifestation of Christ crucified.' He returned to Bormann. 'I was jealous of your way with women, Bubi. So straightforward.'

'I never had any trouble sticking my dick between a woman's legs, but my cock is nothing. You had the power to make whole crowds climax.'

Hitler smirked. 'And come with them, too. I remember that Wagner woman, who was so besotted, saying she sensed an irreconcilable battle in me between feminine softness and bestial ferocity, which responded to your oppressive and silent presence. Trust a woman to complicate things!'

He picked up the Walther again, went through the same rehearsal and put it down, saying, 'Ah, Geli.'

Schlegel, wondering if he would get a rise out of the man, said, 'She didn't shoot herself, of course.'

Hitler turned on him in fury, a transformation to behold. 'How could you possibly know? You would have been a boy at the time!'

Bormann looked interested by the unexpected turn of events.

Schlegel said, 'Ask Bubi.'

Hitler turned to Bormann, shaking. Bormann said, 'It was for your own good. It was his father's doing.'

Schlegel thought, despite himself: Well played.

Hitler turned to him and asked, 'Who was this man?'

Schlegel, to his own surprise, spoke eloquently without naming his father, one of those missing men of history, the background figures who never quite surface.

He explained that the death of the girl was an essential sacrifice.

'I don't see how,' Hitler said, 'other than undoing me.'

'For all your devastation and suicidal state . . .' Schlegel started and broke off, tempted to laugh because just such a state was needed at that moment, rather than an old dolt all of a dither.

'Yes, go on,' said Hitler, interested now.

'The tragedy gave you the one element previously missing. Depth.'

Hitler nodded, entranced. 'Yes. I see it now for the first time. Thank you for explaining. I am the wiser.'

'To become what you became, you needed to love, be loved and be rendered loveless. The loss of Geli was the last piece in the making of you.'

Even Bormann looked impressed at that.

Hitler conceded, 'She *was* a problem in terms of the divine mission.'

Schlegel went on. 'Love lost forged the alchemical solution, and little more than a year later, you were in power.'

'Yes, I was. I never made that connection.'

Bormann asked, 'Don't you want to know who his father is?'

Hitler clapped his hands to his ears and said, 'Too late for that.'

He sat breathing heavily, then more slowly, until he appeared quite switched off.

Eventually he said, 'Perhaps you could fetch Morell. It must be time for my booster shot.'

Bormann said, 'You're being forgetful, Bubi. You fired Morell last week.'

'Did I? Whatever for?' Hitler sat looking lost until he said in a flat voice, 'Well, yes, thank you, gentlemen. Leave me for a moment, please.'

Bormann nodded gravely as he stood and said in his most deferential manner, 'Are you sure you don't need a hand?'

Hitler saw the joke and said, 'Don't start me laughing. I need a moment to myself. Wait outside.'

Out in the corridor, Bormann grew testy as the minutes passed. After five, nothing had happened. He handed a cyanide capsule to Schlegel, who stared at it, wondering if he was expected to swallow it, until Bormann, impatient, said, 'Just make sure you jam it in his mouth.'

At that moment, a muffled report came from behind the closed door, and they rushed in to find Hitler spared by his shaking hand. The gun was still in it, waving around. He gave a sheepish look and said, 'I missed, Bubi.'

'Come on, Bubi,' Bormann said. 'On your feet. Time for a rest.'

Hitler stood willingly – relieved, it seemed, but

337

unsteady – smoothing his trousers until Bormann grabbed him around the neck from behind. Hitler's mouth opened in surprise but snapped shut before Schlegel could insert the capsule. He gritted his teeth and struggled with more strength than Schlegel believed possible. Bormann headbutted the back of the skull and took advantage of the man's stunned condition to place his meaty hands around the throat and squeeze. A grotesque Saint Vitus' dance ensued as Hitler rallied, lurched and resisted while Bormann throttled him. Eyes popping, tongue protruding, but the tongue got in the way and the man thrashed enough to avoid the capsule Schlegel kept trying to shove into his mouth. As he gasped for breath, the tongue moved in and out ever more obscenely. At some point, something shot out of his mouth; what Schlegel realised later was a dental plate. Nasal hair, sprouts of ear hair, that smear of moustache, the fishlike, gaping orifice snapping shut before Schlegel could do anything, stupendous bad breath, wetting himself, then worse.

'Number twos, Bubi,' Bormann grunted.

There was something animalistic about Bormann's brute force. Having effectively controlled and tamed his master, it seemed fitting that the man should die at his hands – in the end, not so different from the physical effort of fucking: flesh on flesh, the untouchable Führer touched and violated. One last effort, the little feet off the ground now, twitching, pigeon-toed; hands clasped over Bormann's hands around his throat, hanging on for dear life, starting to weaken. The left claw undid itself, and the arm jerked up and down – palsy or death throes, it was hard to say. Bormann was grunting like a gravedigger. There was a weird exhilaration to the whole thing.

They ended up on the floor, with Schlegel and Bormann breathing hard from the exertion. Schlegel broke the cyanide capsule inside the man's mouth, thinking: Better late than never.

Dead Time

S ince the war and Evelyn Robinson's lumbering passage through night skies in thirty-one and a quarter tons of flying coffin (including the bomb load, which accounted for just under half its weight), he had made a point of travelling light. Although his life was dedicated to making money on the side – protection, extortion, backhanders, sweeteners, nearly always within an institutional context – his lifestyle remained modest to the point of anonymity.

Later, he moved around a lot, staying mainly in cheap London hotels in Tottenham, Crouch End, Golders Green and Barnet. No one would have guessed from the way he presented himself that he had amassed a fortune. The hotels, perhaps half a dozen, were often little more than boarding houses, combining travelling salesmen and prostitution. These lowly venues formed part of a social network for Evelyn, who seemed comfortable in transit. He may have had a financial stake in these properties; even his accountant, Halliday, was unsure about the extent of his investments. Cash was his preferred method of transaction.

Evelyn was easy-going, sociable and polite when

required, in a way that only someone who has tortured others can be.

When he thought about life, it was in terms of places lived rather than the job, which was too diverse and often too downright impenetrable to summarise. Where he stayed seemed part of a quest to lose the sense of displacement that had always dogged him, which was why he was content knowing that somewhere wasn't permanent.

The beauty of rinsed money was that you couldn't tell that it had been dirty. Its legacy was a history of properties acquired, always in the bleaker hinterlands rather than commercial hot spots. Storage containers and big sheds (in contrast to London's battery-hen office blocks) were among his friends. He had been quick to realise that anything could be going on in those blind buildings, and what couldn't be seen couldn't be known. He was too canny to be a gangster. There was no retinue or show. He had devoted his life to exploiting anything to hand and moving on when it looked like it was catching up with him. He knew what went on in those big sheds and sometimes attended illegal events managed by right-wing paramilitaries as fundraisers. Recently, the police had raided one and found it empty. Evelyn remained sufficiently well-connected that he almost certainly would have been tipped off. By then there was encrypted Blackberry messaging.

He was quick to grasp that, in an interactive world, the faster the communication the slower the process because of the volume to be assessed. Where the world had once been dominated by the high street with its temple of money (bank) and palace of dreams (cinema), now it was all instant transfer and wild speculation, but the rules of behaviour remained the same; only the drive was different, as tribe replaced class while still being mistaken for class.

341

Sometimes he asked himself what his country had done for him other than take him at a young age and teach him to bomb the fuck out of everything. He often woke in cold sweats after being pitched back in his dreams. A recurring one was a failed parachute and falling without end through total blackness.

His career was one of controlled infiltration. Just as 98 per cent of the world's wealth belongs to two per cent of the population, so 98 per cent of the world's crime is committed by the same percentage. He wished in both cases to belong to that two per cent.

Evelyn Robinson, who went on to become a true-blue Thatcherite, was the nation's nemesis, dismantling its institutional heritage into scrap to be sold for profit.

Any official career takes a paragraph. He'd moved from the RAF Military Police to the Met in the late 1940s, serving in vice and narcotics (a sound basic education) before transferring to Special Branch. In the 1950s, he served seconded terms in Kenya at the time of the Mau Mau uprising, being assigned to Military Intelligence and counter-insurgency operations. In the 1960s, he worked in conjunction with MI5, compiling and sharing files on political radicals. (These included the BBC's 'Christmas tree' files, and he was surprised that Katharina Fischer had one because she was suspected of being a Stasi agent.) He collected what was known as 'open source' intelligence, engaged in surveillance and recruited informers. In the 1970s, he was reunited with Military Intelligence in Northern Ireland. Thereafter, the career is harder to trace. He resigned from Special Branch and moved into private security work involving illegal foreign arms deals, which had become a booming industry after the government implicitly endorsed the practice and set up favourable trading terms on the quiet, including reimbursement on defaulted payments using North Sea oil money. In the 1990s, he worked as an adviser to NATO peace-keeping forces in the Balkans.

Even by Met standards, Evelyn was epically bent, with fingers in so many pies that he wasn't sure how many fingers he had. In Kenya, he had begun his affair with Beatrice when she was working on the Rock Hudson picture. Beatrice, who would resurface in Belfast, offered (already said but worth repeating), 'There are only two basic emotions: love and fear. Everything follows from that, which makes the world both endlessly simple and endlessly complex.'

In Belfast, Evelyn became part of crooked ops involving RUC men, with a lot of protection money sloshing around. But the heat was on after several officers were investigated for improved personal lifestyles (speed boats and holiday homes, for which a bent building society manager handed out second mortgages). Unlike them, Evelyn saw far enough ahead to exploit Northern Ireland's future prosperity through the construction business, which was divided up profitably on sectarian lines. With the province heavily subsidised by the mainland government, all kinds of incentives and loans were available. Evelyn was reminded of the way Hanover had been wide open after the war. Many of the protection rackets were a rerun, with companies invited to purchase 'security services', the extortion fees being offloaded into contract tenders, inflated costs and billing for casual labour that never existed.

Evelyn flew to Hanover to ask August Schlegel to invest. ('That's quite a lot of money.') They started buying property dirt cheap to serve at first as rentals and bided their time.

Evelyn found an important ally in Belfast, the crooked Halliday; and lurking in the background the great scandal of the Kincora boys' home, which was where Halliday surfaced. If Evelyn's passage was subterranean, Halliday operated in even murkier depths, doing the books for several Jimmy Savile charities. Evelyn and Savile's peripatetic lifestyles were similar, although there is no evidence that the former had a secret sexual history; that part was claimed by Parker's father, Dominic.

While he was still in Special Branch, stories circulated that Evelyn Robinson's counter-insurgency work involved the torture of suspects. That, back in London, he continued to use techniques learned in Northern Ireland. That he was involved in a drugs deal that went wrong after he was approached by a bent RUC man fronting for a Provisional IRA gang, which had 'chanced' across a load of heroin it couldn't sell locally because of a no-drugs policy on the streets of Belfast. Evelyn agreed to take care of the London end. Whatever went wrong, the boys blamed Evelyn, who protested his innocence – though of course he had ripped them off. The IRA gang was sufficiently incensed to hire a private detective, who wound up dead in a South London pub car park after being run over.

After that, Evelyn decided to move on. He brought Halliday over to cook the books. He set the parameters, and the rest was up to Halliday, who worked in his down-at-heel office on the Holloway Road: nothing that couldn't be walked away from.

They made a further fortune out of the lower, unfashionable end of government bureaucracy: local municipalities with their underbelly of corruption. Evelyn set his course and drove a straight line through everything. He aspired to an invisibility at levels few can be bothered with: council maintenance, perimeter security, waste management, institutional care, the stuff that bores people and is there for the taking.

He and Halliday bought and sold domestic and commercial property through various councils. Halliday ran the newly privatised companies that served them. One riddle, still unexplained to this day, is why they were buying up council property at rock bottom prices and selling it on even cheaper. Halliday used his connections to move into and exploit the uncaring world of institutional care, for both the young and the elderly. The former suited his agenda, as it provided grooming opportunities, and in one of life's ironies Evelyn's wife, Robinson's mother, ended up in a home run by one of his firms. In the 1990s, there was a spell as a NATO adviser, with a lucrative sideline providing sex services to troops stationed in Kosovo. Back in London, Evelyn facilitated the criminal gangs he had cultivated, seeing them as an equivalent to the fashion for Polish builders (faster, cheaper, more reliable, less mouth). He imported the Balkan sex trade into England, which marked the start of a widespread suburbanisation of prostitution, which explained his hotel investments. Sex workers stopped by the front desk and paid commission to the night clerk following their visits.

And lurking in the background, always a notion of bad blood. One of Evelyn's most successful scams involved the blood bank market, selling tainted product to Third World countries using charity organisations as fronts.

Hitler lay purple-faced on the carpet in a pungent odour of shit, cordite and bitter almonds. Bormann had shoved the man's tongue back in, either as a mark of respect or because it amused him. He seemed quite at ease around his master's corpse, as though there were no difference between serving the man dead or alive.

Bormann had sent Schlegel to fetch Linge and Stumpfegger,

whom he found sitting around looking useless. He told them it was done and Stumpfegger should bring his surgical instruments. Neither Stumpfegger nor Linge asked what had happened.

Bormann told Stumpfegger, 'You need to remove the dental plates.'

Stumpfegger knelt down and set to, fishing out the first and chucking it aside. He then announced, 'One's missing. There are supposed to be three.'

Schlegel said it was on the floor.

Stumpfegger picked it up without asking what it was doing there, then extracted the last plate and asked, 'What now?'

'To the oven with him!' Bormann exclaimed.

On reflection, he decided that he and Schlegel would take care of that. An industrial incinerator upstairs was working full blast, burning papers. In the meantime, the other two should prepare the substitute corpses. Linge pointed out that they needed Hitler's uniform for that.

Bormann, incredulous, asked where his spares were. They were all at the dry cleaners and there hadn't been time to get them back.

Bormann pointed to the body. 'Well, you've dressed and undressed the man enough times.'

Whatever reverence had previously been shown to his master was abandoned in an unseemly haste to rip off the clothes. By the time Linge was done, they lay in an untidy heap, leaving the man in his soiled underwear.

A blanket was found to cover the body, and a stretcher. Bormann fetched more booze and said, 'Up the emergency stairs with him.'

Easier said than done; Schlegel, at the rear, had to hold the stretcher with his arms aloft until they ached to prevent the body sliding off. Outside, it was nearly dark. Gunfire sounded blocks away.

The incinerator was in a nearby back building of its own. With the heat from the furnace, Schlegel was drenched in sweat within seconds. Two men wearing asbestos overalls and gloves were burning boxes of papers, using a metal trolley to shovel them in. Bormann told them to get lost. He and Schlegel donned the overalls, placed the stretcher on the trolley and pushed it to the furnace entrance. Each took a back handle.

Bormann said, 'One, two, three, push!'

The front of the stretcher snagged on the entrance. Schlegel had to jam a spade under it to gain leverage. It took several attempts before the handles rested on the lip of the furnace. The stretcher's canvas started to catch fire, so they had to be quick to resume their positions.

'One God Almighty shove,' said Bormann.

The stretcher budged, but not all the way. The body suddenly seemed three times its weight. Halfway in, as the legs startled to crackle, the corpse began to sit up and was in danger of falling off the trolley until one final effort that left both men reeling. The last thing Schlegel saw as he slammed the door shut was the hair burning like a halo.

Bormann had a bottle in his pocket. He swigged from it, and said, ironically or not, 'My Führer.'

He passed the bottle to Schlegel, who couldn't decide whether he was drunk, hungover or both.

Back underground, they found Stumpfegger and Linge sitting around doing nothing. Linge, overcome by an unlikely show of remorse, was sobbing.

'Jesus Christ!' said Bormann. 'Where are the other bodies?'

Before anyone could answer, they were interrupted by

347

Braun wailing hysterically. Bormann nodded at Schlegel to follow him. She was lying on the bed, perhaps not even conscious and crying in her sleep. Bormann surprised Schlegel by lifting her up as she continued to sob, holding her tenderly with one arm while he smoothed the bed and plumped the pillow, leaving Schlegel to wonder if he had it in mind to smother her. He didn't, though, however tempted he was, and laid her back down. Then he stood back and addressed the comatose figure: 'The Führer has committed suicide.'

He muttered to Schlegel, 'Your problem how you solve it, but don't leave her here to be found. Women are women, but they deserve to be treated with respect.'

Was he serious?

They rejoined Linge and Stumpfegger. Bormann asked where the other bodies were. Linge said they were in the guards' cloakroom.

Bormann said, 'Take care of the man. That way, Linge, you can dress "him" for the last time. Make sure he looks his best. We'll do the woman.'

It was hard to tell whether Bormann was trying to get a rise out of Linge, whom no one liked.

Linge said obsequiously, 'Fräulein Braun's favourite blue dress is laid out on her bed.'

They trooped off to fetch the two bodies, which they found unceremoniously dumped. The man looked not unlike Hitler. The woman looked nothing like Braun. She also had a gaping chest wound. Bormann looked at Stumpfegger in disbelief and asked, 'Is that the best you can manage?'

Stumpfegger said, 'Right age, right weight and height, but it's not easy to find an intact corpse, I can tell you.'

'Fräulein Braun won't be best pleased. She looks like a skivvy.'

At that, they laughed in the way one does when something is past a joke.

The bodies were covered with blankets, and they carried them back to Hitler's quarters. Braun's blue dress was waiting on her bed as Linge had said. Bormann produced a clasp knife. As he slit the back of the dress, it made a tearing sound, which Schlegel remembered long after he had blotted out the rest. The whole thing was like a crazy, phantasmal extension of the party with its perverse ceremony and licence. Perhaps even Bormann was pleased it was over. The man's sweating, brooding presence seemed infused with a lightness of touch, and Schlegel saw what an effort it must have been to assume the pretence of total subservience, quite at odds with his own ambitions. There was even exhilaration, hard to detect but undeniably present, fuelled by the massive intake of alcohol. None were staggering, but they were all starting to lurch.

Once the two bodies were laid side by side and covered in their blankets, Bormann said to Linge, 'Take care of the rest. You know what to do.'

Linge recited that there was gasoline upstairs. He had picked a shallow crater where the bodies could be burned, then buried.

'With the dogs,' added Bormann.

Linge looked as though he was about to ask them for a hand, but Bormann beat him to it, saying, 'I'm off for a fuck. I'm about the only one who hasn't had that switchboard operator. Dirty work, but someone has to do it.'

He addressed Linge. 'Time to spread the word. The Führer is dead. He died an honourable death like an officer and a gentleman, shooting himself while taking a cyanide phial.'

He gave a lackadaisical salute, which Linge returned with a stiff arm and a 'Heil Hitler!'

349

'Bit late for that,' Bormann remarked genially.

After Linge and Stumpfegger had left with the man's body, Bormann said to Schlegel, 'Keep an eye on Braun. It's nothing more than a scratch. Up to you what you do with her. It will be every man for himself.' He scuffed the crumpled rug with the toe of his shoe and said, 'I am now legally the Führer of the Fourth Reich.'

He smiled at Schlegel with unexpected warmth, a man on top of his mountain, and added, 'Which was the object of the exercise.'

At that, they were interrupted by the ghostly figure of Braun, standing in the doorway, staring at the dead woman on the floor, head and torso covered, and wearing her dress.

She said, 'Not those shoes. I want the Ferragamo shoes.'

After Halliday had withdrawn, Evelyn Robinson said to his son, 'I hear you're in a spot of bother.'

'Need a mill to pay off some pesky Russians and thought I would try you for a loan.'

'Under normal circs, of course,' Evelyn said as he carried on watching the golf. 'I heard you were doing well.'

'Not as far as the cash cow goes.'

'Then we're both strapped.'

'You don't look that bothered.'

'I'll be dead in three months. Tumour. The inner offensive. No such thing as remission, only undiagnosed illness. Cheers!' He raised his glass. 'Have one yourself.'

Robinson was left contemplating his lie to Michail about his father's medical bills. It hadn't been done with any sense of premonition; just one of those easy lies to distract and create sympathy for a third party.

He said enigmatically, 'Sometimes you make stuff up that turns out to be true.'

His father contemplated the bottom of his glass.

'In fact, I was going to ask if I could borrow off you. There's an alternative clinic in Mexico I have my eye on. Monkey glands and coffee enemas. Bullshit, but I want to see out my days somewhere hot, without HMRC breathing down my neck, being pampered by nice nurses with a private arrangement for a lot of morphine on the side.'

'HMRC?'

The most dreaded acronym in the English language.

'And the Environment Agency. They pay you to get rid of the stuff, usually never ask where, until now.'

'And HMRC?'

'Been after me for years. Turns out Beatrice is prepared to rat on me. She's currently being detained at Her Majesty's leisure. I should warn you, you might come to the attention of the tax man, too, because Halliday set up shell companies in your name.'

'My name!'

'Never told me. Scout's honour.'

Robinson thought that unlikely; oh well, he probably would have done the same in his old man's place.

His father went on. 'I would think of an extended holiday somewhere with no extradition treaty, if I were you.'

'Strapped for cash, like I said.'

Meanwhile, Parker, restless in the car, experienced the first of a series of visions that would plague him until he found Father Roper. A man in a crashing aircraft, reliving Evelyn Robinson's nightmare of being shot down over Hanover, and the forward projection of his subsequent life in the nanoseconds left. Parker saw other deaths: Robinson appearing to drown; perhaps he would. He saw an alternative non-existence for himself, with him and his mother dying in childbirth – a blessing in a way, as it denied Father Roper his ejaculations; he saw his father killed after an altercation with a rent boy, run over on a stretch of wasteland; and his grandfather August Schlegel dying in a ditch somewhere in the east in the summer of 1941.

His phone was off. He switched it on and found several missed calls from Mr Smith, with no message. He foresaw Mr Smith's lonely death in a hotel room, somewhere he couldn't identify, whether by his own hand or assisted he could not say. He thought later, Tel Aviv.

Robinson asked his father about the golden gun, the original of which was not even fifty yards away, in a safe. Without mentioning that he had been trying to sell its replica (which Evelyn didn't know about), he suggested selling the original to raise funds. 'They' were now 'we'.

Evelyn shook his head. 'I was given it by a man who was spooked by it. I suspect there was a hidden motive, because he regarded it as tainted, which is perhaps why I, in turn, passed it on to you, with instructions not to sell without consulting me.'

'It's why I am asking.'

Robinson wasn't generally superstitious, but he wondered if his recent troubles had been brought about by trying to sell its replica.

'Bad karma,' said Evelyn. 'But there might be another way.'

'The man who gave you the gun,' ventured Robinson.

'Yes.'

'Parker's grandfather.'

'Who the fuck is Parker?'

'It's funny how things turn out,' said Robinson.

There was some confusion at first over August Schlegel's name, because Evelyn had always known him as Tieck.

Robinson said, 'He knew Katharina Fischer, Parker's grandmother.'

'We both knew Kate. At one point, she might even have become your mother.'

'That rather stretches the point, but I know what you mean.'

'August is the man to see. He's tricky and secretive, won't talk on the phone. Doesn't do email. How reliable is the grandson?'

'Reliable enough, not especially competent.'

Evelyn said, 'I'll give you something in terms of bona fides he can take. Wait a minute.'

He went off and came back with a cellophane envelope.

'A handkerchief?' said Robinson.

It was folded and had the faintest trace of lipstick.

'August said he was given it by Hitler's mistress. If your man Parker returns it, he will know it's from me.'

Bormann and Schlegel ushered Braun back to bed. She was so woozy that Schlegel wondered whether Stumpfegger had doped her up.

When Linge and Stumpfegger returned for the woman's body, Bormann left with them, and Schlegel knew he wouldn't see the man again. He looked for something to put the ashes in, gave up and fell into a drunken stupor on the sofa on which he had found Braun. He was woken by her calling out. She said she feared she had been abandoned; she had always been afraid of the dark.

'As was the Chief,' she added.

Schlegel couldn't tell if she had taken on board the man's death. She talked about cutting herself.

'I knew all along that he only ever loved her. But why did he have to say? We all delude ourselves. Did he say anything before he died?'

About her, he supposed she meant. So she had taken it in. He said he hadn't been present, so he couldn't say.

He watched her drifting in and out of a troubled sleep. At some point, he must have fetched an upright chair, because he woke to find himself on it. Later, she insisted they drink a toast to the Chief. Schlegel questioned the wisdom of that in her condition and was told to stop nannying.

'He used to nag me all the time. He was a terrible nagger.'

He went off and came back with a bottle of champagne.

'The last one,' he said.

Oh well, he thought to himself, we'll probably be dead before the hangover.

There wasn't a clock in the room, and he had no way of telling the time until he remembered Braun's watch that Fegelein had stolen, which she had been wearing in Bormann's office. He supposed she had taken it off before cutting her wrist. He found it on the carpet under the sofa. He reckoned enough time had passed for the body to burn and went back and explained what he had to do.

'You asked for the Führer's ashes,' he said. 'I have to fetch them.'

She didn't want him to go, saying, 'Don't leave me. I have no one left.'

He didn't care either way about any ashes until Braun demanded they make what she called an 'adventure' of fetching them. She had drunk most of the champagne by then and was feeling 'much better'.

'In some ways, it's a relief, don't you think? Everything feels lighter.'

Schlegel thought that without the man's oppressive presence, the place was revealed for the pointless hellhole it was.

As a final touch of absurdity, Braun insisted on wearing a full-length silver fox fur coat.

'I gave it to Junge. She won't need it now she's gone.'

Something darker might be more appropriate, he suggested, at which she snapped that she had always chosen her own wardrobe.

She took his arm and leaned against him as they walked down the empty corridor to the emergency stairs.

Outside, the battle was raging, but no one was in sight. He hurried her across the broken ground, wondering what she would look like through an infrared sight and hoping the Russian infantry didn't have them.

They made the weirdest couple: Schlegel shovelling ashes into a metal bucket after he realised he had forgotten to bring anything to put them in; her standing back from the immediate heat, which was still hot enough to singe the tips of the fur. Schlegel couldn't tell from the hiccoughing noises she made whether she was laughing or crying; whether she had crossed over into madness or was suffering from some kind of brain fever.

Their return coincided with a lull in the fighting. Not even a single rifle shot. Everything was deathly quiet in the cold moonlight. A man walking with a woman, carrying a metal bucket of still-glowing ashes, in a landscape that says they might be the last ones on earth.

They went back down into the bunker, where Braun collapsed on Hitler's bed, as though her exposure to the outside had used up all her energy. Schlegel looked at the pillow

Bormann had plumped. He got as far as pressing it against her face. She didn't resist, even though her eyes were open, watching, not reacting or struggling. He stopped because of her staring so blankly that she might as well be dead. The bucket of ashes stood cooling in the corner.

Braun slept again, chased by dreams that made her mumble. No way was she fit to travel. There had been talk of using train tunnels as the safest escape route, which was beyond her physical state. Would she even have the right shoes?

She woke and asked what was going on in a voice that suggested that nothing had happened.

He said, 'I didn't know the Führer had a wheelchair.' It was folded at the end of the bed, leaning against the safe that dominated the room.

She said, 'He refused to use it. That fat slob Morell was wheeled around in it more than he ever was.'

He announced that she needed to find some clothes, something practical and warm. They would be leaving soon.

She sighed. 'You decide.'

'I thought you chose your own.'

'Let's not have a row about it. My head hurts as it is.'

He went off and selected a thick jersey, ski pants and rubber boots, which she told him she used for walking Negus and Stasi in the park. There followed a five-minute paean to the adorability of the little mutts, finishing with her telling him, 'I expect you are more of a cat person. Where are we going?'

'Not far. Do you have anything like a deposit box?'

A cheap old metal one, she said, from when she was a girl, a birthday present kept for sentimental reasons. She had her jewellery in it and told him where to find it.

The key was in the lock. He scooped out the jewellery and shoved it in his pockets. As an afterthought, he took the watch as well. He filled the battered box with ashes tipped from the bucket. They didn't all fit, and Schlegel said to himself: At this stage, it's the thought that counts.

Again, as an afterthought, he picked up the Walther from the study desk.

He left Braun to dress and went to Bormann's office, where he helped himself to more booze. He gave the drawers a cursory inspection, thinking there might be cash. There wasn't, but there was the golden gun, so he took that.

Braun was still dressing when he returned. When she emerged, she appeared bewildered again.

'Is there still such a thing as a taxi, do you suppose?'

She told him to wait while she painstakingly reapplied her make-up. Seeing her reflection in the vanity mirror as she left her lipstick imprint on a handkerchief reminded him of watching his mother do the same when he was a child. Braun handed him the handkerchief and said, 'Souvenir,' which left him thinking that this was beyond the logic of any dream.

She would not be talked out of wearing the fox fur, however much of a target it made her.

Schlegel couldn't decide if the woman was heroically superficial or heroically stubborn on her own terms.

Their progress down the empty corridor was a repeat of the time before, except they passed a weaving Dr Goebbels, so drunk that he gave no sign of seeing them.

Schlegel left Braun sitting at the bottom of the stairs, telling her to wait. She grew hysterical at the prospect of being abandoned. He explained as to a child what he had to do.

She nodded obediently. He fetched the wheelchair and the deposit box. As he returned, he passed Goebbels in his room, drunkenly declaiming his old Total War speech, spittle flying.

He got Braun to the top of the stairs and went back down for the wheelchair and deposit box. He found her standing halfway down, her hands gripping the coat collar like a model posing for a photograph.

Schlegel set up the wheelchair outside. No gunfire or artillery; he wondered if there was a ceasefire and the war was lost. A fire in a nearby shallow crater he supposed were the two burning bodies. He placed Braun in the wheelchair and gave her the deposit box, which she clutched with both hands.

'It's warm,' she said, 'which is just as well, because I forgot my gloves.'

Schlegel thought: At last, the man is performing a useful task.

Normally it would have taken fewer than five minutes. Because of bomb damage and fallen trees, it seemed to take forever. At one point, he had to lift her over a fallen trunk.

If Braun was surprised by their destination, she gave no sign. It was almost as if the place was waiting for her entrance, with a door wide enough for the wheelchair.

The Adlon's lobby was full of milling people, undecided about what to do other than carry on drinking. Schlegel pushed Braun through the crowd. No one recognised her, though a few stared at her strange attire.

He heard one woman say, 'Gumboots and fur?'

At the desk, he asked for a room and was told that none was available. He dangled Braun's watch in front of the receptionist, a sour-faced puss not much older than he was, except they all looked as though they had aged decades in days. He remembered her being on the desk the night he had been with Molly Fitzgerald.

The woman made a show of consulting the register. There was in fact a last-minute cancellation; it wasn't necessary to sign in.

'We wish you a pleasant stay,' she said with no apparent irony, pocketing the watch.

It was a smallish room, high up at the back. Schlegel wondered about Molly Fitzgerald. He wouldn't put it past her to have checked back in after leaving Fegelein's.

Braun seemed unaware of events or where she was, other than to complain that it wasn't her usual suite. Outside, the shelling started again, and she shivered like someone with the ague.

He waited until she had fallen into another shallow sleep before going downstairs in the hope of spotting someone he knew; perhaps even Molly Fitzgerald, who would have access to the Hungarian and Irish embassies. Goebbels had talked of using the Italian one as a refuge for women and children.

Schlegel supposed they had a day, two at the most, before the Russians arrived. After that, the Adlon's guests would probably be shot as stinking capitalists.

He spotted Francis Alwynd looking desperate while trying to give the impression of a man you might meet in a queue at an airport. They spoke briefly. Alwynd said he was persona non grata with the Irish embassy, not for any political nonsense but because of an abandoned wife in the Old Country whose brother was high in the government. He was wondering about a bicycle and taking his chances, except he couldn't find one.

His face screwed up in disgust as he exclaimed, 'The last thing we need are bloody nuns!'

Schlegel looked round and saw two habits of such a startling pink that he wondered if they weren't an alcoholic hallucination. He watched them make their way through the crowd, excused himself and hurried after them.

It turned out they were known as the Pink Sisters, from St Gabriel's monastery in Westend, and were nursing in the part of the hotel operating as an emergency hospital, caring for the wounded and giving succour to the dying. Schlegel spoke to the two nuns, who in contrast to the rest looked ageless, with their apple cheeks and serene, unlined faces, and endlessly forgiving.

The sisters took them away in a beaten-up old van they used as an ambulance. St Gabriel's was ten kilometres west, ahead of the Russian advance. Gullible or bribed, Schlegel couldn't say, but his false diplomatic papers and what Braun described as 'a generous donation' to a grateful abbot bought them refuge, which was a welcome relief for its sparse simplicity. They eagerly agreed on the importance of the nuns' mission to have a place of perpetual adoration in Berlin to pray against misanthropy, oppression and the Nazi regime.

Braun said, 'Well, we can forget about the last,' apparently willing to give herself up to a life of penitence with hardly a thought to the past.

Schlegel heard later that she was smuggled out as a Pink Sister on a Lufthansa flight to Madrid.

He made his own strange pilgrimage dressed in a monk's habit, under which he carried the Führer's pistols and a healthy portion of Braun's loot, which had been freely given.

He left before she did. There was no sentimental farewell. She told him to take the ashes to their designated resting place. He agreed for the stupid and logical reason that he had nothing better to do. She would stay where she was for a bit, until she was sure it was safe to leave. It was her suggestion that he travel as a monk.

'It's the perfect cover,' she said, much taken with her own

idea. The monastery would give him a habit; she had already asked. He could make his way staying in similar institutions along the route. She gave him a drawing, like a child's treasure map, with X marking the spot, and he made his passage unquestioned, joining the countless refugees and displaced persons moving south.

Konrad Morgen, December 1946

A curious footnote to the Schlegel affair: Linge, Hitler's valet, claims that only four men knew what happened at the end in the bunker: himself, Bormann, Stumpfegger and Schlegel. No one knows Schlegel, Bormann or Stumpfegger's exact whereabouts. Linge is a prisoner of the Russians. Bormann is either dead or in South America. His secretary, Else Krüger, who is available for interview (another young woman keen to sing from the hymn sheet) – remembers 'a tall young man with white hair' in and out of Bormann's office in the Chancellery in the second half of 1944.

Krüger, a somewhat vivacious young woman, said to have been Bormann's mistress, admitted to being surprised when Schlegel turned up again before the end. She thought his arrival coincided with a visit by Hitler's new head of the Luftwaffe after Göring was fired. One version had the new Luftwaffe man flying into Gatow airport with the test pilot Hanna Reitsch. He then piloted a Fieseler Storch across town to the Tiergarten, close to the Chancellery. When the man was wounded by Russian gunfire, it was left to her to land the plane. This was a few days before the end.

According to Krüger, little seems to have happened after that, other than a domestic contretemps. Reitsch, given her slavish, erotic devotion to the Führer, was aghast to find that Hitler had a woman living with him. Krüger observed Braun exercising her domestic power as First Lady by making Reitsch help entertain the unmanageable Goebbels children. Krüger heard her tell Braun that she was unwilling to sacrifice herself for a man who would betray her with another woman.

She flew out on the night of 28 April. It was all very derring-do, leading to stories (denied by Krüger) that the plane took off with Hitler.

Krüger thought Schlegel might have arrived with Reitsch. This would have been possible, as the Storch is a three-seater. What he was doing there at the eleventh hour, nobody knew, apart from a rumour that it had something to do with Fräulein Braun – or Frau Hitler, as I suppose we are meant to call her. She and Schlegel sound an unlikely pairing as, to my knowledge, they were barely acquainted. Krüger doesn't mention him being part of the break-out from the bunker at the end.

There is no trace of the man that I can find. He spoke of having diplomatic papers. If he got out, I presume he would have made his way to Switzerland or Rome, given that the supposed issuer of his papers was the Vatican, where it is said that the Americans are recruiting for the inevitable conflict with the Soviets. A nervous Vatican is offering immunity to distinctly shady characters claiming to be anti-communist, which is a high card to play now. Those held to be beyond the pale are being shown the back door via assisted passage to South America, where already a flourishing colony of ex-patriates exists.

Rome became a safe haven for wanted Nazis after the war, many of them guests of Jim Angleton's section of US Counterintelligence. They came to include August Schlegel, who found himself ensconced in a comfortable safe apartment with an extensive sadomasochistic library left by the former tenant, a German mistress of Mussolini.

Reflecting on his journey to Rome, Schlegel was surprised by its ease. Bavaria had been reached without incident, a slow passage of waiting in various monasteries until onward transport could be arranged, usually Red Cross trucks distributing emergency supplies; sometimes goods trains; and once or twice private cars. Along the way, he gathered that he should present himself to a cardinal in Milan, to whom he more or less came clean, admitting the habit was a disguise and he had been working close to the top, planning for the battle against communism.

Even though he was accepted, he found himself put on ice, hidden in a Church-run asylum for wealthy drug addicts whose inmates included a fading Italian film star with a taste for heroin, which she shared with Schlegel in exchange for cunnilingus.

By then, life seemed to have little to do with experience or personality, but with a series of moves as everything realigned.

Enter Jim Angleton, doing the rounds for likely recruits among the flotsam and jetsam being sheltered by the Church, who was surprised to find Schlegel in sackcloth and with a head full of snow. He took him to Rome, where Schlegel learned that Angleton, not yet thirty, was now a rising star of counterintelligence, thanks to an address book stuffed full of fascists reinventing themselves.

Angleton, ever boastful, bragged of fixing a secret meeting between the Pope and a visiting Allen Dulles about the communist challenge and the importance of co-opting previous enemies into their alliance.

Angleton struck Schlegel as an academic dabbler whose views were naive and overblown, but he appreciated the fake identity card he was given, which had him as an employee of an American organisation and allowed him a degree of independence. He started going out, desperate for the semblance of a normal existence: cafés, restaurants, visits to the cinema.

He picked up bits of gossip from a decadent SS man who shared the same apartment. He had spent the war in Italy hobnobbing with high society and claimed to know everyone; had been friendly with Eva Braun, whom he had accompanied during her Italian holidays on 'shopping safaris', so-called because of her love of everything crocodile, looking as though she had come back from a trip up the Congo rather than a stroll along the Tiber.

The man was a font of indiscretion. He was able to say that Braun's relationship with Hitler had remained unconsummated, because she had told him that any physical contact would defile his mission. His only love was Germany. To forget that, even for a moment, would shatter the mystical forces of his vocation.

There was more. The man had attended a wild Christmas party in Munich in 1923, where Hitler's fat police file was read out for the guests' entertainment – particularly eyewitness reports of the future leader frequenting a Munich café near the university, cruising for boyish young men.

Schlegel's enforced sojourn was uneventful until he was picked up by the American military as he was leaving a cinema. He sensed they thought they had someone, but didn't know who. He was interrogated by a fat Italian-American and a young man named Glover, who looked barely old enough to be out of shorts. When Schlegel played the Angleton card,

Glover announced that the man was a devious, arrogant son of a bitch, and Schlegel quickly grasped that there was a division between Americans recruiting and those prosecuting, and he had fallen into the wrong hands.

He found himself in a military prison, where thankfully no one beat him up. He was interviewed by Glover and decided to cooperate up to a point, because the boy was open and likeable, the opposite of Angleton. Glover told him he was just eighteen. Schlegel presumed he must be well-connected. He was, with a diplomat father and a family with long-standing connections to Italy. Glover's grandfather had been living in Florence when the war broke out and ended up in an SS camp after being denounced as a Jew, which he wasn't; he had died in captivity the year before, so the young American had no time for Nazis.

Schlegel claimed he had never been a Party member and in the last part of the war he had been conspiring to bring about the downfall of the regime. Not quite true, but he had enough material to produce an anodyne version of events.

Glover spoke openly of his rivalry with Angleton.

'Angleton resents my family. He likes to think he has a lock on Italy and on the Vatican. Jim makes himself out to be an expert on all things Italian, but he doesn't speak enough to order even a carciofi fritti.'

'Which you do?' asked Schlegel.

Glover laughed at that.

'And he's a beaner, too.'

Glover laughed at that, too, being a WASP.

Nothing of consequence happened as a result of these talks, and Schlegel decided he would be incarcerated indefinitely while Glover tried to find out exactly who he was.

Then, one day, he found himself being taken out of his

cell on a stretcher and moved to a suburban guesthouse, to be confronted by Jim Angleton, grinning from ear to ear, crowing that he'd got one over on the little bastard.

The footnote to his rescue was Angleton's carping insecurity about Glover knowing too much, and Schlegel providing Angleton with a solution in exchange for his safe passage to South America.

'Ships sail regularly from Genoa,' he said. 'Show me your file on Glover if you have one.'

Angleton did. The answer was easy: ascribe Angleton's methods to Glover.

He told Angleton, 'Glover has used various informers to hunt bigger fish. One, a Hungarian, worked as an antisemitic propagandist for the fascist government and is wanted for war crimes.'

'You mean, establish the connection between Glover and this criminal.'

'You must have tame press reporters in Washington.'

'That goes without saying.'

'Then provide the Hungarian with a special State Department security clearance and slip him into the United States, leak the story to the press and provide the journalist with documents showing that Glover has worked closely with the man on various covert missions. His career will be destroyed.'

'Easy-peasy,' said Angleton. 'And we'll get you that ticket.'

Which was what happened, except that at the last minute Schlegel received a visitor, none other than Andrey Turkul, who showed up in Genoa, saying he knew exactly who was leaving, when and to where.

'Herr Tieck, a Vatican diplomatic posting to Buenos Aires.'

Having reconciled himself to a life of exile, Schlegel found himself coerced into returning, because Turkul had a copy of

366

Schlegel's file as altered by Bormann, showing him in charge of countless civilian shootings in the eastern territories over the summer of 1941.

He was being blackmailed, but doing what exactly, Turkul didn't say, other than it would be against Stalin. Whether he was working for the Americans or Turkul, again Turkul didn't say.

Schlegel presumed that either Turkul had done a deal with the Americans or they had sold Schlegel to Turkul. It even crossed his mind that this might be Dulles' revenge, to prevent a last-minute escape.

'Hanover, perhaps,' said Turkul. 'Do nothing, just observe and report. Maybe we will use you, maybe not. We need people in deep cover.'

From what he could tell, he had either been forgotten or was a sleeper who was never fully activated, other than meeting a contact twice a month, a man he was told would introduce himself as Richter. As in every walk of life, espionage was full of makeweights and Richter showed no interest in anything other than standards of living among Schlegel's friends and acquaintances: which brand of hi-fi console, quality of furniture, type of car and sexual proclivities with a view to blackmail, which Schlegel suspected was the point when an acquaintance of his, thought to be homosexual, killed himself.

Only many years later, in 1977, when Gehlen – whose wartime outfit had been sold to the Americans, after which he had gone on to become head of the West German Intelligence Service – published his memoirs did Schlegel suspect what might have lain behind all those elaborate dealings.

Gehlen's bombshell was that Bormann had been a Soviet agent all along. It was pretty much laughed out of court, but Schlegel had always wondered who'd prompted Turkul's approach. If Gehlen was correct, Bormann and Turkul might have known each other's real roles, which meant that he, Schlegel, had unwittingly been working for the Russians throughout.

He shrugged it off; too much water under the bridge – his life didn't deserve more than a cliché to explain it. The point was, he had learned by then, anything could be rewritten to fit – Hitler's fate being the obvious example – and the opposite could also be shown to be true. By the time he saw the film *Downfall*, he thought it as plausible as any other version, however full of holes. After all those years, it still told the story that Bormann and Goebbels had wanted the world to hear.

Thanatos

As the Swiss had looked after his money with tomblike discretion, August Schlegel decided to die there. He would make a last will with his Zurich attorney and put his affairs in order. His money he would give away, to whom or what he hadn't made up his mind. He was indifferent to his fortune, around 15-16 million euros: we bring nothing into the world, and we take nothing out. Unlike the buccaneering Evelyn Robinson, he had always been assiduous in his dealings with the tax office, knowing his loopholes. Bank, lawyer and hotel was what it would come down to, then the final business.

He had no relatives, apart from a child by Katharina Fischer, which he had never seen and had no wish to. He had written himself out of the picture without knowing whether she'd had a son or daughter. His wife was dead fifteen years. There would be no funeral service, because there was no one left to attend or that he wished to. He had outlived nearly all those he knew.

So Schlegel, at end of his life, took the train from Hanover to Zurich. He had various cancers – 'take your pick' – and subscribed to a Swiss suicide club which required a membership fee. He had forwarded his medical record. He was on a raft of pills, with side effects, mood swings, unreliable transmission, lassitude and fuzziness, interrupted by vertiginous flashbacks to mass war graves, beatings and near-death experiences. A suicide service was available in Germany, but he had formed an attachment to Zurich during the war and his own country's euthanasia record wasn't exactly spotless.

He had become familiar on the telephone with Benway, director of Thanatos, named after the Greek god of non-violent death, whose touch, Benway patronisingly assured him, was gentle. Schlegel suspected the mythology disguised a commercial edge, for when were the Swiss anything else? Benway was one of those suave cosmopolitan figures (Swiss-German mother, American father, privately educated in England) who switched effortlessly between German, French and English. He made a point of laughing at everything, except himself. Schlegel couldn't decide whether this was a cultivated manner or a mild psychosis. Benway employed an unsettling combination of sales pitch and tedious solicitation; no doubt the man smelled his money.

After saying, 'I can tell you are a practical person,' Benway shared the problems he'd had keeping his clinic open.

'We were twice forced out of residential areas following local protest, after which the municipality wasn't sure if the service offered should be determined by commercial or industrial zoning.'

Schlegel remembered that even Auschwitz had been hampered by local authorities.

Benway went on. 'As a foreigner, you are seen as an anomaly. Swiss residents can be aided in the privacy of their homes. For visitors, it is another matter.'

Schlegel thought it somehow typical that the unwarlike, secretive Swiss should establish themselves as leaders in the field of private commercial death.

For foreign clients, Benway had found himself in the extraordinary position of being forced to attend to their needs in hotels and car parks, because legal loopholes didn't regulate commercial activity in a stationary car, and while any individual could be banned from a hotel, organisations couldn't. Schlegel decided that suited him fine; he would breathe his last in that old haunt, the Baur.

On the way to Zurich, he thought about his first meeting with Evelyn Robinson, also on a train, in its way a *coup de foudre*, recognising each other as two men out for themselves. Evelyn was the more psychotic. Schlegel remembered him behaving like a maniac in a bar in Hanover in 1945, waving a pistol when one night he had insisted that they go to what he called a Kraut joint, a dirty hole off a rubble-strewn street. The conversation stopped when they walked in. The place stank of the bitterness of defeat. The drinkers were ex-soldiers, wearing old bits of German uniform, and violently smashed. One rose on crutches and hobbled to the bar to say they weren't welcome. The men were all maimed, with limbs missing, half their faces blown away, or blind. Evelyn's response was to demand schnapps from the bartender at gunpoint. Evelyn, already drunk, struck Schlegel as unhinged. If he had some kind of flashback to the war, he would probably end up killing someone. They sat by the door, Evelyn loosely holding his gun as he drank. It took Schlegel a long time to persuade him to leave, and then only after Evelyn had fired at a bottle behind the bar. The barman yelped as he was showered with broken glass and dropped to the floor. It happened so fast that everyone jumped. Schlegel's ears were ringing, and the room reeked of cordite. Evelyn looked around for a new target, fired twice and smashed more bottles, before Schlegel dragged him into the street, where Evelyn declared, 'What fun!'

After that, Schlegel decided he had seen enough war to last several lifetimes and cocooned himself by becoming a dull local dignitary, pillar of the community and exemplar of the bland and compromised Adenauer era. Any dirty money had long been laundered. His life since he could write on a couple of sides of paper. His longevity he viewed as a punishment, because he was bored and had been for years. There was his secret double life, because technically he remained a spy, but that had amounted to fewer and fewer pointless meetings with his contact, Richter, and none for years now; he presumed the man was dead. His enviably prosperous but empty existence was how he wanted it. The running commentary in his head was restricted to what he saw: 'Those are the flowers on the table'; 'That is my wife in the next room watching television'; 'This is me driving my Mercedes-Benz' (always Mercedes). Sometimes he had to remind himself that he was no longer August Schlegel, but August Tieck. He found that the split helped him play his elected role.

In terms of near misses, in 1977 the German Intelligence Service found his name on a list of potential kidnap victims drawn up by the Red Army Faction. It was passed on, and he was one of the first to install private security cameras.

In the mid-1980s, a keen young investigative reporter came sniffing about someone known to Schlegel: Dr Hanns Stosberg, senior town planner.

The reporter wanted to know if Schlegel was aware that Stosberg had performed a similar, more controversial task during the war.

Schlegel found the reporter pompous and self-justifying in a way that was typical of the post-war generation (and the Third Reich before it).

The reporter said, 'This was a racially motivated programme, built with slave labour, to turn the town of Auschwitz into a German regional capital.'

Plans included the elimination of any Jewish element, including the cemetery. There were architectural drawings for modern plazas and housing, which would feature all mod cons in anticipation of automatic washing machines and the private motor car becoming the primary mode of transport. Leading landscape architects and botanists would inaugurate procedures for recycling and waste processing. One such consultant was an esteemed Berlin professor of landscape design, one of whose students had already applied to write his dissertation on the subject.

Schlegel didn't point out that much the same could be said of the reconstruction of Hanover, except wages were paid.

'And down the road, the gas ovens,' the reporter concluded, ominously.

'Not built by Stosberg.'

'No, but the point is Stosberg and his associates relocated here and carried on their careers uninterrupted.'

Schlegel wondered if the man had simply copied his old Auschwitz plans for the British. It would have saved everyone a lot of time.

The reporter droned on. 'This includes an esteemed professor of landscape design, who junked his racial invective and reinvented himself as a green ecologist with a worldwide reputation.'

Schlegel asked if Dr Stosberg or his employers and the occupying forces had any opinion on the matter, because he was unaware of any such plans (not quite true) and there was nothing he could add, except to congratulate the young man on digging up such an extraordinary story.

The reporter was under the impression that Schlegel's current construction work meant that he, too, had been part of the Auschwitz development.

Schlegel fobbed him off with his old false papers, placing him elsewhere on diplomatic work.

Schlegel heard afterwards that the reporter had been arrested on unspecified charges; perhaps because of information he had passed on to Richter. There remained a sense that the past wasn't dormant, but it never surfaced in any dramatic way.

Business took care of itself, and he looked back and saw only idyllic summers, skiing holidays and six-week winter breaks in Barbados. His wife was sporty. They played tennis and made passionless love by appointment. His social life at home amounted to dinner parties, including fraternising with the British army and diplomatic corps for the duration of their occupation. Whatever his views, Schlegel kept them to himself. He had the art of being a good listener, while reciting to himself, 'I am empty inside, but that's the way I have made myself.' He thought he managed a better job of it than the hollowed-out men John le Carré wrote about. Apart from a couple of drunken mentions to Katharina Fischer about being in a bunker at the end, he wasn't going to dine out on it; Evelyn Robinson knew, too, but nothing like the whole story. Schlegel had told his wife nothing. No one was going to ask, 'Tell us how you and Bormann got rid of Hitler.'

If he had to summarise his post-war life, it would be a sunny lake and a leisure boat. The boat was nothing fancy, compared to those some had, with a comfortable cabin in which he got his best sleep listening to the lapping of water as he drifted off. He would retain that image for when the time came.

The wish for an assisted death was partly cowardice. He wanted someone in the room, rather than slitting his wrists in the bathtub or messily shooting himself with the Geli gun, which he had kept all those years. His days were numbered and he wasn't sure how to fill them, while being afraid to end them. He wanted to talk to strangers when he drank alone in the hotel bar, except he couldn't see any equivalent to Evelyn Robinson; a chancer by his own definition. He started over-tipping, and the staff were embarrassed because it was far too much, and he saw them thinking that he was an old fool.

The next morning at breakfast in the hotel, a tall young man with dreadful skin approached Schlegel's table. The last time, over sixty years before, his visitor was Allen Dulles; now it was someone who reminded Schlegel of himself, who even more extraordinarily presented him with a photograph of his own younger self.

And there was Braun's handkerchief, also given.

Schlegel knew then that Evelyn Robinson must have been sent him. He couldn't decide whether he was irritated or relieved, though he was at a loss for words when the man introduced himself as his grandson.

In the end, Parker's journey to the hotel had been quite straightforward. He had presented himself at a rich man's house in Hanover where Schlegel had lived all those years (Evelyn Robinson had the address), where he was told by an elderly housekeeper that Herr Tieck had left that morning for Zurich, with no plans to return. Whether the housekeeper was privately worried about her employer or unnerved by the appearance of this troubled young man, announcing with a rather desperate air that he was a long-lost relative, she suggested he try the Baur Hotel. Or perhaps she wasn't so devoted and sent Parker out of mischief or spite (servants are always hardest to read), because she feared her master's generosity wouldn't extend to leaving her anything in his will and it crossed her mind that the so-called relative might be after the man's fortune; in which case, good luck to him.

The only muddle was that August Schlegel had checked in under his own name, paying cash. It is tempting to add that he stayed in or near the room where Molly Fitzgerald had first bedded Hermann Fegelein, but we don't know. Parker thought he had fucked up upon being told that no one called Tieck was staying, until he found himself watching Schlegel at breakfast and saw the ghost of the man in the photograph.

Parker was grudgingly invited to sit.

Schlegel was thrown to find himself with the complication of a relative of whose existence he'd had no idea, threatening by his presence to take him back to a part of his life he had successfully buried. He ascribed to the tall young man in his black suit a symbolic role, perhaps pointing towards another death which Schlegel did not have in mind, rather than swallowing the deadly potion.

So he said, 'I know an angel of death when I see one.'

Parker seemed unthrown by the observation; it confirmed an uncanny feeling that Schlegel had read him perfectly.

Schlegel said, 'Cancer, it hardly matters which sort. Several, competing.'

Parker came with a message, which was only to be expected. He explained the situation with Evelyn Robinson and his son.

'Ah, the begging bowl,' said Schlegel. 'How much?'

He shrugged when told.

'I was always fond of Evelyn,' he said. 'I am happy to write them a cheque.'

Parker looked surprised by how easy it was.

'What about you?' Schlegel asked. 'Do you need money?'

Parker said it didn't interest him.

'Unlike Dr Benway,' Schlegel said, curious for the first time about the young man. 'As you are here now, you may as well meet him. I have an appointment in ten minutes.'

The man remained guarded, but nothing about him seemed unclear. When Parker had first watched him across the dining room, he had appeared blurred, but now it was as though he, Parker, served as a lens to bring him into focus, in a way that reminded him of the uncompromising realism of Grünewald.

Before they left breakfast, at which Schlegel only picked, he said, 'Legally, you have to take the stuff yourself; it can't be administered. Swiss death is like everything else here, a bureaucratic process.'

They met Benway in the private bar room where Schlegel had been entertained by Allen Dulles and Jim Angleton. He wondered what the two Yanks would make of Benway. God knows, they had assisted enough people to the other side via abrupt hospital deaths, unexpected illnesses and so forth. One of their tame doctors had performed LSD experiments on an elephant. Jim was gone twenty years or more; lung cancer – the slow suicide of nicotine and alcohol. Cough, cough! Dulles had managed 75 before being taken off by influenza and pneumonia, though Schlegel had read some-where that it was cancer.

He didn't bother to introduce Parker, and if Benway was surprised it didn't show.

The disturbing thing about Benway was that he resembled a more quietly mad version of Vod, older but with the same embalmed look. The difference was, Benway held eye contact, and Parker wondered if it was some kind of hypnotic trick and whether Schlegel read the man's grasping unctuousness. Whatever the Swiss were, they weren't classy; Roger Federer – sublime, perhaps – tried too hard with his monogrammed kit and off-court deference.

Schlegel seemed to think that his death would take place upstairs in his room. Parker even wondered if he expected it to happen then and there, as Benway had come with a black bag.

Benway apologised for the confusion. The hotel was no longer possible, as that legal loophole had been closed. They now had their own clinic.

Schlegel, disconcerted by this, said, 'I thought I had made my position clear.'

They had been standing. Schlegel sat down, repeating, 'I see,' when he evidently didn't, then saying, 'Perhaps the hotel would be prepared to overlook the matter in exchange for . . .' He rubbed thumb and forefinger in the universal gesture for money. Its crudeness left Parker feeling ashamed on the man's behalf.

Benway coughed apologetically. 'I fear not. We would be liable for prosecution.'

Parker saw that Benway was worried about losing the sale. He spoke for the first time. 'Perhaps you could show us the clinic. I am sure we have time.'

Out of the corner of his eye, he watched Schlegel shrug, then nod.

Benway drove. Schlegel, in a better mood, announced himself impressed by the car, a Mercedes S-class coupé. It was fine if you were in front but the back had little legroom, which left Parker sitting sideways.

Benway kept up a monologue. How they were treated like a cult. How they had been driven out of residential neighbourhoods. How they had first been banished to a commercial zone, where their neighbour was the country's largest brothel.

'A brothel!' echoed Schlegel.

'Thanatos versus Eros, picture that! We blocked planning permission for them to extend their car park. They said our incinerator chimney broke EU regulations. Nothing but squabbles. We were forced to abandon hearses and use rental vans.'

What Benway didn't say was that he had been accused of dumping at least 300 urns of ashes in the lake, but for once Swiss law was on his side, as nothing said he couldn't.

They passed the city limits. Parker imagined a secluded villa and parkland, like an English country house, somewhere you would want to go, but their destination was an industrial estate with giant sheds, block buildings, stacked containers and, sitting there incongruously, a prefabricated, pastel-coloured weatherboard cottage.

Parker and Schlegel formed separate impressions. The building overlooked a scrap of meadow. An attempt had been made at landscaping that looked to Parker like a job lot from a cheap garden centre: wooden decking, an ornamental pond, a bench, struggling shrubbery and a pathetic orchard, with everything mocked by a giant, kilometre-long shed that stood behind. Perhaps it's there where the souls go after death, Parker thought to himself, and this is heaven after all.

Auschwitz had its gardens, too, Schlegel remembered, and regulations done by the book, zoning laws and incinerator

379

chimneys. It was the precursor of these industrial parks with their big sheds and drone-like workers, little more than slaves. Where Birkenau's accommodation was converted horse stables, now it would be shipping containers. The house was, if not a death factory, still in the business of death. Like the first temporary gassing stations in Auschwitz, it pretended to be a cottage set in natural surroundings. The weatherboard house struck Schlegel as a sanitised, commercial successor in manufactured death.

Inside was as one might expect: a combination of IKEA and day-care centre, with neutral beiges and cheerful primary colours, scented sticks, candles and incense-like air freshener to distract from the presence of death.

When Benway introduced them to the clinic manager, Schlegel found himself staring at a woman who appeared to be the reincarnation of Eleonore Hodys. Her ironic expression and almond eyes seemed to recognise him in return, as though she had been waiting for him.

Parker's memory of the next day or so remained vague. Schlegel kept looking at the clinic manager, Frau Hidell, in a strange way. He insisted on going ahead with the procedure and asked Parker to be with him at the end. It was patiently explained that even if they offered their fast-track service, which involved a further charge of several thousand euros, nothing could be done before 11am the next day. Schlegel said he would prefer the evening – 'The dying of the light and all that' – but was told that business had to be completed within working hours.

'What business?' asked Schlegel.

Any death had to be videoed for inspection by the police and an independent doctor to ensure correct procedure.

Parker found something entrancing about Frau

Hidell – the calm voice, a slow politeness that probably masked indifference, a consummate professionalism. It was a perfect performance that didn't waver throughout the rest of the day, which was spent with paperwork, forms and more forms, and an upstairs tour to choose which room. Parker was reminded of a cheap backpackers' hostel. He wondered who had chosen the innocuous pictures on the walls. Schlegel said it was all the same to him.

'There's one that costs more,' said Frau Hidell, 'should you be interested.'

It was done out in the English style, with a sofa in a William Morris print, mahogany furniture, oil paintings, heavy drapes and a comfortable-looking bed with a heavy crochet spread.

Parker looked around as Frau Hidell named an exorbitant price.

Schlegel said, 'Why not?'

There were yet more forms to fill in. Benway had vanished, and Parker wondered how they would get back or whether they would be offered rooms for the night. There was a counselling session he was not allowed to attend, so he sat outside on a bench and stared at the grubby pond. He was joined by Hidell, who had come out for a cigarette, which surprised him as he hadn't associated the place with smoking.

'Your friend seems familiar somehow,' she said. 'Is he well-known? We had a famous conductor once.'

Parker said the man was his grandfather and they'd only just met. He couldn't think what else to add, except that he wouldn't want to die there.

'Don't worry, we know how to make it peaceful and natural,' she said. 'The final moments can be very beautiful.'

It wasn't until then that Parker saw Hidell as entirely

cold-blooded. He wondered what her private life was like. He couldn't picture any children. He supposed the clinic was entirely child-free, yet he thought there was something disturbingly childish about the place, with its unpleasant caring.

Hidell said she would phone for a taxi to take them back and they should return the next day at the appointed hour.

Schlegel was silent in the taxi. Back at the hotel, he seemed uncertain about what to do. Parker was quite out of his depth. It looked like a long night. How does one spend the last hours in the company of a self-condemned man?

'Why are you here?' Schlegel asked, tetchy.

'Because of Morgen, I suppose.'

'Morgen!' exclaimed Schlegel. 'What on earth has *he* to do with it?'

Parker explained how he'd read Schlegel's testament and Morgen's reports on H. and Hitler's death.

Schlegel said, 'Hodys I had forgotten about until this afternoon. That Hidell woman could be her double. I hadn't until then believed in the past returning to haunt.'

'And Benway looks like Vod,' said Parker.

He had to explain, and Schlegel, after looking bemused, said, 'If I am to die tomorrow, I would rather do it hungover.'

They adjourned to what Schlegel called 'the Dulles room' with a bottle of Dewar's whisky, then a second, by which point Parker had only a hazy recollection of what they had talked about: it took days to piece it together, and even then bits didn't fit. It looked like they were there for the duration, because the last thing Schlegel wanted was to go to bed. He talked about a final party in the bunker and how they'd stayed up until daylight getting beyond smashed. He explained about Eva Braun taking his photograph and the handkerchief. He told Parker about mass shootings in the east, illegal Berlin jazz clubs and the slow process of erasure after the war, the summer lake and the pleasure boat, and his heroic dullness compared to that fabulous nihilism he had noticed in Evelyn Robinson.

Parker told him about his life in return, including Father Roper. He could see no reason not to; Schlegel would be dead tomorrow, leaving Parker thinking that perhaps he could finally be released by his confession.

'It's good that these things come out,' Schlegel said, trying to sound more sober than he was.

The Roper business took up only a small part of the conversation. Parker explained about his grandmother, her drinking, her death. Schlegel showed no curiosity about his mother.

Hodys, on the other hand, he did explain.

'She knew too much about the racketeering, which was why they tried to get rid of her, rather late in the day, when she probably should have gone in the general clear-out the year before. Why didn't she? You may well ask. You could lose yourself in the system if you knew your way around. Administration was never that efficient. There was an art to survival, which she had.'

'When did you hear about her?'

'In the summer of 1944. Her name came up as someone who knew the whole story.' Which was what Hodys had said about the women and the penal colony riot, Parker remembered.

Schlegel said, 'The year before, Morgen had failed to make charges of corruption against the commandant stick. Any such further revelations would count for nothing from what I could see, so I told her she needed to come up with something better.'

He could see that she was a canny player; otherwise she wouldn't have survived as long as she had.

'So I wasn't entirely surprised when she told me an entirely believable story about the commandant's infatuation and a less believable one about an actual affair, pregnancy, starvation and an abortion. I spoke with Morgen about this, and we agreed that Hodys was probably exaggerating to strengthen her case and ensure her continued protection.'

But it was an old story, impossible to verify. So Schlegel faked it.

'If it could be updated, I could persuade Morgen to act, so I found a female prisoner doctor who, in exchange for a hefty contribution towards improving ward conditions, was willing to state that she had recently carried out an abortion at the commandant's request.'

This gave him sufficient impetus to have Hodys transferred out of harm's way, in exchange for her co-operation. He saw no reason to inform her of the revised timeline. He had managed to save her life, and it wasn't his fault that Morgen had made such a dog's dinner of her testimony.

'A fat lot of good it did him,' Schlegel said. 'The case was kicked out by the commandant's boss in Berlin, who said it was her word against his and there was nothing to answer.'

Parker said, 'By one account, she was pregnant when she left.'

'Really? Who knows. Anything was possible. It was the kingdom of lies.' He shrugged. 'At this moment, I no longer know or even care. They called it the arsehole of the world.'

They drank, passed out and dozed, woke and drank more, beyond speech. Parker vaguely remembered getting up to vomit and returning to carry on drinking.

At one point, Schlegel asked if he intended to do anything about Roper. Parker said that one day he would confront him.

Schlegel giggled and said, 'As I did with Dulles. The

man was a liar and a cheat, as he proved when we played tennis.'

'My grandmother told me that at her level it was a matter of returning the ball.'

Schlegel looked confused at that and asked, 'Whatever for?'

He said he wasn't afraid of death.

'So many gone before. They give you a cup of ghastly liquid, and you go to sleep. Some people eat chocolate to take away the taste. I'm told the chocolate you have to bring yourself.'

Parker said, 'Robinson would opt for Kinder Bueno. He likes to remove the bottom wafer, break it in two, fold it over and wait until the chocolate melts in the mouth so he can suck out the soft centre.'

'Kinder Bueno, then. Tissues for the bereaved the clinic provides free. I am told if you are physically incapable of drinking from the cup, there is a mechanical hand that performs the task.'

Schlegel wasn't sure whether he had been conscious or dreaming when he saw himself give the golden gun to Evelyn Robinson, not long after they'd met; Evelyn liked stuff that was a bit flash, and Schlegel didn't want to lug it around. He said he wasn't superstitious, but as long as Evelyn kept the gun, it would ensure their good fortune. He didn't believe that for a moment, but Evelyn was impressed. They'd flown with all kinds of mascots, he'd told Schlegel. His bomb-aimer took his childhood teddy bear, stuffed in his flying suit, and never lived it down after they found out.

The Geli gun Schlegel had kept, and he often asked himself why. Perhaps because he knew its secrets and the gun's real role in the deaths of Hitler and his niece, which traced the arc of the man's years in power. The biggest secret Schlegel had discovered was that she had survived, braindead and on life support, for the necrophile pleasure of her uncle; no proof of that, but he wouldn't put it past the man; and it was he, Schlegel, who had switched off the support, her angel of death. Her hair had turned quite white, like his, although she still looked like a child. So he had kept the gun as a true talisman, because he was about the only one who knew she hadn't shot herself (because someone else had pulled the trigger); nor had Hitler, having missed. Even so, he wondered why he had hung on to it.

A taxi fetched them the next morning. Schlegel didn't bother to wash or shave. He cleared his room, packed his few belongings and checked out. He could still smell the drink on himself. His mind seemed to have been effectively wiped. He could remember next to nothing of the night before. Standing in the lobby, Parker looked as though he might keel over. Schlegel paused to watch the hotel go about its business, nodded at Parker and said, 'Let's go.'

It was a hard, bright morning. Schlegel told the driver to stop outside a confectionery shop and sent Parker to buy Kinder Bueno. Parker's hands were shaking as he fumbled the change. He had a vivid image of willingly drinking the deadly potion after Schlegel and Hidell pointed out that it was meant for him all along. He left the shop and thought about walking away, but he got back in the taxi. The driver had the radio on, and a scratchy tune was being played on a balalaika. Parker wondered if Schlegel really wanted to leave the world listening to that. He supposed he should have asked if he had a CD in mind, but presumed the clinic had a library of suitable farewell music, which would waste a bit more time. Schlegel said nothing. It was hard to tell if he was thinking anything at all.

Parker saw death, not waiting but ever-present; saw Christ drive the moneylenders out of the temple; saw the angel of death; saw Bunyan's pilgrim, staggering with no destination or written end in mind.

He supposed Schlegel's last cash transaction would be paying the taxi driver, as it turned out that the fare wasn't on the clinic's account. Schlegel looked blank. Parker paid. It cleaned him out of cash.

Schlegel had made out two cheques the previous night before they'd got drunk. Even though Parker had bank transfer details, Schlegel said, 'I believe some things should be signed for.'

The first cheque was made out to Evelyn Robinson and the second to 'Mr Robinson', after Parker realised that he had no idea what his first name was.

Parker recited in a strange singsong voice to the taxi driver, 'Death is not waiting, it's ever present, except you can't see it,' and wondered where that came from.

Hidell was waiting in reception, wearing a charcoal suit and a white linen shirt and carrying a clipboard. She was gossiping with the receptionist and laughing as they walked in. She composed herself, looking mildly surprised at their dishevelled state. Parker supposed they got all sorts, but 99 per cent would have made more of an effort than they had. He saw a celestial crowd of those who had gone before, some suitably attired for the last formal occasion, others kitted out in Adidas, Nike, Kappa, whatever, old folk turning up in the adult equivalent to babygros as though comfort might ease their passage.

Schlegel thought to himself: This is me standing in a lobby to which I shall not return.

There was, of course, more paperwork. He reconfirmed the terms, ticked various boxes, including one marked 'cremation', which he was sure he had ticked before. He supposed his ashes would be dumped somewhere. He watched a printer rattle out an enormous bill and wondered how much a dose of the magic potion cost, probably no more than a few euros. He had been told by Hidell that terms were normally settled beforehand, but as a result of fast-tracking and staff shortages they were a little behind. Schlegel looked at Hidell and found her polite, deferential and unspeakable. Even so, he pressed on. Parker appeared to have gone yellow. He insisted on handing out Kinder Bueno to Hidell and the receptionist. With the chocolate in her mouth, Hidell gestured: Shall we? Schlegel was offered the elevator. He said he preferred to walk and led the way, reassured that his tread on the stairs was firm, though he found himself wavering on the upstairs landing.

The door ahead: he stood aside to let Hidell open it.

He was asked if he wanted to undress and get into bed. He said no, he would just lie down when the time came.

Various medical trollies had been wheeled into the room. A mini-camera stood on a tripod opposite the bed. They had been joined by another woman he hadn't seen before. He thought of the stretcher that he and Bormann had carried Hitler on. He put the holdall on the bed, thinking of the Geli gun in it, and saw the headlines: 'Man goes berserk in suicide clinic; several dead.' Oh, just get on with it, he thought, but there were more questions, more rehearsals. He was told again that the potion couldn't be administered, he had to take it himself. He was asked again if it was what he wanted. They were all still standing like they were at death's cocktail party. Schlegel asked Parker for a Kinder Bueno.

There were only two left. He wished he had bought another bottle of Dewar's.

'The last for after the poison,' said Schlegel. 'To take away the taste.'

Parker had a flash of Eva Braun – and couldn't tell if it was a real or imagined death – in the split second of biting into the cyanide capsule, realising it wasn't to be the beautiful death she'd wanted, saw the drooling, frothing and convulsions, the snap back of the neck, the rictus grin as though she had finally seen the joke and it wasn't funny, and any dream of escape was in the moment just that.

A pill in a paper cup. Water added. The cup was handed to Schlegel by Hidell, who averted her eyes. He was sitting on the bed, staring at the bubbles as the pill dissolved. If he didn't take it, he wondered how long he had.

Schlegel looked at Hidell and said, 'Not on your life.'

He stood, handed back the cup, picked up the holdall and politely asked for someone to call a taxi.

There was an awkward discussion in the lobby when Parker asked Hidell about a refund. Schlegel left them to it and went outside, wondering whether he had flunked it; if there had been a moment, it was probably when he had ticked the box for cremation.

The taxi was the same as before. Charon, the Styx ferryman, Schlegel thought to himself. The man probably had an exclusive contract with Thanatos.

'Enough of the music,' Schlegel said as he got in and waited for Parker, who when he came said that Hidell had referred the matter of a refund to Benway.

'They're haggling,' said Parker.

'Let them,' answered Schlegel.

The car rental company didn't have a Mercedes. They were all out on hire, so they were stuck with a Volkswagen. Schlegel said to Parker, 'I could go out and buy a fucking Mercedes,' but he rented the VW, thinking to himself it could only end badly.

All he told Parker was, 'About five hours.'

Along for the ride, Parker supposed to himself. He couldn't tell whether Schlegel was Lazarus raised from the dead or if he had already gone beyond and this journey was part of an afterlife. Sometimes Parker felt as though he, too, was taking leave of the world and was left questioning the point of every object: rock, paper, scissors. There no longer seemed to be any proper sequence, with his mind jumping all over: Roper was crowding him, sharper than the faded present. Schlegel appeared parchment-like. Parker saw Roper in the back of the car, sometimes his grandmother, sometimes people he didn't know at all.

What would Roper have told given the opportunity? Not that there was any direct link between the Nazi gold Schlegel had stashed in the Vatican bank and Roper's tenure there, other than the walls remaining the same and Roper being as tainted as the loot that had infiltrated the system. Dirty money, dirty habits, dirty secrets.

The compromised priest would further compromise himself, absconding with Vatican funds and going to ground when questions started to be asked about his past. Roper, getting on now, remained nostalgic for his career of caning, abuse and buggery. He prostrated himself before God, praying that He would allow a way for him to transgress one last time (a lack of boys in the Vatican bank left him contemplating street urchins) before he gave himself to his Saviour's arms.

Schlegel and Parker had only one conversation of significance on the drive, after they had stopped at an empty service station because Schlegel was tired.

Parker asked, 'Did you ever hear of film of the exterminations? Robinson believes it exists.'

Schlegel said, 'Whether it does or not, it remains better unseen. Some things should be held to be beyond show.'

What he didn't say was he knew because he had seen.

Later, in the car, as they neared their destination, he decided to tell after all.

He said, 'There was 9mm cine film shot by the commandant on a camera given to him as a present by Himmler. The commandant was an assiduous shooter of home movies: kiddies, pets, a foal, a slide, a paddling pool, picnics in a summer house, picnics by the river, children swimming.'

It would have been around the time of the Hodys affair, July 1944, when he learned that material filmed by the commandant contained proof of what was going on. A technician who worked for the photo laboratory that processed the footage passed on the information to the underground, and Schlegel was told as much by a prisoner medical clerk whom he had cultivated. Getting hold of the film wasn't difficult as the commandant's house had many collections and deliveries. Schlegel fetched it himself. The films were stored on a shelf in the basement, neatly labelled. He took the one marked July 1942.

The roll contained four minutes of silent material, half of which was family dross, until the subject switched abruptly to what Schlegel realised was Reichsführer Himmler's tour of inspection, which had taken place that month. The man himself could be seen beaming as he pretended to conduct the prisoner orchestra welcoming him, to the evident merriment of his entourage. Otherwise it was dappled orchards, giant greenhouses and reclamation projects shot in colour on a stifling summer's day. Himmler appeared not to object to being filmed despite looking bad-tempered. Then cut: train comes into station. Cut: people get out of goods wagons with their luggage. The camera shows everything done by the book, because it's a general inspection. Considerate prisoner guards in freshly laundered uniforms help people down, politely taking their luggage, pointing the way. A shot of suitcases neatly stacked when they were usually chucked aside. No beatings or snarling dogs to hurry things along. A long, orderly queue awaits selection by polite men in white coats, pointing left or right. Cut to trucks waiting, being loaded. Not many angles, nothing that says death; nothing dramatic or exciting about the footage; a sense of compressed time and random impressions. Almost as though an evacuation has taken place and refugees are being welcomed to a place of safety. No telling what is about to happen; the illusion sustained. Another location. A cottage in woods. Trees. Green. Bucolic. Queues, still orderly, no urgency; even some shared jokes between those in line and medical orderlies. An ambulance with a red cross. Another cut: a queue, naked now, being ushered into the cottage (with bricked-up windows), again almost leisurely. Mainly women and children. To judge by the shadows, late afternoon.

Only afterwards did Schlegel understand the historical significance of this day. A Dutch transport arrived, a pivotal moment that determined the fate of the place. Himmler saw for himself how effective the dispatch was, proof that they could handle the job, and with a second such 'cottage' already established, work could take place around the clock. The day after his inspection, he ordered a huge increase in transportations.

By the commandant's account, Himmler cadged a cigarette, though he didn't normally smoke, and puffed inexpertly on it as he looked through the spy hole while the gassing was in progress.

The commandant also jammed his camera lens against the spy hole (the other facility didn't have one).

Schlegel said to Parker, 'The celluloid failed to process what it saw, other than as an abstract, heaving mass, not identifiable as such. It was as though the film itself had a chemical reaction and refused to capture what was being shot.'

Parker asked if he had told anyone.

Schlegel said he hadn't, as the footage didn't offer incontrovertible proof, and anyway the killings were sanctioned and added nothing to the case against the commandant.

He didn't tell Parker that the final frames had shown everything. He had put the film back where he had found it and told no one.

Whatever Parker had expected, it didn't involve stumbling around a golf course. He hadn't even known that Germans played golf. In a way, they hadn't, because the course was built by the occupying American army as a recreational facility for their troops.

Regardless of what Hitler's mountain redoubt had once been – thanks to Bormann's relentless compulsory purchases and rapid building programme, spoiling natural beauty with a ghastly fortified mini-state – what remained did not conform to Albert Speer's theory of ruin value. The old town survived in its twee, ultra-conservative prosperity, while much of what the arrivistes had built, including the main site, had been reclaimed by nature and was rubble overgrown with trees. The building Schlegel was looking for, about a fifteen-minute walk away, was not signposted, as no attempt was made to advertise the past, and everything appeared very different from when he had last been there.

After parking the car and getting lost, they had ended up on the golf course, where Schlegel finally got his bearings as Parker was about to say they should give up. Schlegel pointed to an overlook. He was sure it was where Hitler had contemplated the view after taking afternoon tea in his tea house, another of Bormann's ugly colonising efforts.

Schlegel said, 'The tea room was his favourite spot, and he strolled down most afternoons and was usually driven back.'

It was a steep climb. Schlegel was wheezing as they struggled on. At the top, he fought to regain his breath and collapsed on a bench overlooking the valley. When he recovered, he became confused because the tea house should have been behind them. It was Parker who pointed out that it had been razed to the ground, leaving only traces of the foundations. He still didn't know what Schlegel was looking for.

Braun and Schlegel had endlessly discussed where Hitler's final resting place should be. Braun wanted somewhere that had a sentimental attachment for 'her and her man', yet was secret and safe. The main house was out of the question, as it had been bombed and had fallen to the Americans, who spent most of their time looting souvenirs. Braun wondered about a waterfall that had been a favoured spot, but she gave up on that because no hiding place came to mind. Then there was a nearby church, picturesque enough to have featured in paintings and jigsaw puzzles. During a rare uninterrupted interlude when Hitler was ill, they had spent hours doing the jigsaw. He had promised that they would visit the church together when he recovered, but they never did, leaving

394

Braun to take lonely walks there on her own. Again, Schlegel pointed out the lack of an obvious hiding place, and Braun despaired.

Finally, she said, 'I know,' drew her childish map and said, 'X marks the spot.'

When Schlegel arrived there late in the summer of 1945, the Americans were easily avoided because they were too busy enjoying their peace. The uncertain pilgrimages of thousands of displaced people made moving around no problem. If people were surprised at seeing black soldiers (and bananas, not seen in years), no one questioned the sight of a priest on a bicycle, which Schlegel had managed to steal. It even had a basket to hold the deposit box.

He put it in its appointed resting place early one morning before anyone was up, performing the task not out of any particular loyalty to Braun, more from a sense of boyhood adventure stories – Robert Louis Stevenson and treasure maps – while he thought that if he landed up in real trouble at some point, he could trade the secret in exchange for his life. Besides, it entertained him that only he and Braun knew, when others would write screeds speculating on the man's death. If nothing else, Schlegel saw himself as burying the past and his own with it.

Parker couldn't work out what he was looking at, other than some kind of weird old futuristic contraption. They had searched around in woods without a path until he'd thought they were going round in circles. It was starting to get dark. They hadn't seen anyone since setting out. When at last Schlegel pointed, Parker wasn't sure what to make of it, standing alone, half-overgrown and incongruous among the trees, bullet-shaped like a small concrete rocket or a Tardis. More prosaically, its door suggested a huge stove or even a public lavatory. It was in every sense sinister and ridiculous. Rectangular slits high up in the concrete to let in light resembled eyes.

It was a Moll bunker, Schlegel explained, also known as a splinter protection shell. Tens of thousands had been produced in the war. They were a common feature of cities, offering cover to those unable to reach a proper bomb shelter. Hundreds had been installed locally, Schlegel added, to act as fortified sentry boxes.

'Bormann had this built for Hitler in case the tea house was threatened. It was bigger than usual and equipped with a telephone and electricity.'

There was never any question that Hitler would use it, but the man was a fan of Karl May Westerns and Bormann flattered him with the idea of a personal redoubt from which to make a last stand. It confirmed Hitler's view of himself as a man of action rather than the sedentary dope addict Bormann had come to despise. Hitler, with a fondness for secret spaces, demanded a hidey hole for personal effects and a supply of food. 'Otherwise it will get stolen by some light-fingered peasant.' Bormann said of course, thinking the man stupid, but obedience to his master's every whim was his watchword.

As it was, the construction of the bunker (with architect's fees for adjustments to the prefabricated model) was a waste of money, as it was never used, although Hitler delighted in inspecting it in the company of Bormann as the world collapsed.

Braun had thought of it was because Hitler had taken her there on the last occasion he had walked to the tea house before leaving, never to return. He told her he didn't know when he would be back. He fretted about her safety and the place being vulnerable now it was within enemy bombing range. He asked her to honour his ritual by going to the tea house as much as possible. Then he walked with her and proudly showed her the shelter and said, if anything happened, she would be safe there, with food for several days and a telephone to call for help.

There was just enough room inside to sit together. Braun told Schlegel that the Chief was in an unusually sentimental mood that day. He produced a silver monogrammed spoon which he had taken from the tea house, wondering if the servants were observant enough to notice they were now one short. He told Braun not to reprimand them. The spoon was his lucky charm and would ensure that she came to no harm. He wrapped it in a monogrammed handkerchief, which he said she could use to dry her tears, except he knew she was a brave girl and wouldn't cry.

'I shall leave it here even so,' he said.

Braun, eyes moist, told him that it felt a bit like sitting in a rocket. She was trying to be light-hearted and suggestive, but Hitler would have none of it, declaring, 'It is the age of the rocket. Remote-controlled missiles will win us the war.' He softened upon seeing her upset and said, 'Consider this your secret rocket that will take you safe far away!'

Braun found him quite sweet when he wanted to be, however desolate she felt about being abandoned.

Schlegel asked Parker if he could open the door to the shelter, as he doubted he had the strength. It was heavy, the hinges rusty but it gave after a few tugs. There had been other visitors, because the walls were covered with graffiti. The place felt claustrophobic and smelled of piss. The dying sun reflected on the walls.

He stood aside to let Schlegel in and watched as he got

down on his hands and knees and started scraping away the earth, leaving Parker to wonder if this was what it came down to: an old man, perhaps not of sound mind, scratching at the ground on all fours in the middle of nowhere.

Before long, a substratum was revealed and a small trap-door with an inset handle.

Perhaps Schlegel, like Parker, sensed the absurdity of the situation, because he grew irritated at being watched and told him to come back in five minutes.

Parker did as he was asked and wandered around, making sure he kept his bearings. They were the sort of woods in which it would be easy to get lost, primeval even, making the idea of a manicured golf course with its pointless taming of landscape – albeit with the traps of bunkers and long grass – appear ridiculous.

Schlegel was sitting on the ground when he returned, with various objects laid out between his splayed legs.

'There are even rusty tins of food left and a first-aid kit,' Schlegel said. 'The telephone has long gone.' He pointed to the battered deposit box. 'Hitler's ashes.'

Parker laughed in disbelief, then remembered what his grandmother had said and decided Schlegel was probably telling the truth; otherwise why go to all the trouble?

The map Braun had given Schlegel had survived, much faded, plus the handkerchief and silver spoon, now black.

Schlegel said, 'The only surprise, apart from it all still being here, is she must have visited at some point.'

He held up a card in a cellophane wrapper – cheesy and kitsch, a Valentine with hearts and angels.

'It's her handwriting.' He read aloud, '"Mein Chef, für immer Dein bis zum Tode. Bald werde ich an Deiner Seite sein, vereint für immer. Eva." Do you understand that?'

Parker repeated in English, 'My Chief, with you always unto death. I will soon be by your side, forever united. Eva.'

Schlegel picked up the box and said, 'I am the only person who knows about these ashes, and now you. Braun must be dead. She suggests as much in her note.' He shrugged. 'She was always prone to the suicidal gesture. Anyway, we are nearly done now.'

Parker carried the ashes back to the car, more or less in a straight line, which took fifteen minutes when they had spent an hour stumbling around looking for the place. They passed a stream, and Parker expected to be told to dump the ashes – good riddance – but they carried on in silence until they reached the car. Schlegel took his bag from the boot, and they got in. He was sweating profusely as he drove out into the dark countryside, climbing ever higher into steep mountains with a succession of u-bends, driving too fast, until Parker was convinced that they would run out of road and go over the edge. Perhaps he shouted for him to slow down, but there was no point. Schlegel gripped the wheel like a man possessed.

Sitting there trapped, staring fixedly through the windscreen, Parker found himself in the grip of his own possession, seeing many deaths in the course of each life; rehearsals, blips, petits morts, because death could play its card at any moment. Flashbacks of previous visions. Evelyn Robinson crashing and burning over Hanover as he had feared; any subsequent life played out in the moment of death, no less real for that. The drowning of Evelyn's son. Goebbels shooting himself (wearing silk socks and yellow silk tie, details *Downfall* got wrong), putting a full stop to the whole stupid opera; entertainment, diversions, this end and that.

Prior to Goebbels putting the gun to his head, Parker saw him present the final scenario as an example of young adult fiction to his eldest brat: 'The Führer cannot be with us for long. He has been called by the gods. He has asked for his ashes to be preserved in a secret casket to be passed down to you, the next generation of believers.' Only fooling! The boy would be dead within thirty-six hours, poisoned by his mother.

At a turning point, Schlegel braked to a sudden stop, turned and went back down, now driving as carefully as a man sitting his driving test. Parker looked at the lights of the town below and wondered at the point of anything.

They pulled into an empty car park in a remote spot, which by day would have been used by hikers. Schlegel became deliberate in a way that reminded Parker of a priest preparing to serve Mass.

He took the bag and produced a small tape recorder and a pistol. When Parker saw the gun, he thought they were about to embark on an absurd parody of the bunker suicide. Although Schlegel struck him as humourless, Parker had a sense of a sick black comedy, or something not far off one, being played out.

Schlegel pointed to the recorder and said, 'I am vain enough to have brought this for any last thoughts, perhaps even entertained by the idea of my disembodied voice being on tape after I am gone. Everything is calmer than I thought it would be ...'

Parker's impression was of it all being stripped down, economical and deliberate.

Of the pistol, Schlegel said, 'This is the gun Hitler was supposed to have shot himself with, except he didn't. Thirteen years before that, it was the gun his niece and true beloved was supposed to have shot herself with, except she didn't.'

Schlegel was grimly aware that the bullet meant for him was by his own volition.

He went on, 'We could continue the tradition: I don't shoot myself and you administer the coup de grâce, then place the gun in my hand to make it look as though I had. Or I just shoot you and live out my allotted span. The question is, how much pain does there need to be?'

Parker thought it could go either way and Schlegel really was in two minds about who to shoot, and said weakly, 'I have never shot anyone.'

Schlegel had been popping pills since the café, and Parker wondered whether it was for the rush to get him over the line. He wondered what they would do if someone else turned up.

Schlegel, who usually restricted his observations to the present, made an exception as he rallied and repeated to himself: This is the gun I will use to blow out my brains, in a rented car in a remote car park.

He recited aloud, 'I expect you have suffered enough in your short life. I need five minutes. It will be obvious when it's done. See that ticket machine over there?'

For a moment, Parker wondered absurdly if Schlegel meant for him to buy a ticket.

Schlegel explained. 'I will leave the tape recorder on top of it with my final instructions. Now go.'

The man had no farewells in mind, and there was no point in Parker saying anything. He was overwhelmed by hostile images as death closed in on Schlegel.

He got out and walked away without looking back, stood at the edge of the car park, staring at the town below. He was unaware of time, except everything was taking a lot longer than five minutes. He saw other visions, flickering like scratchy old home movies projected onto the night

401

sky – random images of the distant continent Schlegel had never got to from Genoa, serviced after the war by burgeoning outposts of Mercedes and Volkswagen and the American United Fruit Company, with military governments eager to be propped up and hire German and American military and security advisers. He saw Morgen examine a secret correspondence between the bunker in the last days and a U-boat pen. The messages from Berlin were signed 'Bubi', a pet name among Munich homosexuals. He saw Jim Angleton in the afterlife – except in his case there was no 'after', only a state of 'in-death'; a posthumous spook, both ghost and spy, a jammed receiver; the only thing since learned was you still keep making mistakes. Jim had not appreciated death's variable offensive, how close the strike was at any moment: road accidents missed by seconds, imminent river drownings when fishing, slipping while wading, at least two KGB plots that could have gone either way and so on, including nights when he could have died from the amount of booze poured down his throat, and even now he missed cigarettes. Parker saw again his own alternative non-existence dying in childbirth; saw again Roper denied his ejaculations; saw his prostrate father dead in a wasteland, his head run over by a car; saw Schlegel dead in a ditch in the east, hair not yet white; saw the deaths of the wee missing. And the mystery of Valerie Robinson, whose death he could never see ... as in a mist, she faded, except he saw the foetus being carried in her belly. Not one death for each of us, but many, projected for death's amusement, for what are our assembled lives if not for that; the surprise was that death had a (childish) sense of humour. Eeeny meeny miny moe. Parker saw what Elizabeth Mouser had seen in the dark, now as clear as daylight: just another lynching. He understood H., his spiritual sister, her death kiss open-mouthed, the slippery, never-ending tongue forcing its way down his throat until he couldn't breathe; an ecstasy of oblivion. They were all death, even his grandmother, ushering Father Anton out of this world.

Then the shot, like a single handclap.

The split second it took the bullet to penetrate Schlegel's brain was his gift to Parker: projecting him into a future and to Father Roper's death-in-waiting. They were standing on a high bridge somewhere – Basel? Sarajevo? – except Roper was already flying. Had he jumped or was he pushed? Parker thought, What does it matter? The world would be saved or torn asunder before the man hit the ground, forever death's flying angel. Parker saw himself as Satan's creature, carrying within him these multiple deaths; then, with Roper's flight, he no longer did, and he knew he would be released. Roper stood shivering on the bridge, a pathetic, shrunken creature. Parker called him 'Timothy' and said he would love him unto death, at which Roper trembled and wept with gratitude, until Parker spat in his face. He had it in mind to push him – the intent was there; 'Bless me, Father, for I have sinned' – but Roper did as he was told and straddled the rail, and when the moment came, he flew of his own accord.

The tape recorder was where Schlegel had said, along with the ashes. Parker wondered if Schlegel was already dead by the time he'd heard the report.

Everything that had seemed so uncertain a few minutes before was now consigned to the past. Death beat its retreat, away with its trophy, and Parker saw only an empty car park on a cold night. It didn't disturb him to look at Schlegel. He'd done a neat job. None of his blood was on the side window. The bullet must still be in his skull, thought Parker, as he had another flash of Roper's everlasting fall. Schlegel looked at

403

peace; why not, he had emptied himself out years before by his own admission. Nothing left to transport.

The car door was unlocked. Parker didn't know why he got in to listen to the tape. It seemed appropriate, like a vigil. He was quite relaxed sitting next to Schlegel's cooling body, and by the great silence that had descended. He thought of the journey from Zurich, which, despite what had been discussed, he now looked back on as a peaceful interlude.

He pressed play and listened to Schlegel talk in a flat, sober way, instructing Parker what to do with the ashes. He was told to give them to Evelyn Robinson, partly as a gift, partly a poisoned chalice – Schlegel said just that – and with Braun's note, which would be easy enough to authenticate, they would be worth a fortune. Evelyn would know what to do with them, split three ways, to include Parker, who thought it a rather cold act of charity, which he supposed he would have to go along with. He was in two minds as he got out of the car and started walking down the mountain. Schlegel's instructions were for Parker to take the recorder, as the tape had a statement about Hitler's end and what really happened as opposed to what everyone had said. Strangling. Ashes. Fake suicides. Doctored bodies. The Adlon. The journey south with the ashes, and how he, August Schlegel, who had spent the last sixty-five years or so as August Tieck, was the last witness to these events.

Parker didn't know what would happen. There was the attraction of unwriting history. He felt at peace, knowing Roper's end was already in motion: the man would fall and fall until the moment came and he smashed into the earth. On the other hand, the ashes would be more filthy lucre, and he wasn't sure if he wanted to become ensnared in any more of Robinson's games. Just as there were many beginnings, there were many endings; and one he fancied mirrored the one that started with people staring at him on the Underground on his way to meet Robinson. The arrangement made for his return was to meet again at the mother's care home, where Robinson would stay until the business with the Russians quietened down. Parker saw himself on the Jubilee Line silver train – Baker Street, St John's Wood, Swiss Cottage, Finchley Road, West Hampstead – clutching Braun's deposit box in both hands in the same way she had done, gloveless, while being pushed in the wheelchair by Schlegel. Instead of getting off at Kilburn, he would travel on to the end of the line. The train was often empty by then. He would leave the ashes on the seat. He rather liked the idea of them ending up in Stanmore and Lost and Found. He would get off, watch the doors shut behind him, cross the platform and, just as the doors were closing, jump on the train going back the other way.

Bibliography

Black Boomerang, Sefton Delmer (Secker & Warburg, 1962)

Bomber Command, Max Hastings (Pan Books, 2001)

Conspiracy of Faith, Graham Wilmer (The Lutterworth Press, 2007)

Dachau Liberated: The Official Report by the US Seventh Army (edited by Michael Wiley Perry, Inkling Books, 2000)

Eva Braun: Hitler's Mistress, Nerin E. Gun (Leslie Frewin, 1968)

I Lived Under Hitler, Sybil Bannister (Penguin Books, revised edition, 1995)

Konrad Morgen: The Conscience of a Nazi Judge, H. Pauer-Studer, J. Vellerman (Palgrave Macmillan, 2015)

The Map and the Territory, Michel Houellebecq (Vintage, 2012)

The Murder of Adolf Hitler, Hugh Thomas (St Martins Press, 1996)

On the Natural History of Destruction, W.G. Sebald (Penguin Books, 2004)

Post Bellum Blues, Finn MacMahon (Bodley Head, 1965)

Tail End Charlie, Ted Church (wordpress.com, 2016)